I0822321

Witches Agenda

Witches Agenda

TYREE

Greg Spicka

Auhere publishing

This book is a work of fiction. The story, all names, characters, and incidents portrayed in this production are fictitious. No identification with actual persons (living or deceased), places, buildings, and products is intended or should be inferred. Yes, it means this story was made up.

Hardback ISBN 978-1-961918-04-7
Paperback ISBN 978-1-961918-03-0
Ebook ISBN 978-1-961918-05-4

Edited by Megan Sanders
Book Cover by "Covers by NAIN"

Auhere Publishing, Gettysburg, Pennsylvania
Printed in the United States of America
First print July 2023

Tomesofauhere.com

This fantasy series is dedicated to Amy H. Without her love and encouragement this world would have never been.

A huge thank you to the writers in the Gettysburg Writers Brigade. Their collective guidance and suggestions on Wednesday nights always have me thinking on ways to improve. Good food, good drink and great conversation.

To all fantasy story lovers that keep this story going, thank you.

"Or should I just kill the both of you now and be rid of your incompetence?"---Tyree

Contents

1

Villainous Intentions

Careless pressure of being mishandled in the icy void is all Abigail can feel as she is tossed around like a toy doll from side to side. She thinks, *Why did I trust that idiot when I knew it was wrong?* Then her worst thought enters her mind while in the darkness. *Olivia...* Abigail can only hope that she is okay. *Klinksly and Se'allt are with her. She will be okay.* Before Abigail can think of worse or better, she is flung into a pale yellow light and the air begins to smell of sour apples and dead grass. She bounces off a cold stone floor that has strange markings that twist and dance with each other in a soft, crimson glow.

A sharp pain radiates throughout her body with every hit of the stone while she rolls to a stop. Something still paralyzes her in the standing position, holding the diamond in both her hands but laying on her right side. When her sight comes into focus, she is on a large stone table and not on the floor. From her position, she can only see part of an octagonal shaped room with smooth polished walls of gold and copper-speckled stone. On the walls are claw marks and splatters of dried blood lit by glowing yellow crystals grasped in boney hands protruding from the stone.

A shadow moves along the wall that she is facing. She can tell the figure is a woman holding a curved, sawtooth-bladed weapon behind her. Abigail panics, trying to move her arms or legs to kick, but nothing happens. Only her eyes can move. Long, muscular, tan fingers with razor sharp nails painted a deep blue reach over her face, grab her right cheek, and turn her whole body easily on her back. The aroma from the fingers is a cross between a warm spring morning after a night of rain with the flowers blooming and an orange hard candy. Her index fingernail slides across Abigail's face with the feeling of a razor cutting flesh.

"Interesting... No scratch," a woman's sultry voice says.

The hand lightly caresses Abigail's face using the back of her nails to stroke her cheek and along the nose with her fingertips. Then the hand gently pulls away a few inches from her face. The muscles of the hand turn it into a claw shape with the nails facing downward. With a heavy plunge, the nails impact her face, causing Abigail's feet to rise for a second from the force of the hit. A chip of blue flies up into the air, flips and hovers for a second, then lightly falls down on Abigail's chest. The hand pulls away, leaving no wounds on her face, but the woman's index fingernail is broken.

"Huh. You broke my nail..." the voice tapers off. "You broke my nail!" The woman becomes enraged. Abigail hears a loud flesh-slapping, slithering sound. The lady comes into Abigail's view, using her tattooed arms to pull herself onto the table. The left arm has a small black tattoo of a wire with thin curved blades protruding from it and spiraling around the arm. The right has an odd symbol of a circle with a diamond on the top. Both arms are adorn with copper bracelets with gold etchings in them that gleam in the light. A gold headband holds her perfect, soft, flowing blonde hair back, lined with small rubies in no certain order.

Her naked muscular upper torso with voluptuous breasts sways as she pulls herself on top of Abigail. A thin gold chain holds a small sheet of light blue silk wrapped around her waist. The lower half is a large, scaly snake of brown, tan, and misty black scales arranged in a diamond pattern along its twenty-foot length. It coils around Abigail's legs. The size of this thing would easily crush most, but Abigail can feel the weight but not being harmed. She lays down on Abigail to bring her face to face.

"What are you? Who are you?" She rubs her finger over Abigail's lips. "No matter, I need not know my victim's name." She draws a two-foot-long curved metal sword that is cut like a jagged saw blade and has a faded steel, black color to it. She raises it high into the air.

Abigail tries to scream or move but can't. The woman slams the sword down on Abigail, and hit after hit she laughs harder and harder, looking up at the ceiling. She slashes left and right and saws at Abigail. Abigail watches every hit, for she cannot close her eyes or defend herself.

No harm comes to Abigail. The woman tosses the sword aside on the stone floor in a furious rage and uses her tail to lift Abigail off the table. She claws at her face with both hands. Again, nothing happens. The woman stands there holding Abigail up face to face, staring at her with those turquoise eyes, thinking of what to do next. She reaches her left hand behind Abigail's head and grabs a handful of hair, bringing her face up against Abigail's cheek and licking her slowly down to the jaw and stops. She pulls her head away slowly, until three inches from Abigail's.

"You still breathe? And your eyes move... How?" She squints at her. "You're a...?" She teasingly grins, rubs Abigail's hair, and notices the necklace. The woman's eyes light up in joy at what she has discovered.

"What do we have here? Such a lovely necklace." She rubs Abigail's chin and lowers her hand to touch the necklace. *Buzzzzzapp!* A small bolt of electricity comes out of the necklace, and she retreats her hand. "OOOW!" she screams in anger. Her snake body whips Abigail across the room against the wall. Abigail can feel each hit of the wall and floor.

The woman picks her up, putting her in a small chamber, about the size of a small closet. She stands her stiff body to face the center of the room and fluffs Abigail's hair, tucking it behind her shoulder.

"There you go now, nice and pretty. Shame though." She slithers to the other side of the room and stops in front of a frosted crystal slab. She wipes her hand across it, and Abigail notices what appears to be another woman with long, black hair.

"Now with her? She doesn't realize the years going by until... I let the curse do its thing." The woman slithers back over to Abigail. "But you, dear..." She grabs Abigail's chin in her palm. "You are going to suffer and watch every agonizing minute of your existence. She steps back, crosses the bracelets, and lifts them into the air. Rising out of the floor, a shiny crystal slab encloses her in.

"And we have time...for you see..." She poses with her hands outwards. "I'm a demon from the dark abyss living in your world." She claps her hands and slithers away, laughing. "We have eons to spend together."

*****

A jubilant Tyree steps out of the portal into a square room with wooden floors and walls. A window is open across from him, lighting the room. To the left, there is a small cot and end table with many melted candles that have dripped onto the floor, creating a cave-like appearance. To the right are many books, papers, and objects from everyday things to the obscure. They are spread about on a large table, desk, bookshelf, and the floor.

Tyree sprints to the desk and slides his arm across the surface to push the contents onto the floor. He sets the red book down carefully and steps back, snaps his fingers, and does a little dance again. The sound of wood being chopped echoes through the window, grabbing Tyree's attention. He looks outside the second-story window, and there is the side yard surrounded by logs being splintered into firewood by his helper, Glaive.

Glaive is a big twenty-eight-year-old fellow, six and a half feet tall, broad square shoulders with muscles to match. His large round face with a square jaw complements the blue half-moon tattoo on top of his bald head. There is a black snake tattoo that wraps around the moon, along the back of his neck, and creeps to his left shoulder blade. The tail comes over the shoulder, stopping above his left pectoral muscle. The head, with its mouth open, stops at his forehead. His shirtless chest reveals scars on his front and back from old combat. The faded dark blue cloth pants he wears have many stains and a few holes from overuse.

"Glaive! Glaive! Get up here quick."

He takes one last swing with the ax before going upstairs to see what Tyree wants. He opens the door and there is Tyree standing there with his hands on the table, humming a cheerful tune. Glaive stands there slack-jawed, watching him with big brown eyes as Tyree hums and swings his hips.

"Uh...why you so happy, chief?" Glaive has a husky voice that sounds like he needs to clear his throat but never does.

"Today, we celebrate!" He tosses a small pouch of gold coins to him. "Go to town and bring back the best wine and drink you can find."

"Uhh, okay." He turns to go downstairs then peeks his head back in. "Chief? Why we celebrating?"

Tyree puts both his hands against his temples and moans in annoyance. "Ahh. Me!" He points at himself and in the air with the other hand. "I have found the Book of Power that Prakdon possessed." He spins around with his hands in the air and stomps his foot. "Go! Before I change my mind." Tyree waves him off.

Tyree watches Glaive walk to town through the window and shakes his head in disbelief. "Why? Why not take the horse?" His attention turns to the book as he leans against the desk and stares at it.

"So... What do you have to offer me?" Tyree rubs his fingers across the cover and opens a random page. The handwritten words are in a strange language he cannot understand. He flips through a few more pages and the same writing. He frantically flips through it and to the beginning. It is all the same language.

"How can this be!" He slaps his hand against the book. "I could read it in the tower, and it showed me the offering ritual." Tyree stomps across the room, talking to himself, "The tower? Don't tell me I have to go back there to read it." After walking in a few circles, his head snaps up with the realization of a parchment he remembers. He searches through a desk drawer and pulls out a rolled parchment tied in a blue string before he closes the drawer. A small brown leather journal catches his eye. The book is old, worn, and has a symbol of a light blue shield with a pure white outline. In the center are golden feathery wings spread between a sword and sunrays. The old symbol of the Skylar Kingdom.

"Yesss. Of course." He remembers this book belonging to his parents and looking through it a long time ago. "It will be mine soon." He tosses the parchment carelessly to the side of the desk and opens to a page he has not seen before. Looking closer, Tyree reads it to discover handwritten notes from his father and mother telling him about his family heritage as a baby. He scans over writings and one sentence stands out.

Remember what we told you for one day you will need it.

He slaps the book on the desk. “What?! Are you kidding me? I was a child. Really?! How am I supposed to remember what you said?” Tyree grabs the red Book of Power again and mumbles under his breath, “Stupid parents.” He turns a few pages only to see mystical writing and symbols that he can’t understand. Tapping his fingers on the desk, he thinks for a moment about what to do, then reaches for the scroll. He unties the blue string and glances over it.

“Yesss. This should work.” Tyree studies the scroll that will allow him to read unknown magic. After twenty minutes of learning in silence, the divination magic of the scroll is erased and transferred to Tyree’s mind. He opens the middle of the book and repeats the words to activate the spell. His hands gleam in the mists of yellow and grays that come forth, gliding down to the book. His heart pounds, watching in anticipation of the letters changing shape so he can read them, but the mist fades into black sparkles that bounce off the pages and roll off the desk, disappearing.

“What?” He shakes his hands violently to make more mist, but the spell fails and ceases. “No, I cast it right! Fatuous spell. It was faulty!” Tyree rips up the now blank parchment and his anger grows into a small rage. He grabs the thick candle off the desk and throws it into the wall, breaking it into pieces. “How am I supposed to read that devilish script now?”

A cool gust of wind blows into the window, stirring the shredded parchment on the wooden floor. Tyree looks around the room he let get so disorganized over the years as he searched for the Book of Power. His face reddens with anger, and he is about to throw another candle when his eyes lock on the flickering flame, then at the ripped parchment. He sets the candle down on the desk and taps his forehead in stupidity.

“Of course! I couldn’t read it because it is not magic.” He picks the red book up, rubs it with his fingers, and murmurs, “It is demon runes.”

Tyree searches through the desk, then over to the shelves, but cannot find anything to read the book with.

He crosses his arms, taps his chin, and thinks. *I remember something about reading dark runes or whatever.* Tyree walks in circles, trying to remember, and laughs aloud. "Ha! Remember what my parents told me when I was a child? I can't even recall when I heard something about dark rune understanding. Ha! The nonsense of it all."

He snaps his finger and smirks with an idea. He pulls out his old spell book from when he was only an apprentice. "Study the simple stuff, the wizard always said." He carefully flips through the fragile pages that he never really took the time to learn. "I guess the old fool, I mean old conjurer, was right after all."

He finds the simple remembrance spell he needs. His finger glides down the paper over the list of spell ingredients he needs and the enchantment words to activate the magic.

"Let's see, a pinch of dried elephant brain powder, pinch of ginseng root dust, and mix with dried fairy dust." He snickers. "Ah yes, I remember drying out that pesky fairy and grinding him into dust." He picks the small green glass bottle off the shelf and shakes it. "Looks like I have a use for you, after all."

Tyree mixes the three ingredients together and reads the words to activate the spell. He pours the dust mixture into his left hand. "Ajatella muistaa." He lets out all the air in his lungs, closes his eyes, and splashes the glimmering dust on his face as he deeply inhales. A moment goes by, and nothing happens. He opens his eyes to a blurry room. Tyree stumbles to his bed, lies down, and falls into a daze.

His memories come and go, from recent to faded. Tyree realizes the spell is working and is not sure how much time he has, so he concentrates on his early years as a child. Coming into view in his mind is his father talking to someone in a dark alley between two buildings. His mother is holding him as a one-year-old baby. His father is arguing with a man dressed in a blue overcoat, but Tyree cannot understand what he is saying.

He sees his father push the man back up against the wall, and this large white diamond with a bluish tint, about the size of a small apple, falls to the ground. The man is sweating as they look at each other to see who will pick it up first. Tyree's father pushes the man away, picks up the gem, and yells, "Meikka!"

The gem turns into a long crystal sword with a faint blue glow. His father has a sinister grin and then runs the sword through the man's chest and drags it out of him. He satisfyingly mummers the command word, and the sword becomes the small diamond again.

During the spell, Tyree calls out, "It can go to the size of a gem?" He thinks of other locked memories.

Tyree is a little over two years old now and laying in a bed with a blanket over his face with just his eyes and nose peeking out. The small room smells of smoke from the wet wood trying to burn in the fireplace. His parents are sitting at a table, and by the partially open door stands a strange man looking nervous as he looks outside into the night. There is a dark-skinned woman dressed in many shades of reds, oranges, and browns with strips of ragged cloth hanging from her arms and legs. Some are loose, and other strands are knotted, clinging to her arms. She is wearing a brown-hooded cloak that hides half her face, but little Tyree can see clearly her one eye is pure white.

She waves her hands back and forth, yelling in a hoarse voice about how, "If the witch, the one that can move earth and water with thought, lives to be their queen, then all is lost." She lowers her hands and points to the fire. "The Mire family will end, never to claim the throne!" Suddenly, the fire roars into a mighty flame. He looks back at his parents. The lady and strange man are gone as the door swings back and forth.

Tyree thinks of more hidden memories that are lined up like closed books in his mind. The spell brings them forth so easily. He relives memories of them wandering around like gypsies throughout the remnants of the old Skylar Kingdom. Traveling to the north and the far south. He sees good and bad times they had. His father teaches him how to use the crystal sword and that if he holds it straight out with both hands and says "Shokki," a small bolt of electricity comes forth.

"Hmm, interesting. I don't recall that. Well, I guess I did." Tyree goes on with more thoughts and gets discouraged when it's mostly about family things that don't matter to him. Then he finds a memory he was looking for, his parents telling him the story about the Book of Power and how general Prakdon became the owner of it. A part sticks out when his mother tells him the details of the book.

"That fortune teller lady said you will possess that book someday, but you cannot read it. You need to find a witch to read that demon rune in the book. Or find a source of magic to do that, but I think none exists."

That memory fades into another; he is fifteen years old. He is in the town of Cragsburg, a mining town in the Southern Kingdom, and has taken his father's crystal cane with him. They sent him into town to get supplies for the next journey after they overstayed their welcome. A group of teenagers starts taunting and throwing rocks at him. One boy comes up from behind him and punches him in the back of the head.

An anger grows so fierce and quick inside him that he drops his bag, twists the knob on the cane to turn it into the sword, and rapidly turns himself with the blade out and sliced the kid's gut wide open. He faces the one that threw the rock at him, who is standing in shock, and plunges it into the boy's chest, killing him instantly. The others run away while the other boy cries, holding his guts in his hands.

A man with a sword, probably a town guard, comes rushing over yelling at Tyree to drop the sword. Tyree runs at the man, screaming for all to die, and the two blades hit each other. The crystal blade breaks the metal sword into pieces. Tyree continues, the blade cutting into the man's face, chest, and right leg before hitting the ground. He sees more armed men coming, and he runs off in fear of being caught.

The spell fizzles, and Tyree comes out of his trance. He looks around the room for a second while his head clears. He rubs his face with his hands, stands up, and smiles. "Oh yeah, I did do that." Tyree reaches for the crystal cane and holds it in both hands. "I can't believe I forgot about the shocking power of this blade. What was that word again? Meikka." The cane forms a diamond with a bluish tint the size of a small apple in the palm of his hands. He tosses it into the air and catches it before putting it in his pocket.

"You could have told me that before I took it into town that day,

Father." He yells out to no one. "But those brats got what they deserved. Ha!" His attention is now focused on the book.

"But I did read you." He rubs the book gently with his fingers. "Just not here though... You want me to read you, don't you?" Tyree lays the book down on the desk and goes to the window to think. The view is of a few rolling hills covered with a mix of beech, poplar, and maple trees. Most of the leaves have changed color to bright reds and oranges, falling on the ground by the cool breeze. Grasshoppers struggle to fly as they are nearing their end of life while the cricket's time has come as they chirp in the shadows. A few miles away, he can see the outline of the tall buildings in town. Minutes go by as he leans on the open window, remembering what the spell showed him of what the fortune teller said. He glances back and grins.

"I do have the book... And I got rid of that queen too... Bonus!" He does a toe tap in celebration and claps his hands. "So the old seeing bity was right after all."

The sun has a few hours left in the day as it begins its journey to the horizon. Tyree notices Glaive coming back from Splinteroak with a large sack.

"It's been that long? What else did he get?" He hurries downstairs to see. Tyree rushes down the stairs as they creak and crack under his weight. He reaches for the lopsided door handle; it is stuck as it usually is from the rusty hinges. He kicks the door and twists the handle at the same time to make it open, then bursts out of the door with his arms wide. "Glaive! Why didn't you take the horse?"

"Well, chief, you took the horse and never brought it back."

Tyree puts his hands on his hips and looks into the sky. "That is right. Damn it. It's at that..." He snapped his fingers." *At that farm Arty boy took me too. We will worry about that later.* "What's in the bag?"

Glaive sets the bag on a small table that is outside. He pulls out a green glass bottle about a foot tall. "I got us a bottle of Garnet City vineyard wine, last bottle too.' He pulls out a small wooden barrel that has a tap on it. "A gallon of Splinteroak autumn ale, fresh."

"And what is in that wooden box?"

"Cake! Can't have a celebration without cake! Strawberry with cream cheese icing."

Tyree's eyes are fixed on the table of goodies. "You're right. Let's drink and eat cake. It's nice out, so we will eat it here. Go get some chairs and goblets." Tyree breathes in the fall's musk air, looks at the setting sun, then thinks to himself. *Tomorrow is the beginning*.

The two gorge themselves on cake and ale, and soon they finish the wine. The sun has set and the lights from Splinteroak shine faintly in the distance. Tyree takes one last sip of wine and taps the table with the goblet.

"Glaive... tomorrow will begin our quest for the Skylar Kingdom."

Glaive responds with a slurred speech, "Pfft, you said that before... Ain't no difference tomorrow."

Tyree gets angry about that remark but lets it go. He reflects on their past paltry attempts to seize a lord or baron to begin the takeover of the kingdom that ended in failure. He tried to con their guards to join him to take over a lord's castle as a start. When that didn't work he tried taking it by force, but hired too few men and the cowards fled from the skirmish. Soon, he will discover the secrets of the book that will lead him to success.

"Either way, my friend. Finish your wine, then get a good sleep. We got business to deal with in Splinteroak tomorrow."

Tyree heads back to his room, grabs the book off the desk, and lays down on the bed, fiddling through the pages. The alcohol overcomes his excitement of the find and eventually he falls asleep, and the book haphazardly falls to the floor, closing itself.

*****

A large crow caws in the late overcast morning on the open window ledge. Still wearing yesterday's clothes, Tyree opens one bloodshot eye to see the crow twitching its head at items on his desk. Before he can even think of reacting, the crow leaps onto the desk, picks up a small green gem, and flies out the window.

Tyree opens both eyes and stands up. His head is thumping as he staggers to the desk to see what was taken. His hands rummage through the clutter on the desk when a slight panic sets in. He looks around for the red book and it is nowhere to be seen.

“That damn bird!” With one big swipe, he rids the desk of everything. “There's no way that bird could have taken the book!” He stands motionless and smiles as he notices the book on the floor next to the bed. “There you are.” He sits down on the bed, lifts the book to his knees, and opens it, flipping through the unreadable pages again.

Tyree waits a few minutes for his head to clear enough to go to the window. There below him is Glaive, spread out in the front yard in the high grass. The empty gallon barrel is laying beside him, split in two. Tyree shakes his head in annoyance at it all. After going downstairs, he makes his way outside to the well for fresh water. Tyree splashes his face with the cool water and takes a sip to wake himself.

Then he taps Glaive's foot to wake him. “Come on, get up. We leave in two hours to go to town, so get ready.” Tyree stops and stares at the old run-down house. Four of the windows won’t close because they are no longer square. There are holes in the roof and the top looks like it’s leaning. Weeds and vines have taken over the foundation, causing cracks in the mortar between the stones. “Huh, didn’t notice that before... Oh well, Skylar Castle will soon be my new home, anyway.”

He heads back upstairs to organize the books that are spread out on the floor and to get himself ready. An earthy smell signals that rain is coming as a breeze blows through the window. Two yellow beech leaves make their way inside, landing on the desk. The site reminds Tyree to gather the gold and other coins. Searching for the Book of Power has left him almost broke after chasing every hint of a clue.

He counts 131 gold coins and 4 silver. Then he looks for the little emerald that was on the desk. “That damn bird! It took the gem.” He fills the little green pouch with the remaining coins. “No matter, I shall be rich beyond the meaning of wealth soon.”

He puts the red book in a secret pocket of his gray jacket and the diamond in the outer right pocket. He is greeted downstairs by sizzling sausage and frying eggs; Glaive is making a quick breakfast before they leave. “Morning, chief, why we go to town today?”

"Nice to see you always think of food. I won't starve with you around... We are going to see a man for information on how to read this book."

"Chief... You spent all this time and coin on a book that you knew you can't read?"

Tyree bites into a sausage and takes a deep breath at the aggravation of his stupidity. "Glaive. I have you around not because you are a good cook but because you swing that blade of yours very well and you follow orders blindly." He then slams his fist against the table, upsetting the food on the plates; the remaining links tumble onto the table and two roll off on the floor. "I don't pay you to think and make senseless remarks."

Glaive grudgingly murmurs, "You don't pay me." He picks the links off the floor and eats them.

Tyree lets that statement go, drinks some water to wash breakfast down, then goes to the front door that is still stuck open. A light sprinkle has begun, and he forces the door shut. "I'm going to close the windows upstairs. You shut the ones down here, then let's get ready to go to town before the heavy rain comes."

"Right, chief."

Twenty minutes later, they are ready. Tyree has a dark gray overcoat on, and Glaive is wearing a worn brown leather jacket with most of the buttons missing. They make their way down the misty weed-covered trail to the outskirts of Splinteroak. They walk an hour to town before the steady, cool rain comes.

"Where we headed, chief?"

"We are going to visit Frederick. He usually has what I need or where to get it. Prices are a little high, though."

It is midafternoon in Splinteroak and even with the rain, many people are still about getting supplies and selling goods as mid-autumn has set in. Tyree walks with his head high, knowing he will be in charge of this town soon. He thinks about what he would change and what he will let be. In midtown, they spot Frederick's purple tower and knock on the door.

The out of square purple door has a wider top and narrower bottom by a foot, opens smoothly, without a creak. Standing there is Frederick, dressed in bright blue silk pants and shirt. Tyree notices he is not wearing any shoes, then Frederick wiggles his toes and smiles.

"Ahh, Tyree, what brings you back so soon? To pay off your debt?"

Tyree clears his throat when reminded of his debt. "Why yes. Yes, I have, and I am in need of other... let's say, business dealings."

Frederick holds out his hand and bends his fingers back and forth. "Let's see the five gold first before any other dealings."

Tyree is annoyed at this pettiness and tries hard not to let it show as he hands him five gold coins.

"Great, great. Now that's settled, what is it I can do for you?"

Tyree looks over his shoulder at the few people out on this rainy day. He points to inside Frederick's place. "Mind if we talk about this in secret?"

Frederick steps back and waves them into a small room about ten feet wide and twenty feet long. Relaxing lavender smoke from a brass dragon incense burner greets them, creating a haze in the room. The wood floor is stained a light brown color but has faded with the trampling of clean and dirty boots over time. A little round table made of metal sits in the middle, with three chairs around. A wall is covered in odd paintings of forest, castles, and creatures. In between them are small shelves holding different shaped bottles. Tyree pokes his head back outside to see the solid stone wall, but on the inside, it has a huge stained glass window with a clear section that you can see the townsfolk walk by.

"You like that little trick?"

"Yes, that is impressive. You can always see who is at your door."

"It took me many years to find that window. And yes, it comes in handy when unwelcomed people come."

"Is that for sale?" Tyree stands in front of the window, looking out at the people getting wet from the rain.

"Ahh, no." Frederick sits at the table. "What is it I can do for you today, Tyree?"

"No easy way to say this, so here it is. I need a demon rune reading scroll."

Frederick's left eyebrow raises. "Really? And you think I would just have one lying around? That is a highly unusual... and let's say, a forbidden thing. If it even exists. Why come here?"

Tyree grins. "You say you have everything someone could need. And well, I need that. Can you deliver or not?"

"Well, I.... But... ahhh, that?" Frederick rubs his face with both hands.

"Can... you... deliver?"

Frederick is nervous. He walks around the room, tapping his forehead. Tyree playfully taps the table in tune with his pacing. Glaive stands there, mesmerized by all the paintings, and has ignored their conversation. Frederick snaps his fingers and claps his hand. "Ah ha! Got it."

"So you have one?" Tyree's excitement grows as his hopes of reading the book get closer. "Great, let me see it."

Frederick raises his hands. "Whoa, hold on, Tyree. I didn't say I had it, and if I did, I doubt you would have the coin for that."

Tyree is enraged at that comment and slaps his hands on the table, causing Glaive to jump. "Don't you ever doubt what I can do! With what I have, I'm going to do whatever I need to, to get—" He pauses for a moment, reaches into his pocket, and pulls out the diamond. Glaive looks at him, expecting Tyree to fight. Frederick's eyes are wide open, but he remains calm. "I will have wealth beyond what you will ever have. So it is best to be on my good side." He puts the diamond back in his pocket.

"Okay, okay, perhaps I meant you didn't have the coin on you this very moment... because that would be about 5000 gold or more for that scroll."

"That much? Absurd."

"Doesn't matter. Because I don't have one." He points his finger into the air. "But... I have a way to see if there is one and where."

"You do? Well then, get to it."

"Ahhh, to get this information will cost you as well. I don't work for free."

Tyree rolls his eyes. "Of course you don't. Why would you help someone out of kindness?"

"Kindness? You? Come now, Tyree, we both know that is not possible with you. I will give you a bargain, though."

“Bargain, huh? Just get on with it. I don’t care anymore. Tell me! Tell me now, damn it!”

Frederick leaves the room with a skeptical look. Through the wall, the two of them hear something large being moved. The screeching of wood being dragged along the floor pierces their ears. Frederick steps out from the beaded doorway holding a rolled map. Tyree and Glaive look at each other, confused.

Glaive chuckles. “Uhh. All that noise for a little paper?”

Frederick walks over to the table and is about to set it down, but he pulls it back. “This is... well, it will tell you where to find a... scroll or something else to read... you know. That will be 100 gold coins.”

Tyree stares at the paper, then back at Frederick. “100? For what? Let me see before I buy it.”

“No can do.”

“At least tell me more.”

“All right. It is a map of the location of Geemend’s Seeker.”

Tyree's eyebrows raise; he taps the table with both hands. “It’s real then?”

“Ahh, so you know what it is? This map will show you how to get to it and how to use the device.”

Tyree stares at the wall. “It is said that this device can find anything by showing you where it is.”

Frederick points his finger in the air. “If! If it exists, then yes. If not, then it will show you that and take something from you.”

“It’s cursed?”

Frederick nods. Tyree doesn’t hesitate to throw the gold onto the table. Frederick gently lays down the map. Tyree quickly unrolls it, tearing a corner. He glances over it, grins, and looks at Glaive standing there. “We got to get some henchman, you know... the disposable kind.”

2

Distraught in The Unknown

After a day of rest to recover from the tower, the next morning it was raining, and Klinksly took young Adam back to the monastery and returned through the tree door spell. Olivia and Arthygus told Barland what happened at the tower many times so they could try to figure out where to start looking for answers. Olivia stares at the chair Abigail broke that Barland repaired. She impatiently smacks her hands against the table until Barland reaches for her hand. “It’s best to be patient. Yeah, it will be hard.”

“I don’t want to sit here. I want to go find her.”

Barland folds his hands together while his elbows are on the table. He has that deep, calming voice that speaks reason. "Now, Olivia, where are you going to go today? Tonight? Or even next week?” Olivia knows he is right but remains quiet and listens with watery eyes and a sniffle. “I know you don’t want to hear this, but with what you two have told me, a powerful magic is at work here. Instead of wasting time wandering off trying to find her, we need to figure out who can help us.”

Arthygus’s voice crackles. “I’m sorry. It’s all my fault.” He buries his head in his hands. “I should have never gone to Tyree. I did not know h’de do something like this.”

Olivia was mad and made sure not to misplace her anger on Arthygus.

She was about to talk when Barland spoke first. "I will not say it's alright, because it's not, but you didn't know he was going to do that. Don't blame yourself."

"But if I didn't..."

Barland's voice gets more stern as he points at Arthygus. "You can't go with what-ifs! That talk leads to nothing good. What is done is done. Let's... concentrate on that."

Klinksly opens the front door, walking into the kitchen after overhearing what was said. He sits on the chair with his head above the table and hangs his hat on the corner of the chair post. "On the way back, I was thinking about Abigail. Not Abigail the friend... but as Abigail the witch queen."

Arthygus lifts his eyebrows in curiosity. "How do you mean? She is the same person."

"Yes, but if the witch community found out she is missing, and so soon after becoming queen... Oooh, the panic, confusion, and chaos it will cause."

Olivia moves her eyes to Klinksly, but not her head. "How so?"

"Well, let's just say we don't want that to happen. So I came up with an idea to give us some time" He looks at Olivia. "I will say she is away learning the queen's responsibilities."

"What? So you are going to fib?"

Klinksly taps his hand on the table, grins tilting his head. "Not really, Olivia. Since she is new and was unprepared to be queen. There is protocol and things she needs to know...As soon as we find her, she will do these things."

"We need to find Abigail soon, not fiddle around with this queen stuff," Arthygus says.

Klinksly, outraged by that statement, slaps his hands against the table. "Queen stuff!? This may not be important to a wizard like yourself, but to us, if Abigail is to be known as missing, then any hope of finding her will be lost because a few people will not want her to be found!" He leans against the table. He looks sternly at Olivia, "I want answers also... I want her back too, more than anyone. If any of you want to have the slightest bit of hope of finding her." Klinksly sighs. "I know someone that may tell us what happened to her and there is a way for him to observe it." The three of them are baffled at Klinksly. "But Olivia, you will need to appear as Abigail."

"I need to what?"

Silence fills the kitchen as the angry gnome sits back down and, after a few minutes, Olivia's calming voice breaks the stalemate.

"Yes, to get answers you will have to appear as her."

Olivia rubs the side of her cheek for a second. "I will do it."

"How? How are you going to do that?" Arthygus looks at Olivia.

Olivia slides the chair back and stands. Klinksly grins because he has seen that confident look on her before. She takes a deep breath and rubs little circles on her temples with her index fingers. Olivia thinks of Abigail, of how she last saw her. The men in the room rub their eyes as Olivia's image begins to blur, and then she appears as Abigail, complete with red hair and the crimson dress. She sways her dress, and it spirals outward, she lifts her arms outward and tilts her hips. "Ta daa."

Klinksly smiles. "I knew you could do it."

Arthygus's eyes open wide at the illusion she did. "That is amazing. And no spell ingredients or scroll?"

Olivia spins around with a welcomed laugh and twirls the dress, then lets the illusion fade.

"So, who do we need to find?" Arthygus rubs his chin.

"Well... Mr. Krew." Klinksly shrugs his shoulders and smirks at them.

"Oh no, not that guy." Olivia huffs. "Isn't he the one that doesn't like Abigail?"

"More like Abigail can't stand him!" Barland chuckles.

"This plane is going to fail. How are we going to ask to find Abigail when Abigail will appear in front of him?"

"Klinksly throws his hat to the ground. "Darn troll toes! Figures a wizard would point that out."

Olivia picks his hat up, brushes it off. "We will tell the truth of what happened."

Klinksly frowns at the idea of telling Mr.Krew the truth. Arthygus nods in agreement and barland shrugs his shoulders.

Klinksly puts his hat back on. "Well, he may have the answers we need, so we need to do what we can. Let's be going now."

Arthygus raises his eyebrows. "What do you mean, he may have the answers?"

Klinksly smiles, stepping off the chair. "You will see." And he heads out the kitchen door to go outside. Barland suggests that the two of them follow, no time to waste, and he will continue to research here at the farm. Klinksly leads Olivia and Arthygus through the tree door spell to the house of Mr. Krew in the cool pine trees. The cloudless daylight sparkles off the snow-covered trees and pine needles on the ground, illuminating the shadowed area in a mystical light. Melted snow turns into ice as it slides into the cold shadow on the black stone walls of the keep where sunlight does not shine.

The scenery impresses Arthygus. "I... like this place. This is what I would want when I can afford it. The location is perfect."

Olivia teasingly pokes him on the shoulder. "Why so dark and dreary? I would like us to be near a town full of people and activity."

"Us?" His cheeks turn red from blushing.

"Uhh, I... mean... I would." She pulls her cloaked hood over her head in embarrassment.

Klinksly makes his way to the door, turns to Olivia, and smiles. "The truth it is then." He gently grabs both her hands. "We have been in worse situations, you and I. I know you can do this because there is no pressure on you. We are doing the best we can right now to help Abigail. You can do this."

Olivia nods her head, hands Arthygus her green cloak, closes her eyes, takes a deep breath and signals she is ready. Klinksly knocks on the large dark oak door.

Arthygus gasps in surprise.

"What is it?" Klinksly asks.

"I'm a wizard? Will they let me in? Will he do something to me?"

The two of them stare at Arthygus with their eyes bulging in the realization that he is right. Olivia shakes her hands nervously, and Klinksly smacks his forehead. The door opens slowly, and Olivia pushes Klinksly and Arthygus out of view.

Klinksly whispers. "What are you doing?"

Olivia shoos him back with a wave of her hand. The door opens and Mr. Krew stands there with that long face of his, giving an unapproving expression at the interruption. Olivia smiles, then quickly throws herself at him, embracing him in a hug. His eyebrows rarely raise in surprise, but this he did not expect, nor did he fight back. "Okay madam, to whom do I owe the pleasure of this... hug?"

"I'm sorry. I'm in terrible need of your help, for something awful has happened to my... friend."

"You must be mistaken. I do not help... people on a whim. How did you get here?"

She looks at him in the eyes as hers gets watery and mumbles, "It's Abigail."

Mr. Krew puts his hand on her shoulder and pats her back, then his beady eyes gaze up and down at her for a few seconds. He offers her to step inside, then closes the door after she passes. Arthygus and Klinksly look at each other in confusion.

"Shouldn't we be in there, too?"

"Well, of course we should. But you being a so-called wizard, maybe not." Klinksly pulls his hat tighter in disgust. "I guess she's got this."

After a few minutes, Arthygus asks, "You think we should knock?"

"I don't know. Maybe give them time to talk?"

"It's cold out here, but comfortable in an odd way."

The two of them walk around, standing at the door, flicking the snow off the pine needles for a while until Klinksly questions Arthygus. "Hey, back at the tower when that chimera attacked us... You really didn't have any magic ready, did you?"

Arthygus frowns at Klinksly and pauses how to answer that. "For starters, I'm still learning magic. It seems to be limited in a way compared to witchcraft."

"For us warlocks and witches, you need to be ready and quick about what you do... If not, well, terrible results could happen when those times arise." Klinksly lowers his eyebrows in thought. "Say, aren't you supposed to have a, what is it? A master or something to teach you?" He laughs. "Don't tell me you are still an apprentice." Klinksly's face is in shock now. "We took an apprentice to a dangerous place?" He lifts his hand to cover his mouth as he gasps.

Arthygus waves his hands no. "No no no, it's not like that."

"Oh? How so? You didn't seem like you knew what to do when it attacked us?"

"Listen, Oland Gregorio, the archmage, was my teacher... my mentor."

Klinksly's eyes light up at the mention of that name. "No, that cannot be. He... killed so many... and Shard, the great silver dragon, destroyed him." Klinksly's voice trails off to a murmur as he looks into the distance. "That was well over a hundred years ago."

Arthygus wrinkles his eyebrows together in disagreement. "Ah no. That couldn't have been him. He left unexpectedly four years ago and left me to carry on with my studies. Besides, what do you mean... killed so many?"

"Witches."

"There has to be a misunderstanding. He was the only wizard that told me to let witches be and don't mess with them. Why do you think I was friends with Abigail?"

"Really?" Klinksly rubs his chin and squints at Arthygus. "How is it your friends with her?"

"She saved me from being robbed one day, and that was the beginning of our friendship. I asked her how she did that and she explained how she moved water naturally while I had to use a spell. We would practice alone together outside of Garnet City."

Klinksly nods his head in understanding. Arthygus flicks more snow off a pine tree. "I was never one to fight, or at least trained to do that. I'm more interested in new discoveries and learning the ways of conjuring."

"Huh. I can see that." Klinksly shivers and rubs his hands against his sides. "You're going to learn to do something. I feel times are coming that call for a need to fight or do your magic."

"I understand. Who do I see about such a thing? Since I have been looking into information about the... um book, I had to keep my head down."

Klinksly smiles. "Well, there is... Wait a second. A witch teaching a wizard? No way will anyone go for that." He raises his eyebrows and points his finger at him. "You're on your own with this one."

Arthygus pulls out a little red bag the size of a walnut. "Look at this. It is a mixture of ground fire beetle, lava dust, and hickory chips." He takes a pinch and sprinkles it on his head, and they fall down to his feet. He wiggles his fingers like a flame flickering. "Lammin!"

A faint orange glow appears around him for a second, then fades. "Ahhh. Nice and comfy. Here you try it."

"What?"

"It will keep you warm... for a while."

Klinksly squints at him while taking a pinch. Arthygus guides him in what to do. Seconds later, the gnome had the same glow and felt a cozy warmth about him. "See? Nice and warm now. That was a wizard magic warmth spell you did."

Klinksly is smiling from being warm. "Okay, this is nice."

"Huh, a wizard teaching a warlock magic. Go figure." Arthygus has a proud grin about him.

"Alright... I get it." Klinksly reaches into his pouch and pulls out a tiny blue acorn with a string on it. "Here, take this and pull the string. It is a bit of witch magic that will give you...clarity."

Arthygus rolls the acorn around on his fingers, studying it. "Clarity?"

"Yes, hold it to your face and pull the string. It will help you focus on what you need to do for a short time." Arthygus holds it up to his face and pulls the string. *Kapow!* The small acorn explodes, causing a faint blackish residue on his face. His hair is slightly smoking and blown back. He hasn't moved and Klinksly laughs. "Oops, it must be the green one." He snickers more and the front door opens, startling them.

Olivia steps outside first, followed by Mr. Krew. Arthygus and Klinksly are frozen in mid-laughter. Mr. Krew steps towards them with his nose held high and his eyes piercing down at them. “I see you have been on the receiving end of what a gnome believes to be...whimsical.”

Olivia hides a smile with her hand while Klinksly smirks and shrugs his shoulders. An embarrassed Arthygus wipes his face off with his sleeve. Klinksly adjusts his hat. “So, Olivia, what did you tell him?”

“Tell me? She told me the truth. Despite what you think, in certain times, the truth needs to be told. Even to those you may disagree with in letting them know the truth.”

Klinksly squints at him, nodding his head. “Okay. What do we do next?”

“I want to hear it straight from the so-called wizard boy as to what he saw. And I mean in detail.”

Arthygus was perplexed by that statement. “Wizard boy?”

“Yes, wizard boy. Now do not question me again about such petty things.”

Klinksly taps his chin again, thinking, and waves Arthygus to stop. “Wait, wait. Before this gets any worse, I can do better than have wizard boy explain it to you.”

Olivia and Arthygus turn to Klinksly in wonder. Mr. Krew raises his left eyebrow in curiosity. “How so, Klinksly, the missing queen’s attendant?”

He ignores that jab at him for losing Abigail and taps his index fingers together. “I can show you. But we need access to the...um... the witch queen’s room at Skylar Castle.”

Mr. Krew stares down at him with a gaze that could make anyone submit to him. “Show me?”

“Yes, I could. It’s just we have no way of getting in there without Abigail.”

“Is that so? Well, my associate, Mr. Blaine, is there at this very moment, cataloging the contents of the room.” He extends his arm to Olivia to hold, and he escorts her to the tree he uses for the tree door spell. Klinksly frowns at Arthygus as they follow him. After thirty minutes of walking through his forest, they come to the tree that takes them to the witch’s colosseum.

Arthygus is mystified at the usefulness of the tree door spell. "That spell is very convenient to get to places quickly. No wonder witches disappear quickly and can't be found."

Mr. Krew opens the door for Olivia that allows them into the arena. "It is more practical than a wizard teleporting into... Let's say solid rock?" He gives Arthygus a whimsical smirk. "That is why you have so few magicians do it once they learned that higher magic. Most die trying... I cannot say I'm disappointed at the results either."

"All I was saying was that it is impressive. You don't have to insult my magics because you don't understand them."

Mr. Krew's demeanor changes to annoyance. He grabs Arthygus's shoulder and points his other finger in his face. "Oh, I understand them all too well. More than you probably ever will, wizard...Arthygus. That's what you call yourself, right?" Mr. Krew rolls up his left sleeve, revealing burnt skin. He speaks in a less harsh tone, staring at him square in the eye. "When some wizard tried to burn me alive, he underestimated me. Your magics are slow and need time to prepare before use." Arthygus's stunned eyes are paying attention to every word because he knows he is right. "Unfortunately for him, he found out that lesson too late... So, Arthygus, I do understand, and you shouldn't assume that others don't." He rolls his sleeve back while the others are quiet.

He leads Olivia through the door to go down the tunnel and again, Klinksly and a silent dejected Arthygus follow them. Once at the door that leads to Skylar Castle, Klinksly notices it is propped open by a brick. The aroma of sandalwood greets their noses as they step in. A smiling Mr. Blaine dips a small pen into a blue ink jar, writing on a parchment.

"I see we have guests, Mr. Krew. What is going on?"

"Yes, we have guests today." He steps aside and in walks Olivia wearing her green cloak followed by Klinksly and Arthygus, who is amazed at the room. "It seems our queen has gotten herself into some trouble."

"Oh? That soon?" He sees Olivia is worried about Abigail. "Excuse me for the comment. I meant to say, "What kind of trouble?"

Olivia smiles at Mr. Blaine. "It's okay. I understand why you said it."

Klinksly goes to the covered mirror. He grabs the cover and pauses, thinking of what happened when Abigail touched the skull. “I’m not sure what this actually is.” He looks at everyone, then quickly removes the cover with one loud snap, exposing the wood and bone mirror with the skull on top. Mr. Blaine eagerly steps over to it and his fingers gently glide across the exquisite woodwork. Oliva cringes at the site of the skull and bone while Arthygus rubs his chin and nods his head in thought.

Mr. Krew cracks a small grin. “This, Klinksly... is the fabled mirror of Burvis Regin.”

“I thought it was destroyed?” Mr. Blaine asks.

“Destroyed? How? By accident?” Arthygus asks as he steps up closer to it.

Mr. Blaine is about to touch the skull when Klinksly shouts, “No! Don’t touch the skull.”

“And why not?”

“When Abigail touched the forehead, it...”

“It what?” Mr. Krew asked in a slow, stern tone.

“It was activated. When she touched the skull, it showed us what was on her mind.” Klinksly lowers his somber head. “It must have been a terrible weight on her to still be thinking about the ghoul. It showed me what she was seeing when the ghoul attacked her and what she was going through. Not only could I see it, but I could hear it too. Awful experience.” He shakes his head.

Mr. Blaine removes his hand from the mirror and steps back. Arthygus steps away as well. Mr. Krew strokes the wood and bone along the mirror and turns his attention to Arthygus. “To answer your first question, Arthygus, it was told that the mirror was destroyed on purpose. In a magical fire that burned so hot that not even dirt itself was left behind.”

“Why on purpose?”

"It was a creation of the famed wizard Burvis Regin. He—”

Arthygus rudely interrupts, "And who is that?”

Mr. Krew sighs and gives him a strict stare. “You need good manners taught to you. Besides, I’m genuinely surprised you have not heard of him, being you are a wizard or sort of.” Arthygus was about to rebut, but Klinksly stepped on his toes and waved his finger back-and-forth no.

“Well, then again, it’s best you did not, for he dwelled in the forbidden arts of necromancy... And anything forbidden only attracts certain people more.”

Olivia peeks closer at it. “If it was destroyed, does this mean there is more than one mirror, Mr. Krew?”

“No. There is only one. Burvis somehow knew what magic it took to make this work. The mirror worked well. It would show others what you saw. Not what could be, but what actually happened. So let’s say you were somewhere and overlooked the object you were looking for. If it was in your memory, then you would observe it.”

"Like when I saw the ghoul chasing Abigail?”

Mr. Krew squints his eyes at him. "Yes. Like the ghoul. You will have to explain that to me later. A ghoul. Like they are around?”

Olivia, Klinksly, and Arthygus all chuckle at that, and Klinksly mumbles. "Oh yeah, they’re real.”

“If it wasn’t for Adam’s mace that did it in, we probably wouldn’t be here.” Arthygus said.

Mr. Blaine has been looking in a book this whole time and snaps his fingers to get everyone’s attention. "It says here that the mirror had a price on how it worked. It took a little essence from the user to activate it. Once it reached a certain level of... essence, Burvis could use it to open a portal to... I dare not say.”

"To where?” Olivia asks.

"The witch Darcey found this out, and she tried to destroy the mirror.” Mr. Blaine reads in silence for a minute. "It looks like there was a fight and Burvis was sucked into the mirror. Darcey didn’t destroy it, but took it for herself.”

"Who is she, and why did she take it?” Arthygus asks.

"She was known as the witch of the dead,” Klinksly says.

Mr. Krew looks over to Mr. Blaine. "Does the book state how it came to be here?” He flicks a few pages, and his eyes get as big as can be. He sits down on a chair. "What is it, Mr. Blaine? What did you find?”

“Very interesting. It seems that certain people were using this device to track down witches that they may have missed. The Knights of Muun in the common year 168 were such people. Until Hagathat retrieved the device and said it was destroyed."

Klinksly removes his hat and scratches his head. "Hagathat? 168? That long ago? I know of the tale of Hagathat that killed Darcey and ended her practice. But how did the mirror survive and get here?"

Mr. Blaine pulls an old parchment from the book and hands it to Mr. Krew. He reads it, then looks straight at Mr. Blaine and hands the note to Olivia. "Please read this aloud, Madam Olivia."

Olivia carefully takes the paper and reads it. "The rest of the covenant only knew it was utterly eradicated. I did not destroy the mirror, for when I grabbed it, I thought it may be a use to future witch queens. I have hidden it in a place only the witch queen can go.

The room is silent. Mr. Blaine takes the note back, folds it neatly, and puts it back in the book. Olivia stares at the mirror. Everyone else looks around the room, not knowing what to say. A minute goes by when Arthygus breaks the silence. "No matter the source of the magic, you still have to be amazed at the function of what it can produce."

Mr. Krew acknowledges him by nodding his head. "It sure is amazing, young wizard. And for Hagathat to see the events so long ago is fascinating in itself."

"Forgive my ignorance, but who is Hagathat?" Arthygus asks.

Mr. Krew quiets Klinksly, who is about to answer, and points to Olivia. "Olivia? Will you explain to your friend who she was?"

She is still staring at the mirror, thinking of what Abigail is going through. She did not fully hear the statement he asked her. "Is it wrong of me to keep thinking of what she is going through because I don't want to think of… if she…isn't anymore?"

Mr. Blaine sees Olivia is overly worried and burdening herself with what-ifs. His hand gently grabs her shoulder and turns her towards Arthygus. "Mr. Krew asked if you could explain who Hagathat is to your friend here."

She fakes a smile at him. "Hagathat? Of course. Um… She was the first witch. In the stories I was told, she was the one that figured out that nature had a magic that could be tapped into with spirit energy and used for whatever means. Like making potions or spells that affect people's minds or body." She looks back at the mirror and whispers. "And also spirit magic mixed with supernatural magic." Her voice trails off again, thinking of Abigail.

"Supernatural magic?" Arthygus is curious about that.

Mr. Krew sets his hand on her shoulder to take over. "Yes, indeed. Olivia is correct. She was the first witch and the first witch queen long ago. Hagathat discovered that spirit magic and supernatural magic are kind of the same. Except the supernatural is more dangerous as it deals with...things we do not fully understand. You can use spirits and bind them inwards to help or prevent...bad things from coming into this world. Or good for that matter, if that is your desire." His long emotionless face gives no sign to Arthygus about what he prefers.

"I believe it spirit magic was in abundance before Muun's time came, according to Mayreea."

"You are correct, Mr. Blaine." Mr. Krew walks over to the mirror and examines it. "So, young wizard, do you know when your magic came to be?"Arthygus looks up and squeezes his lips together in thought. "I take that as a no. Well, I do." Arthygus gives Mr. Krew an awkward look of surprise. "From that look, I will assume you never bothered to look into the opposing schools of magic, then. Yes, wizard. Even though I cannot use your conjuring or evoking of magic, I understand them and the history."

"But why, if you can't use them?"

He gives him that glare of disapproval again. "A good captain of a legion will study his enemy's ways to best him. And so... would I."

"But wizards are not your enemy."

"Oh, no?" Mr. Krew turns from him and focuses on the mirror. "I will let you learn that one on your own, then. For now, come here and touch the skull so we can find out what happened to our new witch queen and ease Olivia's mind for a while."

Arthygus is reluctant, but forces himself to touch the mirror. He withdraws his hand an inch from the skull. "Will it drain my essence? What does that mean?"

Klinksly jumps up on the bed to get a better view. "Well, nothing happened to Abigail when she touched it. At least... she said nothing about it."

He takes a deep breath. "I guess I will concentrate on what happened." With what little experience he has had with magical items, he touches the skull's forehead, closes his eyes, and focuses on when they entered the room.

Remarkably, Arthygus finds himself standing in the same room with Adam, Abigail, and Tyree, but watching everyone, including himself. The diamond is thrown, and Arthygus catches it. Watching from the mirror, everyone is enthralled at what they are seeing. Mr. Blaine has his arms crossed while Mr. Krew and Klinksly are taking it all in. Olivia has her hands half hiding her face, peeking through her fingers while Tyree hits her and talks to her.

As Abigail gets pulled into the door of darkness by that creature, Arthygus feels something envelop him. A faint bright green mist seems to pull red particles from him. He tries to pull his hand from the skull but can't. Now the view is of Adam holding onto Arthygus, who is grasping the dagger that is wedged in the stone, preventing them from getting sucked into the unknown. There is Klinksly smashing the stone and pulling them in.

The green mist mixes with the red particles and again, he tries to scream and pull away from the skull. Nothing works. He hears words that burn his ears and tries to scream even more. The mixed mist retreats into his body.

"Something is wrong!" Olivia yells.

Mr. Krew tilts his head and notices Arthygus's face is struggling. With lighting-like reflexes, Mr. Krew slaps Arthygus's hand from the skull. Mr. Blaine catches him before he collapses to the floor. His vision swirls around the room and gradually comes into focus.

Oliva wipes the sweat from his forehead. "What happened? Are you alright?"

"I need to sit. I'm woozy."

Mr. Krew gets close to Arthygus's face. He inspects him, spreading his eyelids and sees a faint bright green wisp swirl in his eye before it fades. "Are you sure you feel okay?" Arthygus nods his head. Mr. Krew takes a step back from him. "Indeed? What was the last subject we talked about before putting your hand on the mirror?"

Arthygus shakes his head to clear it. "How I'm not your enemy. The skull. I put my hand on the skull, by the way."

Mr. Krew gives him that questionable look again and mumbles, "Um hum."

"So, what do you think we should do?" Klinksly asks as he covers the mirror.

Mr. Blaine grins. "Ah yes. Back to business with this abduction of our queen." Olivia's bewildered face alerts him to clarify more. "Yes, Olivia. Abduction. It appears to us that she was not harmed but taken by..." He then looks at Mr. Krew.

"A demoness from the lower abyss. They have a few names, but she is called a Taraslith. Her real name is hidden very well, like all demons and devils."

Arthygus asks, "And...how do you know this?"

He stands tall and peers down at Arthygus. "Like you, I study and research all kinds of things. Demonology happens to be an interest of mine, since I thought that magic didn't exist any longer." Mr. Krew looks into his eyes one last time. "Perhaps I need to refresh my studies now that we saw Abigail get pulled into a portal."

Olivia perks up with good news. "So does that mean we know where she is? Let's go get her."

Mr. Blaine shakes his head no. "Unfortunately, what we saw only told us she was pulled into a mysterious door. We have no clue where she went...It will take time for us to figure that out."

"Time?! We don't have time. She could be... Or..."

Klinksly consults her. "Olivia. Calm down. Remember what Barland said. We need to figure things out first. Once we figure out where she is, then we can act most hastily."

She crosses her arms, nods her head, and pouts her lips. "How do we find out where she is, then?"

Mr. Krew stares at her in silence. Everyone glances at each other, waiting for him to say something. Mr. Blaine's cheerful voice interrupts the quiet. "First, Miss Olivia, we need to go back to where it happened." Olivia shakes her head no, but before she can say anything, he continues. "To be there is the best way to examine what happened. Perhaps there is magical residue left over that we can identify."

"No, no, no. I'm not going back to that place."

Klinksly slides off the bed. "I will take you. I know how to get there."

Mr. Krew stares down, frowning at the gnome. "Don't you think you have done enough harm already, queen's attendant? You need to stay behind." Klinksly squints at him.

"That is correct, Klinksly, the queen's attendant." Mr. Blaine steps over to him. "We need you to stay safe."

Olivia puts her hands on her hips. "Why?"

"Because if... Well, let me explain it this way. If something happens to the current queen and she can't perform their duties, such as a sudden disappearance or death, then the queen's attendant shall name a successor. In the time of no attendant, Klinksly the gnome in this case, should suddenly disappear or die before naming one. Chaos would arise as to who shall be queen or king."

Olivia waves her hand like she doesn't care. "Then get the next in line to do it."

"Let me say it this way, young witch." Mr. Krew is visibly annoyed now. "We are not royalty. If Abigail cannot be found or has died—yes, that is a real possibility—and if the gnome was to show me where it took place and he too was killed, there is no one else to name a successor. That means other witches and warlocks will try to be queen or king. It would be a free for all and cost many their lives. A witch war, you could say." Olivia sits down on the bed, frowning. "Do you want to be responsible for their lives just because you cannot wait or listen to what needs to be done? I for one am not."

Klinksly is holding his hat in both hands. "He is right, Olivia. I cannot go. I know my station."

"But..." She doesn't know what to say.

“Besides, it was all my fault to begin with, forgetting my spell pouch,” Klinksly says.

“If it was anyone’s fault, it was Abigail’s for going there in the first place,” Mr. Krew says.

Olivia is angered by this. “Don’t blame her. It’s not like she sought that place out. It was an accident that she found it.”

“It was an accident that Renee named her queen,” Mr. Krew mocks.

Olivia’s face turns red with anger, but before she can speak, Arthygus interrupts her. “There is no one to blame. It is what it is and what has happened, happened. But look at us now. We have a duty to get her back until we know otherwise. The situation put actions in motion and people together.”

Mr. Krew looks at everyone and calms down. “Why, Mr. Blaine, the young wizard is correct. There is no blame to go around. Events are in motion, and we need to be in control or ahead of them by working together.” Silence once again takes over the room while they calm down.

Olivia paces back and forth with the others watching her, trying to figure out what to do. She once again thinks of what Abigail would do. “Okay, Mr. Krew. What do we do, and when?”

“Klinksly, I need you to go back to wherever you go for being an assistant and see if you can find anything associated with searching for items of unknown locations. Arthygus... Do you have anywhere to go to look for such items?”

“I don’t, but I know a person to ask in Splinteroak.”

"Frederick, right? Don’t waste your time with him. Go with Klinksly and assist him in his searching. Olivia, take Mr. Blaine and myself to the tower after we retrieve some items from back at Snowcap.”

Olivia squints her eyebrows. “Snowcap?”

Mr. Blaine answers, “That is what we call our home.”

"Oh, that is cute. I like that.” She giggles. "But we have to leave now?”

Mr. Krew’s long face shows displeasure at prolonged questions. “Of course now. The longer we wait, the less magical residue will be left. And so will be the hope of any possibility of recovering...our queen.”

Klinksly steps in front of Mr. Krew. "When and where should we meet once we find something?”

“Let’s meet three days from now at Snowcap. Keep what you are doing a secret. If any word gets out about what we are looking for or doing, well, that would be bad. And this Tyree fellow? We need to see what he is all about too and what he is up to with the Book of Power.”

They all agree. Klinksly hands Olivia bark from the spruce tree from the tower of Prakton that he used to escape Tyree’s spell. Olivia grinds the bark to a powder while Mr. Krew and Mr. Blaine get things ready to go back to Snowcap. Klinksly motions for Arthygus to follow him out the door and back into the tunnel. Once in the tunnel leading downstairs to the arena, Klinksly stops. "To my knowledge, there has never been a wizard in this place. So please respect things and say nothing to anyone if they are here.”

“Got it.” Arthygus is silently excited and takes in as much as he can.

“This Frederick guy. Is he the one we visited after the bistro? The purple tower?”

“Yes, it is.”

Klinksly has a mischievous grin. “We will visit him if nothing turns up in here.”

3

Unlawful Gains

Tyree smiles as he struts through Splinteroak with the map firmly in his hands, protecting it from the steady rain. Glaive follows him a few feet behind, looking at the pretty women that are out. In Tyree's mind, he is already thinking ahead to what life will be like with him overtaking the kingdom. He looks around at all the people and shakes his head in disgust at how the Southern Kingdom is controlled. People standing doing nothing annoy him to no end. *I will make sure everyone knows their place and each one will contribute to my kingdom, my way, that's for sure.*

He passes two Splinteroak guards that he gleefully waves at as they stand in the rain looking miserable. *At least they are doing their job.* Tyree recalls his failed attempts to overtake a lord or two to raise a rebellion. He blamed these failures on lack of trained men, funding, and finding the right men to make them fight for the cause. This time is different because he found the Book of Power; that is all that he needs to succeed confidently this time. He thinks to himself, *All those laughing, denying fools. They will soon know who I am, and the Skylar Kingdom will rise again with me as king.* "Petty fools," he says out loud.

They soon find the place he was looking for. He looks above the door on the stone and wooden two-story building. A carved wooden muffin sign reads Craving Tummy Bakery. The aroma of sweet baked goods reaches their noses. Tyree tilts his head and shrugs at Glaive, who follows him inside. It is a small room of only five feet wide and twenty feet long. A large foggy window covers most of the front wall, but the back has many shelves filled with tarts, pies, and cakes. The countertop has many kinds of muffins and breads laid out to buy. Through the back opening they glimpse a thin brunette lady wearing a blue shirt and pants covered by a dirty white cooking apron from this morning's work. She is using a large wooden peel to pull out pastries from the brick oven.

Coming around the corner to the right is an attractive blonde-haired lady with hazel eyes, about five feet tall and a sensuous body. She is also wearing a blue shirt and pants with a white cooking apron that has a yellow and red flower pattern on it. She greets them with a pleasant smile. "What can I get you two hungry men this morning?"

Tyree stands there in a silent moment of thought, imagining her as his queen, until Glaive gives him a little shove. "Oh yes. Lovely treats you have here."

"What would you like?" She holds up a pumpkin muffin that is freshly made.

"Sure." He leans against the counter with his elbow closer to her and crosses his right leg over his left.

"Um, chief?" Glaive taps him on the shoulder. "Don't you have to say the thing?" Tyree ignores him and gives the lady a smile.

"Your friend is trying to get your attention."

"Well, you have my fullest attention now, sweetie."

She rolls her eyes and sighs. "Oh, great, another one."

"In that case." Tyree places a silver piece on the countertop. He looks straight at her. "Nice day. It's all sunshine and unicorns."

"And rainbows," Glaive says.

She glances at them with a smirk. She takes the silver piece and walks them through the back room. There is a boy keeping the fire under the oven going by feeding it firewood. She moves a few chopped logs aside, revealing a door on the floor with a wrought-iron ring attached to it. The boy grabs the iron ring and pulls the door open, revealing stone stairs that lead into darkness. Tyree and Glaive quickly go down twenty steps when the door closes above them. They hear the sound of logs being dragged over the door.

There is enough room to walk single file with Tyree first. The cool, musty air holds a dull orange glow from a light crystal that reflects off the mildewed stone blocks along the dark hallway. Tyree and Glaive step in small puddles, walking to the light. At the end of the fifty-foot tunnel is a warped wooden door. At eye level, there is a small, square metal plate in the center of the door. Etched into the door by a crude knife are the words, *Welcome to The Devil's Bowels.*

Tyree turns to Glaive with a funny smile. "We're here." He knocks on the door. The little square opens with a brighter light behind it. An unshaven face appears, and yellow teeth are visible when he speaks with a nasal voice.

"How many?"

"Two." The door is unlocked, and a large bar is removed, allowing it to open. They walk past the thin, smelly, scraggly-haired man, and another large man sitting in a chair that watches them go down the hall that opens into a larger room. The secret gathering place for the nefarious is a large square room, forty by forty feet. It's well lit by yellow and white light crystals. The walls are stone blocks covered with many stolen tapestries, hung as trophies. A few cut fingers hang from strings across the wooden rafters, supporting more stone blocks for the ceiling. A long wooden bar with a copper foot hold is to the left of them. To the right, many small and large tables and chairs. The small fireplace warms the area to the far end. A large-bellied man wearing a dirty apron stands behind the bar making drinks for two well-dressed men that are looking in their direction.

There are two women and one man sitting at a table near the burning fireplace. They are wearing typical garments for this time of year. The two ladies have on white ruffled shirts with dark yellow corsets over them and brown pants. The man is wearing deep blue pants with a brown leather protective vest that is unbuttoned over a black long-sleeved shirt. Tyree glances to his right and notices someone he knows. "Gullen Mull. Is that really you? Here in Splinteroak?" Grinning, he spreads his arms wide, walking over to him.

The unshaven, scraggly, thin-faced man lowers his cigar onto the table. His light brown hair is slicked from left to right and cut short. It could be wet from the rain or greasy from not washing. His brown beady eyes stare over the crooked nose that points downward toward his lips. His dirty dark green cloak is thrown over the chair to his side to dry from today's rain. He is wearing a brown long-sleeved shirt that has seen better days but looks very comfortable on cool days. His legs are crossed, resting on a chair, and a small dagger handle peeks out of his black leather pants near the wet black boots. He lowers his head in disbelief, and his throaty, raspy voice demands to be left alone. "Tyree?"

"Yes!" He motions for Glaive to go get drinks from the bar as he pulls out a chair and sits with Gullen. Tyree whispers, "What brings you here? Well, that doesn't matter. I have a proposal for you."

"Oh, really..." His non-caring tone allows him to look elsewhere. "There are plenty of other tables...Go choose one." He waves him off.

"Come now, Gullen. You should at least hear me out. This time..."

"This time? How many times have you failed to lead us to the prize? How many times have you left us when you got what you wanted? And how many times did I have to ask to be paid?"

Tyree leans back in the chair with a blank expression and nods his head. Inside, he feels like beating this guy, but he calms himself down. "I get it. I really do. All the failures... But...Those failures, as you call them, led me to something I was looking for."

Glaive comes over with three mugs of ale. Tyree sips the ale and slides one to Gullen. "Now, what I need is a right-hand man. Are you in?"

A dismayed Glaive smacks the table. "I thought I was your right-hand man, chief?"

Tyree takes a deep breath, shaking his head. "Glaive. You are my left-hand man and always will be. Now, don't interrupt me again." He gives Gullen back his attention. "So, what do you say?"

Gullen gulps the ale. "Say? You still owe me for the last two times you hired me. I'd say pay the two hundred gold now and I'll let you live."

Tyree is annoyed now at the threats and raises his voice. "I have found the Book of Power! Now is my time to rise and take my rightful place as ruler of the Skylar Kingdom!" His self-glorification brings the attention of others in the room. "And I will have riches beyond what you're worth. So, Gullen Mull, again, I ask you. Are you with me or against me?" Tyree lays the red book on the table and flips a few pages for Gullen to see.

"Uh, chief." Glaive is watching the two women and one man coming in his direction.

Tyree glances at them over his shoulder, standing with his hands on the table. He reaches inside his overcoat, which has many small pockets, grabbing a small pinch of chokeweed leaves. The larger woman, who has a round face and wavy, dirty-blonde hair that comes down past her shoulders and a snooty attitude, points at the book. "Ahh, this book must be worth something, Gina. Grab it."

Tyree's eyes stare into Gullen's, who is sipping the ale. "Now look at what you're going to make me do." He whips around quickly and spreads the chokeweed into the air and yells, "Lopeta hengetys!" The crushed weeds turn into a sickly green vapor that quickly surrounds their faces. They choke, gasping for breath while they rub their throats. The man behind the bar bends down and disappears while the other two sit and watch.

Tyree happily turns back to Gullen. "You see. My time has come." He spreads out his arms and twirls in a small dance while moving towards the three of them. "Now what should I do with these three that were about to...rob me?" He watches them choke; the large woman falls on her knees, gasping for air. The man rocks back and forth, falling against a table. Tyree sees a nice dagger under his vest and reaches for it. Gullen's eyebrows are raised in surprise at Tyree's actions, for he has never seen him so bold.

"Ah ha. This will do." He grabs the large woman's hair, tilting her head back. He slaps her hands out of the way, covering her throat. "Here bitch, this will help you breathe, ha." The dagger slices her silky white throat, and he tosses her backwards with a yank of her hair. She flops and gurgles as blood spills out across the floor.

He turns to the other girl. "So, Gina is it?" Her panicked eyes beg for forgiveness while her face turns an awkward purple. Tyree shakes his head, with one side of his lips smiling higher than the other. "You kept the wrong company." The dagger easily slices through her dark ebony skin and deep into her throat. "There, be free of the choke spell." He carelessly lets go, and she falls to the floor, also gurgling.

He turns to the man lying on his back, spread out on the table. "This is a very nice sharp dagger, I must say." He holds it up to show Glaive and Gullen, twisting it. "It's instruments like this that are designed for one purpose in mind." He sees his reflection on the polished blade as blood drips from the edges. Tyree watches a dribble follow the sharp edge to the small, hooked pummel. "Now, I don't know what association you had with those two, but, sadly, it ends now for you." He goes to cut the guy but notices the spell did its job already. "Huh, guess I shouldn't have been talking so much." He crosses his arms and taps the dagger against his forehead. "That is always such a problem of mine." He shakes his head in displeasure and walks towards the two well-dressed men that are frozen in fear, not expecting what they witnessed. A grinning Tyree turns to Glaive and glimpses the red book on the table.

"Now hold on. We didn't see anything," the man in the fancy yellow shirt says.

The other one pokes him in his side with his elbow. "Good one. Yeah, nothing to talk about."

Tyree dashes to retrieve the book from the table, grabbing it with his right hand. He is relieved he is holding it. A small drop of blood falls from his thumb, and the book absorbs it. It even pulls more crimson pasty blood from his hand. Tyree puts the book into his pocket when a deep voice comes to his mind. *Aughh rasgul mensha. The book has awakened and needs to feed.*

Tyree freezes, contemplating if he actually heard that. Seconds go by as the two men squint at him, wondering what is going on. Glaive and Gullen look at him as well. "Uh...chief? What's wrong? Do you see something?" Glaive scans the area for trouble but sees nothing.

The book vibrates in his pocket. The voice in his head is angry; *it needs to feed now.* Tyree's eyes are wide as can be as he looks back at Gullen and Glaive. Gullen pushes his chair to the side and stands with his back against the wall. Tyree pulls the vibrating book out of his pocket, dropping the dagger on the floor.

Tyree lifts the book with both hands in front of him and walks towards the two men. A deep, bloodcurdling, forceful voice booms from the book. "Lasgal kantuc mensha burg lambotta." Glaive, Gullen and the two men hold their ears as the voice hurts them with the piercing sound. The red book quickly opens on its own with a mix of bright red, pink, ochre yellow, and olive green light that shoots forth at the terrified two men.

Their screams are masked as it sucks their very essence into the book with a reverse wailing sucking sound. Parts of their skin blister and peel, followed by chunks being pulled off by the light. Muscle, blood, and other organs twist and get pulled into the book. And just like that, the book snaps shut. Tyree drops it on the floor with the book steaming. He shakes his hands, trying to rid the stun of electricity that is going through him.

A frightened Glaive stands up from under the table. "What was that?" He looks over at where the remains of the two men are. Their clothes have small burning embers on them, but it is the skinless steaming bodies that remain behind. Parts have muscles still attached where other spots are gone completely. The array of colors from the organs disgusts Glaive as some slide out onto the floor. The rancid smelling bodies slowly tilt and fall face-first to the floor.

Tyree picks up the book, looking at it before putting it away. He turns to Gullen. "Well, what do you say?"

Gullen is shocked at what he just saw. Since the last time he was with Tyree, he thought of him as a whiny man that didn't get his way. He always complained when things didn't work out. Now he sees him with something powerful that may prove useful. "Say? I'd say we can discuss what needs to happen next."

Tyree smirks and motions for them to leave, pointing at the door. The two men on the other side of the door are playing a card game as if they heard nothing. The thin man quickly looks at Glaive coming through the door and back at the cards. Gullen follows closely behind. Tyree thinks about not leaving any clues behind and a thought occurs to him to burn the place, but then notices one hand move on the corpse and claw at the floor. He scuttles to the door, leaving it open a hair.

Once past the second door, the thin scraggly faced man begrudgingly gets up from his game to shut the door and lock it. Tyree glances down at the door lock. He twiddles his thumb and index finger and quietly murmurs a few words, casting a lock spell on it. “No one will unlock it without magic or breaking the door down completely. We can’t leave any hint we were here.”

“Hey, chief. What about the women upstairs that saw us come in? Instead of killing them, can I take them?” Glaive said.

“No, Glaive. I’m afraid that will bring even more unwanted attention to us.”

“How come, chief? We will have them with us.”

Tyree shakes his head at Glaive’s stupidity. “Because people will search for them and soon find us. I can’t risk what we are about to do because you fancy a lady. Keep it in your pants, for now.”

Glaive is disappointed. “But, chief, they are too pretty to kill, and they make wonderful cakes. Like the strawberry I got for us yesterday.”

They walk up the stone steps, and Tyree also feels they are too pretty to kill. He decides killing them would also be a problem. “Do you have some spell that could erase their minds?” Gullen whispers.

Tyree pauses, reaches into his overcoat, and pulls forth a small vial containing dried holly berry dust and wisteria seeds forced into a swirling black and maroon vapor. “This should do the job.” Once up in the bakery, Tyree tricks the two ladies and the boy into smelling the vapor by saying it is a new berry flavor he would like in a pie. After sniffing it, they have a blank expression and look at Tyree’s hands, waving back and forth. “Unohda tänään. Forget all about today. You will never remember to-day.” Faint images come from their ears into Tyree’s hands. Once he sees themselves, including Gullen entering the bakery and leaving, he crushes the memory, and it vaporizes into nothing.

Tyree motions for the others to leave, and he soon follows. After a few minutes, the ladies and boy come too and go about their business with no question, as if nothing is wrong. Glaive and Gullen are outside across the street, waiting for Tyree. He comes over to them with arms wide and snaps his finger. “See? Nothing to worry about. But let’s move away from here and talk.” The three of them head towards the outside of town.

*****

Back down in the Devil’s Bowels, the two watchmen are still playing cards when they hear a chair break in the other room, followed by a muttered scream cut short. The larger man, being lazy, points at the door. He has a voice that is like constantly chewing food. “Go see what that was.”

The thin man gives him a sneer. “No cheating now, just because I’m winning.”

“Ahhh, you're just lucky...as usual.”

The thin man opens the door partially and seems confused at what he sees. He hears the guy behind the bar shuffling around on the floor but does not see him. The other side of the room is dark, and he steps in noticing the bodies on the floor. He is shocked and stutters, trying to get the attention of the barkeep. Coming out of the dark corner, sliding one leg and hardly lifting the other, is the skinless body. The man freaks out and jumps over the bar, screaming. “Wilbur! Wilbur! What is that?”

He keeps an eye on the thing coming at him and taps Wilbur, who is bent over. He lifts his hand to his face and sees a pasty bloody goo on his fingers. The man slowly turns his head down to see Wilbur, but Wilbur is lying in a pool of blood with his head ripped open. The grayish bloody body is staring at him, then opens its mouth. Parts of Wilbur’s brains fall out and the creature jumps onto the thin man. “Ahhhhh!”

The large man slams his fist against the table. “Damn it. Can’t you guys do anything? What is going on?” He grabs his small sword that is on the table and struggles to get out of the chair. Once he gathers himself up, he smells burnt rancid flesh and hears a slight wheezing. He looks up to see both creatures in the hallway that used to be the two fancy men. “What the...” He drops his sword in a panic and tries to open the door to no avail. The creatures tear into his head and flesh as his hands grasp the small opening on the door, trying anything to get out. Then all is silent but for the munching of flesh.

*****

Tyree, Glaive, and Gullen Mull reach the outside of Splinteroak. The rain has turned into a light mist with a cool breeze. A few farmers are tending to their crops with covered wagons. Tyree looks around and people are far enough away and too few to hear what he has to say. "Alright. Now that you see what I'm capable of, want to listen to me now?"

Gullen pulls his hood over him as the mist picks up. "So you are saying you finally found... that book?"

Tyree stands tall, proud that he has indeed found it. "Yes. And it's the beginning of what I can do...What we can do."

"What is the reason you searched for the book?"

"This book was the secret that allowed General Prakdon to be so successful. And now I have it to help with my conquest for the kingdom. Nothing! Nothing will stop me."

"What are the plans now?"

"Now? Well, I need a few men. Good ones to go on an expedition."

"Huh. Why and where?"

"The why is none of their concern. The where is to the west of the Northern Kingdom."

Gullen shakes his head. "That is your problem with getting good people to do the job. It is their concern why. What's in it for them? How much are they getting paid or what percentage of the prize? That is why you always fail or they quit on you. I don't know why I stayed the last two times. You still owe me."

"That's just it! You will get paid ten times more. No! A hundred times more, soon." A minute goes by in silence while they look around. "So, what do you say?"

"It just so happens I'm in town for a job. Meet me in two days at 11 in the morn, a mile past the guard tower on Garnet Road. You will need to prove yourself to the others." Gullen takes a step back, then walks towards Splinteroak. Tyree shrugs his shoulders before he and Glaive walk back to his place.

*****

Two days later, Tyree and Glaive are walking in warm sunshine after a few days of rain. The autumn leaves are at their peak, ready to fall. Tyree walks with the crystal cane, and Glaive has his curved pole arm blade on a shorter shaft strapped to his back. They casually walk past the guard tower outside of town till they run into Gullen, hiding behind a large bush.

"Quickly, behind here." Gullen waves for them to get behind the bush.

"Alright, Gullen. We are here, so now what?"

Gullen peers around the bush, looking down the road. "Okay, Tyree, if you need hired hands, and I mean good ones, you have to prove yourself to them."

Tyree is taken aback. "Prove myself? I do not need to prove myself to you or anyone."

Gullen sighs. "Listen, they don't know who you are or even give a crap about you. You help with this job by...showing your superior ability. Then maybe they will follow." Tyree rubs his small beard for a second or two, thinking.

"What is the job?"

"In about an hour, three wagons will come down this road, each ten to twenty minutes apart. They have on good authority that the third wagon has a chest of gold coins in it."

Glaive shrugs his shoulder against Tyree. "That's just what we need, chief."

Tyree frowns at Glaive. "So. Could only be a dozen or fifty. What's so special about it?"

Gullen has a smile from ear to ear. "Ahh. But this is special. It is the payment chest for the Splinteroak guards coming from Garnet City." Gullen looks down the road. "They will have Garnet City soldiers on the third one. Guarding it. So you know it's special."

Tyree taps Glaive on his shoulder. "Not a hundred gold, Glaive... Not a hundred. But maybe a thousand coins plus." Gullen smirks, nodding his head. Tyree pats him on the back. "Good. This can work. Where are these men at, and what is the plan?"

Gullen points down the road near a hilltop. "There. They plan on attacking it from the hilltop."

"No. No, no, no! That will not do. Are these men idiots? Take me there now if this is to be done right."

Gullen leads them to the hilltop away from the road so not to be seen. They walk through scrub bush, trees, and thickets that annoy Tyree, getting his coat stuck on thorn branches that reach out at him. Soon, they come to an area of less scrub bush and about a hundred yards away they see five individuals that are near a fallen tree. Two of them are sitting on it, two others are standing, and one has his foot on the log adjusting his black boot.

"Is that them?" Tyree whispers. Gullen nods his head. "Tell me who they are."

"Well, the large dark-skinned one, looks in his thirties with his foot on the tree, is Ryan. The leader, you could say." He is a large muscular fellow with short black hair and a trimmed beard, dressed in brown and red leather armor and brown leather pants with a long sword sheathed on his side.

"The two thin young ones sitting on the bench are brothers, Brak and Brace. Very quick, they are. You know, with their hands and fighting skills." They appear similar but are not twins. About five feet tall each, Brak has long dirty-blonde hair while Brace's is cut extremely short. They wear green clothing with silver armbands. Brak has a black leather vest with many knives on the inside. Brace has two hand axes of copper and gold on his sides.

Gullen points to the one standing looking in their direction, holding a faded dark brown bow. "That one there is Kade, from the far southeast. She doesn't talk much, but boy, can she shoot a bow. That girl also has this weird round weapon she throws. I've seen her cut the fingers right off of those holding swords with that thing." Kade stands about five foot seven at twenty-eight years old, with long jet-black hair that is crown braided from both sides of the temple to behind her head then intertwined as one, stopping below her shoulders. She has a few stragglers that hang over her pale forehead above her elongated brown eyes. Her dark maroon leather pants, pink shirt, brown leather knee-high boots, and a pinkish brown cloak make her stand out among the group.

"You see that small grimy one in the dirty brown robe that is too big for him? That's Buggs. He will steal anything. They shouldn't have brought that guy. He doesn't think and causes problems for others and yet, he gets away." He has unkempt knotted brown hair, black beady eyes, and yellow teeth with some missing. The man is bony from lack of eating properly and his face has sunken eyes with black shadow around it, giving an unappealing look.

Tyree nods his head in understanding and murmurs. "Is that so?" Tyree gets in front of Gullen and picks his pace up, heading towards the group. They notice him proudly walking through the bushes and stepping on fallen branches, snapping them without a care in the world. When he gets thirty feet from them, he speaks, "Vedä." He holds his left hand out in a claw motion and stomps his feet when he stops. A flash of green comes from his palm and quickly grabs Buggs, dragging him towards Tyree.

Tyree pulls the diamond out of his right pocket. "Meikila!" The crystal sword springs forth, and he stops Buggs at his feet. Before anyone can react, Tyree slashes into Buggs with several swipes of the blade. "Why?" He hits him again. "Did they bring a worthless piece of trash?" He slices into the now lifeless body. "Disgusting. He is full of fleas." Tyree shakes his head and walks to the group, who are all now standing shocked. Gullen emerged from the bush.

Tyree recoils the blade back into the diamond and holds his hands out wide. "Friends… We all knew he was going to ruin this. So, in good faith, I solved that problem for you."

Ryan stands tall at six-foot-five and has a husky tone in his voice. "Why do you think he was a problem?"

Tyree claps his hands and stops a few feet from Ryan. "Because none of you stopped to help him." They all look at each other, perplexed. "You know I'm right. But enough of that. What is your plan with the wagon now?"

Ryan looks over at Gullen. "Wagon? Gullen, who is this guy?"

Tyree waves Gullen off. "Friends, I'm here to help. Gullen has brought me here to make sure this goes right. And it will. Then I offer you way more than what is in the chest that will come soon."

With a thin voice, Brace says, "You just want a share of the gold."

"Or all of it to yourself," Brak says with a similar voice.

"If I was here to take it for myself, all of you would be like that bug thing back there. Dead." A smiling Tyree holds his hands out to everyone. "But I offer a chance of more work after this successful endeavor."

Gullen looks at Ryan with an unpleasant grin. "Just tell him the plan and listen to him. And yes, all of you would be dead by now if he wanted."

With hesitation, the group looks around, and eventually Ryan speaks, "Alright then. When the wagon reaches the top of the hill, we are going—"

"Wrong!" Tyree interrupts. "Certain failure."

"How so?" Ryan said.

Tyree stands in the middle of them, spinning and pointing at each one. "The first failure would be, as soon as all of you jump out at them, the point guard would alert the driver and they would speed off...Downhill!" Tyree makes a whoosh sound and slides his hand downhill like a speeding wagon. "And they would leave you in the dust. With nothing."

The group looks around at each other again. "And the second thing?" Brace says.

"Glad you reminded me, kid. If you were lucky enough to stop them, these are soldiers. Not guards."

"Ahh, what's the difference? They would go down just as quick," Brak says.

Tyree smiles and claps his hands in delight at telling them the ignorance of their plan. "These are Garnet City soldiers. From that statement, I take it you never tangled with one. Well, by the time you try to open the back door, two of you may be dead and the rest will be captured when they open the door... You'd surely lose."

Kade speaks with a smooth, far southeast accent. "I don't lose."

Tyree smirks, putting his hands on his hips. "Ahh, sweetie, don't tease yourself. If you didn't lose, you wouldn't be here with this company now, would you? Let the men speak on this matter."

Brak and Brace crack up laughing, and Brace stumbles off the log. Kade gives them a look that forces them to stop laughing but snicker behind her back. Ryan motions for Kade to step back. "Okay. So what do you plan on doing, then?"

"Ah, glad you asked. The way I'm going to do it will leave no reason to be tracked or sought after. If by any slim chance you would have been successful, they would have tracked you down." Tyree notices a few wooden crates on the other side of the log and points to them. "What's in the crates?"

Ryan lifts his left lip up in confusion. "What? It's water, apple juice, and vegetables. Now forget that. Tell us your plan."

"Not just apple juice, but fresh pressed juice we got an hour ago. That old man never saw us," Brace says, giving a high five to Brak.

"Perfect then." Tyree rubs his hands together. "This is what we are going to do." Tyree has Glaive empty a crate and put in the water, apple juice bottles, and carrots. Next, Tyree pours a little bright red liquid into each bottle that dissipates quickly with little heart-shaped puffs of vapor popping out of the top.

"We will not harm the soldiers or do anything that may cause them suspicion. That will break the charm I'm putting on them. When Glaive tells you to go," he points at Gullen, "I want you to get in the back and pick the lock." He then points at the brothers. "Then you two hop in and get the gold out of the chest as quickly as you can into the crate that Ryan will hold." Brace and Brak look at each other and nod their heads, laughing with excitement. Tyree looks at Kade. "You...sweetie. I need you to keep an eye out on the road from behind for anyone and for the next wagon." She huffs and turns her head. "Hey, you should be thankful I'm including you in this. After all, that's what you do best. Watch, right?"

"What about me, chief?"

"Glaive... you need to watch me for the signal to get the others to move and keep an eye in front of the wagon. Okay?"

"Right, chief."

Kade sarcastically mumbles. "Oh, hey, I see the wagon coming. I guess a woman can do something after all." She moves off into the bushes to hide. Tyree grabs the crate with the bottles and heads out to the road between the two hills at the lowest point. The others hide along the roadside in bushes, waiting for the sign.

Tyree keeps an eye on the enclosed carriage approaching while walking on the same side of the road and in direction. He hears the trotting horses getting closer, and he begins his plan by dropping carrot bunches onto the road. Tyree bends down with the crate to pick up the carrots but falls over, causing the driver to quickly stop the horses from running over him. The hoofs stop right in front of Tyree's head. For a second, he thought he was going to get run over. *Stupid fool, I should just kill him now.* But then notices Glaive peering out of the bush for the signal and he regains his thoughts. "Oh, heavens meeee! Don't run over me!" He hides his face with his arms.

"You there. Out of our way!" The driver said.

Tyree gets on his knees and pushes carrots in front of the horses that start eating them, stomping their hoofs. He scoots the crate to the side and lifts his arms up in the air. "Sorry, good sirs. But it seems your horses have taken a liking to my fresh carrots." He reaches into the crate, pulling out a bottle of apple juice. "Perhaps you need refreshment as well? I have fresh pressed apple juice and nice crisp, clear water too."

The driver and point guard look at each other in agreement and the soldiers in the back of the carriage open a small slot and inquire what the holdup is. The driver motions nothing is wrong, and the point guard scouts the area and heads down to Tyree. Before he can get to him, Tyree whispers over the bottles to activate the charm spell, then smiles. "Your choice. Apple or water?"

The soldier pops the cork out, releasing the strong sweet apple aroma. He smiles and takes a small sip. "Oh...Oh this is fresh." He gulps more down, thirsty.

Tyree looks into his eyes and waits for the pale red haze to appear. "Ahh, friend, it is good, isn't it?" The soldier nods in agreement while drinking more. “Hey, you should really get your friends to drink some. After all, they work hard too.”

The soldier turns back to the wagon. “Hey, Ackley. Get down here and try this juice. It is the best I ever had.” The driver motions for the others in the carriage to get out. The back door opens, and five well-armored soldiers step out. They stretch from a long-awaited break and head over to Tyree. After they all drink the juice, they finally convince the driver to come down to enjoy the juice too.

Tyree keeps their attention away from the carriage and gives Glaive the signal. In a matter of five minutes, Tyree notices the brothers and Ryan head back into the bushes. Kade is waving that the other wagon is near.

“Okay, friends. I’m glad you enjoyed my apple juice. But don’t you think you should be on your way now?”

“Oh yes, yes. Thank you, kind man.” The driver orders the soldiers to go back inside the carriage while he and the point guard hop on top. Tyree stands to the side of the road, smiling and waving. After they are out of sight, he tosses the crate to the side of the road and sprints to the group. They all lie low till the last carriage goes by.

Tyree looks at all the gold in the crate that Ryan is holding. “See, now let’s head back to my place and discuss a way to get more. That is, if you want more.” The group looks at Ryan, waiting for him to say something.

4

Inquisitive To No End

Two days ago, while Tyree was planning on visiting Frederick, Olivia took Mr. Krew and Mr. Blaine to the tower of Prakdon, while Klinksly and Arthygus headed back to the colosseum. She is very nervous about going back, but is determined to help find Abigail. To her, it is better than sitting back at home doing nothing.

They arrive at the mountaintop on another cloudy day and are met with freezing rain and heavy wet snow coming down to obscure the view again. Olivia cautions them about the chimera that is here and notices their faces are like little children in a candy store for the first time. They regain their composure to the hazards as she points out the body of the decomposing ghoul and Se'allt's grave. Mr. Blaine scrapes bark off the tree they came out of for his door spell. They waste little time in getting Olivia to take them to the spot Abigail was taken.

She has difficulty going down into the depths of the sunken tower again without Klinksly by her side. Each creaking sound or rock falling, she would jump back and do the little eek sound she does, thinking another ghoul is going to jump out. The light crystals create unwelcomed shadows that spook her. Mr. Blaine comforts her and ensures they won't allow anything to happen to her. Before they get to the last room, Olivia stops. "Do you have any...special abilities?"

Mr. Blaine is crouched over, looking at the scribings on the wall. "This is an odd time to ask such a question."

"Well, I need to know in case we... run into something."

"Valid point," Mr. Krew says.

"If you need to know about us, rest assured that we both know many spells. My ability may not help us here...I'm able to tell if someone is telling the truth or lying. Same goes for writings too. If they are false or misleading, I can tell." Mr. Blaine goes back to examining the scribings around the door frame.

Olivia glances at Mr. Krew, waiting for an answer. He hesitates to tell her, but gives in. "I have two, actually. I can control someone by taking control of their body. And the other? Let's hope you don't have to see that. I shall say nothing more."

Olivia nods, going into the room. The dull yellow light crystals light up the room and, to their surprise, they see the shattered remains of the creature Adam destroyed. "Eww, that smell is horrible." Olivia covers her nose.

Mr. Blaine scurries over to the spot it exploded at. He picks up part of the back skull with two black spikes protruding from it. "Amazing, Mr. Krew." He holds it up for him to see.

Mr. Krew's eyes widened in astonishment. "That stench? The spines? Look at all the mess...It's a black-spiked devil!" Discovering this puts him in a sort of delightful mood. He reaches for the skull part that Mr. Blaine is holding out to him. "It's still warm? But how?" He focuses on the spines, and it hits him. "This devil should have not been here? This type of banned magic was the first doors to be closed, so it was said." He turns to Olivia, who is standing stunned at the news. "What happened here?"

"I...I don't know. I wasn't here, and they didn't tell me this part."

"But you came through here? Didn't you?" Mr.Blaine said.

"Yes, but we were in a hurry to find Abigail and the others. We just kept going."

Mr. Blaine stands looking over the mess. "Speaking of hurry. We should get to the spot before more magic dissipates."

"Agreed." Mr. Krew puts the skull parts in a little cloth sack.

Olivia guides them down the secret door that was left open and to the room where the enormous stone statue is. The appearance alone amazes both of them. Olivia stands near the exit, reliving the image she saw of Abigail being taken on the mirror. She tries to stand strong but gets teary-eyed, wondering what is happening to Abigail. Mr. Blaine notices this while Mr. Krew opens his old black leather hardened bag.

He retrieves a glass vial containing a white swirling smoke. He looks at Mr. Blaine with an unknowing expression. "I have not had the chance to use this ingredient until now. Thought I was never going to." He hands the vial to Mr. Blaine, who waves him off, pointing to Olivia. Mr. Krew raises his left eyebrow. "Really?"

"Yes. She needs to be a part of this. Let her see it."

"Very well. Here, Miss Olivia, take this vial and hold it. Nothing will happen to you." Mr. Krew moves her to a general position where they think the magic was used. With her holding the vial, he uncorks it and a little white wisp follows. He dips his left index finger into the swirling white smoke and takes a deep breath. "jäljittää" (yalee-he-ta) The smoke follows his finger as he makes a large circle with his hand.

The smoke spreads and slowly thins out into the air. After a few seconds, Mr. Krew sees the spell didn't work properly. "Perhaps this spell was not what I was thinking it was."

Olivia feels a tiny vibration from the vial. "Um... Mr. Krew?" The small bottle shakes side to side and up and down. She is now holding it with two hands.

"Don't let go," Mr. Blaine says.

The smoke puffs out like water on a fire. They watch in wonder as the smoke creates lines in the air. First it fills the outline of a seven-foot tall by three-foot wide rectangle. Mr. Krew is immersed in what is happening and murmurs, "There's the door." The smoke goes off to the side and a jagged sawtooth circle forms around the door. On the left side, a human skull takes shape and to the right an elongated skull with horns curved back appears like the statue before them. The smoke forms more symbols but turns to a sickly green.

"No!" Mr. Krew slaps the cork back into the vial and takes it from a stunned Olivia. "Clear the smoke! Clear the smoke!"

The three of them wave their hands quickly to dissipate the smoke, which they easily do. Olivia sniffs the air. "Why do I smell rusty iron and burnt flesh?"

"It is not what I expected. But also, I'm glad it worked." Mr. Krew sternly looks at Mr. Blaine. "You are going to get your wife to do a cleansing on us. Just to be safe."

"What just happened?" Olivia asks, shaken.

"That was a recall spell. Or some call it a retrace spell. It is to figure out what type of spell was used and, in this case, what spell opened a doorway," Mr. Krew says.

"It's not good," Mr. Blaine says, packing up his things.

"What do you mean...not good?" She backs up to the door.

"The spell worked. It identified that a potent magic was used and opened the doorway as the smoke showed us. But...something tried to open the door from the other side..." Mr. Krew's voice fades off as he points to the chains on the wall. "Mr. Blaine, tell me if I'm wrong, which is rare. Weren't there the remains of a skeleton hanging on the wall when we witnessed in the young wizard's memory?"

Mr. Blaine wiggles the chain with dust falling to the ground. "Yes, there was."

"We lingered too long. Gather everything, and let's leave."

Olivia watches Mr. Krew close the bag when a chilling touch penetrates her leg. She swipes at her leg only to feel something cold and boney. There is a skeleton hand and part of a forearm grasping her. She screams, kicking her leg forward, but the hand does not release. Mr. Blaine grabs the boney arm and pulls it away. In doing so, he notices a faint red mist that fills in the missing parts. An image of a skeleton wearing a robe with a crown made of silver bones on top of his skull lays on the ground. Every part is a red mist fading into small wisps away from the bones. The jaw opens to speak, but nothing is heard.

"Sagoil!" Mr. Blaine yells, and the hand releases Olivia. She jumps back into the hallway as the mist disappears from Mr. Blaine's sight. "We must leave! We came unprepared for this."

"Why? What is it?" Mr. Krew asks.

The skeleton hand fades into the wall with small crumbles of rock and dust falling to the ground. The three of them step outside the room with Olivia and Mr. Blaine leading the way, only to have Mr. Krew remain behind. He searches through his bag and finds the red vial he was looking for. He pokes his finger with a needle to draw blood and dips it in the red liquid. After drawing ward symbols around the door frame, he says a few words awaiting the glow of the writing. He puts the vial away, stepping back as the wards glow bright, then fade.

"What is he doing?" Olivia asks.

"He is putting a quick seal on the door to keep...that in there. Now keep moving." Mr. Blaine gives a push to Olivia to move.

They quickly make their way out of the tower and tread lightly to the tree door. Olivia opens the door, and they step inside. When the spell ends, she lets out a deep sigh of relief and rubs her ankle. After coming out of the pine tree onto the snow of Mr. Krew's place, Mr. Blaine rushes in to find his wife. "Mayreea!"

Olivia and Mr. Krew make their way into the warmth of the keep. Last time here, she didn't make it beyond the entrance hall of the keep and is uncomfortable about how dimly lit the place is. She can hear Mr. Blaine talking to someone and Mr. Krew confirming they all need cleansing. Mr. Krew goes off to a room on the left to rummage through a book to satisfy his thoughts on the boney hand.

"Miss Olivia? Mind coming in here, please." Mr. Krew firmly requests.

"Sure." She walks past an open door that looks like the dining room and suddenly stops. Standing beside Mr. Blaine is a woman just as tall in a golden yellow sleeveless dress. The dress reflects the candlelight in little sparkles and compliments her perfectly smooth ebony skin and hazel eyes with a tint of yellow. Her black and brown hair is parted in the middle and braided tight in flawless spiral locs hanging down the back of the neck to slightly above her waist. Gold bracelets surround both her wrists and a fine gold belt with unusual etchings on it lays at her waist. Wide bands of gold and a small sapphire gem cover her neck. "Mr. Blaine, is this beautiful woman your wife?"

The smile he gives is all Olivia needed, and she rushes into the room. "Mr. Blaine! How dare you not say anything about her?" Olivia giggles at the sight of her in a beautiful dress. "You have the most intriguing brown eyes I have ever seen. How did you ever get so lucky to find such a wonderful woman?"

"Well...I... Lucky I am, I guess."

Mayreea's voice is ethereal with an off accent. "Blaine. You should take lessons on compliments from this charming woman." She reaches for Olivia's hands and holds them.

"Olivia is my name."

Mr. Krew walks to the doorway and rudely interrupts. "Oliva! When I say to do something, I need you to do it."

"I was admiring Mayreea."

He stares at her with a condescending look but does not push the issue. "I need you to remove your boot so I can see where the hand touched you."

"Oh, very well." She presses her lips together in disapproval and murmurs. "Just like Abigail sometimes."

She removes her boot, revealing five thin blueish purple claw marks on her ankle. Olivia rubs them. "They are still a little cold, or my foot is numb. What could have done that?"

Mr. Krew feels the spots and confirms they are still cold. "Well then, no doubt about it now, Mr. Blaine."

"A cold that is felt like no other through the touch of the bony hand," Mr. Blaine says.

Olivia pulls her eyebrows together and frowns. "And what does that mean?"

"You, dear Miss Olivia, have been grasped by the remains of a lich," Mr. Krew explains with his head held high.

"What is that? It's not so bad then if it only does this."

"How wrong you are. You should already know not to take things at face value, Miss Olivia."

"Well, sorry. I pay little attention to skeletons or whatever these things are. It's not my vibe."

Mr. Blaine sees she is not getting the point and that Mr. Krew's patience is thin at the moment, so he intervenes before it gets worse. "What my colleague is trying to tell you is that there are different undead. And this bony hand that touched you was not a normal skeleton but a lich."

"Okay, so what is a lich?"

"They were once a strong wizard or enchantress that dedicated themselves to the forbidden magic of necromancy so they could continue on even after death of the body. One power they have is the chilling touch, which affects your very soul, sapping part of your life force from you. No other skeleton has that ability."

Oliva rubs her foot and the cold spots. "Well, it's not that bad."

Mr. Krew shakes his head. "Of course not. Because it was only reforming back into itself. Lucky for you and us... its power is reduced at the moment. Mr. Blaine, we need to find out who that is."

Olivia claps her hands together and taps her toes against the stone floor. "Oh, I know. That sinful man Tyree said it was the remains of General Prakdon himself. Remember? From what we watched in the mirror?"

Mr. Krew smiles at her. "Yes, you are correct. If this Tyree fellow was right, then that means the general was a wizard and will have to be stopped. We have to do more research on this. In the meantime, will you, Mayreea, give the three of us a cleansing so we can't be seen or tracked from what may have seen us?"

"I sure can. Let me change and get my things to do this."

Olivia's eyebrows curve inward. "Tracked? Nothing followed us?"

Mayreea smiles while helping Olivia take off the other boot. "Nothing that you can see, but the unseen may have tracked you. Some spirits are curious by nature and may cling to an individual to see who they are or what they are up to. Others may have a sinister purpose in reporting what one does. So I am going to prevent that from happening and shoo away any unwelcome spirits."

After a few minutes, Mayreea brings in a few light candles and sets them around the room. She holds a small bouquet of smoldering sweetgrass, sage, and cedar shavings. After circling the three of them with smoke while chanting in a language Olivia does not know, she then blows a fine stone powder into their faces and it floats to the floor.

"There... all done. Any residue from the chance meeting back in the tower is all gone now." Mayreea sees the faint outline of wispy hands that get caught by the powder and taken to the floor, but she remains quiet about it.

Olivia is relieved that anything that was on her is gone, but she is still concerned about her ankle. "My ankle still feels cold. Can anything be done about that?"

"Not at this time. We never had to have a cure for that because they were supposed to be only stories to scare off people from places," Mr. Blaine explains.

"Get some rest. You're welcome to stay the night here...Just in case." Mayreea notices Olivia looks worried about it. "We have a spare room."

Mr. Krew frowns at the notion of that but concedes it may be best. Mayreea takes Olivia by the hand to show her the room. Mr. Krew and Mr. Blaine go into their library to go through books about what happened for the rest of the evening.

The guest room's ceiling and top part of the walls are stone painted black, with deep red, bright red, and pink roses painted along the top in a variety of green stems going in all directions. To her, they almost look real. The dark brown wood dresser has a fine polished look that reflects the light of the candle that is on it. The plush bed has fluffy soft pillows shrouded in pink silk and dark red silk sheets folded over, beckoning her to sleep.

Giving in to the tiredness of her body, she strips down to nothing and slides into bed. The cool sheets feel good across her body while she twists and turns, feeling the smoothness of the silk. Not too long after, the candle scent puts her to sleep. Mayreea opens the door to check on her, only to discover she has already fallen asleep. She picks up Olivia's clothes and cloak, folds them neatly, and sets them on the dresser. She is about to leave when the sheet comes off Olivia as she turns. Mayreea is appalled by all the cuts and scars that are on her. She covers her back up and tucks her in tight. *What happened to this poor child?* she thinks and closes the door.

Olivia dreams about gliding a few feet above the grasses that are black and white with dark clouds obscuring any vision beyond a hundred feet. Then the grass changes into the color of greens and yellows, and the scent of salty air hits her. She has no control over where she is going. She comes into a small seaside town with buildings and shacks pushed up against each other tight. The recent rain made the streets muddy. The clouds disperse more so that she can see the tall mast of ships on the docks.

A little girl, about ten years old, goes rushing by her crying, followed by three boys in their early teens that are laughing and throwing mud at her. Olivia feels herself stop and stands in the cold mud. She watches the little girl trip and fall into the mud. The boys surround her, grabbing clumps of mud and raising their hands to hit her with it. Olivia tries to cry out to stop them, but nothing happens.

The clumps of mud make her already dirty dress muddier than it was, but one boy hits her in the face, causing her nose to bleed. "Serves you right!" the larger boy says.

The boy is reaching down to grab more mud when he is pushed from behind, causing him to fall face first into the mud. The two boys turn to look at who did that with mud balls in their hands. Standing there is a thin boy of eight years old holding a worn-out wooden practice sword. He is barefoot and wearing old blue pants and a brown dirty shirt. His thin, long blonde hair covers the first two missing buttons.

"Aww, the kid thinks he is going to hurt us. Get him!" the larger boy yells. The little boy avoids being hit by the thrown mud balls and kicks the still sitting larger boy between the legs. He smacks his sword on his chin and jumps over him, causing him to fall backwards. Now he stands between the girl and the three boys. He motions for the girl to run.

The two older boys come at him with arms swinging that he deflects with the wooden sword. He smacks them in the hands and legs with it while they scuffle. The larger boy stands, grabbing a crab trap that is on top of a crate. The little boy smacks the hands again of the two boys, causing them to step back. Olivia wants to yell watch out, but again nothing happens. She watches in horror as the larger boy hits the little boy over the head with the crab trap, busting it to pieces and causing him to collapse into the mud.

The three boys stomp and kick him until he is bloody and covered in mud. The little boy looks through parts of the busted trap laying on the ground and watches the larger boy snap his wooden sword in two. Olivia feels bad for this little boy, who then jumps up from the muddy ground with part of the broken wooden trap in his hand. He swipes at the larger boy, cutting him in the face.

The boys are about to hit him again when they run away. The little boy is about to chase them when he is grabbed from behind by a town guard that stops him. Olivia can't hear the guard as the clouds slowly close in on her. She looks around and notices a woman wearing a white skirt with her belly showing and a white long-sleeved top and has the blondest long hair she has ever seen. The woman is out of place with the scenery, as if she doesn't belong.

Olivia suddenly wakes up, confused about where she is at and what she just saw. *That dream was so vivid...so real. Aww, hope that little boy is okay.* The candle on the dresser is almost out, so it must be near dawn. She pulls the covers over her and falls asleep again.

She awakens to the aroma of sweet pastries being baked. Olivia lays there and for a second, it's like she is back at Renee's while she bakes the berriemuffs. Her thoughts turn to sadness as to all that has changed in the last two months. From Renee's passing to Abigail being taken. Olivia gathers herself up and regrets not practicing her craft sooner, like Abigail tried to get her to do. She takes a deep breath. "Time to face the day as a big girl now."

*****

Back at the colosseum, Klinksly and Arthygus look at a vast room lined with books; the light crystals don't even cover all of it. Arthygus puts his hand on the gnome's shoulder. "I'm a bookworm, you can say, and love to discover something new...But this? We don't have the time."

"No. No, we don't." They stand there in awe and disheartened about all the books.

"I guess we should start with a visit to Frederick first. See if I can get a location spell? What do you say, Klinksly?"

Klinksly thinks for a moment, and a smile comes to him. "Well, I could eat more of that delicious cake at that bistro place. Wait. A location spell? Why didn't you say something in the first place?"

"Well, I don't have one in my collection of spells. But I believe Frederick does."

"And how will that work?"

Arthygus points his finger in the air. "It will be better that I show you how it works than tell you."

The two head off to Splinteroak through the tree door spell Arthygus thinks is very convenient. It suddenly hits him why most witches were not caught. He has to learn the teleport spell soon to make his future journeys easier; he thinks to himself while walking through Klinksly's forest. After eating at the Wobbly Table Bistro again, they make their way in the rain to Frederick's front door.

Arthygus taps the little bell on the side of the wall by the door. Klinksly gives him a peculiar look. "What did you just do?"

"I tapped the bell."

"What bell?"

He taps the bell again. "This one right here. You don't see it?"

"No."

"That's right, only wizards can see the bell."

The door opens quickly. Fredrick stands there dressed in bright blue silk pants and shirt, but this time he has his shoes on. "Stop ringing the bell. I heard it the first time."

"You seem agitated today, Frederick," Arthygus says.

"Of course I am. I haven't any time to get ready with all these interruptions." He rubs his forehead with his hand. "What brings you by this afternoon, Arty?"

"Arty?" Klinksly smiles at him.

"We are in need of a locate spell. Do you have one?"

"Ugg, can you come by tomorrow? I'm very busy trying to get something ready."

"No, we can't. This is very important," Klinksly says.

Frederick shakes his head, annoyed. "It's always like that, isn't it? The world will end if I don't get this or that, right? Well, let me tell you. It's not the world that will end. It's your little world, and sometimes you just have to wait because my little world is too busy at the moment for your whatever."

"I have gold." Arthygus shakes a small cloth pouch that clinks when he shakes it.

Frederick stares for a second, then smiles. "My world is not too busy to accept the transaction of coins at the moment. Come in, come in." He holds the door open for them to come in.

"That was a quick change of mind." Klinksly jabs Arthygus in his side.

"After dealing with him for a while, you learn how to speak his language," Arthygus whispers.

The small brass dragon incense burner is still smoldering, and the room is a haze. The three of them sit at the table. "A location spell, you say? What did you lose? Perhaps it may be cheaper to buy another one? It's not like you to lose something."

"Um. Well, I can't go and buy a 'new' one."

"Why not? You know the cost of that spell, right?"

"Yes, I do. But it's not a thing. It's a person I need to find."

"A person? They better be important for a price like that."

"I believe they are," Arthygus says in a somber tone.

Frederick nods his head, snapping his fingers. "Right then. Let me see what I can come up with." He departs the room while the two remain seated.

Klinksly looks around at all the nic-nacs, paintings, and odd things in the room. "What does this guy actually sell?"

"He is a dealer in...strange magic items and such."

"What did he mean by important for a price like that?"

Arthygus takes a deep breath and sighs. "I was going to use a location spell a long time ago when I was told it should be of the utmost importance."

"Why is that?"

"Because it will take a small part of you, part of your thinking or intelligence in a way. Use the spell too much and you become dumb, relying on it because you will forget where you put things."

Klinksly nods his head in understanding and goes back to looking at objects in the room. After hearing a lot of moving and banging from the other rooms, Frederick comes in with a large bright green leather book with gold trim and end protectors. Frederick smiles. "I do not have a single spell. But it is in this spell book."

Arthygus frowns. "How much for the book?"

"Book? We just need the one spell. Rip it out and sell it to us," Klinksly commands.

Frederick's eyes open wide. "Rip! Oh no, no, little gnome. It doesn't work like that."

"It's okay, Klinksly. I got this," Arthygus says.

"Besides. With what else that is in here, it may help you with your magical journey. I will give you a deal since you bought and sold here for quite some time. Let's say a thousand gold pieces."

Klinksly's jaw drops at the price. Arthygus shrugs his shoulders, tilting back in the chair. "Alright, I have about five hundred in gold back at my place. Would you be willing to take a brooch of youth? Or my collection of gem powders?"

Klinksly pulls his sword out and lays it on the table. "This is a very sharp and quick blade. Its former owner was Skeel, the wererat prince...Till Olivia killed him. This has to be worth more than a thousand gold."

"Klinksly? What are you doing?"

Frederick is surprised at all they are offering as he picks up the sword. He looks down the length of the blade to see how straight it is, then swings it left and right. It cuts through the air and is balanced perfectly. "This is an exceptional blade, for sure. I believe it is one of the ever-sharp blades."

"Ever-sharp?" Klinksly rubs his head. "I have not heard of them."

"They are rumored to never dull, even hitting stone or metal by mistake. They allow the user to strike quickly. More than usual. There should be a matching long sword too. But where that is, I'm not sure, or who the owner is. Skeel, huh? That's impressive."

"So it should cover the cost of the book?"

Frederick lays it back on the table. "That blade is worth well over five thousand gold, little gnome." He pauses for a bit. "So I have to ask. Who is so important that you are willing to give up such a valuable blade? And you, Arthygus, giving up your gems? You have been collecting and buying them off of me for years."

Klinksly shrugs his shoulders. "Tell him."

"Well, it's our friend Abigail."

"Oh yes, Renee's friend. Didn't you two find her already? I guess she has a habit of wandering off."

"Yes, we did. She was at Barland's recovering from a ghoul attack."

"A what!"

"That will be a story for another time. But we were at the tower of Prakdon, and she was taken by some demon lady in a portal. We need to find where she was taken."

"What?!...What?" Frederick shakes his head in disbelief and spins around the room with his hands in the air. "The tower is real? You were there?"

"Yes, ghoul, chimera, and all," Klinksly mumbles.

"What? Really?"

"Yes. That is why I need the locate spell. Do we have a deal?"

Frederick thinks for a moment. "Arty, you always are a good customer. I can't take your sword, gnome, but I will take the brooch you were talking about. That will be an even trade."

Arthygus grins, reaching for the book. "I will go right now and get it. I'll be right back."

Arthygus rushes out the door and leaves Klinksly behind. Klinksly puts the sword back in his sheath and opens the spell book. He is curious about what is inside but he cannot make out the scribings.

"Funny thing is, if you were here just an hour ago, I could have sold him a map to Geemend's Seeker. But another customer got it first."

"What is Geemend's Seeker?"

Frederick raises his eyebrows. "You don't know what that is? It is a magical device that can let you know the whereabouts of anything. Without paying the price of a locate spell." He turns his head to the side and grins. "But if the item is destroyed or doesn't exist, then the seeker takes...Well, you don't have to worry about that now."

"Huh...okay. Who was in here that bought the map? Please don't say it was that assman Tyree. He is the cause of all this. Abigail's disappearance and all." Klinksly's eyes open wide at Frederick's shocked face. "No...? What was he after?"

"How do you know... He did that to her? Tell me what all happened."

By the time Arthygus gets back, Klinksly has told Frederick about how Tyree met them to the encounter at the tower. Frederick remains silent, wondering what Tyree is up to. Arthygus hands over the brooch for the book, and the two hurry back to Arthygus's place. Frederick waves them goodbye, looks around at a few people in the rain, and closes the door. Klinksly doesn't tell Arthygus about Tyree on the walk.

Arthygus guides the gnome through Splinteroak to the far southern side. A cluster of two- and three-story wood and stone buildings line up tightly against each other. They go to the last one on the right. He opens a door with a key, and they walk up three flights of stairs. A door is at the top of the stairs, but it has no knob.

"How do you open this door?"

"It's a wizard's door. Thief proof." Arthygus reaches to the top right, makes a turning motion, and the door opens.

Klinksly grins and laughs. "Unless the wizard is also a thief."

Arthygus stands there perplexed at that thought, rolls his eyes, then goes in. It is a small room that has a chair and a table with many books on it. Some are opened while others have feather markers between the pages. There are books stacked haphazardly on shelves, along with jars of stuff and odd things. He clears off the table and opens the new spell book to read over the location spell.

Arthygus reaches for an orange powder and a charcoal stick that he uses to make three orange dots in a triangle pattern and a charcoal line that connects them. He lights the orange dots on fire and they snap and sparkle with a dancing flame. "Okay, when I speak the words, inhale the smoke and keep your eyes closed. We should see the same thing, if you'd like to try it."

"Sure. Will it hurt?"

"No. Just concentrate on Abigail." Arthygus puts his hand on the first fire and connects the others while he speaks. "What I have lost has me in a bind. Now I need help with what I cannot find. Paikantaa esine."

Their darkness is lit by a deep blue spiraling light that makes a large ring in their minds. Within the ring, a sight forms of green and brown grass fields that follow a road, then they lift over the town of Splinteroak. The vision ring climbs higher and higher as they soar over the forest, past Garnet City, heading east. They see the shorelines of the Magelic Ocean and turn south, going over the Skarpur Peak Mountains, then they lower down to the warm tropical seas. They cross over light blue and azure waters that lead to crystal white beaches with many elms, palm trees, and large grasses before they come upon a city. The docks are full of fish retailers in their colorful booths and buyers of all sorts. The ring stops at a sign that reads Teal City Wharfs.

Their vision takes off again over the great city of stone structures, some towering four and five stories tall. Flying at treetop level now, they leave town going northwest. The ring slows down and passes a roadside sign that reads *The Road of Hope*. But someone scratched "lessness" after hope. The road has weeds growing on it from being less traveled.

The ring picks up speed down the road leading into a forest of palms, elms, teak, and rosewood trees contented by lush green vines. An array of colorful flowers bloom here and there in clusters. They are not sure how far the ring traveled because of its speed, but it stops at a large stone peeking out from a fallen tree. It looks like the tree is hugging the stone the way its branches have fallen.

They travel into the forest, passing all kinds of plants, birds, and a few primates in trees when it comes across flowing waters that it follows upstream till they reach a small waterfall about two hundred feet tall. They go up the waterfall to a top of a large, barren, tan, rocky plateau about a mile wide sticking out over the jungle. The vision ring floats to the middle of it, where it goes through an outline of a stone door and down into darkness.

The magical spell takes them down further into the dimly lit passage where it can go left or right. Heading left, they twist and turn in the tunnel and come into an octagonal shaped room with smooth polished walls of gold and copper-speckled stone. On the walls are claw marks and splatters of dried blood lit by glowing yellow crystals grasped in boney hands protruding from the stone.

The ring slowly crosses over the large stone table to a slab of frosty crystal against the wall. A faint image of a person is in there, and the ring gets closer. The image comes into focus and reveals it is Abigail standing there magically paralyzed. The ring backs up to turn towards something else when suddenly a woman's mouth with sharp teeth appears screaming into the ring. Arthygus opens his eyes, jumping back, and Klinksly screams and falls to the floor.

"Ahh, troll toes! What was that?"

Arthygus shakes his head to clear his thoughts. "That was what took her, I guess. But quick, let's write down what we saw and where she is."

After making sure every detail was in the parchment, they decided to have ale. Maybe a little too much for Klinksly, but he thought he deserved it. They rest for the day before joining the others back at Snowcap.

5

New Obsession

Brak and Brace stand there looking at the gold. They say at the same time, "What do you mean, more?"

Gullen remains silent, but Ryan asks, "Isn't this enough?"

"I just want my share and to go," Kade says.

Tyree looks at the ground, then joyfully spreads his arms. "Friends and sweetie over there. Of course, you can take your share now and wander around or even perhaps go back into Splinteroak to spend some of it. But the guards are not stupid, and when the charm wears off... Well, they will look and look hard for the thieves. So let's go to my place to divvy up the share. Kutistua!" Tyree throws out a small grinding of yellow crystals over the crate of coins and it shrinks to the size of an apple. He picks it up and slips it into his pocket. "See. Easier to carry it."

They are shocked at what happened. "Hey! That is our gold. Give it back!" Brak yells.

Tyree walks away, back towards his place. "If you want your share, then follow me. If not, then you're not getting anything because I'm not waiting around like a fool to be caught. We have to go past Splinteroak." Glaive and Gullen follow him.

"He is right, you know," Ryan says to the others. "We can't linger here any longer. Let's follow and see what he has to offer or take our share."

The rest of the group gather their things and follow Tyree back to his place through the falling leaves, staying outside of town.

A few hours later, they make it to Tyree's place. He lays the small crate on a table in the room with the fireplace. "Glaive, get a fire going." He turns his attention to the crate again. "Suurentaa!" The crate returns to normal size. "See, I am no thief." He smiles at them. "Now do you want to split your half among your friends and leave or listen to how to get more?"

Ryan runs his hands through the gold coins. "Split my half? Oh no, we split this evenly."

"No can do. I did most of the work and led us away. Half is mine. If not, you want to see what I can do to you?" Tyree reaches his hand in his pocket for the red book.

"If you take your half and split it now, that is more than you would have made this entire month," Gullen says. "I saw what he can do; you have no defense against him. No need to be greedy now."

Kade slips her hand through the gold. "There are at least five thousand here. If we split only half, that is not enough for me to get back home, but it will be a start."

Ryan then speaks to his people. "It's up to you to take your share now and leave, but I want to hear what he has to say to earn more before I choose. So what is your grand idea, wizard?"

Tyree slides a chair from the table and stands on it, looking over everyone. "I need a select group of experienced individuals like yourselves to travel with me to the Knorrwind City. From there, I will give directions where we need to go to get... a certain device."

"So. How will that give us gold?" Ryan said.

"Not only gold, but how about a position leading the army we will raise?"

"Army?" Brace says.

"That's right. I will raise an army to take back what is rightfully mine!" His voice gets more agitated. "I am Tyree Keir Mire! Rightful heir to the Skylar Kingdom. I will take it back now that I have the Book of Power that General Prakdon used!" He pulls the red book out of his pocket and holds it high into the air for all to see. "With the secrets in this book, we cannot fail! So how will it get you more gold and power? The more we hire and the more we conquer, the more spoils we will... you will get. Be it people, places, or treasure. I'm only interested in enough coin to hire and pay for the cause. The rest you can have."

The room is silent, then Brak and Brace laugh. "Ha... You king? Book of Power?" They slap hands together. "We will take our share and leave, crazy man."

This action infuriates Tyree, and he doesn't hold back. The book trembles in his hand, and Tyree is lifted into the air above the chair. A deep boom bellows from the book along with that voice. "*Aughh rasgul mensha! You will follow him or your life will not be your own.*" A faint green flash comes from the book and hits the boys' eyes.

Brak and Brace have a flash vision of them being burned alive and torn apart by weird black stringy humanoid things only to serve afterwards looking like twisted, sad zombies. They look at each other, shaking at what they saw. "Did you see that?" Brak asks. Brace nods his sweating head in fear.

"I guess we need to follow you then," Brace says.

Tyree floats back down to the floor. "Good choice. And the rest of you?" He holds his hands out, expecting an answer.

Ryan, looking at the boys, turns his attention to Gullen and Kade. "What do you two think?"

"He owes me 200 gold, anyway. I've seen what he can do. So I'm going to follow this out and see what happens," Gullen says.

Kade slowly looks over at everyone, noticing the boys are quiet and not themselves. "Even if I take my share now, it is still not enough to get me home without doing other things. Tyree, will we be getting paid as we go or what?"

Tyree squints at her because he hasn't thought of such nonsense, then comes up with an idea. "Listen. I understand coin is all you think of. For now, we will use this money to get us horses. We will travel in style and comfort so as to not bring attention to us. *If*—and I mean a careful *if*—an opportunity comes along to... acquire more coin, then so be it.

So, sweetie. If anyone objects, I will put you in charge of the gold. That way, we keep things honest between us." He points his finger at her with a grin and a wink.

Ryan asks, "Just how do you plan on recruiting people for an army? Who would even be foolish enough to go after the Skylar Guard? That would be a problem."

Tyree pauses for a second to think about what he needs to say. "There are those that dwell south of the Sharp Peak Mountains."

"Those are just scattered bandits and roaming bands of murderous thugs. Maybe an orc pack or two. They claim allegiance to no one but themselves," Gullen says.

"All the better to hire or entice them to join. Once I figure out the secret that Prakdon used, it will be as easy as pulling the wings off a fairy." Tyree claps his hand on the book.

"Why do we need to go north, then?" Kade asks.

Tyree nods his head for a moment. "There is a device that will help me decipher pages in here to better understand what the general did. This part of the journey comes first before no other. That is why I need your assistance."

"Do you have a map of Eastern Essalon?" Ryan asks.

"Glaive. Get the map!"

"Uhh. What map, chief?"

Tyree slaps his forehead with his hand and looks at the others. "He really is good with the blades. But other things... The brown map of Essalon."

"Oh, right, chief." He digs through a few rolled up maps, comes to the table, and lays it out, putting candles on the ends to prevent it from rolling up.

Ryan looks over it, gliding his fingers from Skylar Castle to the Northern Kingdom. "You know, with bandits, they only will be loyal until there is an opportunity to further themselves elsewhere. They spread thin the Southern Kingdom soldiers, protecting the borders between them too. Thin, but there are many. The Northern Kingdom is closer to the castle, so the troops would have less travel to do, and since not much is going on up there, the men are fresh and ready. But getting them is the problem because they are loyal to King Boreas."

Tyree is impressed by Ryan's assumption. "How do you know all of this?"

"I used to be a soldier for the Eastern Territories before they tried to become under one rule. I don't care about that, so I left."

"Is that so?" Tyree taps his forehead in thought. "So you see, you will be very useful to me... to the cause. What do you say?"

"I'm not looking to join any... cause. Even if you were to be king, I don't think any of us would join a cause."

"I'm not joining unless it is to earn enough for me to get back home," Kade says.

Gullen steps forward, closer to all. "I'm going to follow Tyree for two reasons. One, to see where this goes, and two, he already owes me two hundred gold and I want to be paid."

This irritates Tyree, who grabs a handful of gold and shoves it into Gullen's chest. A few coins fall to the wooden floor that Gullen can't hold and spin and tumble to a stop. "There! That should shut you up!"

"Hey! That was part of our split!" Brace says.

Tyree gives him a nasty look that causes Brace to back down after what he saw in his vision. "Are you brats worried about a measly few gold pieces when tens of thousands more are waiting for us?" There is silence in the room, and Tyree thinks of a way to calm everyone down from this pettiness. "Listen, all of you. I appreciate all of your skills, even you, sweetie. So why don't you go along with me to the Northern Kingdom, get what we need, and after learning more, you can decide to go your own way... With your share, of course, or continue with me."

"He does have a point, you know, Ryan," Gullen says. "It will get us out of this region and onto something else. At least we can travel without looking over our backs for once. Besides, we have nothing else planned yet."

Brak and Brace smile, look at each other, and say at the same time, "Ooo, fresh places to rob."

"What say you?" Tyree points his fingers at Ryan and Kade.

"I know this will take you further from your home, but what do you say? If you're in, then I will be too," Ryan says.

"Great! We got ourselves a party then," Tyree says, clapping his hands together in delight.

"Wait, I didn't say yes or no." Kade slaps her hands against the table.

"Of course you are going, sweetie. Why not? You need the money, and you're in good company. Besides, you're in charge of the coin. So I would count it up so we know what we have... exactly." Tyree goes into the kitchen to find some wine. "Choose any room but mine to rest in. Glaive and Gullen, why don't you take some coin and go get us horses for tomorrow's travels?"

Kade stands motionless with a snarl and her hand on the round blade. She looks at Ryan, who is still waiting for her answer. "I guess... for now." She sits at the table and counts the coins with the help of the brothers. After counting it, they come up with 5,345 gold coins. Kade gives Gullen 500 for the horses and supplies.

A cloudless morning arrives with early birds chirping for acknowledgement. The sun's rays wipe off the cool night's dampness on the colored fall leaves, and the air begins to warm. Tyree has laid out a course to get to the Northern Kingdom. Tyree has them dress like normal travelers and keep their armor and weapons hidden under a blanket on the horse they are riding, but within easy reach if needed. He ensures them that they do not need to bring attention to the group and to do as he says on the journey. They look at Tyree with snarls as he is dressed in his usual black and gray clothing that doubles as leather armor.

Tyree mounts the horse from the right side of the horse, while all others mount from the left. He looks back at everyone with a renewed energy. This time, he is not searching for clues or false information about where or what something is, only to come up empty-handed. Tyree is excited because there is a purpose now with a destination and the next step to his goal of taking the kingdom for himself. A chill goes through him as he smiles back at everyone.

"It will take us ten days to get to the Central Kingdom. In three days, we will go through Merchants' Pass." His horse strays to the left of the small path leading out from the house. He controls it with the reins. "There is a respected inn there that I've always wanted to stay. And now... I have a reason, *we* have a reason too. So come now, friends, let's begin this journey to claim the kingdom."

Kade whispers to Ryan, "Claim the kingdom... not with me." Ryan nods his head at her and encourages his horse to move.

Glaive guides his horse up to Tyree. "Chief, you look different today."

"And how is that, Glaive?"

"Well, you look... happy, chief." Tyree turns his horse around to trot down the path. Tyree thinks he is right. For the first time since being told he is an heir to the throne of Skylar in his youth, he is happy. For many years, he was met with nothing but failure and heartache, keeping his identity secret for fear of being hunted down or not believed. Tyree smirks while riding past Splinteroak, knowing he will soon be the ruler of this place and more.

Throughout the day, they travel north on Old Kingdom Road which leads them to Merchants' Pass. On the eastern side of the road, they watch the forest retreat further away, opening up to grasslands. To the west, small rolling hills covered with waving grasses and small patches of maple and ash trees appear to be giant waves that never splash against a shoreline. In the far western distance, the tops of the Carnassial Mountains can be seen on this cloudless day.

The further north they travel, strong breezes try to rip the remaining clinging leaves from the grasp of branches. Small children near the road wave at the passing travelers, never knowing who they are, while their farming parents tend to the last of the fall harvest. Pulling corn from the stalks, the last of the dying vegetables from the ground, melons and pumpkins that will soon be cooked into wonderful desserts. Kade gives a simple smile and a wave at a little girl while Glaive holds his hand up high and waves to all of them.

A couple of these places are so small they just have names like Dowds Farm and Endless Work Homestead. Tyree chuckles at this and then thinks about how he will rule the farming community. He grins and thinks to himself, *I will treat them fairly. After all, they will be feeding me and my army*. He goes on thinking of what his council will be like. Who he will appoint and so on. Before they know it, the day passes without incident, and they come across a small town called Wheatland Plains.

The town has around thirty buildings, mostly storage barns full of summer crops and a few teamsters buildings that house wagons that deliver goods to distant towns and cities. The rest are personal houses scattered about in no order, and a few inns and taverns. Tyree picks out The Pampered Traveler Inn to rest for the evening and heads that way. Lantern lighters are beginning their routes of lighting lanterns and light crystals as the sun sets in the orange and red sky to the west. The cool air of the night is pushing away any warmth the day has created in the fall season.

Tyree stops his horse near the tavern and dismounts. He has a cautious look about him when the others stop near him. "Now I'm only going to say this once." He looks at Brak and Brace. "No one goes out and…brings attention to us. What we are doing needs to be kept a secret. I will not tolerate any…deviations…Got it?"

"Why is he only looking at us, Brak?"

"Because if something happens, it will be because of you two," Ryan says.

Three teenage boys come out a side door of the inn and approach the group. The oldest one speaks. "Hello, masters and guests. May we take your horses and barn them for the evening?"

Tyree smiles at them while grabbing a sack off his horse. "Yes, you can. We are staying for the evening, so feed and wipe them all down." He firmly grabs the boy's arm and pulls him in tight to whisper in his ear. "Extra gold if taken care of properly… and if any gear goes missing, I will skin all three of you alive in front of the whole town."

The boy's eyes bulge out in horror, then he smirks. "Yeah, right," he mumbles.

Gullen Mull hands the reins over to the boy. "Yes, he will. I have seen it; it's not pleasant." Gullen grins and heads off to the inn.

The boy's smirk disappears into worry with his eyebrows raised, looking back at Tyree. “Okay, guys. We leave these alone. Now let’s get to work,” he says to the other two boys.

Gullen enters the tavern first, alone. He is greeted by the smell of beef and spices roasting on an open pit in the middle of the tavern that stirs up his hunger. To his left is a small hallway that leads to a woman behind a desk and straight ahead are many people sitting around tables while others are up at the long stone bar. Three musicians are playing joyful music. One has two small drums, the girl has a flute, and the third man has a guitar. Gullen chooses to sit at the bar alone and orders food and drink. The fancy room has painted walls of violet and gold outlines. Tapestries of different colors that have animals on them—bear, deer, boar and one with a lion— decorate the room. The place is clean and well-kept for upper-class patrons, they can tell.

Tyree and the rest make their way into the tavern and choose a large table. They have a good meal for once. After all the food and drink are gone and the musicians have stopped playing, Tyree turns to Kade. “Okay, sweetie, go pay the people for the food and our rooms.”

Kade huffs at him. “Really? I’m not some handler for the group, you know. I—”

Tyree cuts her off, pointing his finger at her and smartly says, “No, you're not, but you're the one holding the coin.” He grins at her. “That is your job.” He sips the last of his ale as drops roll down off his short beard. Kade pushes the table hard while standing up, knocking cups and goblets over. She storms off to go pay for everything.

“Someday, you are going to really make her mad,” Ryan says.

“So, what of it?” Tyree says.

The boys laugh. “You may end up with an arrow in the back,” Brak says.

“Well, the guy did deserve it,” Brace adds.

Tyree remains silent, stands up, and looks at everyone. “We leave at dawn. No exceptions.” He heads off to get the key to his room.

Ryan looks at Brak and Brace. “Let’s enjoy a nice rest for once.”

The two grin and snicker at each other, then nod at Ryan. “Alright, we’ll stay in tonight. Besides, my belly is full,” Brak says.

Brace pokes him in the belly. “Yeah, mine is too. Maybe I will take a stroll to walk it off.” He winks at Ryan.

“Well, I’m not your babysitter. Let’s see where this goes.” He finishes his last sip of ale he liked and looks into the bottom of the cup. “Hum, going to get another and head up to the cleaning room.”

“This place has a cleaning room?” say both boys at the same time. Ryan smiles and walks away to go upstairs to his room and Glaive, who remained quiet all this time, asks for more bread and drink before he retires for the evening.

The flickering candle by Tyree’s bed gives off a rosy aroma while he lies on his back holding the Book of Power. He scrolls through pages to see if he can understand anything. “I’ve read you before...but that was back at the tower. Then you talked and did that thing to those in the tavern. Why can’t I understand you?”

He continues to go through the book, when a drop of blood slowly slides along the page and drips onto the bed sheet. “What do we have here? Why won’t you talk?” Tyree shakes the book to see if it will react. He pauses at the thought of being injured or worse. As he is about to close it, he recognizes a word. “Oh, what do we have here? Wielder. Yes, that looks like wielder to me.” His finger glides over a few words, and he can decipher another word. “Book. Ah ha. Book. And master!” He smiles at the assumption he came up with. “The wielder of this book is its master! Of course.” Tyree closes the book and sets it beside the candle. “You will do my bidding soon, once I learn your secrets.” Tyree falls into a slumber with thoughts of controlling the book.

*****

The early morning arrives. The boys are awakened by the morning attendant in the cleaning room. They enjoyed the warm waters so much that they didn’t realize how tired they actually were. They jump up to gather their belongings, and Brace looks out the frosty window to see that the sun is about to crest over the small hills. The boys scramble to get dressed and rush downstairs. Brace, who is shirtless, stumbles, trying to keep his pants up, and Brak, who has his shirt on, and is trying to put his pants on, only ends up tumbling down the stairs head over feet.

His black leather boots fly out of his hands as he protects his head from the wooden stairs. When he stops tumbling, he opens his eyes to see Kade, Gullen, Glaive, Ryan, and Tyree standing there looking down at him. Brak is laying on his back with his pants around his feet. He grins and slowly reaches for the pants to pull them up. "Ha, at least we're not late."

Tyree frowns, and his eyebrows are curved in. He turns around, says nothing, and heads out the door. The others leave silently as well, except for Kade. She grins and laughs, "Now I know why you are just boys." Then she walks away.

Brace helps Brak to his feet and hands him his boots. "What did she mean by that?" Brak asks.

"I'm not sure." Brace passes him and speeds up to go outside to catch up with the others.

The stable boys bring all seven horses out. Tyree and the others look them over and all seems good to go. Kade pays the boys for their service, and they trot north through town in the early sunlight. The day is looking to be cloudy but no rain. For a few hours, they trot past a few more farms and orchards till the road becomes narrow with patches of tall grasses that have turned brown at the end of fall. A lone leafless oak tree stands along the road from time to time. The wilderness is on both sides and seems to never end until they reach Merchants' Pass. This is not the first time Tyree has been on this road, but it has been a long time; he was a teenager when he dared to get close to the Central Kingdom.

Glaive pulls his horse a little closer to the daydreaming Tyree. "Hey, chief. There are men off to our left in the tall grasses following us," he whispers to Tyree and guides his horse away. The others now see what Glaive is talking about.

Tyree is about to get his horse to gallop, when a dozen yards ahead, a tree falls in front of them, blocking the road. Tyree stops the horse and looks for an escape route, but men come out of the tall grasses, shrubs, and trees on both sides. They are surrounded by men and a few women dressed in leather armor. Others are in dark clothing. All of them have some sort of weapon drawn—short swords, maces, clubs and two of them have bows with an arrow knocked, ready to be drawn.

Kade has her hands on the circular weapon attached to her hip. Tyree knows what is about to happen, and looks back at the others with a wink in his eyes. "Follow my lead, and do what you have to do," he calmly says.

He steps off the startled horse and walks out front with his arms spread wide, looking around. "Aright! This doesn't have to get messy. Now, is your leader here?" Tyree notices three men with unshaven, grinning faces come closer, glancing off to their right side at a man in black stained leather with no weapons drawn. He seems to be cleaner than the others. He is clean shaven, has combed back long brown hair, and looks to be in his thirties. He gives the slightest nod that most people would not have noticed, but Tyree does.

Coming from the other side of the road is a large, dark-haired man wearing chain mail armor and wielding a sword with both hands. "That would be me. Now give us everything and then go on your way."

Tyree rubs his chin and pulls the diamond from his pocket. "Everything? Is that so?" He holds the diamond up high in the air. "I guess you all will have to fight over this." Everyone stops coming closer. Tyree knows what to do next, for he has done it many times. He has the pull spell down pat and is thrilled to show it off. "Muuttaa." The diamond changes into the crystal cane. The men and women marvel at the sight and move in, eager to grasp the cane.

"I will only speak to the actual leader." He glances at the man in the black leather, raises both his hands, and stomps his foot. "Veda!" The green wave of magic comes forth too quickly for the man to react. He is drawn towards an evil grinning Tyree.

The man screams, "Attaaack!" His feet are being dragged against the ground trying to stop himself, but to no avail. The cane turns into the crystal sword, with Tyree holding the point at the man being dragged to him. The man pulls a knife from his belt and thrust it forward into Tyree's side as the crystal sword penetrates his chest simultaneously. All the others stop and gasp. Tyree was lucky; the sword cut into the heart and killed him instantly.

Tyree pulls the bloodied blade from the man and lets him slump to the ground. He turns to his group, grinning. "Well? You heard the bandit leader...Attack!"

This startled the bandits as those they were going to rob suddenly jump and dart in different directions. Seeing their leader being killed suddenly causes one of them to yell, "Kunk! We need you now!"

Tyree slips between two horses while he holds his right gut. He feels a burning pain and his hand is wet with blood. Gullen Mull slides off his horse and becomes a blur. A bandit near him swings a mace, only to have it go through the blur, causing him to spin more than expected. Gullen appears beside the man and runs his wavy bladed dagger upwards into his gut, under the ribs, causing injuries that immediately drop the man, leaving him gasping for breath. Gullen then lunges at another, standing stunned at what is happening. He slashes the man's throat, grabs his sword, and throws it at another that is near, hitting them in the leg.

Kade throws the circular weapon, and her eyes follow it. One man after another it hits near the throats or arms as they try to block it. It slices four bandits before returning to her hand. While the weapon was in motion, she slid off the horse, grabbing her dao sword from the sheath. A long, thin, curved, polished blade that has gold and rose-colored etchings of flowers along the spine. The black, polished wood grip has gold etchings of leaves and a dragon tail. The small, gold round guard is plain, but it has two tassels about a foot long that are split. One is gold and the other black.

She spins with the sword and thrusts it into the chest of a bandit that was rushing her. She lets go of the blade and ducks as a sword-wielding bandit misses her and strikes the man she hit. Kade sticks her leg over the ankle of the man and trips him forward, pulls her dao out of the other's chest, and stabs him in the back. The bandit tries to scream in pain, but nothing comes out.

Before Brak and Brace can jump off their horses, a woman yells, "Kill them, Kunk!" pointing at the boys. The small trees part like soft curtains when an ogre comes charging out between them. The orange and tan-skinned beast yells as slobber drools out from its large square teeth and slack jaw that doesn't close. Its black straggly hair is all matted and twisted with small bones intertwined in it. Kunk is wearing small shields on his forearms and bands of black, gray, and putrid green leather. Parts of metal plating are sewn in here and there. The huge halberd polearm acts like a normal ax in his hands. The horses neigh and stand on their hind legs. Brak takes control of his reigns and guides the horses away from the ogre. Brace tumbles off his horse and draws his axes.

Glaive and Ryan look at each other and nod. They rush after the ogre immediately. Glaive's massive size pushes a bandit to the ground that was coming at him. Ryan, who is just as big, slices the fallen man's chest open with his sharp sword as he runs past. The ogre pushes the other woman bandit out of the way and swings overhead with the large pole arm. Ryan and Glaive dart out of the way while the halberd impacts the ground and sticks. They both rush the ogre with Glaive hitting the ogre's shield on his arm while Ryan thrusts his blade into the gut of the ogre. Kunk roars, releases his grip on the pole arm, and back hands Glaive, sending him tumbling across the road like a thrown child's doll.

The three snarling bandits approach Tyree with their weapons drawn, ready to hit him. The two bandits off the side of the road with bows aim at Tyree when suddenly a flash of silver crosses their line of sight. Kade's circle blade cuts through both bows and returns to her hand with a glowing silver light, leaving the archers stunned. The three men, including the one with chain mail and the enormous sword in both his hands, look like they would do massive damage to him with their weapons raised ready to hit him. Tyree knows he can't physically overtake these three, so he does the next best thing he can. He pulls yellow dust out of one of his many pockets and sprays it towards the men, covering them. "Hidas!" he yells. The men begin to slow down from the spell cast.

Brace dodges left and right, avoiding two bandits swinging their weapons at him. He lunges forward and teasingly slaps the backside of one with his ax. He knows he is much better than these two and plays with them, unaware that an archer has drawn a dagger and is approaching from behind. Brak is still getting the horses under control, away from the melee.

Kunk attempts to grab Ryan who fends off grab after grab, with his sword cutting its arms and hands, further angering the ogre. One hand finally grabs Ryan's head like a small pumpkin and squeezes it. The pain causes Ryan to drop the sword. But then the ogre's chest explodes, spewing blood everywhere as Glaive's weapon is run clean through from the back. Ryan falls to the ground, grasping his sword. The ogre screams in pain and turns to smack Glaive again as he ducks. Ryan and Glaive exchange hit after hit, slice after slice of the crying ogre until he falls dead. A female bandit is frozen in fear at what she witnessed with Kunk. Ryan stares at her, seeing what her next move is, but Glaive, in a frenzy, throws his weapon with all his strength at her. It impales her gut, knocking her backwards to the ground.

"Did you have to do that to her?" Ryan asks Glaive.

"Uh sure, chief, I mean Ryan. You know, take advantage when you can to live, right?." Ryan nods his head in disbelief but knows he was right.

Brace is making the bandits even angrier by slapping them, when Kade runs up behind the one man, kicks him in the back as she jumps off his head, flips in the air, and throws her dao sword at Brace. His eyes are wide open in shock as he ducks. The sword makes a fleshy thumping sound, followed by gurgling. He turns to see the archer drop the dagger he was holding, Kades sword in his throat. The other bandit now sees Kunk drop dead as Kade grabs the bandit's mace from him, spins, and knocks him out with a smack to the back of the head. Brace stands looking at Kade with a frown. "Aw. You spoiled my fun." He reaches for her blade, pulling it out of the dying bandit. She hits the other one in the head, cracking his skull with the mace as he was about to get up.

Tyree smirks, turning his sword back into the diamond and putting it back in his pocket. He approaches the man in the chainmail armor who is looking stunned, moving very slowly. "Well, well, this sword looks enormous. I never used one like that. Mind if I try?" He laughs, twisting it out of the man's hands who is trying to react, but Tyree is moving faster than him. The sword is very heavy for Tyree, and he clumsily holds it. With the others now looking on after their fights are over, Tyree steps back and takes a big swing at the man's neck. Tyree did not have the skill or strength to do a clean cut. The sword impacts the jaw to the back of the head and only goes halfway through. The man slowly cries out in a low tone that makes Tyree laugh.

He lets go of the blade and spins in a circle, clapping his hands and laughing. “Ha! Didn't expect that sound. That is funny!” The man falls to the ground in slow motion from the spell. The other two bandits try to turn to walk away, but Tyree pulls his dagger and stops in front of them. He pulls their weapons from them, carelessly tossing them to the ground. “Now you know what it feels like being robbed.” He reaches into a small pouch on the man’s side. The pouch contains a few coins. Tyree looks up at them. “Or maybe not!” He slices the throat of the one man and thrust his dagger into the other’s chest, killing them.

Brace and Kade are standing next to each other as Ryan watches on. Brace hands her sword back. “Here you go,” he murmurs, trying to figure out what he saw Tyree do.

Kade wipes her blade clean on the cloth of a fallen bandit. “Yeah, ah, ha. Not sure what to think of that, either.”

A body flops to the ground behind them, and they all turn to see. There is Gullen Mull holding his bloody dagger over the last female bandit. “What? She was trying to get away,” he says with his gravelly voice.

Tyree looks over at everyone, holding his side, which has blood coming from it. He counts twenty-three dead bandits and an ogre. “Well done! Well done, I must say!” He claps at everyone, then sees Brak coming back with the horses.

Tyree motions for them to get the bodies off the road so as not to draw attention as much as possible. He is beside his horse, lifting his shirt to see a long gash in his side gut. He puts ointment on, and it burns, causing him to draw a breath between his teeth and moan. Kade sees this but says nothing. After the bodies have been moved, the boys take the time to loot them and show each other what they got while mounting their horses.

“I am impressed… Really,” Tyree says as he gallops his horse away and the rest follow. Even though his side hurts, he smiles now, knowing he has people that can handle their own. *These people will definitely get me where I need to go to get that scroll. No problem*, he thinks. "About time," he mumbles to himself.

"You do know this was not our fault? Right?" Brak says to Tyree who laughs at the remark.

6

Hopeful Discussions

Early in the morning, a well-dressed Mr. Krew walks into the dining room where Mr. Blaine and Mayreea are seated eating breakfast, still in their night-time silk clothes. Mr. Krew sits across from them, unfolds a black cloth napkin, and sets it on his lap perfectly. He gives that disapproving look but then smiles.

"Quite an eventful day yesterday, wasn't it, Mr. Blaine?"

He takes a bite of a bagel coated in peach jelly, then wipes his mouth. "It certainly was...interesting."

Mr. Krew fills his plate with sausages, scrambled eggs that have bacon, pepper, salt and parsley mixed in, and one over-buttered biscuit. "Looks like we have new studies to do. This time with an expedited importance."

"Shall we put our other discovery off for a while?"

Mr. Krew nods his head and takes a bite out of the biscuit. His thoughts stray to another problem that has been bugging him. He stares at the plate of food and twirls the eggs with his fork. Mayreea notices this is not normal for him to not answer without looking. "Something wrong with the food I cooked, or is there something else bothering you?"

Mr. Krew grins, taking a bite of eggs. "Of course not, Mayreea. Your meals are always beyond my expectations." They are shocked to hear that compliment from him; he'd said nothing like that before.

"What is on your mind? Did you figure out the results from yesterday already?" Mr. Blaine asks.

"No. Not fully yet. I was thinking about Abigail."

"How so?"

"I was thinking more about her mother, Adrianna. She was a dangerous woman, from what I remember. I thought the Anseim gang killed her and her daughter." He takes another bite of eggs. "And yet here is Abigail claiming to be her daughter, Renee's passing, Abigail becoming the witch queen, granting us permission to look for the Covenant Diary. Then getting taken by a demoness into the unknown. I cannot figure out what all this means at the moment."

"Does it have to mean something?" asks Mayreea.

"No, but don't you see something is not right? Look at the timing of it all?"

"Yes, I admit there are odd events going on. In time, we can explain them," Mr. Blaine replies.

"Either way, we need to figure it out. Something is happening. I can feel it."

"Again, how so, Mr. Krew?" asks Mayreea.

"The statue we saw below the tower is related to all this somehow, and we have to find out who that represents. And I have a hunch, I know. It's just I don't want to be right."

Mayreea laughs. "What? You always make it a point when you are right." Mr. Blaine grins at him as well.

Mr. Krew sets his fork down on his plate, puts his arms out on the table, and looks them in the eyes. "When Muun arrived, the first doors to be closed were the death magic, or the necromancy door. And again, Abigail was attacked by a fully powered ghoul. And Mr. Blaine...the skeleton hand that reached out for Miss Olivia. That was something more, wasn't it?"

Mr. Blaine pauses and nods his head. "Yes, yes, it was."

"So, Mayreea. If I'm right, somehow, this Tyree fellow allowed a force more powerful than we are here on Auhere to reopen that particular door." He takes a bite of sausage, followed by a drink of fresh apple juice.

There is quiet stillness about the room while they think of what was said. Mr. Blaine breaks the long silence.

"And what of our queen, Abigail? Do we leave her wherever she is at?"

Mr. Krew stares at him slowly, taking a bite of the biscuit. "It is going to be difficult to find her, but I believe it can be done. But in time before the worst? I don't think so."

"We have to try."

"Yes, we do, Mr. Blaine." He slams his fist against the table, causing the silverware to bounce and jingle. "If we do nothing with the knowledge of what happened, it will not look good on us. Besides, that is not us either. We will do something and as quickly as we can. For if we save her, it will go down in writing that we, Mr. Blaine, saved her. We have to, not only because Abigail is our witch queen... She is a friend of Miss Olivia's, and I think she cannot bear to sit aside and lose her."

"I see that too. There is something more to Olivia as well," Mayreea says.

"Ah, then you do think there is more to all of this than happenstance?" Mr. Krew grins in knowing he is right.

"More to what?" Olivia pops around the corner, surprising all of them. Mr. Krew is a little worried about how much she heard. Olivia smiles in delight at all the breakfast food. "This smells delicious. May I?"

Mayreea points at a chair. "Of course you can. I set out a plate just for you." Olivia scoops eggs and sausage onto her plate. The cinnamon pastry that has white cream on top is the first thing she takes a bite of. She gives Mr. Krew an uneasy look.

"What are we going to do about Abigail? Did you figure out where she is?"

His long face shows he is not sure. "Let's get hope out of the way. We are working to figure out what happened. She may not even be in this world... and if that is the case, we cannot do anything about that. Her fate is in her own hands then." He sees her freeze with a mouth full of eggs, getting teary-eyed. "Nothing is easy being a witch or warlock, Miss Olivia. How our queen got herself into so much trouble in the first few weeks of her reign is beyond me."

"She didn't ask for this! Abigail had no idea she was going to be named until that day. Neither did I. Renee kept us in the dark."

Mr. Krew is motionless, considering what she said. "That doesn't change what happened to her. We are going to decipher what we learned from yesterday to give us a direction to go in until we...find her."

Olivia calms herself by eating more of the pastry. "Maybe Klinksly has found some information out?"

"I doubt it. That library has a tremendous amount of books and scrolls to go through. That would take him at least two months, even with ten people," Mr. Blaine says.

Olivia reaches down and rubs her leg where the boney hand grabbed her. "It's still a little cool, you know.

"I remember reading stories of them of a few witches and people encountered, mainly treasure hunters. In addition to retaining their magic spells and other powers, the longer it holds the victim, the colder they get till their body slows down and...eventually stops working." Mr. Blaine says.

"Is that why my leg is still cold?"

"I'm not sure. It wasn't even at full power, so your leg may heal in time. Isn't that so, Mr. Krew?"

"You will be okay. It's not as cold as yesterday, correct?" She nods in agreement. "See, now that is that. I must get back to go over what we saw yesterday and figure out who that statue is. That will be a start. Wonderful breakfast as usual, Mayreea."

Olivia perks up. "What do you need me to do?"

"Why don't you help me for a moment while those two go do their thing?" Mayreea asks.

"We have a whole day before the gnome and the young wizard friend come back. I will give you something to do later," Mr. Blaine says, walking out of the room.

Mayreea and Olivia sit there while she eats the remaining biscuits. "These are delicious. How do you make them taste so good?"

"It's nothing, really. I love cooking with all kinds of herbs, spices, and even magic once in a while." Mayreea gives a careless grin. "But the secret is, you make sure whatever you are cooking with all blends in together."

"That is what Renee would say when she made her sweets."

"She is...or was exactly right." She changes the subject quickly. "So, how did you and Abigail meet?" She puts her hand to her mouth, acknowledging the mistake. "Maybe that is not the right subject, either."

Olivia finishes the biscuit. "It's okay..."

Mayreea smiles and picks up a handful of dishes. Olivia does the same and follows her into the kitchen. While they clean the dishes, Olivia talks about meeting Abigail for the first time when she was younger. "I'm sure I was about eight years old when me and my parents met her. We grew up together before my parents disappeared."

"That's right. That's you, then?"

"You know about my parents?"

"Sophia and Alastir. I knew him well. He would come by and get herbs and spices from my garden for meals."

"Really? I thought it was my mother that did all the cooking."

"I know little about her. She would come with him sometimes. She seemed to be quiet and out of place when they were here. He would talk about all the herbs that he got for your mother."

Olivia looks over at all the dried plants and herbs hanging from rafters in neatly tucked bunches. From shortest to tallest, with not one out of place. She is saddened at the moment.

"What is it? I didn't mean to bring them up."

Olivia squeezes her lips together and frowns. "No, that's not it. I just feel sad for not trying harder to find my parents. Renee said she would take care of..." Her voice goes silent at a revelation.

"Care of what?" Mayreea grabs Olivia's shoulder and turns to look her in the eyes. Anger takes over Olivia. "What is it, girl?" Mayreea asks with concern.

Olivia stomps her foot against the ground. "I'm so stupid! I always made fun of Abigail for when she got mad at Renee for not telling her things. And she did the exact same thing to me about my parents!"

Mayreea lets Olivia go and takes a step back from her. "Did she have reasons?"

Olivia leans against the water basin, looking at all the soap bubbles slowly pop. "Reasons? Why would she not tell me of my parents? Was she really looking or just didn't want to interfere with what happened? She always told Abigail it was fate and leave it at that."

"Really? Leave it at that? Fate is a peculiar thing. Some people believe it and others don't." Mayreea dips her hands into the soapy water and hands a plate for Olivia to dry.

Olivia unconsciously grabs it, thinking of all the times she could have asked. "I am so stupid. Abigail was right. I am too naïve. Now, every day it is getting too late to find out what happened to them." She continues to dry the plate over and over until Mayreea grabs it from her. Olivia then says in a soft murmur. "It may already be too late."

"It has been what? Thirty years now since they...went?"

Olivia nods in silence while drying the dishes. Nothing else is said until they are almost done when Mayreea states, "Even though time has gone by, don't give up. There may still be someone that knows something out there."

"You think so?"

"Besides, maybe Renee had her reasons not to give you false hope or to spare you any heartache while she was looking into it. Maybe Renee had information that she was not able to tell you in time?"

Olivia lifts her head with newfound excitement. "Her passing came suddenly, and maybe she didn't have time to tell me. But, she also said recently she found nothing about my parents too. Maybe I will go visit her place and look around."

"That is a good thing to do to get peace of mind," Mayreea says.

Olivia stomps her feet against the ground and waves her arms in the air. "I can't! Not now. I have to find Abigail first. I have that to deal with... with that and Klinksly wants me to pretend to be her while she is missing."

Mayreea is surprised at what she mentioned. "Only you can decide what is a priority for you. We are helping in any way we can." She pulls wrapped meat out of a stone icebox and turns her nose from it. “Eww, it is spoiling. Shame really. I was going to use this tomorrow.”

Olivia peers into the icebox at the frost and frozen mist. There are a few other wrapped meats in there. “What is that?”

“That is a creation of Mr. Krew. He captured a small ice elemental and kept it in there,” she explains with a smile.

An idea suddenly pops into Olivia’s head. “That is nice. We have a heated cleaning tub back at my place. What are you going to do with the meat?”

“Probably toss it out over the cliff side. Let the animals take it.”

“I can get rid of it for you,” Olivia says with a grin on her face.

“Help yourself.”

Olivia grabs the wrapped meat and puts it into a sack. “Before I go get myself ready, do you have honeyed oats or grain?” Mayreea gives her a curious look.

*****

Olivia was gone most of the day with thoughts of returning to her home, but decided she didn’t want to be alone. More importantly, she did not want to be away when news of Abigail's location was discovered. Olivia knocks on the dark doors, and Mayreea lets her in. She is back in time for the evening meal when she is led into the dining room to see dinner is served.

“Miss Olivia. You are making a habit of visiting us. Please, have a seat,” Mr. Blaine says. She smiles and sits down, looking at all the wonderfully cooked vegetables and roasted chickens. “Where were you off today?”

“Oh, I had to get away and take care of a few things.” She smirks because that is what Abigail would say to get away for a while.

Mr. Krew still has that long, drawn-out look of annoyance while reaching for a biscuit. “Do not consider this a second home for you to come and go as you please.” Olivia nods her head in silence.

“Here, take this.” Mr. Blaine hands her a small book that is five inches wide and seven inches tall. It has a blue leather cover and is kept shut with black twine. “I think you might find it interesting to read. See if anything comes of it.”

"What is it about?"

Mr. Blaine smiles at her. "It is for you to figure out if it means anything or not."

They pick at the chicken that was roasted with butter, garlic, parsley, and thyme. It was so delicious that everyone was quiet for some time. Halfway through the meal, Olivia's curiosity gets the better of her. She can't hide it very well; Mr. Krew is annoyed by it, so he stops it. "Miss Olivia." He doesn't even look at her while he butters a biscuit. "If we had found information of importance, we would have told you."

Olivia fills her mouth with stewed carrots that were cooked in maple syrup and sprinkled with cloves. She understood what he was saying and didn't reply.

Before he takes a bite of the steaming biscuit, he looks at her. "I am not in the business of giving false hope...But we don't give up either. Especially when it's the witch queen..." He realizes he needs to say more to comfort her, but he does not.

Throughout the rest of the meal, Olivia listens to the three of them discuss possibilities, theories, recollections of times past, and suggestions about what to do next. Soon, she finishes, grabs the book, and excuses herself to the room she stayed in. She walks down the dimly lit cold stone floor till she comes to the door. Oliva looks down the hallway that continues for about thirty feet then splits left and right. She swore she saw a shadow move and wanted to investigate, then decided against it. She slips into the room and slowly closes the door. A dark humanoid shadow slowly peers around the corner, watching Olivia shut the door.

Olivia clears her thoughts, undresses, and slips under the covers. The candle is still lit and gives off enough light to look over the book. She flips through the pages, stops, reads a small section, and looks over a drawing or two. It tells of a tale of a boy named Gillespie. He was an acolyte of the Church of the Father. He was fascinated with wizard magic and witchcraft. Gillespie would secretly learn their ways. When he became older in his twenties, he already mastered enchantment spells. Learned a little on spirit witchcraft along with his normal priestly prayers of protection and summoning. It proved that magic and prayers can be shared. He was found by the church to be casting spells, even though to help people, he was labeled as evil and was to be executed but escaped. Never to be seen again. Soon she yawns a few times and falls asleep from the busy day.

Olivia has a deep dream again. She finds herself standing in a general goods store near the docks. There is a man in his forties, enormous belly, full brown beard and hair, wearing gray pants and a white shirt that has a few stains from today's work. She can actually smell the many wax candles near the window as two women look in at him. The aisle is full of everyday items, from lamp oil to bread boxes. Other shelves carry fishing gear and tackle to clothing at the opposite end of the store.

Olivia hears the ocean waves slapping the rocks near the shoreline. She peeks through a foggy glass window and notices a tiny sandy beach that has a few row boats and dinghies beached. Boys are tying and holding them while people get out of or into the boats. Olivia hears a glass lid being opened and turns to see the little blonde-haired boy from the dream she had before. This time, he is around ten years old. He pulls out a blueberry sugar stick and smiles.

At this time, Olivia notices the two women looking through the window scuttle off quickly and not looking back. Two dirty and scraggly sailors, wearing seafaring garb of blue and gray colors, rush in with daggers drawn and approach the man behind the counter. One is tall and thin while the other is a bit shorter and muscular. The taller one grabs the man by his beard while holding the dagger to his throat. They yell at him to give him all the gold. The shorter man holds out a dirty, whitish cloth bag that has brown and crimson stains on it and reeks of fish.

The young boy rushes past Olivia with the sugar stick in his mouth. His little body slams against the one holding the dagger, causing him to drop it, but not the shopkeep's beard as he screams in pain. The boy slides to his knees, punching the shorter man between the legs. The shorter man bends over, and the boy grabs the bag from him, covering it over the man's head. He then causes him to trip, falling backwards. The shorter man knocks a few wooden and metal cups and plates that were neatly stacked off the shelves.

Olivia yells out to watchout, but no one can hear her as the large man has regained the dagger and is about to slash at the boy. A loud wooden thump is heard, and the large man drops the dagger, falls to his knees, then falls flat on his face. Standing behind him, holding a wooden club for just these occasions, is the shopkeeper. The boy kicks the shorter man between the legs again as a town guard steps in after the fleeing women give notice.

The insignia of Traders' Wharf sticks out to Olivia. The boy runs behind the counter, unseen by the guard, and the shopkeeper covers him with a sack quickly. Images fade while Olivia is pulled through the wall and up and over the small fishing town. She glides away from the shoreline and town to open grassy fields on small hillsides. A slight cool breeze is blowing off the ocean, and she smells the salty air. Oliva glides down onto a small sandy hillside covered with green and brown dune grasses. She feels the cool blades between her toes and flapping against her knees from the breeze-driven grass.

Below her, she sees the boy again, laying on his back between two tall grasses. This time, he looks to be about fifteen. His hair has gotten longer, to his shoulders. He appears to be cleaner and have better clothes, though they still look ragged with holes and patches. He is reading a book that is very worn and a few pages are missing.

Three other older teens come walking by with sacks of feed and notice the boy. One of them has a scar on his face. Olivia recognizes him as the boy that smashed the crab trap over the boy when he was younger from the other dream. He drops the sack and turns at the boy. "Well, well. Look at what we have here."

"A street rat that is lost," says one of the other boys. The other two drop their sacks as well and hold up their fists.

"I've been meaning to get you back for doing this." He points at the scar on his face.

The blonde hair boy slowly closes the book and speaks with a silvery regal voice, "I guess I left my mark then."

The larger older boy goes to kick him while he is laying down but gets tripped by the blonde-haired boy. He falls to the side of him, and the younger boy rolls away to stand up. The older boy gets to his feet, cursing at him in anger, "There is no one out here to help you this time!" He sees the boy standing there with both hands behind his back. "What? So poor that you have to hold up your pants, street rat?" He lunges at him.

The blonde-haired boy pulls out two cut hickory sticks about two inches thick with carved hand holds and two feet long. He whacks the fist of the larger boy, then pokes him in the stomach a few times and hits him on the back of the head, stunning him, causing him to fall. The other two boys look on in awe and step forward with fists drawn. One pulls a knife out. "You will get it now."

The young boy stands his ground and says nothing, staring them down, ready to intercept their fists. They stop shy of him when he raised the sticks in a defensive position. They stare at each other for a few seconds, then the older boy moans. The two boys grab the older, help him up, and they go back to the sacks. The younger boy's blonde hair is flapping in the breeze, covering his face, and he remains perfectly still, watching them as they leave.

Olivia's attention is turned uphill, and she notices that woman again wearing a white skirt with her belly showing, a white long-sleeved blouse that has thin decorative gold chains connected from her wrist to her waist, and the most impressive golden blonde hair that she has ever seen. She is standing there smiling but looking straight at Olivia. Before Olivia can speak, she is jolted out of her sleep, taking in a big gulp of air.

After a few intense breaths, she looks around and is safe in the room she was staying in. The candle is almost burned out. *Now that wasn't a coincidence. Was it*? She thinks to herself. *What is going on? I don't have dreams like that.* She rolls over to her side and thinks of the dream and the little boy. *I wonder if he is real. I wonder if that woman is real?*

*****

On the day Klinksly and Arthygus are to return to Snowcap with their findings, a sudden knock wakes them up. Arthygus slowly opens his eyes. Loud, quick banging confirms he is not dreaming. He rolls out of bed and gets his thoughts about him. Klinksly is laying on a small couch that is falling apart. Arthygus taps him on the shoulder. "Hey, watch this."

Arthygus steps up to the door, waves his hands in a counterclockwise motion, and whispers, "Nahda lapi." The door fades so he can see what is on the other side. He turns back to Klinksly. "Don't worry, they can't see through it," he says with a grin.

Standing there banging on the door is Frederick. Arthygus opens the door quickly. Frederick has his head turned looking down the staircase, so his fist impacts Arthygus's face.

"Oops, sorry about that."

Arthygus rubs his eyes as Frederick pushes his way in and shuts the door quickly. Both Klinksly and Arthygus notice he has a worried look about him.

"Um, this is a surprise. You never visit me. What do you need?"

"It is not what I need, but what you two need."

Arthygus and Klinksly are confused. "What do you mean?"

"Arty, you have been a good customer of mine for a while, even helping to discover things for me. So I went back and forth last night about an...issue." He steps back, looking around the room.

Arthygus holds his hands out in confusion. "Where is this going? Did I do something wrong? Was it the wrong brooch I gave you for the spell?"

"No, Arty, you didn't. Listen, after you left the other day to get the brooch, the gnome here told me why you needed the location spell."

"He did?"

"Yes, I did. What of it?" Klinksly says to Frederick.

"Well, it is a good practice of mine not to say anything about what other customers buy or sell to me." He winks at them. "Confidentiality, you know, that sort of thing. I can't have customers buying from customers and cutting me out. Not good for business."

"Okay, again, what does that have to do with me? I sold nothing to anyone."

"Of course not. What I'm saying is, after the gnome told me the story, I went back to what I needed to finish when this thought came over me. I felt bad that Abigail was taken, but I need to tell you something else. It is about Tyree."

"Go on," Klinksly says firmly.

"He came in looking for a demon rune reading scroll—"

"A what?" Arthygus and Klinksly say at the same time.

"After you told me about the Tower of Prakdon and how Tyree got a hold of the Book of Power, and after yesterday's events, I realized he couldn't read it. That is why he needs that rune reading scroll."

"What events?" Arthygus is confused even more about what is being said.

Frederick waves his hands in a dumbing down motion. "Okay, you didn't hear? Over at the Craving Tummy bakery, two...zombies or undead creatures attacked the place, killing four people. Is the Book of Power in demon rune? General Prakdon supposedly had undead as guardians? Tyree was just here with it? He stated he would have more wealth than anyone and would do anything to get it. Coincidence?"

The two are silent. Arthygus turns to Frederick with a stunned look and whispers, "In the tower, there was this statue of some type of demon. We fought a devil and ghoul, too."

Frederick scratches his head in disbelief, looking at the gnome. "You said nothing about fighting a devil."

"Well, I... uh wasn't there for that part."

"Then that is it. He had to be responsible for that attack somehow," Frederick says.

"What do we do now?" Arthygus nervously paces the room, looking at Klinksly.

"At least we know where Abigail is. Now we need to know where Tyree is going." Klinksly falls back onto the couch, and Arthygus slaps the table and sits down, frowning, trying to think.

Frederick looks at both of them with his hands out in confusion. "I know he can't read it until he gets to Geemend's Seeker. That device will give him the location of the scroll, if it exists."

Arthygus smiles. "So I need to use the locate spell to find the seeker and beat him to it!"

Frederick shakes his head in shame at what he heard. "No, no, no, Arty."

"Ahh, wizards, they just don't see the obvious," Klinksly says, scratching his head and then picking his hat off the floor from last night's sleep.

Arthygus squints, figuring out the hints and his face lights up at the realization of what they were saying. “Oh...you mean locate the scroll and get that before Tyree?”

Klinksly laughs with a high pitch. “No wonder us warlocks and witches are smarter than wizards. You can’t see what is right in front of you without help. If I was able to do the locate spell, I would use it every day to find things.”

Frederick raises his finger at the gnome. “If you were to do that, with each use, it would take away a little part of your memory to the point you would need to keep using the spell to find everyday normal things and eventually it would take the memory of the spell itself and you’d be nothing but a forgetful meat puppet at that point.” Frederick then tilts his head in thought. “So let me get this straight. A young wizard and an old gnome who is a warlock in the same room? You do know witches are still sought after to kill, right?”

The three look back and forth at each other for a few seconds when Frederick speaks again. “None of my concern. I have always been neutral to my customers, and I want to keep it that way.”

“So why tell us about Tyree?” Arthygus asks.

“If he is up to no good, and if he can read that book, then I don’t want that to happen. It would be bad for business... with lack of people around and all.” The two are silent, staring at Frederick, awaiting what he will say next. “So? What are you going to do?”

Arthygus stands from the chair and points his finger in the air as he always does when he knows what to do. “We know how to find Abigail. We now have a glimpse of what Tyree is up to. So let’s go back to Snowcap to see what they came up with; that will decide our next move.”

Klinksly grins. “That sounds like a plan. When can leave...”

“What is it? Was I followed?” Frederick asks.

Klinksly goes over to the window and peers out. “I don’t think so. I just got a whiff of something delicious coming from outside. Huh, there is a guy with a cart that has muffins and cakes!” Klinksly storms off outside, almost stumbling down the stairs.

Arthygus shrugs his shoulders at Frederick, who chuckles. “Apparently, he has not been to Splinteroak until recently to enjoy all the good food.”

“Arthygus.” Frederick puts his hand on Arthygus’s shoulder. “Whatever you are going to do, you better be careful. These are dangerous people. And I hate to say it, but I worry about you.”

“Aww. That's nice of you.”

“No, it’s not. I mean, I worry because you are a good customer, but you don’t know how to handle yourself. I’ve watched you around town and see how you avoid conflict.” Frederick then slaps him on the chest jokingly. “That's it. That's your best asset. Avoidance.”

“What do you mean?”

“I know you had no training in fighting or anything like that. I’m just saying be careful and find someone to give you a few pointers if you are going out looking for a bad individual.”

“I know. I get what you're saying. There will be others I trust around me to help.”

“Yes, good. There may be a time that they may not help you. Here, I got this for you to help with your journey.” He pulls out a slim package wrapped in a fine black cloth.”

“Journey? Who says I’m going anywhere?”

“Listen, Arty. Something is going on. Certain magic doors were closed a long, long time ago. If by Muun or whoever. There were unknown people who did not like that.” He waves his hands as if to imagine smoke disappearing. “She vanished. Was her work done or?” He hands him the package. “Doors to the unspoken arts were closed. That's why we have seen no undead for centuries.” Frederick glances through the window outside at Klinksly buying muffins and other people happily walking by, hurrying to who knows where on this cool sunny morning. He then murmurs. “And now we have some... right here in our town of Splinteroak. And Tyree with the Book of Power was just here? Yes, Arty, you are going on a journey to find answers. This is why I’m giving you this.”

Arthygus unrolls the cloth and finds brown leather pants and a light and dark brown leather armor jacket. The jacket has four horizontal strips about two inches wide that start with a red, orange, blue and then a dark purple. His face lights up with excitement as he puts it on.

"The colored strips are for wizards; you put your spell ingredients in there. It is a very useful magic to have. For example, take the mint tea leaves and hold them off to a particular spot or color and think of storing them. They will be absorbed by the armor. Then, to retrieve it, just put your hand near the same spot and think of the mint tea leaves in your hand. And then there you go. Tea leaves in your hand. But you have to think clearly, and it only has what you put in it."

"Wow! This is awesome. Where did you find this? Why haven't you shown me this before?"

"That's not important now. I'd like to see you come back. And you must inform me of what you find and if you find any relics you think I may buy."

"Oh thank you, thank you." Arthygus is sliding to the left and right, pretending to be in a fight. "This actually fits, and I can move freely in it."

"Good..." Frederick then says softer. "Good." His thoughts turn to when his late son used to wear that. *May it bring you a better use than it did him*, he thinks to himself. He turns towards the door and opens it. "You be careful...And bring me back something magical that no one has." He smiles and closes the door.

Arthygus sees something is amiss with him and yells through the door, "I will, and thank you again!"

A few minutes later, Klinksly comes into the room with a bag of assorted fruit muffins and one in his mouth. He suddenly stops when he sees Arthygus in the new leather armor jacket. He swallows the rest of the bite of muffin. "Now that is a leather jacket for a wizard! That look is you." Klinksly takes another bite while offering the bag to Arthygus. He grabs a muffin and eats it as well.

Arthygus searches through neatly rolled up parchment on his shelves —one of the few things in the tiny apartment that is organized. He grabs a few useful ones and lays them on the table beside a large blue and gold book. Klinksly looks on, wondering what he is doing. Arthygus unrolls them, flattens them out, and puts them in the book's front. Once he closes the book, he taps the four corners from left to right, bottom to top. The book shrinks to the size of a small walnut, and he puts it into his pocket with a grin, looking at Klinksly.

He also rummages through an old, beat up travel trunk and pulls out an old brown leather backpack that has a few patches sewn into it. After gathering a few potion bottles that he meticulously fingers through, he packs a few clothes before Klinksly's patience wears thin.

"Come on already. Is this how wizards travel? Takes just as long as baking bread."

Arthygus snickers at him. "I wasn't prepared last time, and we knew what we were getting into. Now I want to be helpful this time, and we don't know what we are getting into. So I'm taking my time to be sure."

"Ah, good point." Klinksly sits back, crosses his short legs, smiles, and waves his hand. "Continue on, grand wizard."

"Oh, I suppose witches are up and ready at a moment's spur?"

Klinksly smiles and nods. "Em hum."

Arthygus plays around, putting spell ingredients in the new jacket. He gets used to installing them and retrieving them, which impresses Klinksly. "Before we go back to Snowcap, maybe we should bring Young Adam and Abbot Garret too," Arthygus says. Klinksly nods his head in agreement with a mouthful of muffin. Crumbs fall out of his mouth and onto the floor.

Once he is finally ready, the two head out of town to a tree they used before and make their way to the Dianeeta monastery. Arthygus is still impressed with how they use the tree door spell, and he wonders if magic like this exists in the wizard realm.

7

No Matter the Cost

An hour has passed since the bandit encounter on the road to Merchants' Pass. The clouds are now hiding the setting sun, and the air is getting cooler. Tyree stops and dismounts from his horse, clearly in pain. His jacket and pants have blood stains on them from the cut the bandit leader gave him. Riding the horse didn't help matters, either.

"What's wrong, chief?" Glaive aska, pulling his horse up beside him.

"It's nothing."

"It's nothing? Lying to us is not a good way to start out," Kade says. She pulls her horse beside him and slides off. "I saw you get cut."

"What? Ah, whatever. No big deal," Tyree says, pulling up his shirt. The gash is deeper than he thought. He then wonders about the Book of Power and how it absorbed blood. *Will it heal me or tear me apart like those two men?* He says to himself.

Before he can think about it more, Kade lifts his shirt and demands Brak to hand her a bottle of water. "What are you doing?" Tyree asks but does not retreat or stop her.

"Looks like it is about to get infected," Kade says.

"Again, sweetie, what are you doing?"

"Going to prevent infection so you can get what you want and we get our gold." She has Brak pour water over the wound, and she wipes off the dirt and dried blood. She pulls a little red glass compact from her side pocket, opens it, and puts her finger in it. Kade rubs this green ointment over his cut, causing him to snarl.

Tyree takes a deep breath. "Okay, that stings." He shakes his head from side to side and laughs.

"The burning will only last a second or two." Kade watches it foam up with lots of little green and red bubbles. She wipes away the access. "Looks like it will need to be sewn." He frowns at her, and she grins back. "I have what you need."

Tyree rolls his eyes, getting annoyed. "If you must...At least I killed the one that did this."

The rest of the group tend to the horses while Kade spends about twenty minutes sewing him up. He suspects she is taking a little longer than needed every time she pokes the needle into him. Two men on horseback followed by two draft horse drawn covered wagons approach. They are followed by four more men on horseback that are well armed coming from the north part of the road. They wave and speak small talk, and Tyree's group does the same.

She finishes sewing him up. Tyree feels better, and he moves to his side. "Ah, that is better. Thank you...Kade."

Kade squints her left eye in disbelief. "What? No sweetie remark?"

Tyree smiles at her, then looks in the distance at the passing wagons. His attention is drawn to the blood that he spilled on the road and all the hooves and human footprints. "There is the possibility that someone will find those bodies and guess we are going to Merchants' Pass."

"How they know it's us, chief?" Glaive says.

"They don't, Glaive! I'm just using that term." Tyree is very annoyed at the moment. "We need to be seen as innocent travelers. We cannot go to Merchants' Pass."

"Then where do we go?" Gullen asks.

The boys laugh at the same time. "We can handle anything that comes along. Look what we just did," Brace says.

"We do not need to draw attention to ourselves! Got that!" Tyree looks to the east and sees the runaway mountains. "There." He points eastward. "We will go through the wilderness for now and sleep in the open. I know a place where we can cross the river safely. It will add a day or two to our journey. That should get us away from searching eyes."

"That's alright with me if that gets us off this road," Ryan says.

They all mount their horses and leave the road, heading into the tall grasses and thorn bushes.

*****

Back at the site of the small bandit skirmish, six Garnet City soldiers on their routine patrol, riding on horseback, are going northward on Old Kingdom Road. Suddenly, the last soldier cries out, "Hold on!"

The other five slow the horses and turn. They are all wearing brown cloth pants with red shirts and have on silverish gray cloaks bearing the Garnet City emblem—a three-fingered silver claw holding a maroon garnet that has 4 sides like a diamond going to a point. The leader, Sergeant Mashawn, is dressed in his chain mail armor, as he always is when on patrol. The highly polished chain glistens against his dark ebony skin. "What is it, Luis?"

Soldier Luis hops off the horse and heads into the scrub bushes on the side of the road. He moves branches out of his way and stops immediately, cringes, and covers his nose. "Uh, er...Sergeant."

"What is it?"

"Bodies, sir. Lots of them! All dead!"

"Draw weapons!" The soldiers react quickly and draw their swords. "Conner, Evan, remain on horseback and go northward about a mile, then come back...Report anything!" Sergeant Mashawn dismounts, followed by the remaining two soldiers. "Kadeem, Miles, go to the other side of the road. Be careful, be ready, and report anything." He heads toward Luis with a sword in hand.

"I count at least 19...Maybe more."

Sergeant Mashawn is bewildered at what he is seeing. It is clear the bodies were tossed and quickly tried to be hidden. "Is that?" He steps over and on a few bodies to get to the enormous figure. He uses his sword point to move branches aside to look.

"What is that orange color, sir?"

He stares at it and murmurs. “It’s an ogre...A dead ogre.”

Miles and Kadeem come back to the sergeant. “Nothing over there. From the amount of blood on the road, it looks like whatever happened, happened here,” Miles says while bending down, rubbing the dried blood in the dirt.

“What is that?” Kadeem asks.

“Ogre!” Luis yells in excitement. “I never saw one before.”

“Neither have I. What’s it doing here so close to Splinteroak?” Kadeem asks.

“Search the grounds! If anything or anyone is out there, let me know,” the sergeant orders.

After twenty minutes of searching, the other two soldiers come back. “Sir, nothing unusual to report,” Conner says.

Sergeant Mashawn gathers his men in a circle. “What do you think we have here?”

“Looks like someone lost,” Luis says, laughing.

“Was it a robbery?” Miles asks.

“Was it a robbery gone bad? They all look like bandits to me,” Evan says.

“If so, where did the survivors go, or where are the victims?” Kadeem asks.

Sergeant Mashawn smiles. “Good. Good ideas. You are learning well. If you remember the reports, we are getting news of bandits being more brave. Especially the one group that started taking over others in the area, Banda Krada.”

The soldiers shake their heads, looking at each other for an answer. “Is that the report that a farmer stated a large figure remained in the woods and was going to let it lose if they didn’t get what they wanted?” Evan asks.

“Yes. It may very well be the enormous figure was an ogre,” the sergeant says.

“If so, then who did them in?” Luis asks with his eyebrows squinted in concern and looking around.

“That is what we need to find out. Who is capable of doing this and then hiding the bodies poorly, as if they almost wanted to be found?" the sergeant ponders. "Luis, ride back to Splinteroak and tell the major what happened here. We will mark it and head to Merchants' Pass. That has to be where whoever did this is heading."

Luis mounts his horse and gallops south. The others mark the area with torn cloth tied to tree limbs and then head to Merchants' Pass.

*****

The sky slowly darkens as the sun sets behind the mountains in the west, bringing the cool autumn night air once again. Tyree and the others have been mostly quiet except for Brak and Brace, jokingly telling exaggerated stories of what they did to the bandits back there. The group has been weaving in and out tall grasses and around small maple and poplar tree outcroppings that are too tight to pass through.

Tyree is first to round a corner of tall grasses that opens into a small clearing. Ahead of the clearing are more trees turning into a dark forest. The ground is covered by mostly fallen brown leaves with red and orange ones scattered about. When the rest come around the corner, Gullen spots something to the right of the clearing. "Looks like an old burnt house."

They trot the horses over carefully and scout around. Tyree waves for Glaive to dismount and get closer. The rock foundation remains and is four feet high, with parts of it collapsed here and there. Where a door once was is now a burned out opening with weeds that have died from the cool weather setting in. The roof collapsed into the house and burned away. Glaive kicks a few charcoaled boards away, and he notices a blackened skeleton hand sticking out. He taps it with his foot, and it crumbles.

Glaive frowns at it. "Well, chief, someone wasn't lucky." He walks around but really can't notice much as it is getting darker.

"What? Are we going to sleep out in the cold tonight?" Brace complains.

"No way. Not after the other night. I want to be pampered. You said we were going to travel like rich people," Brak says.

"Enough!" Tyree yells. "Quit your damn whining before I do it for you."

Gullen dismounts his horse and goes to the side of the house around scrub trees that have grown in and out of the house. "Hey, there is a small barn. We can stay in there."

"See, accommodations. Now get it ready for us since you wanted to be pampered," Tyree says as he laughed at them.

The boys clear out a section of the barn to sit and sleep. There is enough room for the horses to come in too. They get settled and eat what food they have left. Tyree walks outside to think under the night sky.

Ryan sits next to Glaive, offering him an ale. "Is Tyree really heir to the throne?"

"Uh, yes."

"How do you know?"

"Chief told me. He has never lied to me."

"But how do you know for sure?"

Glaive is silent for a few seconds; he drinks the ale and smiles. "Good ale...It didn't matter if it was good ale or bad, you told me it was ale."

"So?"

"So, it doesn't matter if he is or isn't. It's that he is going to be either way. So it doesn't matter. I'll just help him. I have nothing to lose."

"What I saw in that...that vision or whatever. He definitely has some sort of power," Brak says.

Ryan thinks for a moment. "Okay then. Let's say he is meant for the throne. How is he going to take it? How come we have to go to that place to find a device?"

"Yeah, why not use the book now?" Brace asks.

"Why don't we use it?" Brak suggested.

"It's because I can't read it fully yet," Tyree whispers, startling everyone.

"Ah, heh heh." Brak chuckles. "How...how long were you standing there?"

"Long enough." Tyree goes to the center of the barn with his hands on his hips. "Listen. I understand your hesitation going along with me.

After all, you are out to get a few coins and live week by week, not knowing how many coins you will get or when you will get caught. That's right, not *if* but *when* you will get caught."

Brak waves his hand in a non-caring motion. "Pfft, I will never be caught."

"Maybe so. For now, I offer something bigger. A chance to be someone besides what you are now."

"Did he just insult us?" Brace whispers to Brak.

"I offer you a position by my side where you don't have to steal or hide anymore."

"How is it you think you are the heir to the throne? The Baran line ended with the death of Prince Euan some 500 years ago," Ryan says.

"I'm not of that line. I am of the Mire family that last rightfully ruled Skylar."

"All those families that called themselves true rulers... never were. That is why the kingdom was divided."

Tyree snarls his lips at Ryan for saying that, but he keeps his composure and speaks in a calming tone. "Until the split of the kingdoms, my family, the Mires, had ruled successfully, if I might add." Before anyone can refute that, he continues by pointing his finger at each person. "But we were unjustly run out by people that were selfish, spread lies about us, and wanted the kingdom for themselves. And where did that get them?"

Tyree reaches into his jacket pocket. He pulls out a gray bound book that has gold and silver edges decorating it. He tosses it to Ryan. "Here, you will find the lineage of all the families since the reign of Baran. You will notice I am the last one mentioned. So yeah...the kingdom is mine to take."

Brak and Brace scuttle over to see the book with Ryan. They read through the impressive list of names, dates, and times of passing. Ryan looks at Tyree, who is smiling. "Well, sure enough, your name is in here."

"Yeah, at the end, ha ha," Brak says.

Tyree points his finger at him, also laughing. "And that is the important part."

Brace, who is standing in front of Ryan, looks perplexed at the book upside down when Ryan notices him. "What is it, boy? Don't know how to read upside down?" He gives a bellowing laugh.

Brace rips the book from his hand and looks closer. "On the contrary. I am well versed in the reading arts and upside down. But this..."

"What?" Brak asks.

Brace has everyone's attention. "Looks like someone took the time to write another lineage upside down using the existing spaces between the normal writing."

"What does it say?" Gullen asks.

"Yeah, read it aloud," Brak says.

Brace fiddles through the pages. "It says here that King Tavish and Queen Fenella had a daughter as well. Princess Alison. The queen sent her away after her brother, the prince, was killed. She had all records of her erased, but two that will confirm her heritage."

"What?! That cannot be! I am the rightful heir to the throne. Besides, that was centuries ago. Surely, the lineage has died off."

"Tyree. When did you get this book?" Brak asks.

"Only a few years ago. Passed down by my father. Why?"

"The last entry is of a Caden Tavish, CY 525 was born. Had a son in CY 554."

Gullen lays his head back against a pillow made of old straw. "Not so long ago. The lineage is alive then."

"No! It can't be!" Tyree says.

"Maybe they don't know. If they did, someone would have come forward a long time ago," Ryan calmly says.

"Yes, that is right." Tyree grabs the book from Brace.

"Ha, in front of you the whole time and you didn't see it," Brace jokes.

Tyree smacks him on the back of the head with the book. "Thanks for bringing it to my attention." Tyree frowns and puts it back in his pocket. He picks out a spot in the corner to sleep. "It matters not. I have...We have the Book of Power. It will help us unite the kingdom at any cost. Where I rightfully belong. And we will give it a new name, too."

"And what name is that?" Glaive asks.

"I'm open to suggestions...From the ones that want a position beside me."

The rest go silent, thinking of names, while Kade has sat there silent the whole time near the door, occasionally peeking out. She does not believe she has a part in this but wonders about the other man. *Is he still alive? Should I stay and find out?* she thinks to herself. Her thoughts stray to her home. It has been many years since she ran through the bamboo forest and clear running streams. Her journey chasing clues and hints to the Black Diamond of Truth had led her to this area, but nothing ever came of it. It is always a dead end for her. She has spent everything searching for it. Now she has to go home a failure. Everyone falls asleep while she ponders what to do.

*****

The sun rises on the chilly morning as a few raindrops fall. Tyree is already up and outside, going over a few spells and looking at the Book of Power. He came to a conclusion about the others on the journey. He goes back into the barn, confident about what to do.

"Listen, everyone, I am going to the location of Geemend's Seeker so I can find a scroll that will let me read the rest of this book to take the kingdom." He holds up the red leather book for all to see. "So who is with me at least to that place?"

Ryan nods, followed by Gullen, Glaive, and the boys. Kade shrugs her shoulders. "I have no choice at the moment."

"At least you're honest. I mean, come on, sweetie, you could have run off with the gold by now. You know you want a place by my side." Tyree gives her a wink and goes back outside.

After getting the horses out of the barn and mounted, Ryan, Brak, Brace, and Kade put their armor on before they travel into the dangerous wild. "We are going to need food," Brak says.

"Yeah, where is the nearest town?" Brace asks, looking around in all directions, only to find tree after tree.

"It has been about ten years since I was near here. I believe there is a bridge close by to cross the river. There was a copper mine that was discovered and should be a booming town by now," Tyree says, leading his horse through scrub bushes.

Ryan looks back at the burned-out house and at Kade. "Apparently, not for that household. Keep an eye out."

"I always do," Kade says as she was last in line, following everyone through the bushes.

Ryan has only known Kade for about a year now, but she always is aware of her surroundings by not fully trusting anyone. That gives Ryan some comfort when they rest.

The rain sprinkles off and on with steady downpours for a short time. Tyree leads them through small woods of leafless birch and chestnuts. They have about four hours of sunlight left when Tyree comes out into a clearing and can hear the river ahead. A cluster of willow trees hides the view of the bubbling water. The rain has stopped, and the crisp air is getting cooler. The rest of the group come out into the clearing and allow the horses to graze on the remaining grasses that still live in the fall air.

"Brak, Brace, get off the horses and go to the willows. Locate the bridge to cross the river."

"Why us?" Brace asks.

"Because he asked you two idiots to do it," Kade smartly responds.

"Yeah, yeah," Brace mumbles. The two slap each other while they go to the willow trees. Brak stretches his back, and Brace does it likewise.

"Which way you think it is, chief?" Glaive mumbles.

Tyree looks north and then south. "I'm not sure. There should be a sign of chimney smoke or something burning. I just don't see it, but I know we are close." He then whispers to himself, "At least I think so."

The two boys disappear into the willows. After searching for the bridge, they take their time coming back to the group. They both suddenly stop, looking at the ground. Brak reaches down and picks up a rusty broken sword blade. He inspects it. The blade looks to be the center part and is bent slightly. The edge is gone, with dirt and grass clinging to it. They both look around for the other parts but find nothing. Brace tosses it to the ground, and they continue towards the group.

"What is it you found?" Ryan asks.

"Just a broken blade. But you won't believe what is on the other side of the trees," Brak says.

"How far from the bridge?" Tyree asks.

Brace pointed to the willows. "Well, it's right there, but—" Tyree cuts him off.

"Ha! I knew it. Damn, I'm good." He gets his horse to trot towards the willows, with Glaive following.

Ryan squints at Brace as he gets on his horse. "But what?"

"Well, it's destroyed."

Gullen, Kade, and then Ryan guide their horses to the willow. Tyree comes out the other side and is in disbelief at what he sees. The large brown and gray stone sections from the bridge archway have collapsed into the river in huge chunks, almost like it was smacked down long ago. Three scour aprons remain where the arch ring bases were in place at one time. The bridge was a sight to behold, easily a length of a hundred feet or more and thirty feet high at the midpoint.

"What happened here, chief?" Glaive asks.

Tyree, looking confused, scouts the other side of the river. The outline of where houses once stood is now covered with weeds, thorn bushes, and trees growing out of them. Parts of walls remain, but most are knocked down and burnt. Large piles of rock and dirt that are just as high as the buildings once stood reveal this is the copper mine that Tyree knew years ago.

"Funny how most of the bridge fell into the flow of the river. It had to be pushed," Ryan says.

"Huh, but by what?" Gullen asks.

"A flash flood?" Brake suggests.

"No, a flood would have carried it a few feet downstream and carried the little pieces away," Kade says.

"By something big," Ryan whispers.

"Whatever. Looks like that was a long time ago and not our problem." Tyree looks up the river and then down. Both surfaces are smooth, flowing brown water from tree sap runoff. Near the fallen bridge parts the water ripples the most. Some spots you can see only a foot or two deep before it gets too dark to see the bottom. "It is shallow enough for the horses to cross here."

"Really? Cross here?" Kade grudgingly asks.

"Yes, here!" Tyree says, annoyed.

"Fine then, Your-Majesty-to-be. You go first," she says.

Tyree tightens the reins on his horse and nudges it forward to the riverbank. The horse hesitates, but Tyree, using his legs, urges it on. The hoofs sink into the soft sod and eventually into the mud along the bank that has a three-foot drop. Tyree struggles at first, but then the horse splashes into the brown water. They sink up to the horse's belly with the horse's head bobbing forward as it struggles to go through the moving river. They soon get to a shallow part to where the water is only covering halfway up the legs of the horse.

Tyree sarcastically says, "See! With a little guidance, you too can follow your...King!"

"Uh, let's go," Kade says. She huffs as she goes next in the same route through the water as Tyree. Next is Glaive, Gullen, then Ryan, followed by Brak and then Brace. They stay close to the remains of the blocks from the bridge, zigzagging their way across. Past the halfway point, Tyree's horse sinks into a deeper section, getting his feet wet up to his knees. The horse is nervous but continues on his own to get out of the river.

Brace's horse enters the deep part as Brak's attention is drawn downstream. A ripple is flowing against the current quickly. Brak is stunned at what he sees. An enormous, bright cobalt blue, crocodile-like head with two pale white horns arches back. The head is at least five feet long and three feet wide at the base of the jaw and a foot wide at its peak. At the base of the head, the horns are three to four feet long and come to a point.

Brak is horrified, but before he can scream, the creature blitzes with lightning-like speed at Brace. The many rows of teeth are like fine daggers stacked one after another. The creature almost looks like it is smiling as Brak watches. Brace has no clue what is about to happen as he tightens his grip on the reins going into the deeper water. The jaws grab the horse by the neck. With an enormous splash, they are gone. Brak watches the creature's body slither past. The bright cobalt blue color fades into a deeper blue. It has six legs per side pushing it along.

Ryan turns around to see the creature swim by. It is at least forty feet long. He notices Brak paralyzed with fear. "Run! Run to the shore quickly! Draw weapons!..Now!" Ryan doesn't have to really force his horse to move quickly; it wanted out just as bad.

Tyree glances back to see nothing but people panicking. He doesn't waste a second at guessing and moves his horse closer to the shore. Brak's horse chases the others on its own while Brak is motionless.

A loud splash gets the attention of everyone. Rising out of the deeper water is the creature with Brace's horse in its mouth with Brace hanging off of it. The monster is twenty feet out of the surface and notices the group going to the shoreline. It clamps its jaws shut, slicing the horse into two pieces, causing massive amounts of blood to spray. Brace falls into the water, followed by the halves of the horse. The creature sprints across the river, giving very little time for them to dismount.

Kade urges her panicked horse away from the scene as she dismounts, throwing the circled weapon at the creature. Glaive stands in front of Tyree as he gets the diamond to change into the crystal sword. Ryan is waving on Brak to make it to the other side. Gullen jumps from his horse and becomes a blurry image, going behind a tree.

Kade's round, bladed weapon bounces off the back of the creature's head. Once on shore, they truly see the size of it. The twelve, five-foot-long deep blue to mauve-colored legs hold a massive snake-like body that has bands of cobalt blue and dark blue scales. The tail extends another fifteen feet after the last set of legs. It easily moves aside small trees and crushes bushes beneath its body as it slithers towards Glaive and Tyree.

Glaive is ready to strike at it, but the head is too large and coming fast. He pushes Tyree out of the way and lunges himself to the ground. The creature's massive head strikes the dirt with a pounding that shakes everyone.

Ryan, seeing the opportunity to strike, swings his sword at the creature's back. The blade barely chips the scale as it rears its head to look back at Ryan.

"Oh crap," Ryan says.

Tyree sees what minor damage it did and tosses the crystal blade to Glaive. "Use this!"

Kade's circle blade comes back to her hand, only for her to throw it again at the monster's eyes. Brak makes it to the shore and goes near Tyree. The blade impacts above the left eye and sticks into the scales. The creature snarls at Kade as she takes a step back with fear in her eyes. It whips its tail against Ryan, sending him flying back into the river.

The creature takes a step towards Kade when Glaive cuts deep into its one leg with the crystal blade. Kade draws her bow. Ryan pulls himself out of the river. The creature quickly pounces over Glaive, knocking him to the ground, then hops and slithers past Kade. She readies a shot and lets the arrow fly. Tyree grabs Brak off his horse, and they hide behind a fallen wall covered in vines. The creature moves slightly to the left; Kade's arrow misses, flying off into the trees.

Ryan grasps his sword and is alongside Glaive who is charging at the creature. Kade is about to let another arrow fly when the monster stands on its last two rows of legs at thirty feet tall. It coils its head back then thrust it forward, sending an unexpected bolt of bluish white static electricity at them with a buzzing clap.

The flashes edge past a diving Kade. Ryan and Glaive watch with wide eyes as the electricity hits the ground, arching in their direction. The arcs are bouncing, twisting, and then impacting both of them. Ryan, being wet, gets shocked and thrown back. His sword flies off to the side with white and blue sparks popping from it. Glaive yells as the shock jolts through him and is absorbed by the crystal sword. Steam comes off both of them.

Tyree smacks Brak out of a daze and hands him a small lump of coal. He gives Tyree a confused look. "What is this?"

"Listen, we can't beat this thing. I need you to climb up it and put this near its eyes or head at the very least, so I can cast a spell."

"I...What? You want me to do what?"

"Do this! Now!" Tyree grabs his shoulders and shakes him. "I know you can."

"No. We can." They both look up and there is a soaked Brace standing behind them.

Brak smiles at his intrusion. "You're alive?"

Brace grabs the coal and runs. "Bet I will get it to the top before you."

"Oh, you're on." Brak runs after him.

The creature slithers back down, darting at Glaive. He hardly has enough time to regain his composure with the blade when he is hit with the chest of the creature, sending him tumbling across the ground. He continues to roll as the monster tries to stomp on him. Glaive is on his back, up against blocks from a fallen wall. He holds the blade out, slashing at a foot. The creature pulls back and strikes with its mouth.

Kade lets another arrow fly, only to have it ricochet off the banded scale. Gullen comes out from a tree to a stunned Ryan, helping him up and giving him his sword back. Glaive rolls to the left as the massive jaws strike the rocks again. He swings the sword at the mouth, hitting it, causing a few blue scales to fall. The creature quickly steps back from him, giving the fortuity for Brace to climb on its back.

The creature doesn't feel him until his axes tap the side of the scales. Brak suddenly runs beside the creature, yelling to get its attention. Glaive stands and yells, also coming at it with the crystal blade drawn. The creature's large foot trips Brak and then pins him to the ground. He yells out in pain.

Brace climbs up the back, and the creature twists side to side. He is only about ten feet away from the base of the horns. Brak is screaming in pain, and Glaive swings the blade into the front chest of the creature. Lager scales crack and break from the underbelly side.

"Its belly is weaker!" Glaive yells.

Kade runs towards the tail with her dao sword drawn. Ryan runs towards the creature again. Tyree stands off to the side with his hands steaming a black shadow mist, waiting for them to do the job.

Brace is swung and almost loses his grip. He swings his ax into the scales to have something to hold on to. This only causes the creature to sway faster. The others step back as the creature bucks and swings its body wildly. The ax comes loose, and Brace relies on his reaction and intuition. He lets go of the ax and jumps off the creature's back with the monster's head twisting to the right, away from Brace as he does an upward back flip. The head comes back as Brace grabs Kade's blade to hold on to. The beast shakes its head to the left and right violently. Brace's legs are pulled outwards as if someone is tugging them.

Everyone else is standing further away while the creature spins in uncontrolled circles with Brace hanging on for dear life. Gullen runs through the legs of the creature and grabs Brak before he is stomped to death.

The blade digs into Brace's hand and pain is setting in. He can no longer hold on. With a mighty pull, the blade comes free, and he pushes the coal lump into the broken scale of the monster. He tumbles uncontrollably through the air, yelling, "It's there! It's there!"

Brace lands into a scrub bush that cushions his fall. The creature coils into itself and then looks right at Tyree, who calmly walks out from the fallen wall. The creature thrust forward with its mouth open to consume him. Tyree gently holds his hands up with the black vapors coming out above his head, pointed at the creature. "Pimeys kuluttaa!" The black vapors shoot from his hands with blinding speed and envelop the monster's head, creating a total globe of darkness around it.

The creature stops. It twists and turns, growling in anger. Tyree motions all to be quiet and gets to the horses as quickly as possible before the spell expires. Gullen waves them in his direction as he tends to all the horses but Tyree's and Brak's. Brace runs towards Tyree, around the spinning monster, to get Brak's horse. The others sprint away and around the creature as it arcs another bolt of electricity in its general direction. The electricity cracks in all directions, burning small dead trees and bushes.

Tyree and Brak race northward, away from the creature. After ten minutes, they wait till the others catch up with them in a small clearing. Gullen is holding Brak, who is in pain. Brace dismounts immediately and helps Brak to the ground.

Kade comes up to him and starts feeling his chest. "Where does it hurt? Can you breathe?"

"Oww, it hurts... a sharp pain!" Brak grabs his chest.

Tyree remains on his horse, looking at Glaive. “Go back and listen for anything.” Glaive nods, hands back the crystal blade, turns his horse back, and goes into a cluster of trees.

“It’s his ribs. I know it, they’re broken. No one could withstand that stomping,” Brace says.

Kade unbuttons Brak’s black leather vest, then gives him a smirk. “Sharp pain, huh?”

“Yeah, it hurts... It won’t stop. I’m dying, ain’t I?”

She reaches under his vest and with a quick yank, Kade pulls out a bent dagger. The edge of the blade pierced his skin. “I’m surprised not more of your daggers stabbed you, honestly.” Kade stands up and faces Ryan. “He will be okay; just let him catch his breath.”

“Ha, you stabbed yourself,” Brace taunts.

“And you. Where did you go after falling from that mouth of whatever that was?” Gullen asks.

“All I saw was darkness and blood. I swam back, well, more like walked against the current to get to this side.”

Tyree dismounts his horse and puts his hand on Brace’s shoulder. “You did an amazing job. That showed real spunk.”

Brace smiles and jokingly kicks Brak, who is laying on the ground. “You hear that? Spunk.”

Tyree bends down to look at the cut. “It all worked out in the end. You did good too.” He frowns at Brak and pats his shoulder.

“I told you they come in handy,” Ryan says.

Tyree smiles, thinking he needs to keep this talented group together. “You all did good.” He looks at Brace and Brak. “The next time we come across any treasure, you two get first dibs...How's that?” Tyree mounts his horse as Glaive comes back.

“Nothing going on back there, chief.”

Brace and Brak mount Brak’s horse together. “You hear that? First dibs," Brak says.

“And I got Spunk.”

“Oh great, more food for your egos,” Kade grumbles, riding past them.

Ryan passes them, smiling. “You did good...Now shut up about it.”

"Where to now?" Gullen asks.

"We ride north till sundown and into the night. Merchants' Pass should be nearby," Tyree says.

They travel quietly along the river and away from it. The rain has stopped, and the clouds part, allowing the partial moonlight to help them see the area. After several hours, they see the lights of merchants in the distance. Tyree guides them to an inn he knows—The Frothy Lager. Only three rooms were available at that time of night. Tyree got his own, and Kade made sure she got the other. Everyone else shared a room. It wasn't long before they all fell asleep in dry, comfortable beds—or chairs and floors for the others.

Tyree holds the red book in front of him again. *No matter the cost, I will achieve my goals*, he says to himself.

"Ashguul masheen," whispers a deep voice from the book.

8

Discoveries

Olivia awakens in the darkened room again. *The candle must have gone out*, she thinks. *How long have I been asleep?* She gets out of bed and feels her way along the wall to the door and opens it to allow the hallway light in. *They really need windows in this place*. Olivia gets dressed and is tired of these clothes. It is early in the morning as she walks the cold stone hallway to find that the others are not up yet. She uses this time to go back to her place and get a change of clothes.

Olivia steps out of the aspen tree near her home. Once again, she gets sad at the thought of Abigail and how mad she was at her at this tree. She wishes she could take it all back and have her here again. “I’m sorry!” she yells into the air. “I’m trying to find you, Abigail. I really am.”

The flowers are all dead and have fallen off from the morning frost. The slight wind gives off that eerie howl through the leafless aspens that, oddly, she enjoys. Olivia makes her way back into her home and opens the kitchen door to see the morning sun that has risen over the ocean has lit the room through the brown stained glass. The breeze blows a few dead flower petals onto the floor and stirs the dust up, giving off an unusual spectacle of dust and light rays sparkling in unison across the room.

The stairway that leads upwards is dark, and for a second, she can almost see Abigail apologizing to her before she went upstairs to the cleaning room. Olivia closes her eyes, standing in the middle of the kitchen. The house seems so lifeless since her parents are gone and now Abigail. She can almost see her mother cooking over the fire and her father helping with the herbs, showing her what to do. Olivia smiles at that thought when she is startled to hear her father.

"Olivia, dear, will you hand us the plates?"

She opens her eyes, and there before her is her father reaching out to a young Olivia. Her mother has her back to her with her rich, flowing black hair tied into a ponytail with a butterfly clamp her father made for her. Olivia can smell the food, hear them talking and watch her younger self give him the plates. *I remember this. I drop the plate*, she thinks to herself.

The plate slips from her fingers and breaks against the floor. "I didn't mean it, Papa."

Her father pulls back his long brown hair from over his eyes. "It's my fault. I should have reached further. Now go get the broom."

Olivia is bewildered at what is happening. *It must be a memory mixing with my illusion*, she thinks. She steps in front of her father and looks into those hazel eyes that she has not seen in two decades. He watches the younger Olivia with careful eyes that she never noticed when young. He smiles at her cleaning up the broken dish. Olivia sees the care he had for her, then he turns to give a kiss on the cheek to her mother. Olivia knows the love he has for her, as if nothing can tear them apart.

Her mother, in return, holds and hugs him. Olivia wonders and slowly reaches out to them both. To her surprise, they are solid but have no heat. She doesn't care, and she tears up and hugs them both. "I've missed you so much. Where did you go?" They have no reaction to the older Olivia even being there as she continues to hold them.

A gust of wind slams the kitchen door shut with a clang, startling Olivia as she does that little "eep" of hers and the illusions disappear in an instant. "What happened? What was that? Did I just do that with a memory?"

She hurries upstairs to the guest room where Abigail stayed. Olivia stands in front of the closed door, closes her eyes, and takes a deep calming breath. Her eyes open, and she enters the room. There is a twelve-year-old Abigail looking out the window like the first time she was there. In her little brown dress and with messed up auburn hair, she stands on her tiptoes to get a good view.

"This is the best view ever. If I had your family and this house, I would never leave."

Olivia smiles at that memory and is about to turn away when young Abigail stops her with her words.

"Can I be your bigger sister? I would never leave you...I don't want to be alone."

Olivia stumbles to the door, tearing up and shuts it. She doesn't remember hearing that. She rushes down to her room, rummages through drawers, and pulls out a dragonfly pin made of silver and stone. A young Abigail gave it to her when Olivia was nine years old. Olivia breaks down and cries at all that has happened and is about to happen.

After a few minutes have gone by, she gathers herself up and takes a deep breath. "I can do this. They need me. I need to get Abigail back. I can't let her down...I can't lose her too." Olivia changes clothes and finds a maroon, square neck, shirred-ruffle hem dress. "Perfect."

She puts it on, and it stops above the knees. Then she slips on a pair of black leather pants followed by aged leather boots that have many golden buckles, tied at the top with black leather strings. Olivia then rolls her hair in a long ponytail and ties it shut with her mother's butterfly clamp. She then grabs her father's old black leather jacket that fits her comfortably. She slides a few pouches of her ingredients and a mortar and pestle.

Olivia looks at herself in the mirror. She smiles and clasps the dragonfly pin onto the left side of her chest, over her heart. On her way downstairs, a memory stops her at the broom closet. *No, can it still be there?* she thinks to herself. She opens it and feels in the back. Her hands feel something cold and metal. Olivia cannot believe it is still here after all this time. Her father's saber. She draws it from the black scabbard and the silver blade shines like new. A few unidentifiable markings are etched in the blade near the pommel. Other than that, it is plain looking.

She remembers her father telling her to never play with it. It can do a terrible thing. "Ugg, silly. I thought I would never swing anything again." She clamps the scabbard on the jacket, grabs a dark brown cloak from the hanging rack, and heads out of the house to go back to Snowcap.

*****

Olivia steps out of the pine tree into the cold fresh air near Snowcap keep. She stops for a moment to see the sun cresting over the mountains in the east, creating sparkles in the snow. Olivia closes her eyes and takes a deep breath. She gets it now why Abigail loves the silent cold. The cold seems to cleanse all that is wrong and create peace within. "I hope you are okay."

Olivia opens her eyes when a sun ray taps the side of her cheek, warming it. The sunlight makes a snow-covered pine tree glow with the rays reflecting in all directions. After staring at it for a minute, the natural spectacle fades as the sun continues its journey across the sky. Olivia smiles and takes that as a good sign. Once again, she walks to the large doors of Mr. Krew's home and walks in.

She hangs the brown cloak on a bird claw hook made of iron. Olivia peeks into the dining room, but no one is there. No warm and toasty breakfast waiting for her or anyone. *Maybe no one is up yet*, she thinks to herself. She continues down the hallway, peering into the next room.

To her surprise, Mr. Krew, Mr. Blaine, Mayreea, Abbot Garret, Young Adam, Klinksly, and Arthygus are sitting around a large white wooden table. It has black and gray twisting vine designs along the legs and edges. They are all quiet and look at Olivia as she comes around the corner. Arthygus smiles and is the only one to stand.

"Wow, you look stunning," Arthygus says.

Klinksly shoves his elbow into him, grinning. Mr. Krew's face remains towards Olivia, but his eyes frown at Arthygus's sudden interruption. Olivia blushes at Arthygus's comment.

"Good to see you again, Olivia," Abbot Garret greets.

"Where have you been, Miss Olivia?" Mr. Krew asks.

"I went back home to get a change of clothes. I needed to do that." Then she had an idea to test her ability. "Guess who I ran into?"

Before any others can answer, Mr. Krew responds, annoyed, "I don't play guessing games."

Olivia smiles and looks behind her. She steps aside, holding her hand out. Walking around the corner into the room entrance is Abigail, in her full maroon dress with the black corset and her hair loosely flowing half over her face. She waves at all of them. "Hey everybody."

Everyone's eyes are as wide as can be. Klinksly stands on his chair with his mouth wide open in surprise. Mr. Krew and Mr. Blaine stand, scooting their chairs back with a screech. "How? How did you escape the demon lady?" Arthygus asks.

"What? How?" Young Adam asks.

"Indeed. How did you do that?" Mr. Krew parrots.

"And to think we just found out where you were," Arthygus comments.

Olivia is happy at what she can do until she hears those words. "You—You know where she is? Is Abigail alright? Is she hurt?" The illusion of Abigail suddenly fades when her thoughts are disrupted.

"What?" Klinksly yells. "What happened to her?"

Olivia now realizes what she just did might not have been the best choice. "I'm sorry, I didn't mean too...I mean..." Everyone looks at her for an explanation. "I found out I can do illusions from memories, and I wanted to test it." She leans up against the door and blows a strand of hair away from her eye. "I didn't mean to cause—"

Mr. Krew interrupts and stands beside her, grabbing her hand. "I understand perfectly why you did that. If it could fool us, then it will make others think our queen is still around." He gives the slightest grin at her. "There is no shame in getting to the point. Job well done." He then offers her a chair at the table.

"Your illusions are getting stronger," Arthygus says.

Olivia feels relieved at what Mr. Krew said. "So, you know where she is?"

Klinksly, who is still standing on the chair and at eye level with those that are sitting, smiles and frowns. "Yes, we do, but there is another problem we need to tend to."

"Another problem?" Mr. Blaine asks.

"Problems are a way of being told how to overcome obstacles in our journey. Think of them as brief hints in guiding us along," Abbot Garret proposes.

Olivia laughs. "If Abigail was to hear that, she would scream."

Abbot Garret nods his head, smiling. "Yes, she would. Now, Arthygus, what is the problem we need to deal with?"

Arthygus and Klinksly tell of how they saw where Abigail was through the location spell. Then they tell the tale of what Frederick told them about Tyree. How he is searching for this scroll so he can understand the book and that he is on his way to Geemend's Seker. Everyone is silent in thought after hearing this.

Mr. Blaine rubs his chin. "Geemend's Seeker. I have heard of that story."

"So it is real? Has it been found?" Mr. Krew asks.

"Well, Frederick sold him a map to the seeker, and he doesn't sell anything with false leads," Arthygus says.

"That you know of. He will sell anything, false or not, to make a profit." Mr. Krew shrugs it off with a wave of his hand.

"Okay, fine and dandy, but what about Abigail? Where is she?" Olivia asks anxiously.

"You are right, Miss Olivia. Important things first," Mr. Blaine says. "From what you have told us, she should be about...Here." He points to a blank spot on the table, then touches it with his hand. Part of the tabletop slowly changes into a map of Esalon.

Arthygus is very impressed. "This is...wait. This isn't witchcraft magic."

"No, it is not. It is an old relic of magic we came across many years ago," Mr. Blaine explains. He rubs his fingers across it, zeroing in on Skylar Castle, then making the map move southward. He follows the map with his fingers from the description and directions Klinksly gives him until he comes to a large, reddish-brown to tan stone plateau in the middle of the forest.

"Is that?" Klinksly asks.

"I believe that is what we saw in the spell. Don't you think?" Arthygus asks.

"Yes. Yes, I do. Before the ring went deep into it"

"Is that where she is?" asks Olivia.

"If it is, she is in there." Arthygus looks closer. "I don't recognize the words. What is that place called?"

Mr. Blaine leans over and squints at the words. "It says...Con Del Mal Forest." He looks closer at the rock plateau. "And this reads...Mujer Malvada Plateau, if I read that right." He glances over at Mayreea.

"Well, close. Con Del Mal Forest means...with..." she stops mid-sentence like she saw a ghost. "It cannot be."

"What cannot be?" Olivia asks.

Mayreea taps Mr. Blaine's arm and rushes out of the room. Everyone looks at each other, then at Mr. Blaine. "What? Sometimes she gets excited. She will be back."

Mr. Krew changes the subject back to Tyree. "Until she comes back and tells us what she knows, let's figure out what we are going to do about Tyree."

"How is that supposed to help Abigail?" Olivia cries. "We know where she is, so let's go get her."

Mr. Krew takes a deep breath. "I know it is tough at the moment to seem to do nothing when we are actually trying to figure this out. But being irrational or irresponsible without planning will get you nowhere fast."

Olivia sighs, crosses her arms, and sits back in the chair. "That's all we seem to do is think," she mumbles.

Mr. Blaine changes the subject quickly before it escalates between those two. "How are we going to find where Tyree is going without the map?"

Olivia frowns and pouts. "Just have Arthygus use that location spell again. But instead, if that seeker place is going to tell him the location of the reading scroll, find the location of the scroll before him. Done and done."

Mr. Krew's eyebrows raise as high as they have been in a while, for not much surprises him. Klinksly takes his hat off and slaps it against Arthygus, smiling. "Ha, didn't I tell you witches have more common sense than wizards?"

Arthygus is motionless. "I didn't even have time to say that." He goes back to thinking that using the spell again might harm him.

"I like that idea, Miss Olivia. That way, we don't need to waste time tracking him or hoping that he is not that far ahead. Nicely thought out," Abbot Garret says.

Olivia feels better after that compliment and smiles.

"How does this location spell work? Mr.Arthygus?" asks Mr.Blaine.

"Well, um."

Klinksly takes over the explanation. "When we did the spell, he asked for what needs to be shown, and we saw in our minds where she was." He grins at Arthygus, who still has an uneasy look about him. "Oh yeah, and the spell takes a little part of you, too."

Olivia perks up in concern, and Mr. Krew stares at Arthygus. "Do you know how your magic works versus ours?"

"Not really. I mean, I know how wizard magic is."

"And that is?"

"Well, depending on what type of spell or how educated you are at it, you are tapped into the plane of magical energies." He demonstrates with his fingers. He creates a small bead of blue light about the size of a grape on his fingertip. "Once you conjure or summon the magical energy, you transform it into whatever you want or need." He blows on his fingers, speaks a word, and the light grows to the size of an orange, lighting up the room better. "Before you access it, you need to know the vocal tones, ingredients if needed, and the appropriate thoughts of the spell." Arthygus then lets the light fade. "It is tricky. If you do not stay focused or are not educated enough on the spell, disastrous results can happen. I am not clear on how witchcraft works...but magic takes a little of you with each use."

"Interesting. You give a little of yourself freely when in prayer to the greater powers for assistance. And yet you seem reluctant to give up this... extraordinary power," Abbot Garret says.

"With prayers I have discovered in this book, they are asking for a lot from me. Something I'm not sure I have in me to give," Young Adam says.

"Ours is less summoning and more on using the natural magical energies that are all around us. Plants, animals...people," Olivia says.

"And that can be quick and even more powerful than tapping into the magic plane. Tell me, Arthygus, do you know the history of wizard magic and witchcraft?" Mr.Blaine asks.

"That is something I try to stay away from. It is confusing and I was told something bad may happen if I pry too much."

"Let's just say we got the poor end of the spell," Mr. Blaine says.

"Hum, excellent lessons. Good indeed," Mr. Krew says.

"With evil!" Mayreea announced to the room as she walks in. "Con Del Mal is With Evil Forest and Mujer Malvada is Evil Woman Plateau."

"Oh, lovely," Klinksly jokes.

"I read that in a story once, long ago. Does anyone know the Curse of Tangeo?"

They all look at each other, expecting someone to answer, but no one does.

"All right then. The short version of the legend is this. Tangeo was a protector of those that traveled the forest on the Hope Road. He would outwit thieves, bandits, and those that would bring harm to innocent travelers. Tangeo was very deadly with two blades if needed, but he rarely used them. He made a fool of the wrong man one day and embarrassed him in front of his men. So the man kidnapped Tangeo's love, Catalina. Cursed him and offered her to a demoness."

"Oh, that is horrible," Olivia whispers almost to herself.

"But, Olivia, the curse is still active. Tangeo is doomed forever to look for Catalina, but he can never find her. And once a year, the curse brings her back to him and then takes her away, reminding him of his actions that lead to this hell. He cannot die, nor can she."

"That is really awful. Why would someone do that?" Olivia asks.

"So what does this have to do with Abigail?" questions Arthygus.

Mayreea signs. "There is a deadly consequence of this curse if those should go actively searching for her or now Abigail if she is in the same place."

"Huh?" Olivia's dumbfounded eyebrows lift. "Deadly?"

"We need to find an expert of curses. They are strong and should not be messed with," Mayreea declares.

"Who do we get?" Arthygus asks.

"We know nothing of curses," Abbot Garret adds, looking at Young Adam who shrugs his shoulders. They all look around and then all eyes end up looking at Klinksly.

"What? Why are you looking at me?" He slumps back into the chair.

"It is because you are the queen's assistant, Klinksly the gnome. And you have access to...certain parts of the witch queen's athenaeum."

Klinksly stares off into nothing, smirks, then grins. "I guess I do."

"And why is that important?" Young Adam asks.

"There is supposedly a tome in there that has most, if not all known, witches, warlocks and even wizards' names and their specialties listed," Mr. Krew explains.

"I've heard of this book but never saw it. Heck, I have not been to the athenaeum." He leans back in the chair, and Mr. Krew stares at him. "Alright, I will go and take a look." Klinksly stares back at Mr. Krew with a motionless expression as if waiting on something. "Oh, you mean go now?" Klinksly points out towards the door.

"Yes, queen's assistant. We do not have the luxury of waiting while Tyree is in motion and now, according to Arthygus's location spell, a demoness may know as well," Mr. Krew says in a firm tone.

Klinksly slides off the chair, grumbling about being an errand gnome, and heads to the door. Olivia gets up to go with him, but he stops her. "Sorry, Olivia, this has to be done by myself. Besides the queen and myself, witches are forbidden to enter those sacred chambers."

Olivia nods and gives him a hug. "At least it won't be dangerous like our adventure, huh?"

"Yes, it will be boring. No wererats to...deal with, you know. I won't be long." They smile at each other as he walks out the door to go into the hallway.

"Now that task is underway, let our wizard friend cast the location spell, shall we?" Mr. Blaine says.

Arthygus gives an awkward smile and pulls out his backpack to get the spell ingredients. He pulls out orange powder and a charcoal stick to make three orange dots in a triangle pattern and a charcoal line that connects them. He lights the orange dots on fire, and they snap and sparkle with a dancing flame. "Okay, when I activate the spell, it will show me... Who wants to see it also?"

"How do you mean?" asks Mr. Krew.

"I mean, I think those that are going to retrieve the scroll should see this too." Everyone is quiet, looking around at each other, and Arthygus smiles. "Also, if you are just curious to see, we all can take part."

"Well, that is a splendid idea. If Abigail can take me in that door tree thing...spell, then why not a chance to see real magic or...sorry, wizard magic," Abbot Garret excitedly states. Young Adam gives him the most perplexed look.

"It is called a tree door spell," Olivia explains.

"Yes, now let all of us see this location spell. Will it affect us as well?" Mr. Krew questions.

"I don't think I want to see, I mean, if it shows her...I'm already too upset about it." Olivia says.

"And why not?" Arthygus asks.

"Neither do I. I have no place in this so it's best I don't know. Just in case," Mayreea says as she softly grabs Olivia and stands away from the table.

"Who else does not want to participate?" Mr. Krew asks. No one else says anything, and he looks at Arthygus to begin.

"It will only harm the caster, I think...Okay, when I speak the words, inhale the smoke and keep your eyes closed and focus on the demon rune reading scroll and nothing else. Arthygus puts his hand on the first fire, causing it to smoke, and connects the parts while he speaks. "What I have lost has me in a bind. Now I need help with what I cannot find. Paikantaa esine."

Everyone breathes in the smoke. Their noses tingle, and an image of a deep blue spiraling light ring forms in their mind. A view becomes clear inside the glowing ring. They are above Skylar Castle, looking down at the blue rooftops. The ring turns westward and flies to the Woodland Kingdom. It lowers to treetop level and passes through the kingdom and over the lush green valley of the elf lord's territory and into the Lífvana Hills. The growing trees fade to tall shrubs and grasses in the tall hills that are barely mountains. The ground becomes barren and only shows gray, brown, and black rocks for miles around until an outcropping of dead trees comes into view. A warning sign lies broken on the ground, and the ring passes over it for a second to show the words *Djöfla Gardur*.

The ring hovers close to the ground and stops at a fallen tree from a long time ago. One branch seems to point at a small pile of rocks in the distance. The ring turns towards the rock pile, and it has the silhouette of a robed man pointing downward. The ring follows to where the image is pointing and comes upon a hidden crevice.

The crevice is small, and the ring stops at a word scribed into the rock. *Baladain.* The ring quickly goes into darkness. Nothing is seen for a few seconds until a faded, eerie, olive-green light comes into view. A black stone door lies in front, and the ring passes through it into darkness again. A faint reflection of the glowing ring illuminates a rolled-up parchment on a pair of hands made of stone. The smoke dissipates and the spell ends.

A few of them cough and clear their heads. Mayreea comes up and rubs Mr. Blaine's shoulder. "What did you see?"

He responds with a muted tone, "Baladain."

Mr. Krew stands and walks around the room. "Baladain. It has to be that place."

"What is that place?" Olivia asks.

"It was only a legend and lost to time. It is said to be the birthplace of death magic and the first place that Muun closed in the stories," Mr. Krew explains.

"We can send no one to that place," Mr. Blaine declares.

"Why not? If the myth of Muun is real, and she did that, then there is nothing to fear," Abbot Garret says.

"True. The death portals were the first to be closed. But if that was the case, then how did a ghoul survive and now Arthygus, you tell us of zombies rising? It may very well be that a small portal has reopened in Muun's absence," Mr. Krew suggests.

Everyone didn't realize Arthygus was silent. They look at him for a response to Mr. Krew's question. His jaw is open slightly with drool coming out and his eyes are looking off to the side.

Mr. Krew shakes him on the shoulder violently. "Seems our young wizard suffered the spell's effects. Snap out of it."

Arthygus clears his head from the spell and recalls what he is doing here. "Huh? Oh. I'm alright. What was I doing?"

"You casted a location spell." Mr. Blaine says.

"Again? So soon?" Thoughts of the location of the scroll pop into his head. "Okay. It's coming back to me now."

Olivia is getting agitated. "Okay, fine. But how is all of this going to help us with Abigail?"

Abbot Garret stands and claps his hands together. "Now, Olivia, as our fine, well-informed hosts have said, we need to gather as much information as possible to know what we are dealing with. It is not like we are dealing with the pesky gnolls that Abigail dealt with at a moment's notice. We seem to be in a very dangerous territory, the unknown. If you rush in, you...or *we* could be the victims also. Who would help Abigail then?"

Olivia frowns and sighs, kicking her foot against the floor. "I know. It's just hard to sit here when we know where she is at now."

"Help is not always running out and knocking down doors to get what you need. Sometimes we are guided to see what is right in front of us."

Olivia grins. "If Abigail was here, you know what she would say to that, right?"

"Yes. Yes, I do. Heard it firsthand...Look at all the talent you are surrounded by in this room. All with the goal of getting Abigail back." The room is silent, and Mr. Krew is nodding his head in agreement. "Let's look at what we know now."

Arthygus raises his finger in the air. "We now know the location of Abigail and the reading scroll."

Young Adam raises his hand as well. “We also know Tyree is up to something with the Book of Power. He needs that scroll to read it before the book's true power can be used.”

“But what is his end purpose and how long has he been planning... whatever?” Mr. Blaine asks.

Abbot Garret sits back down. “And what of this curse that may involve Abigail?”

“Mr. Krew? You have remained silent,” Mayreea says.

His thoughts stray back to when he was younger and part of a group that searched old ruins in the mountains. He can still hear the screams and the last thing that he heard his friend say. *“We should have planned before we came here.”* This was before a young Krew fell off a dark cliff and into a river below. Mr. Krew grins and stands up. “We have a well-disciplined group here, Olivia. Patience is needed at the worst of times.”

Olivia’s soft, sweet voice pierces everyone’s heart with one question. “Then what will be done about it?”

Everyone looks at each other for an answer, but no one speaks. They hear the large entrance door open and close, followed by little footsteps coming down the hall. Klinksly pops around the corner.

“That was quick. Did you find anything?” Arthygus asks.

Klinksly walks to the table and lays a small splinter of wood on the top. “Yes, I did. Don’t ask, please. But yes.”

Mr. Krew’s long face is requesting an answer. “And?”

“Well, when I looked into... a name stood out with this splinter between the pages. She has a long history of being the go-to for curses. But she stopped. Last recording was about 75 years ago.”

“So she could be dead?” Olivia asks.

Mayreea picks up the splinter to examine it closer. “It is soft and pliable. Smells like sand. A palm perhaps. What is her name, Klinksly?”

“Masika... Witch of curses.”

Mr. Krew claps his hands together before anyone else can speak. “We now know what must be done. We need to retrieve the scroll before this Tyree fellow gets ahold of it, and someone needs to go seek this Masika woman.”

Olivia stomps her feet and puts her hands on her hips. “Okay, finally. Klinksly, Arthygus, and I will go get the scroll and someone can go see the curse lady.”

“Um, no can do, Olivia,” Klinksly says.

“And why not? What now?”

“Remember? I have to stay behind to do my job. I have to go back to the colosseum. People are wondering about our queen, And i recommend you stay as well.” Klinksly explains.

Mr. Blaine stands and points at the map on the table again. “I have figured out where Baladain is. It lies beyond the elf kingdom. It may very well be dangerous and a long journey. Who here is healthy enough to travel?”

“Why not use the tree door spell to that location?” Young Adam asks.

The room goes silent, and Mr. Krew chuckles. “If only it was that easy. There are rules or laws we follow. We are warlocks and witches, not lawless barbarians or common thieves.” He slams his fist against the table. “The Elven Lord, Sigurdur, forbids us to use his forest for such a purpose.”

Olivia perks up and smiles. “You mean one or more of us would travel through the elf kingdom?”

“Well, yes. But those that go would need a valid reason to travel through their domain. And they rarely let anyone do so,” Mr. Krew elaborates.

“So, who will do what?” Abbot Garret asks. Once again, the room goes silent. Some of them sit and point at the maps while others pace the room for a while. Olivia’s belly rumbles, followed by Klinksly’s. She rubs it, looking hungry now.

Mayreea sees this. “Since I won’t be going anywhere, let me get breakfast ready. Klinksly, would you join me?”

The gnome smiles and quickly follows her down the hallway. “Now, this is one problem I can help solve.”

Olivia taps her head, and Arthygus stares at her. He looks her up and down, realizing how beautiful she is. Olivia keeps her head to the floor and looks up to see him staring at her. She blushes and a thought comes to mind. “I’ve got it!”

“And that is what, Miss Olivia?” Mr. Blaine prompts.

“Arthygus and Young Adam are best suited for getting the scroll,” Olivia begins.

“But they have little experience in tough situations,” Mr. Blaine argues.

“I know, that’s why I will go get someone that will be perfect for this task. My friend Waldron.” Olivia smiles confidently. “And Abbot Garret can go with Mayreea to see the curse lady.”

“Now hold on. Why Mayreea and not Mr. Krew or myself?” asks Mr. Blaine.

“As much as I would like to go on this journey, we are far more useful here getting as much information as we can on Baladain and this Tyree fellow,” Mr. Krew chimes in.

“I know…Who is going to be the one to tell Mayreea?” Mr.Blaine asks.

“Well, Miss Olivia, it has seems you have taken control and made a most excellent suggestion,” Mr. Krew says, and with that, he and Mr. Blaine quickly leave the room.

The rest of them look at each other. Olivia shrugs her shoulders and sits down.

“I, for one, am up for an adventure. I have been cooped up far too long in that old stone monastery,” Abbot Garret says. Young Adam gives him a smirk. “What? At my age and after what Abigail opened my eyes to, this is an opportunity that Dianeeta is giving us to grow, explore the world and gain knowledge.”

Mayreea and Klinksly come into the room with breakfast biscuits and eggs and hand them out to everyone. Olivia and Arthygus eagerly grab one, followed by Young Adam, then Abbot Garret.

Mayreea speaks with a joking tone. “Where did the mighty duo go?”

Everyone looks at Olivia, smiling, and she holds onto her biscuit and draws her arms into her chest. “They left the room because I have to tell you that you are going with Abbot Garret to go see the curse witch.” She grins, hoping nothing will happen.

“Oh, that’s all.” Mayreea smiles, gently puts down her biscuit, and walks out of the room.

“Huh, wonder why they made a fuss about—” Arthygus is cut off by Mayreea screaming at Mr. Blaine and Mr. Krew in another language. Her voice has a southern island accent, and they can tell she is not happy.

“Kind of has a hypnotic flow, does it not?” Arthygus asks.

Abbot Garret nods his head and is about to say something when she comes back into the room; he quickly puts a biscuit in his mouth.

“I’m sorry, I didn’t know you were against going anywhere,” Olivia says.

“Oh, no.” Mayreea waves her finger in the air. “I’m not mad at you. It’s those two cowards that let you do the dirty work by telling me that I’m mad at.” She leans against the table and grins. “Besides, I would like to go. Get out of the house and all.”

While they were eating, the two gentlemen came back in with a few books in their arms to go through. It is decided that after they are done eating, Olivia will take Arthygus, Young Adam, and Klinksly to Waldron’s place to see if they can recruit him. Mayreea will take Abbot Garret and see where the tree door spell takes them.

Everyone is at the large wooden entrance door that is wide open and the cool fresh midday air rushes in, pushing aside the late morning breakfast aroma. Mr. Blaine kisses and hugs Mayreea goodbye. “Be safe, my dear.”

“Always.”

Abbot Garret firmly shakes Young Adam’s hand. “You are definitely growing, Adam. A year ago, who would have thought we would be here, doing this?”

Adams smiles. “Eyes open right.”

Mr. Krew holds onto Olivia’s arm. “As soon as it is all good, get them as close to the woodland kingdom as possible. And under no circumstances go with them. Come back here...” He then gets close to her ear and whispers, “Please.”

“I will. Klinksly will make sure of it.”

"I hope so. It looks like the queen's assistant has turned more into Olivia's assistant."

The six of them head to two different trees. Olivia opens her tree door spell and, one after another, they disappear into the yellow and green sparkles. Mayreea grinds the remaining splinter in her mortar and pestle until it is a fine powder. She casts the spell, looks back at Mr. Blaine, smiles, and walks into the spell followed by a waving Abbot Garret.

*****

Mayreea guides Abbot Garret through her pink glowing forest. Many trees are present from high peaked pines to low, moss-covered black willow swamp trees. They come upon a large palm tree. She opens the tree door spell and cautiously peek out. She pulls her head back in. "Well, Mr. Abbot Garret, you may have too much clothing on."

"Garret. You can call me just Garret." He peeks out to see what is there. They are along a wall of palm trees outside of a small oasis. The air is hot and dry. The sky is bright blue with no clouds, and as far as he can see there is light tan and white sand dunes in all directions. In the distance, he can see a large square building with two tall stone monoliths on each side. "I guess that is where we need to go?"

"I believe so."

*****

Olivia pops out of the tree next to Waldron's house under the oak tree, followed by the others. The air is cool, and most of the leaves have fallen from the trees, all but a few stragglers. The leaves crunch beneath their feet as they come around the corner of the house. There is Waldron surrounded by eight gnomes with worried looks on their faces.

"There! They are the cause of all this!" a gnome angrily yells.

Olivia, looking happy then confused, approaches them. "What do you mean?"

A gnome speaks in his language at Klinksly. "It's all your fault. If you wouldn't have gone and robbed them!"

"What are you talking about? I'm no robber! Who dares call me one?" Klinksly responds in gnomish.

Waldron steps between them and speaks common tongue. "Calm down. It's not their fault... Well, it is, but they didn't do it on purpose."

Olivia looks totally confused. "What is going on? We came for your help and now we are being accused of what now?"

"After you killed Skeel and the gnome took his sword, Klatzz, the wererat king, has blamed the gnomes of Mushroom Cove for his death and has a small army coming within hours to claim the sword back and kill all the gnomes," Waldron explains.

Olivia is stunned. "This can't be. It's not like I sought him out. I was trying to get away." Her mind races with many thoughts. "What do we do now?"

9

Cursed Ambition

Tyree extends a day of rest at the Frothy Lager Inn due to the coming rain. After two days of skirmishes, everyone's bodies are a bit sore, and no one is dissenting to the idea of a day off. Tyree remains in his room, studying the Book of Power. Glaive and Gullen take a walk around Merchants' Pass to taste the various foods and look at goods being sold. Ryan soaks in a warm cleaning tub to rid himself of the chill from falling in the cold river and being shocked by the creature. Brak sleeps the day away, recovering from his minor injuries.

After cleaning off and changing clothes, Kade and Brace visit the wandering vendors on horse-drawn wagons. She browses through different cloth material and finds a roll of gold silk is partly hidden under other less desirable cloth. She quickly grabs it, rubbing it between her fingers.

The old merchant man tries to get her attention. "Ah, you like that, do you not?"

Kade keeps rubbing the silk between her fingers and staring off into the distance. Brace notices her watery stare. He looks at the old, wrinkled man that has a flat top hat, a bushy gray mustache, and eyebrow hairs that needed a trim a long time ago. "She gets like that...sometimes," Brace tries to explain with a perplexed smile. He is about to wiggle her shoulder when he watches a tear slide down her cheek. He has never seen that from her.

"What is wrong?" Brace speaks in a calming voice.

Kade turns to Brace, tosses the silk back onto the wagon, wipes her face, and walks away. Brace shrugs his shoulders at the man. "Women?" he says and hurries after her. He steps in front of her, walking backwards while she continues forward. "Hey, what's going on?"

"Nothing, it's nothing. Mind your own business."

"If you liked that silk, then why not buy it?" Kade turns to walk in a different direction away from Brace. "Tyree won't know if you spend a little of the gold."

Kade grabs Brace and takes him to the side of a building out of the way of prying ears. "I don't want to buy it. Now leave it be."

Brace smiles at her. "Okay, okay... So what is bothering you?"

She waves her hand at him to brush it off. "It reminded me of home...That was all." She walks back out to the main part of the street.

"Oh, that's all? Where is your home? Hey...where are you from, anyway?"

Kade didn't want to answer the question, but she found that talking about her home calmed her. "Oh, after all this time together, now you want to know? Fine. I come from Jin Si Cheng City."

"Whose a where's now?"

"Jin Si Cheng. In the far southeast lands of Dangso Tung." Brace's eyebrows raise in bewilderment; he is silent. Kade exhales in disgust, shaking her head. "You really need to be educated about the world and all its offerings."

"But I am."

"No...you're not. Do you even know what my city name stands for?" Brace crosses his arms, tapping his chin and looking into the air, thinking. "No, you don't. Now end of story," Kade commands in frustration.

"Well, if I had a home, I would be talking about it all the time."

"Is that why you are following Tyree? You think that fool is going to offer you a home?"

Brace stops walking, and Kade takes a few steps before also stopping.

"He was the only one to offer me something." He snaps his fingers. "And Brak too."

Kade nods her head. "If that suits you, then…fine. Go for it."

"Wait, you are going to leave?"

Kade shrugs her shoulders and walks away. "We will see." She remembers her home and the lies that sent her away. *Soon. I will be home soon*, she says to herself. The two walk around for a few hours, looking at items being sold. They buy dried fruits and meats, along with fresh vegetables for tomorrow's journey. Soon, they run into Glaive and Gullen and go back to the Frothy Lager Inn.

*****

Tyree relaxes by studying the red Book of Power. The etchings are enticing him even more to find Geemend's Seeker so he can find the scroll to understand them. Page by page, he rubs his fingers across the ancient runes. "Prakdon ran his fingers across these very pages. Now I am." He ponders in what way General Prakdon used this power to gather an army. *What commands did he utter?* "What strategies did you come up with? Why were you so undefeated until that day?"

"Well, I'm your master now. And I will command the power to do my will. And I won't hide in a tower. We will go places." The book gives off a warm vibration for a second, startling Tyree. He grins, thinking the book understands him. "What secrets will you reveal to me?"

Tyree searches for the portal spell page in the book. "Why did you show me it?" He comes to the page he believes it is on. "Was it because I was in the tower? Or…was it you wanted a victim?" His eyebrows squint in thought. "And what happened in the Devil's Bowels? What spell was that to pull the life energy from those two men?" He stares at the book cover. "Did I summon you, demoness? What is your name?"…*Does this book control you?* he thinks to himself, grinning.

Midafternoon, he hides the book in his jacket pocket that is hanging over the chair. He retrieves his spell book from the other pocket to browse over. He notices the small rod he used back at the tower and grabs it. "I wonder…" He concludes once he reaches the seeker, he will be able to go back at any time thanks to the rod of teleportation. "It's a shame I have to be there first before I use it." He slams his fist against the table, remembering seeing the girl and gnome disappear into a tree. "Damn witches! That's how they escaped so quickly! They go through trees. I must learn how to do that."

Tyree laughs hard and giggles. "Well, I know one witch that is going nowhere anymore." The rest of the day, Tyree learns his spells to his memory for use later. Wizard spells disappear from the mind when used. Occasionally, he takes a break to look out the window and observe people walking on the streets dreaming of ruling the kingdom.

*****

Ryan and Brak meet Kade, Brace, Gullen, and Glaive downstairs in the inn for a much welcome dinner. They feast on ale, wine, and seasoned fish and meats, as well as share a loaf of freshly baked bread.

"How do you feel?" Gullen asks Brak.

"Eh, a little sore from being stomped on by that...whatever it was."

"Yeah, what was that anyway?" Brace says.

Confused, they glanced at each other, unsure what to say. Brace stands and speaks with a slightly louder voice. "Did you see how I climbed the blue monster's back?" He waves his hands in the air, recreating the moment. "How I was flung from side to side as it was trying to flip me off."

"Yes! I thought that was amazing to watch!" Glaive says, raising a goblet in the air only to encourage Brace to speak more.

"Right! At least someone appreciates what I can do."

"Uhh, well. It looked like you were a goner for sure," Glaive says.

Brak lays back against the chair with his arms crossed. "You got lucky, that was all."

"If we weren't in a river, I'd say you pissed yourself when that multi-legged creature took Brace and his horse underwater. The look on your face..." Ryan shook his head and laughed.

"I was worried about Brace. Or I mean his horse. Besides, that was water that splashed on me!"

"Uh huh," Kade says.

Brace taps Brak's back teasingly. "Aww, you were worried about me."

"Was not."

"Were too. You just said."

People sitting near them are captivated by their storytelling. One man in particular approaches them. "How did you get away?" He is wearing fine brown pants and a maroon dress shirt with a small insignia of a Garnet City soldier—the three-fingered silver claw holding a maroon garnet. He is a short fellow, about five feet tall, and has short black hair with a light tan complexion. They all glare at him and are quiet. Brace swallows a sip of ale nervously.

The man sees this and eases the situation. "Forgive my intrusion. I was listening to a wondrous tale."

"It wasn't a tale. It—" Brace is cut off by a poke from Ryan.

Another person wearing stained brown trousers and a ripped green shirt walks up and leans his drunken body against the man. He has longer brown hair that has not been washed in a few days. "Oh, is my buddy Luis bothering you?" The man hiccups, then burps. "He is always up for a good story. Come, buddy, let's listen to the ale some more." He pulls on Luis's arm to get him to move.

As Luis turns, he asks, "Wait, I want to hear what happened."

"It's another tall tale..." The man stumbles and burps again, leaning against Luis. "Travelers always have to say something they are not.You know, tall tales and such."

"But it's true! You calling us liars?" Brace questions.

The two men turn to them. "No, no." Luis waves his hands.

The other man staggers forward. "Friends, I do not know...*burp*...you. I mean no offense. I like a good story also." The man lets out a loud, deep belch that others laugh at. Even Brak and Brace chuckle.

"So where was this monster at? What did it look like?" Luis asks.

"Yeah, tell us," a woman sitting near them adds.

"Tell me a story," another man says, raising his mug in the air.

Brace looks at Ryan for permission. "I see no harm in a tale. Go ahead."

Brace explains the story of where they were crossing and what they encountered, including him climbing the monster's head to put the lump of coal there. The crowd is on the edge of their seats as Brace stands on the chair, telling the tale for all to hear. He actually likes the attention for once. People clap and whistle in admiration, while others wave their hands in disbelief.

Kade whispers over to Ryan and Gullen. "From the way he says it, we really did a good job together."

"Or just got lucky," Ryan remarks.

"In the past, Tyree mostly looked out for himself if he got what he wanted. But this time he sees something in all of you to save. That surprised me," Gullen mentions.

"You say we should follow him?" Ryan asks.

"I would...for now. I for one would like to see this Geemend's Seeker he is after. You do know if it works for him... it can work for us, too," Gullen points out.

"What does that mean?" Brak asks.

Gullen leans in to make sure most can't hear as Brace describes their encounter with the monster. "We each can use it to find what we are looking for." He smirks, leans back in his chair, and claps as Brace finishes his story. The others follow his lead and clap.

The inn patrons join in.

"That was a good one," a woman yells.

"To make up. There is no creature like that," yells another man.

"I enjoyed the tale," laughs another.

A loud crack shatters the noise as an old man slams a crutch across a table. The room goes silent. The old man has faded blue eyes that match his pale skin, perfectly trimmed gray hair, and is a little on the chunky side. He is missing his left leg from the knee on down. His red and black checkered shirt matches his dark brown pants; a worn belt barely holds them up. "It's true," he says with an overbearing raspy voice from too much smoking.

The people in the inn watch the old man. One of them says, "How would you know?"

"It's from the old copper mine...isn't it boy?"

Brace is still standing on the chair and puts his hands on his hips. "Why yes. Yes, it is, good sir."

Kade squints at him. "He does have manners."

"The beast caused that place's demise...and took my leg!" He looks around at everyone, then over at Luis. "You are aware of that too...soldier man. At least you should have been told about that place."

Luis steps forward. "Yes, it is true. But none of the recruits believed it. After all, that happened, what, thirty years ago?"

"And I ain't no spring chicken! I was there and saw how fast that monster chewed through our horses, men, women, and babies. Sparks flew out of its mouth, burning the houses that people were hiding in."

"How did you escape?" Brace asks.

"Like you, I tried to attack it with my blade. Only with my leg in its mouth, it picked me up and shook its head violently. My leg popped off, and I flew into the river and was washed downstream, away from it."

"So you didn't—"

"No! I didn't escape. I was taken away by the river. My destiny was to tell of what happened there and to live with this awful memory."

"So what was the monster?" a man asks.

"That beast is called a behir. At least, that's what the elves used to call them," the old man says.

Brace touches his lips with his one finger. "A behir huh? Sounds fitting enough. Where did it come from?"

"No one knows. King Rashaad forbids anyone to go near there. But the elves said it was a clever hunter and a dangerous foe to go after. Some believe it hoards a treasure from those it eats, but that is hogwash. Wizards used to seek them out for whatever wizards do and they paid a hefty price for its innards." The old man points around the room.

"Perhaps that is why it killed so many people. They tried to kill the unkillable!" Another man says.

Most people wave their hands in the air in disbelief and go back about their business. They resume drinking and eating while others watch Brace and the old man. Luis walks away. The drunk man leans against a wooden support beam, watching. The old man holds up a goblet of ale. "A toast to encountering the behir and living to tell about it. You must be a strong team to defeat such a beast. Bet nothing can stop you after that." The crowd cheers and clinks their cups and goblets together, laughing.

Luis turns his head back as he is walking out of the room. *A strong group, huh? Maybe one able to defeat bandits?* he thinks to himself.

Brace steps off the chair and the rest finish their meal. The old man hobbles away across the inn toward a warm fireplace. The drunk man finishes his ale, then staggers away. After an hour, Kade lays gold coins on the table and the group heads to their rooms to rest for tomorrow's journey.

"That was some good storytelling, but you didn't have to call me a weenie hiding between the monster's legs," Brak says.

"Aww, it was just a bit of fun...for the story, you know," Brace says as they head upstairs.

Luis heads out of the inn into the dark streets. "The lantern boys are running behind tonight," the drunk man says to Luis.

"Yes, they are." Luis walks away from the door as more people leave. "How do you burp like that when only drinking water?"

"Just a little ale does the trick," Ray asks.

"What do you think? Is it them?"

"I would say it is a strong possibility. But come on, it looks like they did all of us a favor."

"I know, I know. But it's what Sergeant Mashawn wants. Let me know if you come up with anything else."

Ray staggers back into the inn. Luis walks away while Gullen appears as a blur around the corner, hearing what was said between the two. He waits for a few minutes and sneaks back into the dark alley, climbing up to the open window of his room.

*****

The morning sun glares through the window, illuminating the room. Smoky meats and ale still linger in the air. Tyree is getting packed for the day's travel when there is a knock at his door. He opens it to find Gullen there with a frown. "We need to talk." Gullen explains what happened last night and what he heard the two men talk about.

Tyree angrily busts through the door of the other room, breaking the top hinge so the door sticks open. Glaive and Ryan jump out of bed. Brak and Brace roll around on the floor, instinctively grabbing their weapons.

"I'm not even going to say anything about last night, but that was foolish." He slaps the table with his hands. "How many times do I have to say we need to keep a low profile? We do not need to bring attention to ourselves at the moment," Tyree says in a calm voice.

"Huh? What do you mean? I didn't do anything, like steal or get into any trouble," Brace points out.

Tyree smirks. "This is not the time to explain, but listen to me now. Brak, go get your horse and ride north out of town by yourself for an hour. Find a good secluded spot to flag the rest of us down." He stares at Brak while he lays back down on the rug. "Now!" He stomps his foot on the floor.

Brak stumbles to get his stuff packed. "Okay. I got it."

"Now, Gullen, I want you to leave town thirty minutes after Brak and go north also. Ryan and Brace, you two will leave together thirty minutes after Gullen."

"And what of me?" Kade asks.

Tyree turns to her. "You will leave with Glaive and I."

"Uh. What is all this for, chief?" Glaive asks.

"Well, with someone's story last night, the Garnet City soldiers are inquiring about the bandits we did in the other day, and they think that is us. I don't have time to deal with this nonsense."

Brak is packed and heads out the door to leave the inn. The rest quickly pack their things. "Speak to no one," Tyree emphasizes as he goes back to his room. He glances outside the window and watches Brak leave town on his horse. *At least that part is out of the way*, he says to himself. Before he turns away, he notices three Garnet City soldiers approaching the inn. One tall dark-skinned man in full chainmail armor and two shorter soldiers with lighter toned skin.

Tyree asks the others to come down soon and gestures for Gullen and Kade to follow him to the inn's front door. Ryan, Glaive, and Brace watch from Tyree's window. Tyree walks outside and bumps into the large soldier. Gullen and Kade come out of the swinging doors and walk past them, laughing as if nothing was going on.

"You there, stop," Sergeant Mashawn orders.

Tyree blows a light blue powder into their faces and whispers, "Maaginen Ehdotus." The powder turns into a quick sparkle and goes into the soldiers' noses. "Look at me and me only," Tyree says.

The soldiers turn towards Tyree with their eyes twinkling a light blue color. Tyree grins in satisfaction that the spell is working. "Friends, what is your hurry this morning?"

Sergeant Mashawn frowns at Tyree. "We must hold those two and the others."

"Why?"

"We think they are involved in the slaying of people south of here, and they need to pay for the crime."

"Why do you conclude they did that?"

"From the story they told last night of defeating the monster at the old copper mine."

"Is that so? See how happy and peaceful they are. I suggest you check out the old copper mine first to verify the tall tale. You know how people are...with that sort of thing."

"Yes, that is a good idea."

"Well...go now." Tyree watches the three of them turn around and head back into the center of town.

Ryan watches the soldiers leave through the window. "What did he say?"

"Oh, being a wizard, chief has a way with words," Glaive says.

"Oh, he's waving us down," Brace notices.

After Gullen departs, Ryan and Brace leave as well. Soon Tyree, Glaive, and Kade leave town, mixing in with other travelers going north for a while to avoid being seen.

Kade pulls her horse next to Tyree. "Why did you have us leave separately? We are stronger together, you know."

Tyree trots along on his horse, grinning at her. "Sweetie, sometimes strength is not needed to overcome a...situation. We had to make sure we were not seen as a threat."

"Why not?"

"I guess Garnet City soldiers found the bodies we... you know. After last night's story that was told, we became of interest, and I cannot stop for any minor reason such as that. So I had people leave by themselves and blend in. No one would even think for a moment that one or two people could have done all that killing to so many people."

Kade nods her head, then asks, "How did you get those soldiers to leave?"

Tyree laughs. "Sweetie, that's one of my many talents. I suggested they look for the blue monster to verify our story that it does exist."

"And they believed you?"

"Well..." He smirks. "A little suggestion spell sprinkled in with the truth definitely helps."

"Oh. So what will happen to them?"

"Ha ha ha! I didn't think about that. Thank you for the amusement. I guess they will meet the creature and get eaten. Ha ha ha!"

Kade gives the horses space by separating from Tyree. "See, chief always has a plan. And here we are, casually on our way, with no worries," Glaive says. Kade is silent while Tyree smiles at what Glaive has said.

*****

An hour later, Sergeant Mashawn and Luis lead the other four men south along a trail going to the old copper mine. They meander through scrub bushes and around thickets. The sun is a welcome warmth from the last two rainy, chilly days. The wet ground keeps the horses' hoofs quiet.

Kadeem and Conner are in the rear, talking. "Keep your eyes and ears about, men," Sergeant Mashawn orders.

"Why are we going to the copper mine to begin with, sir?" Kadeem asks, looking confused.

Conner whispers to Kadeem, "Glad you asked and not me."

"That man told us to check for the monster to verify their story."

"But sir," Miles interrupts. "We already know it is there from the reports telling us to tell others to stay away."

Sergeant Mashawn stops his horse and looks at Luis. He knows this already. *Why am I going here?* He says to himself. The fogginess in his head begins to clear, and the blue sparkle in his eyes fades. He shakes his head from side to side. "Men! We have been duped by a user of old magic!"

"A wizard?" Miles asks.

"Yes." Sergeant Mashawn says nothing more and turns his horse in disgust to gallop back to Merchants' Pass.

*****

Farther north, Brak is waiting for everyone to arrive. He chose a place near a small stone bridge that crosses a stream. There is a little cottage near it and a lady outside selling baked pies and cooked fish for travelers. He makes small talk with the middle-aged lady and takes samples of the fruit pies.

Eventually, Brace and Ryan arrive and wait for Tyree, Glaive, and Kade. Brak and Brace end up buying an apple pie and splitting it between them.

"You better hurry and finish that. Here comes Tyree," Ryan warns.

Tyree frowns at the two with crumbs on their faces, wolfing down the pie. Brace pokes Brak, acting like it's his fault.

"Everything okay so far?" Tyree asks.

"Yes, it is," Ryan confirms.

Tyree dismounts his horse to stretch for a moment. He leads the horse to the stream so it can drink and waves everyone over to him. "We cannot draw attention to ourselves. I must get...No. *We* must get to Knorrwind City."

"Yeah, but that is easily a two-month journey at best from here," Ryan points out.

"What do we do in the meantime?" asks Brak.

"We continue on. Stop in small towns for supplies until we reach Keskella City. There is something there I need to retrieve," Tyree says.

"Keskella? That would mean we will be close to Skylar Castle," Brace says.

"Ooo, I've always wanted to break in there," Brak says joyfully.

"Yeah! We can finally do it," Brace agrees, smacking Brace's hand.

Tyree looks at them furiously, and before he can say something, the two back off from any plans of doing so.

"You know, we were just kidding. A dream more like it...really," Brak says.

"As I said, no distractions. We need to pull this off, and you all will be rewarded well."

"And what is the plan? Can you at least tell us that?" Ryan asks.

"When we get to Keskella City, I will tell of the plan."

"But that is what, twelve or thirteen days from now?" Brace asks.

"Eleven, if we take no more extra days to rest. But we address that when the time comes." Tyree says. Tyree is in a hurry but is learning to be more patient now that he has the Book of Power.

Kade thinks she is making a mistake going north, taking her farther away from where she needs to go. "Tyree, what does the seeker do again?"

"Why the questions now about it?" Tyree tightens the saddle strap on his horse.

"I just want to know."

Tyree stretches himself before mounting his horse. "Ah, sweetie. You want to use it for yourself."

"Ah, um." Kade's eyebrows lower and she lifts the left side of her lip. "Yes."

"Well, of course you can use it. All of you can. Consider it a perk of getting me there."

"Okay, well, how does it work?" Brak asks, listening to their conversation.

Tyree motions for everyone to gather around him. "Alright, listen carefully. Geemend's Seeker was thought to have been a legend, a story to tell during food and drink. But it was real. Lost through time. Glaive and I discovered a map that leads to this seeker."

"More like paid for it." Glaive chuckles.

Tyree is annoyed at Glaive for disrupting his speech. "That is not important. What it does, though, is allow you to see whatever you're trying to find. It will show you the location." Tyree points at each one of them. "But you have to know, it asks a price from you and you best know for sure what you are looking for."

"I'm for one am game," Gullen says.

Kade thinks to herself, *Maybe I can use this to know where to go*. "I'm in as well."

"Great!" Tyree claps and gives the signal for his horse to head towards the north road. "That is why we need to get to Knorrwind City. That is where we begin our exploration for the seeker."

Brace, Brak, and Ryan simper at each other, mount their horses, and follow Tyree. As winter approaches, the merchant caravans are making their final journey northward, and Tyree instructs the group to mingle with the other travelers to avoid drawing any attention. Brak and Brace make small talk with the other travelers as they normally do, but give the ruse of meeting up with parents up north when asked.

Near the end of the day, they arrive at the border of the Central Kingdom, a small outpost camp that had a town grow around it over time. The stone and wooden walls at the side of the road force travelers, horses, and carriages to enter through one point. The twenty-foot-tall wooden walls have posts placed in a line for at least a hundred yards on each side of the large iron gate that is supported by thick chains. Young guards stand on top, looking down but pose no real threat. They are more ceremonial than used in today's times.

The Central Kingdom tapestries hang from the stone wall that supports the iron gate. The ten foot long by four feet wide white fabric has a blue border and a massive, golden, leafless tree in the middle. To the left of the tree lies a small green building signifying the Woodland Kingdom. To the right stands a building with a hue of blueish purple and a wall, which belongs to the Eastern Province. An orange building, which is the Northern Kingdom, is located above the tree. A wall of mountains lies beneath the tree, with a single deep red dot that is the Southern Kingdom. The dot represents Garnet City. The tree is from the old Skylar days of rule.

There are around two hundred people waiting to enter through the gates. Donkeys are braying and horses snort once in a while. A few dogs bark while sitting on wagons with their owners. Children play and run around after the long ride. Tyree motions for all to gather near him.

"Alright, now we stay together."

"What is this place?" Brace asks.

"All main roads to the Central Kingdom have entry points that people are taxed on," Ryan answers.

"Taxed? Why, that is roadway robbery!" Brace says.

"Can't we go around? Through the woods or something?" Brak suggests.

Tyree's bossy voice once again takes control. "No. It is best to pay the small tax and move on."

"What's the tax for, anyway?" Brace asks.

"Inquisitive today, are we?" Ryan comments.

"I'm opening my mind to be up to other cultures. You know, be worldly," Brace says, looking at Kade, who grins back at him. Brak frowns in confusion, not knowing what is being said.

"Since the Skylar Kingdom was separated, the Central Kingdom has no king or family anymore to rule them. Only a cluster of lords. Three or four? I'm not sure. They tax travelers coming into the kingdom to help pay for services like soldiers, city guards, and such," Ryan explains.

"The Southern Kingdom doesn't tax travelers that enter there," Brak points out.

"No, they don't. They also have a wealth of gems in those mountains that lie behind them, too. This kingdom is a central hub for trading among all the other kingdoms, including ones from far away continents," Ryan says.

Brak squints his eyes, thinking of something. "Wait a second. If there is no king, why is it called the Central Kingdom?"

"It is out of respect for the old days. All the other kingdoms agreed to that... That will change soon," Tyree comments. He wonders how knowledgeable Ryan is; he will be a great general for him. After an hour, it is their turn to enter through the gates. They all dismount their horses to walk them through the gate. Two men are wearing light gray pants, long-sleeved shirts made from cloth, and white vests with the old Skylar crest on them. The one light-skinned man is holding a small coffer filled with silver and copper coins, and the other darker skinned man is holding out his hand.

"How many?"

"How many what?" Brace's forehead creased in confusion.

"Idiot." Tyree pushes Brace aside. "Six of us."

"Six, huh? That will be six silver or hundred twenty coppers."

"That much?" Brace scoffs. Tyree's brows draw together, and his lip snarls. Brace immediately shuts up.

"Here you go." Tyree hands him three gold pieces. The man looks up with a broad grin and before he speaks, Tyree says, "No bother for change. That's for all of you doing a great job." The man steps aside and lets them through.

"Next," he is heard saying as the coins clink in the coffer. The group spends a quiet evening at the Days Gone Past Inn. Everyone is tired and rests well throughout the night. Kade made arrangements to have the horses groomed and fed for the evening. Morning comes, and all are refreshed and ready to go.

*****

For ten days, through rain, fog, sunshine, and chilly winds, they traveled north. Sleeping out under the stars, sneaking into barns for the night, and staying at inns when they were in small towns. They mostly kept to themselves to stay out of trouble.

The day comes when brown rolling hills come into the distance. The blues skies are sprayed with high wisps of thin clouds carried by the chilly winds to the east. Clusters of trees on the hills and below them have lost their leaves in the fall. No more annoying bugs and butterflies flutter about from the cold. Weeds and grasses have long since been dead, cracking and crunching beneath the horses' hooves when they stray from the road looking for something to eat.

They arrived at the initial hill on the road and started to trot upward with a slight tilt. Tyree arrives there first and stops his horse. The rest of them stand their horses next to him. He points at something in the far distance that can barely be made out.

"Look. You can see the glistening towers between those two hills."

"What? I don't see anything," Brak says.

"Me neither," Brace agrees.

"It's Skylar Castle," Ryan confirms. Kade squints and sees the small reflective towers twinkle. Gullen smiles at the notion of visiting it.

"See, Glaive, I promised we would observe again the amazing limestone towers that ascend from the granite shelf that rises like a king over his subjects." His thoughts stray to acknowledge that this time is different. As soon as he can understand the book, he will be returning with an army to take over the kingdom.

A few minutes go by before Ryan asks, "How?"

Tyree snaps out of his thoughts. "How what, Ryan?"

"I know you are thinking about taking over the kingdom. So how? How are you going to do it?"

"With the army I will raise and the power behind the book." His arrogant tone changes to a more somber one. "I will give them one chance to surrender and join....or be utterly destroyed with no chance of rebelling... Each and every person."

Ryan knows that will only cause more uprisings and wars against him but remains quiet. He urges his horse forward and slowly trots down the hill. The others follow except Tyree. He watches the glistening towers for a bit, then continues on.

"How long to Keskella City?" Brace asks.

"We should be there by nightfall," Ryan answers. Their pace quickens even when the horses are tired. The threat of a seasonal storm is approaching from the southwest.

"Might be in for the first snowfall, perhaps?" Gullen suggests.

"That would be a little early, but it looks like a doozy either way," Ryan says.

Tyree grins and thinks to himself, *Perfect. This just might work after all.*

They come upon Keskella City when cresting a steep hill. From their viewpoint, the city is scattered with stone towers and tall buildings, and each gap is packed with smaller buildings constructed of stone and wood.

Many chimneys are spewing out smoke from fires that are for cooking and warmth. Parts of the city have tall walls where other locations have none. The outer edges of the city spread out among many farms and orchards, and livestock graze on the crops that have been harvested. A mile away is the monumental Skylar Castle, dwarfing the size of the largest building in the city.

Their eyes widened in amazement at its immense size and the glistening light reflecting off the speckled white limestone walls, creating a captivating aura. The windowpanes, shutters, and rooftops, with their light and dark blue hues, twinkle in the shifting cloud shadows, almost entrancing the onlookers. The long, triangular flags—white, gold, and blue—flap in defiance of the coming breeze. While sitting on their horses gazing at the wonder, Tyree is thinking of his plan for tonight. His coy grin reveals something is up when he looks at Brak and Brace.

"This is amazing," Kade says.

"I always wanted to visit Keskella. They say you can get almost anything here."

"They're not wrong." Tyree said. "We head for the Brundar Inn. I've always wanted to stay there." He snaps his heels to get the horse moving.

"Can we stay an extra night?" Brak asks.

"A night? I believe we earned a few days of relaxation," Tyree said.

As they make their way into the city, they encounter a variety of people. Even gnomes, a few dwarfs, and an elf are spotted walking around. A variety of people wearing anything from shabby clothes to the most luxurious garments can be seen. Eventually, they find the Brundar Inn, a huge three-level building created out of stone and brown brick. Gold pillars form an archway at the center with lavishly decorated carriages parked in front and workers of the inn assisting people in and out of them. The window frames are painted white, and the glass is frosty so you cannot see into them clearly, but they are lit from the inside and silhouettes of people pass by. Along the rooftop are small statues of men holding various objects. They hold a wand, a book, and a sword. In between them, three stone gargoyles with snarling mouths look down at the people.

"You will enjoy this place. Kade, get the gold ready, sweetie." Kade's narrowed eyes and lips press together, clearly showing her displeasure at being called sweetie. She lets it go for now.

As the storm draws near, people gather their items outside and shut windows. The group lets the stable boys take the horses and go inside. Everyone gets their own room but the two boys. After eating a good meal without Tyree, they all head to their rooms. Brace and Brak are stopped by Tyree before entering the hallway.

His wide, sly smile startles them. "Boys, tonight is the perfect night," he whispers.

"For what?" Brak asks.

Tyree leans in between their heads. "Tonight, the three of us break into Skylar Castle." The boys are wide-eyed. "Now go get an hour's rest and come back to my door. I will explain it all," Tyree whispers and walks away. He stops and points at them. "Tell no one."

Brace and Brak face each other with raised brows, but not sure if they are delighted or fearful.

10

Emboldened Idea

Olivia's mind is spinning at what she has done. *Am I the cause of this?* She thinks to herself. The gnomes are grimacing at her as the cause of what is coming. A frowning Klinksly is trying to convince the other gnomes that she is not the cause of the forthcoming attack by Klatzz, the wererat king. Olivia bites her fingernails and turns away from the stares of the gnomes.

Waldron's soothing voice calms her down. "Alright. Putting blame will not stop this. We need to figure out what to do."

"I guess I will go and tell Farlan Darby the bad news," Glambell, the gnome, says. He is the head of the eight gnomes and is slightly taller than the rest, including Klinksly at three feet and two inches. His brown trousers and shoes, coupled with the small green leather coat, obscure his muscular build.

"Wait. Before you go, tell me again what is coming here?" Klinksly asks.

"Oh, you know," another angry gnome yells.

Klinksly removes his hat and points at the gnomes while firmly stating, "No, I do not. Now, kindly tell me!"

The gnomes grumble among themselves. "Why do you want to know? Not like you can do anything about it," Purgsul mumbles.

"We so can. After all, Oliva took care of that nasty wererat prince! If you knew what we went through, you wouldn't be pointing fingers at us right now," Klinksly says.

"Yeah, we know. That is why Klatzz is coming," Glambell retorts.

Klinksly slams his hat on the ground, and his face turns red. "So then tell us what is coming so we can figure out a plan!"

"Plan! Alright, Mr. Smart gnome," Purgsul spits back.

Glambell stops Purgsul with an arm across his chest. He speaks in a calmer tone, "They have men, goblins, and wererats, of course."

"What are we hanging around here for? We need to get back to Mushroom Cove to warn them.'

Klinksly is about to say something, but he had no plan. Olivia weeps over the consequences of her actions, attempting to figure out what to do since she came here for help. Arthygus and Adam are confused at what is going on. Waldron, glancing at them, wonders who they are. Arthygus smiles at Waldron, and Young Adam gives a friendly wave.

A twig snaps uphill, and Waldron is quicker than the rest to react. He spots a gnome tumbling down the hill, frightened and out of breath. The gnome lifts himself against a small tree. He waves at them and screams. "They are coming, they are coming." He collapses to the ground.

Everyone rushes up the hill to give the small gnome a hand. "Flingar! Flingar! Hold on, we are coming," Glambell calls.

Waldron gets to him first to see if he is injured. "Where do you hurt?"

"I'm not. Just tired. Been running the last two hours." Flingar inhales deeply to catch his breath. The high-pitched wheezing makes Arthygus chuckle a little, then he coughs to cover it up. Olivia is the last to arrive and is more distant than the others.

"What is it? What did you see?" Glambell asks.

"Oh, just two or three...hundred!" Flingar jokes.

"Whaaat?" all the gnomes, including Klinksly, say at once in their little squeaky voices. It makes Arthygus chuckle again.

"Can't be. Klatzz doesn't have that many wererats," Purgsul says.

"Oh, it's more than rats! Much more."

Waldron lifts Flingar up to stand. "There you go now. Describe to us what you saw coming this way."

Flingar brushes himself off and stands tall for a gnome. "First, there are many goblins. A few hundred at least. A dozen men or more. Then I saw them."

"What?" a worried gnome asks.

"Bugbears! Probably thirty. But that's not all."

"You mean there's more?" another gnome says.

"Yes!" Flingar hops around, telling the story, waving his arms. "As I was sneaking between bushes and trees...orcs!"

"Orcs too?" Klinksly asks, slamming his hat against the ground.

"Orcs were surrounding Klatzz, the wererat king. And guess what he was riding?" Flingar points his finger at everyone. But no one answers. Their eyes are wide at what he is describing. "A giant rat that would dwarf any enormous horse! It has sharp claws that will tear through anything we have as armor for sure!"

"No, you must be mistaken," Glambell says.

"It's true! And the rat is wearing metal armor, too."

"How much time do we have?" Waldron asks.

Flingar points his finger in the air, counting things that are not there. "I'd say three, maybe four, hours at the most."

All the gnomes throw their hats down on the ground and stomp their feet in a circle at the horrible news from Flingar. Waldron inhales deeply while looking up the slope at the trees, attempting to come up with a plan. Klinksly places his hat back on his head and caresses the sword pommel against his side.

"I guess we need to go tell Farlan Darby what is coming," Glambell says.

Klinksly draws the blade out from the scabbard, raises it high into the air, and squints at the others. The gnomes can now understand how unique it is and why Klatzz insists on having it back. "Go...I will hold off what I can."

"You can't possibly hold them off. Not without help," Waldron says.

"No...he can't," Glambell agrees.

"Yes, I can...for my part, mostly. It will buy time for Farlan to figure out what to do."

Glambell points to the gnomes. "I need two of you to run to Mushroom Cove and warn Farlan of what is coming...Now!" Two gnomes race off down the path.

"What are you going to do?" Flingar asks.

Glambell stands beside Klinksly. "I'm going to fight by his side." The remaining gnomes agree to help hold off Klatzz's horde for as long as possible.

Waldron nods his head. "Alright, we will do what we can. I would suggest those of you that are good with bows head over to that hillside, behind the pines."

Olivia looks on, not believing what she is hearing. *This is all my fault*, she thinks to herself. Her hands are shaking at the thought of the gnomes getting hurt. *I need to do something, but what?* Olivia turns her back on them, trying to think as her eyes get watery. "What would Abigail do? Abigail! Oh no, what about her? No time for that now. She wouldn't get help; she would do it on her own."

Olivia is pacing back and forth in circles, talking out loud to herself again while everyone else watches her. She flails her arms, huffs loudly, and stamps her feet in indecision again. She freezes for a second when an idea pops into her head. A broad grin grows on her face as she turns to see all of them staring at her. "I got it! I will be right back!" Oliva rushes towards the tree by Waldron's cabin.

"Wait! Where are you going?" Klinksly calls.

"Olivia?" Arthygus yells.

Not looking back, she flails her arms in the air. "Don't do anything yet. I have an idea!" She continues down the hill over fallen wet leaves and slips twice, almost falling from being in a hurry.

"Wait!" Before Klinksly can react, she disappears into the tree door spell. His gaping mouth is breathless as he stares at the spell sparkles fading before hitting the ground.

"Ahh, who needs the troublemaker anyhow?" Glambell says.

Klinksly turns towards Glambell with his brows pulled together and adjusts his jacket collar. "We do." The tone of his voice makes it clear he is not kidding.

"And he is right. What I saw her do to Skeel. She will be more of a use than all of you put together," Waldron says.

"Well, that may be, but she is not here now, is she?" Flingar retorts.

Klinksly tilts his head at Waldron, who is squinting back at him, knowing Flingar is right. "We will come up with a plan before she gets back," Waldron says.

Young Adam steps forward in front of everyone. "We are here now, in this time...together. Outside powers have brought us here for a reason. Now is not the time to doubt what we can do. What Olivia can do. I thoroughly believe we were brought here to prevent Klatzz from even entering Mushroom Cove."

A few seconds of silence go by. Klinksly claps his hands together in approval at Young Adam.

"If you believe that, then that is all I need too," Waldron calmly says.

The raised eyebrows of gnomes show they are surprised and encouraged by what he said. They put their arms on each other's shoulders and smile. "Okay then. This is what we will do," Glambell says, knowing they are facing certain death.

*****

Oliva makes her way through her growing tree door forest. She has been going to various locations just to get bark off of trees so she can open a door spell. She stands in front of an aspen and takes a breath. "Okay, I can do this. I need to do this." She shakes her hands vigorously. She takes a step back from the tree. "No. Stop this!" Olivia forces herself to move forward into the tree.

She steps out of the tree onto a small hillside full of aspens. A large watermill, supported by a gray stone building, is turning from the gushing stream, with brown leaves floating and twirling in it. The grinding of stones inside is heard as it crushes the fall's wheat harvest. Olivia slips past the trees behind the mill down to a dirt road. She casually crosses the wooden bridge as a horse-drawn wagon passes her; the driver smiles and waves at her. Olivia instinctively waves back. Her eyes open and mouth drops as she spots the outer limits of Garnet City and why she came. Her pace quickens with excitement and panic.

Garnet City is easily three times the size of Splinteroak. Olivia walks slightly uphill towards the main gate entrance to the city. She visited the city a few times with her parents when she was younger. After her parents' disappearance, she tried to come but turned back halfway through her three-day journey from her house due to sadness. She hasn't been here in years, but she sets her emotions aside to focus on the important tasks she has now. People are coming and going, hustling about. Farmers, fishermen, supply caravans, and people are everywhere. Garnet City soldiers and city guards come and go from an outpost building on the outside of the great stone walls.

The colorful stone buildings look like artwork that is lived in. Fine sculpted statues of important people of the past sit along the ledges of buildings. A few have small dragons and mythical creatures on them as well. One catches Olivia's eye as she slows down. A white stone chimera is pouncing down on guards bearing spears. A few pigeons sit on top cooing. Olivia's head tilts in a strange thought before she rushes on.

It was hard for her to ignore the clothing shops and food markets while she weaved through the crowds. After twenty minutes of walking and sprinting down cobblestoned paved streets, she rounds a corner and comes across the center of town. There is a perfect grass-covered circle a hundred yards wide with a smaller oval of red maple trees holding onto their withering maroon leaves in the last warm days of fall. The maples are spaced evenly at twenty-five feet. At the very center of the grass circle and the maples is an exquisite stone statue carved from granite. A man dressed in miner's clothes holding up a large garnet gem the size of a pineapple. The statue is of stone, but the gem is formed of stained glass to represent the garnet.

Olivia stands motionless, in awe of what she is seeing. Beyond the circle is an enormous brownstone castle, complete with white window frames and maroon shutters with gold trim. Deep red shale squares cover the roofs and tower tops. At each corner of the castle stands a tower which is a hundred twenty feet tall. Each has small slit windows, one space away and above the other in a spiraling setting. Two massive black iron griffon claw hinges are attached to the two dark stained oak doors, both of them ten feet wide and fifteen feet tall.

A line of cleaning maidens enter from the side. Olivia notices this and has an idea. She looks around for a dark spot to slip into. *Okay, I can do this. Think, think*. She presses against her temples and thinks of appearing as one of the cleaning maidens in their white and maroon dresses. Her image changes from the black leather pants and maroon dress to that of the maroon and white dresses of the cleaning maidens. Olivia rushes over and gets last in line.

"A little late, are we?" one of the elderly ladies asks.

Olivia smiles and gives a nod. "Um hum."

The grinning elder gives her a basket containing cleaning cloth and a scrub brush. "For that, you get to clean the queen's privy."

Olivia nods her head and keeps quiet. *How am I to see the king now? Will he be there?*

"Okay, ladies, off we go." The head mistress claps her hands. "Start on the guest floor and work your way up as usual." The ladies stand tall and proper. They produce a fake smile while doing their duties. The head mistress grabs Olivia's arm. "You. I don't know you. Who are you?"

Olivia's image flickers for a fraction of a second when she is grabbed. The lady lets go and stands back with an unfocused gaze. Olivia grins while rubbing a little circle above her eye, hoping her suggestion powers work. "Silly headmistress, you know me. You asked me to cover for the one who is sick today...Remember?"

The lady tilts her head and nods. "Oh yes, Laila is sick."

"Yes, that is right. Now I should go about my duties. Shall I not, headmistress?"

"Yes, yes, go without delay." She purses her lips and narrows her eyes, watching Olivia scuttle to the end of the line and head into the castle.

Olivia makes it to the door before the guards close them. She stands in a large room with a plain brown stone floor with one large old carpet that was bright yellow at one time but now faded and dirty from use. There are three doors that are closed and one open with the clinking and clanking of pots and the aroma of bread being baked. She can see it is the kitchen as staff come and go. *This must be the workers' entrance. Now how to get to the king?* A few of the girls stop smiling and discuss what to do first. Three of them walk past Olivia.

"Well, come on. Don't just stand there. Follow us to the queen's chambers," a girl prompts. Olivia's dimpled smile shows relief as she follows with a bucket in hand. They go through the far left door and up a spiraling stone stairway that takes them to the third floor. A cleaning girl opens the small plain wooden door, and they step into a hallway. A grandiose garnet red rug with a silver leaf pattern lays down the length of the hallway. On each side of the walls are beautiful tapestries depicting woodland scenes on one side and oceans on the other.

"There is your door," a girl says, pointing down the hall.

Olivia walks slowly down the hall, admiring the scenes. She hears the other girls knocking on the doors before going in. She does the same and peers into the room. There is no answer, and she figures this is a good time to figure out what to do. The door closes gently, and Olivia looks around. The air is warm and moist, and a little steamy. There are small water vases near hot rocks that sit in an iron tub over burning coals. A pine incense stick burns in a waterfall carved from a small amethyst stone sitting on an end table. Different shades of blue, violet, and silver silk sheets hang in a crisscross pattern, obscuring the other walls in the room.

Olivia lays the bucket down and spins around the room, viewing all the sheets and wondering what to do now. She taps her forehead. "Think...Think. Come on, you can do it." She spots a chair and sits for a second. "Uuuh, this is silly. What am I even doing here? This was not a good idea." Her thoughts of what had happened over the past few months catch up to her, and she can no longer bear the heartache. Her eyes wet, she plops her face into her hands, sobbing.

"This is too much for me. I can't do this...But Abigail. The gnomes. What am I to do?"

A splashing of water startles her, and a sympathetic woman's euphonic voice speaks out from behind the silk sheets. "You are here now, so what is not such a good idea?" she asks.

"Uh, who's there?" Olivia can hardly see a silhouette of a shapely woman standing out of a tub behind the violet silk sheets.

"Do you mind handing me my robe near the warming rocks?"

Olivia reaches over and grabs the red robe. Her hands sink deep into the soft material. She stands still, grasping it with both hands, adoring the warm soft feel when a cough is heard from behind her. Olivia jumps and doesn't turn around but hands the robe behind her. A few seconds go by, and the robe is lifted away from her hand.

The lady speaks in a calm, demanding voice. "You're not one of my cleaning girls. Who are you?"

Olivia turns around to see a tall, elegant, sensuous ebony woman with long hair that was once black but now has tints of gray on the ends. She closes her robe. Olivia squints at her. "Imene?" she whispers.

The lady's eyes perk up. "What did you say?"

Olivia turns to pick up the bucket and heads towards the door in a hurry. The bucket grabs the silk sheet and drags it along. That causes her to spin and trip. She gets tangled while pulling a few others down as the thin ropes break under her weight. The lady shakes her head in utter amazement at what she sees, a lump of blue silk wiggling like a giant worm. Suddenly, it stops.

Olivia cries. "Why? Why is this happening to me?" She tries to stomp her feet, only to kick air. Olivia screams, "I can't take this anymore! Will something just go right for once?"

The blue silk carefully gets parted around Olivia's tearful face, and the lady is smiling down at her and helps Olivia out of the tangled mess. She stands there, defeated, and mutters the most insane thing with a grin. "At least I wasn't getting clawed to death this time."

"Oh child, why would you say such a thing?"

Olivia is frozen and at a loss for words.

"You called me Imene. Only a few people call me that, and I'm afraid I do not know you." Olivia is nervous. "I ask again, who are you?"

Olivia is shocked that her illusion is still working but is hesitant to say. "I'm not...Please don't take me as hostile."

"Dear, why would I think that? If you were, our actions would have a different ending."

"I was told when I was a child that if you look for the truth—"

Imene finishes her sentence with a peculiar look. "You will find comfort in the end."

"I hope that holds true." She grins and lets the illusion of the cleaning girl fade. Slowly, Olivia appears in the black leather jacket with the dragonfly pin, maroon, square-necked, shirred-ruffle hem dress, and the saber by her side.

Imene takes a step back. Olivia puts her hands out, shaking no. "I'm not here to hurt anyone...I was going to ask for help." She steps back and relaxes herself. "You probably don't remember me. I'm Olivia."

There is silence in the room. Imene looks at her up and down. "Sophia. That is your mother."

Olivia's eyes open at the mention of her name. "You know who I am, then?"

"Yes." Imene is skeptical. "How did you change yourself? What did you do to me?"

Olivia shakes her head. "I knew I shouldn't have come. Please, can I go?"

Imene smiles and reaches out to her hands and holds them. "Child, I did not know you possessed your mother's magic, and clearly you are not here to cause harm or you would not ask to be excused. So why are you here?"

Olivia thinks for a moment about what to say.

"Come on, out with it."

Olivia squeezes her arms together across her chest and grits her teeth. "For starters, I'm a witch, not an enchantress like my mother. That was my ability to do illusions."

Imene nods her puckered forehead and motions for her to take a seat. "Now tell me why you are here."

Olivia takes a deep breath and starts from the beginning, from how her friend became the new witch queen to finding Klinksly the gnome in the goblin cave. How they made their way through the goblins and giant rats to get out, and how she took Skeel's sword. When they woke up and met Waldron and then accidentally killed Skeel at the river crossing. Then how the gnome Farlan Darby was able to get them home. She explained in rough detail that she went back to Waldron to help train her two friends, only to discover that Klatzz, the wererat king, was coming to destroy their village.

"So you see, it's all my fault, and the gnomes need help."

Imene stands in silence, then lifts Olivia up by her hands and hugs her. "So that is why you said at least you are not being clawed to death." She holds her tight, and Olivia reaches back to hug her. She hasn't felt a motherly hug in ages. It makes her smile with her eyes closed. Imene lets go. "You have been through so much and yet you are here to help others. Who did you expect to see?"

"Well, King Rashaad..." Her face grows pale when she realizes who she is in front of. "Excuse me, Your Majesty. I'm sorry for forgetting the formality. I didn't expect—" Imene cuts her off.

"No, call me Imene. It has been a while since I heard that. I'm a little tired of Queen Pemba lately."

"So now what?"

"You didn't come prepared to talk to him, did you?"

"No. Just getting to him was going to be the hard part."

"He has a lot going on with the sudden appearances of gnolls and orcs in the southern mountains. The troops are spread thin. So what would you say to him? Why should he be bothered with the gnomes?"

Olivia looks down at her feet. She hadn't thought this through. *Why would he help the gnomes? This is not his fight.* "Or is it?"

"Excuse me?" Imene says.

"I'm going to be truthful with him and repeat what I told you. Then I will add it doesn't matter if his troops are thin. The Southern Kingdom soldiers have a reputation for getting things done no matter the danger. Mushroom Cove is under the Southern Kingdom's lands and protection. Besides, I doubt any king would let another so-called king wreak havoc upon his subjects without repercussions."

Imene stands smiling at her. "That is indeed a good argument for me to send our troops there," a strong, rich, male voice says.

Olivia peeks around Imene and is confounded to see King Rashaad standing there with a towel wrapped around his waist. He still has a muscular build for his age. His ebony skin glistens with water drops yet to be dried.

"But sadly, if you say he is upon the gnome village now, my soldiers would not make it on time."

Olivia's broad smile makes Rashaad raise his eyebrows. "Do you trust me? I can get your men there in minutes through my tree door spell."

Rashaad and Imene look at each other with narrowed eyes.

*****

Moments later, in a hidden courtyard behind the castle, one large oak tree stands at the center. A few older guards stand watch. A variety of thirty men and a few women stand in two tight rows. Ten of them have bows while others have various swords. One man stands out in front of them. The polished steel armor gleans against his ebony skin. He wears the dark red colors of the Southern Kingdom under and around the armor. His hair is bushy and unkept, and he lightly taps the long sword by his side.

Queen Pemba steps forward, wearing her ceremonial red gown of going to battle. King Rashaad walks along the troops with nods of encouragement. He stops and stands beside the queen.

"Troops! There is a call for help, and we have answered. I will be straight with you. You are all fresh recruits, but you have been training for weeks. With the guidance of Prince Trajan here, you will be victorious." He pauses in thinking of what to say, then motions for Olivia to come over. "Troops, this is Olivia. The gnomes of Mushroom Cove are being attacked by Klatzz, the wererat king. Olivia has had a brave journey to get here to warn us of this intrusion into the kingdom's lands. I will not stand for that. *We* will not stand for that, and *you* will not let that happen. You will not let any harm come to the gnomes."

He turns to look at Imene, who nods back. He takes a deep breath. "I am ordering you to follow her without question or judgment as both the Queen and I trust her. Is this understood?"

The troops all yell back in sync. "Yes, Your Majesty."

"Good. Now follow her through that...tree."

Prince Trajan looks confused, and the troops look at each other, wondering what to do.

Olivia walks over to the large oak tree and activates the tree door spell. She speaks loudly so they can hear. "Well, come on, the gnomes don't have all day. And stay in line and don't go anywhere but where I tell you."

They are all motionless. King Rashaad looks straight at the very confused prince kneading his face. "I gave you an order."

Prince Trajan reacts by turning towards the troops. "We have our orders. Now follow me." He walks towards the tree, and the others reluctantly follow.

"Remember... You are Southern Kingdom soldiers now!" King Rashaad calls. That recognition gives them a little encouragement, and they hustled to the door.

*****

Arthygus's attention is drawn by a yellow, greenish light that sprinkles out of a tree and mixes into the rising mist, followed by Olivia. His heart races, and he rushes to her, instinctively hugging her. They both almost fall to the ground, but Olivia holds them both up, surprised.

"Are you okay? Where did you go? Don't disappear like that." Arthygus looks directly into her eyes, then let's go with his face red and chin trembling. "Uh, I mean... Sorry...I was worried."

Olivia's eyes are blinking fast, and she blushes. She taps him on the shoulder as she walks by. "It's nice to know you care. I'm okay."

"Don't run off like that, missy!" Klinksly says with his hands on his hips. "Where did you go?"

Everyone's darting glances tell her something is coming from behind Olivia's tree. Prince Trajan steps out, followed by many other soldiers. The few gnomes and Waldron smile as they welcome the intrusion.

Klinksly's jaw drops, and he looks at Olivia. "What? How?"

Olivia jumps and claps her hands. "Oh, I have an idea or two."

"Plan."

"Huh?" She tilts her head.

"They are called plans. A and b. You have the first part of a plan, then a second part. Hence, a and b."

The prince walks past them and scouts over the area. The remaining gnomes step out from the bushes, and Waldron, Arthygus, and Young Adam stand there, staring back. "This is it? How many more are hidden?"

The gnomes look at Waldron to speak. "This is all there is," he says.

"A handful of gnomes, two boys, and a woodsman? Really?"

The gnomes nod their heads in unison.

"Against what? A rat and henchmen?"

Glambell chuckles. "Ha, you wish it was just a rat."

"Well, he is," Flingar says.

"A big fat one at that," Purgsul adds.

Prince Trajan lets out a sigh. "That should be easy enough for us. Now step aside and let me think."

"Think?" Waldron questions. He walks up closer to Prince Trajan so others can't hear. "What do you think is going on here?"

Trajan looks at him with one raised eyebrow and nose in the air. "It doesn't matter. I'm here to stop this menace."

Waldron smirks and shakes his head in disbelief. "It matters. A leader always finds out what they are up against, and if you had any wits about you, you would be asking what is coming."

"How dare you speak to me that way—"

Waldron cuts him off quietly. "Don't you see I'm speaking out of earshot of your troops so they don't hear? I'm trying to help you and not belittle you."

Trajan stands tall, and it hits him about what Waldron is doing and lowers his princely stance. "Alright. What is actually coming?"

"Death," Klinksly says. Neither of them saw him sneak up behind them.

Trajan is startled and steps back. "If you can't see me coming, then how are you to see the enemy? Humm." Klinksly gives a little wink of distrust.

"Now let's not be rude. They are here to help, and we welcome that," Waldron says.

"So what is coming?" Trajan asks.

"Hundreds of goblins, orcs, bugbears and a giant rat that the king rides," Klinksly lists with a smile. "So we will give it to them..." He teasingly punches the prince in the thigh.

"And don't forget the wererats and a few men that are with them," Waldron adds.

Trajan looks over at his men, turns to Waldron with a grin, and walks towards his troops. The prince orders the ones with the swords to stand in two rows, one behind the other and spaced apart. The archers are ordered to stand behind the swordsmen. He gives orders when to fire.

Glambell comes up to Waldron. "What is he doing? Does he know what he is doing?"

Klinksly scratches his head in dismay. Klinksly shakes his head. "I don't know. Why don't you go over and tell him?"

Glambell goes over to Trajan and doesn't hold back any pleasantries. "Ah, Prince, sir. But this is not where we intend to do battle."

Trajan squinted with his brows together. "What?"

"Yeaaa, it's going to be uphill further. I would have your archers there and there." He points up the hill at a cluster of pine trees. "And have your swordsmen create a line from that bush to that tree to funnel the goblins to."

"How will that work? You need to meet them head on."

"No, you can't here. This is not an army versus an army on a flat field. We need every advantage we can get out here. Us gnomes know these hills very well and know how to use them to our advantage."

Prince Trajan concedes the gnomes know more and orders the archers to follow the gnome archers. He then leads the swordsmen up the hill and sets them in a line with him out front.

While walking up the hill, Waldron and Klinksly get near Olivia, Arthygus, and Young Adam. "So, what brought you here to begin with?" Waldron asks.

"It was Olivia's idea. Ask her," Young Adam says.

Waldron looks back at her. "Well?"

"We need your help... or thought we did." She looks at all the soldiers with worried looks on their faces. Before he can ask, another gnome comes running down the hill, falls, and rolls.

"Lasgar, is that you?" Flingar yells.

"Yes! Yes! Help me?"

Waldron, Prince Trajan, and Flingar run to help him. He is cut up and bleeding. "I thought you died?" Flingar said.

"The last hit I took sent me over a small ravine, and I hid from them." He grabs onto Flingar in horror. "There are more goblins behind Klatzz. We got to..." Lasgar passes out.

Waldron and Flingar carry him downhill. "What is going on?" Arthygus asks.

"Just more goblins coming," Trajan says, walking past them to his troops.

Klinksly turns towards Olivia. "Was there a Plan B?"

Olivia perks up. "Yes, but you have to come with me in case."

"What? Leave? I can't leave now." He then squints his one eye at her. "What do you mean, in case?

Olivia grabs his arm and starts back down the hill. Trust me on this one." Klinksly doesn't resist and follows her.

"Great, the ones that caused this run off," Glambell says.

"She knows what she is doing," Arthygus snaps. "I hope," he murmurs under his breath, watching her last image disappear into the tree.

Waldron has Arthygus and Adam stand off to the side near Lasgar. He points at Adam's mace. "Can you use that?"

"Sort of, that's why we—"

"Great. You two stay here and help get any stragglers or help with the wounded."

Waldron then sits on a log tending to his bow a few steps away from Prince Trajan. He watches him tap his sword pommel. Waldron has seen this before. The hidden war before the battle. The war no one sees. There is no weapon to help become victorious over this foe.

"This is your first actual battle, is it not?" Waldron asks.

Trajan stands tall with his chin out and turns towards Waldron. “Why would you ask such a thing? I am Prince Trajan, son of King Rashaad of the Southern Kingdom. I know how to swing a blade. Besides, what would some woodsman know of battle?”

“Oh, he knows plenty.” Klinksly chuckles. “He’s a knight of old.” Waldron waves at Klinksly to hush.

Trajan looks Waldron up and down, seeing him differently.

Waldron points at the prince’s hand, still tapping his sword pommel. “I don’t doubt your skills. I just don’t see a leader.”

“You don’t?” Prince Trajan squints at Waldron but dares not ask more.

“You're quiet. Waiting for known combat is the hardest part. And that is when a leader should shine among their troops.

“How so?”

“The dread silence grows fear and doubt in their minds. Klatzz knows this. He waits till you think of what-ifs and you begin to second guess your choices? Catching you off guard and unable to lead your men. That is when he will strike.”

“How do you know what is going on in my mind?”

“I can see it in your eyes. I can see it in the men also. Some are nervous while others are too eager for what awaits. They do not know about battle yet, and surely, they don’t know how to stop the war in their minds now. They wonder who will be going home after this? Who will become part of this forest forever? Will they die side by side? Will they see loved ones again? I have thought this many times. This is where a leader steps in and breaks the Curse of silence.”

“Well, I...Yes. I was thinking that.”

“Be honest. You have no clue what is about to happen.”

Trajan’s eyes light up in surprise. “Alright. Let’s say I don’t. What can I expect?”

“Good. You’re asking questions now,” Klinksly says.

“You are going to see the genuine horrors of what battle is all about. Unspeakable things are going to happen to your men and the enemy. A few, maybe even you, will be stopped in their tracks at what they see. Tragically, those who are untrained cannot protect themselves, and the enemies use this to their own advantage. Can you deal death when the time comes? Can your men kill when needed? Will your indecision and lack of leadership allow everyone to perish? Will the small triumphs and tragedies never be spoken at the table over a good drink?"

Prince Trajan looks over at his men. The archers are behind pine trees on the hillside while the swordsmen are standing in a row. From here, he can tell they are nervous. He turns towards Waldron. "You're right. I have only given orders about how to use the weapons in training, never in true combat yet. What should I say?"

Waldron frowns at that response, wondering why the king would send an inexperienced prince into a situation like this? "Follow my lead." Waldron steps forward so the few gnomes can see him. "Gnomes. Klatzz is coming. He will not stop until we make him stop. And we will. Lie low and quiet. Don't think about anything...When the time comes, just do."

Waldron doesn't want to outshine Trajan and points his hand at the prince, who then steps forward. "Men...I...We..." He stops, takes a deep breath, and stands up tall, remembering his father's inspiring words to the troops. "You are Southern Kingdom soldiers. We are representing Garnet City. You must live up to the standard they set. We will not fail, we will not let Klatzz reach Mushroom Cove, we will not let the gnomes perish, no matter what comes forth to us. Here we will learn to stand and fight to the last man. There is no retreat. Remember your training and focus on that. Stay on plan and we will be victorious. We are Southern Kingdom soldiers!"

The men give a quiet rally cry, lifting their weapons into the air along with the gnomes.

Klinksly and Waldron are even inspired by that speech. "That was good. Really good," Klinksly says.

Waldron pats him on the shoulder. "I guess you have a knack for speeches when you know what needs to be said."

Trajan smiles and is about to respond when a loud, snapping sound of a tree limb echoes down the wooded hillside. Everyone's attention is drawn uphill.

"Are you ready?" Waldron asks.

Trajan is anxious and draws his sword. “No.”
“You never are.”

11

Innocence is Lost

Another loud crack of splintering tree limbs reverberates down the darkened hillside. The sun has started its descent behind the hills, creating leafless tree silhouettes that give a haunting presence. Loud groans and yelps echo over the sound of many feet stomping down the hill. The air turns foul with the dried pond scum stench of goblins and from the pungent aroma of the greasy, grungy fur of the wererats and gnolls.

The men and women clench their weapons in anticipation of what they think is about to happen. Their hearts race while others tremble. Some watch little bugs crawl around on the leaves, wondering if this is the last peaceful thing they will see. The gnomes kneel deeper to the ground, making sure their arrows are close at hand. They roll them to make sure they're evenly spaced, but it doesn't really matter. It's something they do because they're anxious. Waldron taps the prince's shoulder with a smile of confidence and heads towards the left hillside opposite of the gnome archers.

Trajan stands before his troops, holding his sword and lightly tapping his foot. Glambell stands beside him with his short sword and gives him a quick rictus grin. Young Adam is holding his mace with both hands and looks silently over at Arthygus. Nothing needs to be said as Arthygus nods back with a forced smile. He reaches for a few of his spell ingredients that are now in easy reach with the leather armor that Frederick gave him.

The stillness is shattered as a wave of goblins emerge from the shrubbery before Trajan and the troops. Stronger goblins have makeshift armor of broken metal, leather, and scraps of cloth, while others have nothing on. All of them have some sort of twisted sword blade, ax, and clubs with spikes. They range from pale, sickening yellows to various green shades. A few of them are actually bright orange. The goblins scream and curse in delight at the chaos they are about to release.

The troops are wide-eyed at what horror appears before them, including Prince Trajan. Unexpectedly, Young Adam steps in front of Prince Trajan. He holds the mace towards the goblins. "Tulkoon valo!" he screams with authority. A brilliant flash of pure white light spews forth in a wave, enveloping the goblins. They shrill as the first few rows collapsed to the ground and those that were lucky enough to hide their eyes were still blinded. Arthygus is amazed at what he did.

Trajan raises his sword into the air. "Archers! Fire at will!"

Waldron releases his arrows at the ones not affected by the light. A volley of arrows come from the pine trees on the right. The archers and gnomes hit their targets, dropping them.

Trajan sprints past Adam towards the goblins that are wriggling on the ground. "Attack them all!"

Glambell and the troops follow with swords in hand while the archers pick off goblins. A clash of steel and metal clink and clank through the valley as the first rows of goblins are slaughtered. The soldiers only see what is exactly in front of them and nothing else in the frantic melee. Their minds go blank, and the raw training kicks in. Others just swing to survive.

Without thinking, Adam joins the melee, swinging his mace back and forth like a farmer does with his scythe on wheat, easily tossing goblins to the side.

Waldron notices goblins breaking off to go after the archers farther up the hill. "Protect the archers!" He points at the young wizard. Arthygus scrambles, runs behind the troops, and gets Adam's attention.

"Follow me." He runs to the pine trees with Adam in tow.

More goblins push aside the shrubs, climb over their fallen spawn, and try to leap at the soldiers. Trajan swings back-and-forth non-stop, dropping goblin after goblin. Green blood is covering him as it splatters and sprays in each direction. The soldiers fight on but grow tired of the never-ending swinging of their weapons.

Waldron has used up his arrows and jumps down the hillside, slashing with his blade. Trajan watches out of the corner of his eye. Waldron and his sword move in unison, striking more than one goblin per stroke. He spins and twirls and the sword keeps striking, never retreating for a swing. The blade cuts effortlessly through flesh and bone. Three, five, seven goblins cleaved in seconds.

This encourages Trajan even more. "Fight! Move forward We are winning!"

A large rock rips through the tree limbs and down at the soldiers. It lands on two goblins, smashing them to the ground, then bounces into the chest of a soldier, crushing his ribs and killing him instantly. The two that were beside him look at each other in shock. Another rock bounces off a tree onto a goblin, killing it and heading to Trajan. He dodges, and the rock continues down the hill harmlessly.

"The rocks! Archers! Kill what's throwing them!" Trajan orders.

They look uphill as more goblins come at them. Behind them, two colossal figures stand twelve feet tall, reaching for more rocks. They are grungy, semi bald, slouching and covered with fur clothing of bears, deers, and what looks like human skin. Large, square, crooked, yellow-brownish teeth stick out in different directions of their saliva-dripping mouths. Huge dark brown eyes search for victims to throw rocks at.

"Giants! Hill giants!" an archer yells.

"What do we do now?" another one asks.

"Take them down!" screams Trajan.

The archers shoot uphill at the figures but are not sure if they are hitting their targets.

Arthygus and Adam reach the archers and gnomes to see ten goblins coming at them. "What do we do?" Arthygus asks.

"Kill them."

"How?" a panicked Arthygus questions.

"Just do something." Adam stands ready with his mace.

Arthygus remembers a simple spell. He thinks of the ingredients he needs, and the leather armor produces it quickly. "Tyontaa!" he yells, spreading the ingredients and waving his hands in a crossing outward motion. A compressed wave of air comes out in front of him. It hits the goblins, pushing them back, dropping their weapons as they tumble.

"Well done," Adam commends.

Arthygus smiles then is standing in fear when a large bugbear jumps over the tumbling goblins rushing at him. He roars, swinging a wooden club with nasty metal spikes protruding from it. Arthygus's eyes are frozen open, and he does not move as the club comes down at him. *Clang!* Adam's mace stops the club inches from Arthygus's face. Adam pushes back, but the bugbear does not move the club. Instead, he presses harder against Adam.

"Move!" Adam screams.

Arthygus gets pulled back by a gnome, and the archers let a few arrows loose into the bugbear. It screams but still stands. The bugbear lifts the club above him and swings down at Adam, who jumps out of the way. The club hits the ground with a thud. A gnome charges with his sword and slashes at the bugbears' leg. Another arrow hits it in the arm. He raises the club and swings low with a mighty grunt, catching the gnome. The spikes impale him and send him flying into the pine trees screaming. The lifeless body falls through the branches, smacking the ground.

Arthygus is trying to stand when Adam's mace contacts the back of the bugbear's head, splitting it open, sending matter onto Arthygus. The creature falls with a soft plop on the pine-needle-covered ground with Adam standing there breathing heavily with blood dripping off his mace.

Before Adam and Arthygus can consider what just happened, another barrage of rocks tear through the trees at the soldiers below. Adams rushes at the goblins that were blown back by the spell and smacks them with his mace till they are dead. Adam shakes off questionable thoughts that start to haunt him of what he is doing.

Trajan, Waldron, and the remaining soldiers are tiring, but they still fight on. The goblins halt the charge and step aside as yips and howling begin. Gnolls and bugbears rush down the hill, pushing aside small branches and weeds while the two giants throw more large rocks at them. Three more soldiers are killed by the rocks before the onslaught of gnolls reaches them.

Gnolls jump with blades pointed outwards and soldiers clash against each other. Trajan thrusts his sword through the first gnoll, the second one pushes him out of the way. His sword blade flexes and breaks inside the gnoll's body. Trajan falls and gets rolled and stepped on as gnoll after gnoll pushes through. Two more soldiers are killed by the ferociousness of the gnolls.

Waldron slashes left and right, moving along. "Keep moving! Don't stay in one spot!" he yells to the soldiers. Fear is setting in. They are not moving as fast. Weapons are becoming lower and lower with each swing. The archers are running out of arrows. Adam is charging at the gnolls from the side, smashing them with the mace. The situation is looking dire for them.

The gnolls force Waldron, Glambell, Adam, and the remaining thirteen soldiers into a circle surrounding them. Arthygus, the gnomes, and archers are still hidden in the pines. Two large trees uphill get ripped from the roots and tossed aside. The gnolls back off a few feet and howl, then go silent. A giant rat, larger than a draft horse, steps between the hill giants. On top of the rat is Klatzz, a huge muscular wererat surrounded by other smaller rats, wererats, and orcs. He has a chest plate of silver and gold that bears a black eagle emblem with its wings spread. A gleaming silvery blue longsword is waving in his hand.

"Feazt on flezh today! Tatze the humanz! Eat the gnomz!" he yells down through the small valley.

The gnolls take a step forward. Waldron ready's his sword when a thunderous, deafening boom explodes above Klatzz. He is blown off the giant rat. The orcs and wererats near him fall to the ground, and the giants cover their ears.

The two clashing armies all gaze uphill at what the loud boom was.

Standing beside a large oak tree is Olivia with her hands on her temples, eyes closed, and Klinksly holding his fireworks wand, grinning.

"It's about time," Glambell says.

Klatzz is stunned and wobbles while getting up. Seconds go by until he focuses on Olivia and Klinksly. Klinksly pulls out Skeel's sword, holds it in the air, and points at it.

"You want this? Do you? Do you, mouse?"

Klatzz hisses at them. "Who are youz?"

Klinksly turns around and bends over. He rubs the sword across his bottom. "Ahh, got that itch. This is a good bottom scratcher, is it not?" He shakes his bottom side-to-side in a mocking motion.

This infuriates Klatzz. "Killz themz. Bringz me blade!"

Klinksly turns to face him and runs the sword between his legs like a child pretending to ride a stick horse and waving his arm in the air. "Whew, weee, this is like what I did to Skeel. That's right, we killed him!"

"Stoppppzzz!" Klatzz screams. "I killz them myzelf!" He pushes a few orcs out of the way and charges up the hill.

"Almost," Klinksly whispers at Olivia.

"What are they doing?" Waldron asks.

"With her? I don't have the faintest idea," Adam says.

Arthygus wants to say something but keeps quiet, knowing she has a plan. He whispers to the remaining archers. "Whenever something happens, be ready and aim at the gnolls surrounding our friends. The archers slowly and quietly ready themselves.

Klinksly is still hopping around in a circle. "Ride the wererat! Step right up and ride the wererat!"

Klatzz swings the sword in anger, and it easily cuts through a four-inch-thick dogwood tree, shocking everyone, including Klinksly, who stops. Klatzz snarls in delight at seeing the gnome fear the blade.

"A few more steps," he whispers.

"I willz enjoy ripping you apart like you do to Skeel, witch!"

Olivia opens her green eyes that stare down Klatzz. She points at him. "Burn the rat!"

A cone of fire comes from above and behind Olivia and engulfs

Klatzz. He drops the sword and rolls on the ground to put out the flame. Patches of fur are burnt off, and parts of skin have turned red. The chest plate remains undamaged. Klatzz rolls himself to his hands and knees and looks at Olivia.

Everyone sees a large shimmering image become visible, a chimera standing fifteen feet tall behind Olivia and Klinksly. Wisps of smoke drift out of the dragon's mouth. The huge wings fold in behind its back. The lion's head is still and grinning, staring at Klatzz. Its tail flickers slightly in anticipation of pouncing. Olivia has been taking meat and honeyed oats from Snowcap to feed it in secret.

"Is that?" Adam asks.

"It can't be that one," Arthygus says to himself.

Waldron narrows his eyes. "What is that? What did she do?"

"Just go with it. Looks like it's on our side," Adam says.

She points at him again. "Get him!"

The chimera wags its lion tail, springs over Olivia, and pounces on Klatzz the wererat.

"That actually worked," Klinksly says in amazement.

"You doubted me?"

The chimera clamps the wererat in its mouth, shaking its head back and forth. The plate mail straps tear into pieces from his teeth.

"Well, yes."

"I almost lost it listening to you hop around." She chuckles.

Klatzz gets tossed over into the trees. The plate mail separates from his body and gets stuck on tree limbs as he falls to the ground with a thump. The chimera looks back at Olivia for what to do next.

"I had fun with that." Klinksly looks at his sword, then spots the sword Klatzz dropped sitting in the grass. Its gleam almost beckons him.

Olivia points at the bugbears and orcs. "Go on, have fun." The chimera pounces downhill at them. The dragon's head spews fire and bites while the lion's head tears its teeth into them, biting orcs in half. The goat's head is jabbing them with its giant horns. The front paws are smashing them into the ground. Orcs and bugbears try to swing the weapons at it and miss as the creature is too quick. A few hit it, but no actual harm is done at the moment.

Waldron and Adam look at each other as to what is going on. Arthygus orders the archers to fire. The arrows hit the confused gnolls, which is Waldron's cue to start swinging again. Adam and the soldiers fight on as well. Trajan pulls himself out from under a gnoll.

"I'm down to one arrow," a gnome says.

Arthygus's face lights up with an idea. "Here, give me that." He grabs the arrow from the gnome and lays it on the ground. Arthygus thinks of two identical butterfly wings and the ingredient comes out of his leather armor. He crushes them into a powder and sprinkles it over the arrow. "Klooni lisaa toistaa." Gnomes and archers watch in amazement as the arrow reproduces itself over and over. At first, Arthygus is proud of what he did, but then soon realizes that the duplication is not stopping.

After an immense pile of arrows overcome the gnome, Arthygus scrambles to find the original arrow. "Help me look for the first one and snap it!" Archers are taking the arrows and aiming them at the gnolls and bugbears. Arrow after arrow flies through the air into them. The gnolls and bugbears spin in confusion with the soldiers attacking and the archers shooting at them.

Trajan rolls to his hands and knees when he feels a sharp pain work its way up his back. He is kicked and rolled over by a huge bugbear. Trajan is lying on his back, using his hands to block the wide dull blade coming down at him. He clasps the blade between his hands and guides it to the ground. Wham! The bugbear's fist impacts the prince's jaw, dazing him. He is lifted into the air and tossed aside like a rag doll. Thoughts of his mother and father swirl in his head as he reaches his final moments of life. He closes his eyes as he hears the bugbear stomp quickly up to him and, oddly, the whistling of the blade coming down at him.

All goes dark as a heavy weight falls upon Trajan and the pain intensifies. *This is not how it's supposed to feel.* He opens his eyes to discover the bugbear laying on top of him. With his back hurting, he squeezes out from underneath the now dead bugbear. There are three arrows stuck in him. Trajan crawls out and stands to see no one near him, just arrows flying everywhere. *Who saved me?* He grabs the nearest weapon and goes back to the melee against the gnolls surrounding his troops.

Up at the top of the hill, orcs have come out of their daze and charge at Klinksly and Olivia. Klinksly runs to grab Klatzz's sword. It is twice the size of the gnome, yet light to carry. Olivia activates a tree swing spell and crushes dried leaves in her hands. She pulls back her arms hard and tree limbs bend and arch towards her. She trembles, struggling to hold back the energy of the pulled tree limbs. The orcs are almost upon Klinksly when Olivia screams, "Hit the ground!"

Klinksly doesn't even think and flops in the grass. Oliva releases her clenched fists. The arched tree limbs lash out under released pressure, striking the orcs and sending them flying downhill. Klatzz's giant rat jumps out from behind a large row of thorn bushes, spotting Klinksly. It wobbles quickly at him with its jaws open wide, dropping saliva everywhere. Klinksly struggles to get up.

The chimera suddenly stops and spots the larger rat. An orc falls out of its mouth onto the ground, moaning. The rat stops quickly when it spots the giant lion staring at it. The paws of the chimera crush the fallen orc into the forest floor as it leaps through the air after the rat. Scrub brush parts as the giant rat flees through bush after bush, dodging left and right from the grasp of the chimera. The two disappear over the next hill, out of view of Olivia and Klinksly.

Klinksly lowers his head. "Well, okay then." He quickly makes his way over to Olivia. Goblins and orcs rise out of bushes, and those that were hiding behind trees make sure the chimera is gone. They raise their weapons and approach Olivia and the gnome surrounding them.

The soldiers are tired. They are covered in blood, both their own and others. The gnolls and bugbears are stronger than they thought. Their training has only been against themselves and wooden dummies that never fought back. Adam notices Prince Trajan fighting by himself outside the ring of gnolls.

Adam has a thought enter his head. He remembers a prayer in the book he found and thinks this is an appropriate time to use it. "Prince! Take this!" Trajan glances over to see Adam's mace fly over the gnolls and bugbears. He lets go of the weapon he was using and reaches tall into the air. The mace handle lands perfectly in his grasp. A broad grin takes over Trajan's worry as soon as he feels how light the mace is.

The first swing impacts a gnoll's head from behind, killing it instantly without a single yip. He bashes another, then another. Down they fall with hit after hit. He smashes a bugbear's leg, snapping the bone easily. It yells in pain and swipes at Trajan, knocking him to the ground. Trajan rolls over and to his feet quickly and hits the bugbear square between its eyes. He hears the skull crack as flesh and blood spray in the area.

His soldiers, Glambell and Waldron, witness this and are encouraged to do more as they struggle to swing their weapons. Adam stands tall with his hands clasped together. He closes his eyes. His hands unclasp and a simple gold circle a few inches in diameter appears. His right hand grabs it and raises it into the air. "Palauttaa voimat!" A faint, golden glow instantly encircles the soldiers in a globe with Adam as the center.

They pause a second as an energy surges through them, restoring their strength and courage. "To arms! Fight like you never have before!" Waldron yells.

They all swing faster, harder, and with more determination to succeed. Gnolls and bugbears are now on the defensive. The soldiers are now killing the gnolls. Bugbears are still harder to kill, but now, two or three soldiers are attacking one bugbear, taking them down. With Trajan on the outside of the circle and the soldiers fighting on with renewed spirit, they eventually break the surrounding circle of gnolls.

They rush to the prince and form a line behind him. Waldron and Glambell stand beside him. A pause happens on both sides. Flingar has the archers stop but draw an arrow. Arthygus is frantically looking for the original arrow as the pile is getting bigger and bigger.

The remaining ten gnolls and four bugbears stand in their line, gasping for breath, waiting to charge again. They growl, bark, and yip, trying to intimidate the soldiers. They look back without fear and eagerness to put the gnolls in their place. Prince Trajan raises the mace, holds it, then lowers it forward quickly.

A volley of arrows whiz past them and into the gnolls and bugbears with precision, dropping most of them. Trajan rushes, followed by Glambell and Waldron. A swing of the mace sends a bugbear to the ground. Glambell the gnome jumps on it and thrusts his sword deep into its chest. Another swing by Trajan knocks another to the ground. Waldron slices his sword into that fallen bugbear, spins, and deflects an attack by a gnoll. A soldier runs his sword through that gnoll as Waldron continues onward.

For the first time, Trajan and the soldiers fight as one unit. He encourages them forward, finding his own courage to overcome fear. They follow without hesitation. Not another soldier is lost as the last gnoll falls from the hit of the mace.

Flingar pushes a tree branch out of his view to see more clearly. There is Trajan standing above the others on a large rock sticking out of the ground with the last gnoll slumping to the ground. Waldron, Glambell, and the soldiers all looked at him. His chest is breathing heavily as he looks around at the small conquest.

"You should be proud of your prince," Flingar says to the archers. They briefly take in the sight when Trajan points uphill.

"Archers! The giants! Take out the giants before it's too dark!"

They scramble to get closer for a better shot. Arthygus pops out of the pile of a thousand arrows, holding the original one. "I got it!"

"Good, now what?" a muffled gnome's voice is heard under the pile.

He snaps it, and the spell is stopped. Arthygus stands from the pile and is stunned to see what has happened to the soldiers. "What did I miss?" He watches Waldron and others sprint uphill.

Klinksly runs up to Olivia. "Turn your back to me, missy! It's about to get ugly."

Olivia puts her hands on her hips and frowns. "Missy?"

"Olivia. Okay. No time for..." Klinksly sets Klatzz's sword between them and draws his short sword in time to slash at a goblin that ran up to him. He kills it with one hit. "Pick up the sword!"

"It's too big for me." Olivia draws her father's saber from her side. "I don't like this, Klinksly!" The orcs are getting closer and see her fear. Two of them take their time, watching her struggle with the blade.

"Remember the cave. The river. You can do this. Start swinging," Klinksly instructs.

Another goblin rushes in. Their swords bounce off each other. Klinksly pushes his blade downwards along with the goblins and immediately comes up and slashes the goblins' throats. A heavily armored orc steps in and raises a large, jagged blade. He knows if he stays to block the blow, it could hit Olivia, so he jumps forward at it. The gnome's shoulder impacts the center waist of the orc, knocking it back slightly. Their eyes meet, and the orc's weapon hovers for a second before swinging down at Klinksly. The orc's blade strikes the ground as Klinksly rolls between its legs. He sees the weak spot in the metal armor and thrusts his sword upward, wounding the orc.

Olivia steadies the saber as an orc tries to grab the blade from her. She swipes upwards, cutting the hand off. The orc screams in agony and tries to strike at her with the other hand holding an ax. Instinctively, she slashes back. The ax is being held by a hand as it sails through the air and lands on the ground. The now handless orc screams at her and is pushed aside by another sword-wielding orc.

The orc swings wildly. Olivia steps back as the blade flashes past her face. An anger begins to grow inside her. She swipes back twice, killing the orc. Her eyes moisten at what she did. Before she can think, another orc gets closer to her. Olivia's lips curl and she grinds her teeth. Two more quick slashes and the orc drops. Another one steps in to take its place. Olivia has an anger in her now that won't stop.

Orcs run past Klinksly, ignoring him. He turns to see something strange with Olivia. She now steps after the orcs. She moves like an expert as she spins and twirls. Orc after orc drops. Some with their heads barely cut off as they flop to the ground. She screams in a rage while slicing them.

Klinksly is about to approach her when a giant appears. He tosses a rock at him and misses, crushing the wounded orc. He scrambles to get up. Just as he stands, the giant bends over to grab him. Once again, Klinksly dives and rolls. The huge hand slides right by him.

The orcs and goblins are running around in a disorderly fashion. The giant is smashing the ground after Klinksly, eyeing him hungrily. Klinksly rolls down the hill, away from the fight, into thicker trees. The giant spreads the trees like a child playing with sticks.

Olivia yanks the saber from the orc's chest. She notices the giant trying to get Klinksly. Olivia becomes herself for a second and gulps at what she did to the orcs. Her jaw drops and eyes squint at the horror of the blood, body parts, and dead orcs around her. She hears Klinksly cry out. A furious rage grows again inside her. Pushing aside any kindness, she runs at the giant chasing the gnome.

Thud! A tree branch lands on Olivia's forehead, knocking her backwards and into a daze. A large shadowy figure stands before her. Her eyes focus and before her is Klatzz. He reaches for the saber still clenched in her hands. She swings, and he pulls back. He kicks her with his clawed feet. Olivia cries out and swings again, but misses. He steps back farther, then leaps into the air at her.

Trajan leads the others uphill. More orcs and goblins fall at the hands of the soldiers. Waldron notices Klinksly going over the hill. He moves to the edge of the line, killing a few goblins along the way. Waldron grabs a soldier to follow and races to the hillside after Klinksly.

The other giant comes out from the pine trees, startling Arthygus and the archers. It grabs an archer and rips her in two. They all run in different directions. The giant throws the still-screaming upper torso at them, followed by the lower half. It knocks an archer over and he falls to the ground. The giant sees this and stomps on him with a bellowing laugh. Arthygus hears the strangest pop of the body under the tremendous weight of the giant's foot. The giant does not see him, nor the gnomes that start shooting arrows at it. Arthygus pulls out his spell book and rummages through the pages, looking for a spell.

Trajan is making headway up the hill. The goblins flee but are stopped by a row of wererats. Few are in human form while others are half rat half man. Adam has since picked up a war hammer from a dead orc and wishes he had his light mace.

Waldron and a soldier are close when he spots Klatzz's sword in the grass. "Get that sword!" he yells at the soldier. He runs over and picks it up. He stands motionless at its marvel. How light, sharp, and precise the craftsmanship is. “Go to the prince!” Waldron commands.

The wererats and soldiers clash. Prince Trajan swings the mace, breaking the jaw of a wererat. The soldiers’ weapons hit them, and they are shocked to see no harm as they bounce off the skin. Wererats laugh, tearing into them with their claws and swords. The goblins wait till the time is right to attack.

Klatzz has landed on top of Olivia. He reaches back to swing his sharp claws into her but stops. Both are motionless for a second. He lifts back a bit. Her saber has penetrated his side and pokes out the back. Olivia has no emotion and gives the most evil smirk. She twists the blade right before he can swing down at her.

Klatzz’s high-pitched squeal echoes down the wooded hillside, causing the wererats to look back. Olivia kicks him off of her, and she scoots back on her bottom, away from him. Klatzz stands and looks at his wound. He rubs his hand over it and licks the blood from his long, clawed fingers. “It’z takez more than that to hurtz me.” Olivia quickly stands up.

Waldron is undecided on which way to go. Help Klinksly or Olivia? Thoughts of Melisanday race through his mind. The memory of not being there to save her still haunts him. He darts towards Olivia as quickly as he can.

The dozen wererats jump and tackle Trajan, trying to get the mace from him, while three others run uphill at Klatzz. The soldiers are trying to hit them but to no avail. They pile on him and pin him down. Levi, the soldier with Klatzz’s sword, runs down the hill at the pile of wererats. With his speed and motion, he swings the brighter blue gleaming blade at the first wererat. The sword hits below the shoulder, cutting clean through. The creature’s lungs are cut, and he can see it trying to scream.

He swings again as he runs, cutting into the two wererats, killing them as he sprints by. Levi comes upon the pile of wererats clawing into the prince and does not stop. Levi holds the sword straight, uses his speed, and impales two at the same time. They scream and wiggle as he pulls the sword out from their bodies. He swings wildly to the left, then back to the right, cutting wererat after wererat.

The soldiers back off to give him room. Levi is tiring. "Here!" He tosses the sword at a soldier standing near him. She begins to cut into the wererats as well. The remaining ones let go of the prince and go after the female soldier. "Here!" She tosses it to Adam.

He looks shocked. The wererats charge at him and he tosses it at another soldier. That soldier grins and swings the blade into the first wererat that charges at him. Trajan regains his footing. He and the soldier with the blade finish off the last of the wererats as the soldiers surround them with no room for escape.

Arthygus slowly spreads iron shavings and cloth straps along his arm, causing static electricity to build. "Salama shokki!" A bright yellow electrical arc comes from his arm. A flash of yellowish light followed by a loud clap of thunder spreads up the hill side. Pushing aside two large pine trees, a smoldering twitching hill giant stumbles backwards and falls. The gnomes look back at Arthygus with his gaping jaw and he is surprised as much as they are. The archers take aim along with the gnomes and finish the giant off.

Levi points to the hillside where the gnome and other giant are at. He hands the prince the sword, who hands Adam's mace back to him. He gladly takes it, dropping the war hammer. The prince guides his troops and gnomes to the giant.

Klatzz lunges forward. Olivia steps aside, slashing with the saber. Klatzz swipes at her, scratching her face. This angers her even more. She swings wildly at Klatzz. Hit after hit. She pushes him back. He risks getting cut and grabs her by the arms. They struggle at first to gain the upper hand. Klatzz lifts her high into the air. Her feet dangle, trying to catch something. He spreads her arms out wide.

"Thiz iz whatz I do to youz, whatz you do to Skeel." He stretches her arms to the point they are about to pop out of the socket.

She is suddenly tossed by Klatzz as Waldron's sword impales him in the side. "Noz! What stickz mez!" The two exchange blows with Waldron blocking with his sword. The wererat swings his tail, tripping Waldron.

Olivia sits up, looking around, confused. The saber is off to her side. She reaches for it but stops. Olivia remembers her father talking about the bad thing. She realizes what it is. There is anger inside that weapon. She quickly sheaths the saber in the scabbard.

Waldron slices at Klatzz's tail, cutting it. He notices Klatzz's wounds are healing. Klatzz jumps on him, swiping and clawing at him. Olivia has no choice but to draw the saber again. This time, she thinks of positive thoughts of her father.

There is a deep loud scream from over the hillside then silence. Trajan and his troops rise over the hill with Klinksly after defeating the hill giant. They rush uphill to get to them.

Olivia slashes at Klatzz. He lashes back at her. Waldrons swipes at him. They go round and round—sword swipe, claw slash, sword swipe—until a loud thump gets their attention.

There is the chimera holding a dead giant rat in its vast mouth. The chimera lets it fall, and it rolls down the hill and stops before Klatzz. Oddly, the chimera can feel Olivia's fear of Klatzz. It leaps into the air towards Klatzz, and Olivia and Waldron step aside.

Klatzz's mouth snarls, knowing what is about to happen again. He is grabbed by the mouth and swung side to side. The chimera flings him into a tree, then pounces on him with those great paws. After a few minutes, he brings him over and proudly drops him in front of Olivia. Klatzz is slimy and bloody. They can see his wounds are slowly healing.

Olivia puts the saber back in the scabbard. Trajan and Klinksly had made their way over. Waldron asks Trajan to give Olivia the sword. He does so. She grasped the sword, confused.

"You know what must be done," Waldron says.

"Goez ahead…Tryz." Klatzz laughs. "Youz a nobodyz. Youz nothing but a scared girlz. Iz will never stopz! I willz hunt youz down again. Killz the gnomez next time. Iz will tormentz everyone. Iz will take you away and eatz you in the deadz of night. Slowz and alive likez. Little girl."

Olivia points the sword at Klatzz's face, wondering if she can do it. Their eyes meet with hatred staring back at her. She never saw herself kill Skeel. Now she is here, facing Klatzz.

"Youz can't doz itz." Klatzz laughs more and pulls himself up a little.

"Evenz if you tryz, you can't doz it. No weaponz can harm mez." He lets out a squealing laugh.

"I will do it. And with ease," Trajan says.

Waldron stops him from going farther. "She needs to do this," he whispers.

Olivia's hands quiver, holding Klatzz's blade. She fights with herself about what to do. She can't bring herself to kill something looking back at her, not fighting back. Klatzz lifts himself up and is about to grab his blade when she pokes him in the chest, piercing skin.

"Noz! Thiz can't be? Mez own blade."

Olivia puts her foot on his chest, keeping his back to the ground. "This was never your blade. You need to be stopped." She looks over at all the dead bodies of the goblins, orcs, and wererats, but it's a few dead soldiers and gnomes she sees that get to her. "This is all my fault. All of it."

"Yez...yez it iz. They all die becauze of youz." He reaches for the blade. "Youz pay for whatz you do. Now givez me blade."

Olivia's hand is on top of the sword pommel. She knows his evil needs to end and applies a slight pressure but cannot bring herself to do it. A hand gently lands on top of hers. Her lips quiver as she sobs. She squints and averts her gaze away from Klatzz.

Klatzz was used to delivering fear and using it. Now he feels its repercussions for the first time.

The hand firmly pushes down on her hand. Klatzz's skin pops, and he draws in a deep breath. The blade slowly goes into him, through his ribs, and into his heart. She can feel the thumping of the heart reverberate through the sword, making her uneasy. *What have I done?* She watches as the wererat king's eyes open wide as he stares at her in disbelief, then slowly fades away without uttering a sound. The sword is still.

Olivia follows the arm to Waldron standing beside her. He looks at her with a sad smile and nothing is spoken between the two. He helps her pull the sword out of Klatzz, and Olivia lets go of it. She takes several steps back with her hands covering her cheeks. Klinsky grabs her hand to try to comfort her.

"It needed to be done," Klinksly says softly.

She turns to him, sobbing. "But why me?"

Glambell and Flingar are holding the last wererat. It is wounded but alive. "What should we do with this one?" asks Glambell.

"Let him go," Olivia's soft voice says. "You are a witness to what happened." A blank stare comes over her face.

The wererat changes into human form. Bits of gray fur still sprout here and there over the dirty skin. He tilts his head and sneers. "Yes. I got it... And who are you, anyway?"

A bit of anger still resides from the blade in Olivia. She snaps, grabs him by the throat, and stares into his beady eyes. "I am the one that killed Skeel. Now I killed Klatzz" She gently lets go of his throat, turns, and walks away. The words of Klatzz are still in her head, saying she is a nobody. She stops, stomps her foot, turns her head back slightly and firmly yells, "I am Olivia! Witch of illusions!" Everyone is silent, watching her walk downhill toward Waldron's cabin. Klinksly has not seen her act this way. No one can see the dark circles forming around her eyes and the tears that flow. Her face grows pale, and her lips shake as remorse sets in at what she has done. Olivia refrains from wiping her tears so others will not see.

But Waldron knows.

12

Grains of knowledge

The dry hot air rubs against their faces. Mayreea and Garret's hands cover their eyes from the blinding sun. The two black monoliths about eight miles away seem like they are dancing from the heat. In the far distance, a large gray mountain range looms over the desert as far as they can see in both directions.

"Guess that is where we need to go?"

Mayreea looks back at the palm trees and flowers. They are watered very well. "Yes. Could be a two-hour walk."

"We can do it. Nothing out here to bother us."

They walk across soft tan sand on top of the dunes. They wander on top as long as they can and meander down in between them. Sometimes they walk across rock that has been beaten hard by centuries of the sun. They walk through small crevices where scorpions and small lizards hide in the tiny shadows.

"Which desert do you think we are in?" Garret asks.

"I'm not sure. I wonder if the book of witches has locations where they reside."

"We could be in the Glasair Desert…That would be the better choice."

"Why is that?"

"Two reasons. The Glasair is west of the Carnassial Mountains. So we are closer to home."

"And the second?"

"The other large desert is past the Magelic Ocean. The Ramaal Al Shaytan Desert. I wouldn't want to be there."

"Why not? You know a lot about places?"

"In my youth, my studies involved logs of world travels. I have read of places that people have visited, other cultures and such. But also limited script on places not so visited. Ramaal Alshaytan translates into the sands of the devil."

"Is that so?" Mayreea forces a smile and a laugh. "Let's hope we are not there."

They climb another dune that flattens out. It is a few hundred feet wide. The fine dust blows along the bottom from the soft breeze. Mayreea's foot sinks a little deeper than normal. She goes to pull it up when a thin twirling tentacle of sand whips out, spiraling up her leg to her knee.

She screams out as it tightens its grip. Garret, who wasn't too far behind her, kicks the sand tentacle, grabs her shoulder, and pulls her back. The sand dissipates in the air and drifts away in the breeze.

"What was that?" he asks.

Before she can answer, a wave of sand comes at them. It is a foot high and twenty feet wide. It lifts them into the air slightly, causing them to lose their footing and fall to the sand. Mayreea is on her side, and Garret has fallen on his belly.

The sand explodes underneath them, sending both tumbling through the air. Garret is tossed to the side of the dune, getting the air knocked out of him. Mayreea flops right in front of the sand creature. It is shifting and twirling like a sheet in the wind. No eyes or head can be seen.

Mayreea lifts herself up. A sand tentacle lashes out at her and misses as she ducks. Another comes from the same side and grabs her around the waist. The sand twists and slaps Mayreea against the sand floor.

She rubs her hand across her gold waist belt. "Hengen Valtikka!" A clear, shimmering image of a silver scepter appears in her hand. It has a yellowish outline along its foot length. She screams and, with a mighty swing, hits it square in the center.

Half the sand flies into the air in different directions. The bulk of it steps back. It is regaining its form. Garret climbs to the top, gasping for air. He notices small shiny flakes of sand floating around the creature and an idea comes to him. The sand creature whips its tentacles at him while he is staring. Both hit him in the back as he turns. The sharp sand particles act like blades cutting through his robe and into his skin. He falls to the ground again.

Mayreea swings with the shimmering scepter. This time, the creature is ready and wraps a tentacle around her arm. It lifts her off the ground. She released the scepter, and it drops into her other hand. A swift roundhouse swing and the tentacle holding her crackles apart.

The sand creature twirls, and the sand flies everywhere and to the ground. They both cover their eyes so as not to be blinded.

"Did you destroy it?" Garret asks.

"I don't—" The creature lunges from below, enveloping Mayreea. She is hit with sand particles before a tentacle comes up and surrounds her legs, waist, and arms to her chest. A large tentacle rises high above everything else, like a giant arched blade about to come down on Mayreea.

Garret reaches into his pocket and pulls forth a small, blue, glass vial. He pops the top with his thumb and pours out a small drop of clear sparkling water. "In a time of need, Dianeeta, I ask of you to drench this creature to end our peril. Lage Vann!"

A cone-shaped deluge of water spews forth from his hands, covering the sand creature. The huge blade blows apart in the breeze, with sand particles landing harmlessly around. The creature sinks into the warm sands below.

Garret rushes to Mayreea and helps her up. The scepter has since faded away. They hurry away from the dune.

They cross solid rock and more dunes before rounding one. They see the two large black monoliths made from black marble with white and gold veins. A ten-foot-wide square base supports the ninety-foot-tall structure. They are spaced apart by a hundred feet. To the outside of them are three date trees, and between them are two large pots of blue lotus flowers.

Behind them is what has their attention—a large brown and tan building standing just as wide but only thirty feet tall. A huge dune is covering the sides, back and top—either by design or it has been slowly creeping over it. In the middle is a large door painted black with gold trim and decorations of a long-forgotten script.

"Now that is impressive. Dianeeta is showing me things I never thought I would see. There is a reason for all this."

"You think so?"

"Yes, I do." He cheerfully walks towards the center of the building.

They take a few minutes to get there. As they near the steps to the center, they are greeted by a heady scent of fresh, clean sheets of silk and rain.

"Hum, smells delightful," Garret says. He approaches the blue lotus flower to take a deeper whiff when two large, muscular, ebony men step out from around each monolith. They are bald and wear black tunics with gold trim from waist to knees only. Each has a long-handled ax. The pole arm reaches twelve feet in length, and the gold ax blade resembles a half-moon shape.

Garret backs up quickly as the two men blankly stare at them.

Garret nervously clears his throat. "Ah, hello. We are seeking council with Masika."

The men stare at them and not a muscle moves. Garret looks back at Mayreea and waves her to come.

"Oh, this can't be good," she whispers to herself.

Garret walks up to the two men who react with lightning-like reflexes and swing the axes at Garret but stop in front of his face.

"They are sharp." He takes a step back. "We mean no harm. We need to see Masika. If this is not the right place, can you guide us to the appropriate... place?" He grins.

The door unlatches and slowly opens halfway. A young, tanned woman appears wearing a thin white dress with a splash of turquoise at the bottom. Her thighs and legs mostly stick out while the dress is pulled between them. Her top hardly covers her breast, and a thin strap comes up around her neck to hold the dress. A wide gold and black necklace covers her throat. She has short black hair with gold loop earrings. Her dark eyes gleam at Garret.

"What is it you want?" She speaks with a silvery voice.

"We would like council with Masika."

Only the woman's eyes move, glancing over them. "She has since passed away. Whatever dealings you had with her, done is done. Now be gone."

Mayreea and Garret gaze at each other in disbelief. Garret taps his forehead, thinking of something to say. "It's not by chance that two strangers show up at your door seeking help, when they may be the ones to help you." He turns to Mayreea with a sly nod and smile.

The woman stops part way through the door. "You have piqued my interest. Let them in."

The two men slowly raise their axes and step aside. Garret bows at them as he walks past, and Mayreea follows him.

They enter a large room, thirty feet long and twenty feet wide. It has a short ceiling, only ten feet tall. Along the walls are small palm plants in vases. The walls have paintings of a river with men and women working farm fields and catching fish.

On their right side, where a wall should be, is a large opening. A parched sycamore fig tree stands in a small muddy pond. More like a thick soup. A statue of a man titling a large vase is moist, but only a drop of dirty water drips out from time to time. There are small channels coming from the base of the statue to a round depression on the stone floor and to the tree.

"Who are you?" she asks.

"Ah. I am Abbot Garret."

"My name is Mayreea."

"And where do you come from?"

"We are from Esalon. My monastery is in the wilds near Splinteroak. West in the Southern Kingdom."

She glares at Mayreea. "I live near the northern mountains where the ice lords reign. Though I am not part of them." She pauses for a second. "And who is our host?"

She points to a large stone table near the corner. The benches have oversized white silk pillows to sit on. "Sit. I'm Jomana. Masika was my grandmother."

"And can you tell us what desert we are in?" Garret asks.

Jomana scratches her temple. "Desert? The Glasair, of course."

Mayreea and Garret wink at each other. "That is good to know," he whispers to her.

Garret twitches and is uncomfortable in his chair. He rubs his back under his robe. When he pulls his hand out, it has blood mixed with sand on it.

Jomana snaps her fingers and two small, tanned children, about nine and ten, come around the corner. The girl is wearing a white dress with a turquoise outline and a top that covers her shoulders. She has long black hair tied in a ponytail. The boy has a shaved head and is wearing a white tunic with a black outline only. "Nubia and Zahur, go get the figs and pomegranate juice for our guests."

"Oh no, I'm fine, really," Garret says.

"How did you get cut?" Jomana asks.

"It was some kind of sand creature. It lashed its tentacles out at us."

Jomana's eyebrows raise. "The sandling? How did you survive it?"

"Escaped more like it," Garret says.

"We got lucky," Mayreea adds.

"You do not get lucky with the sandling. It protects that oasis ferociously."

"We used knowledge to make it go away," Garret says.

A few moments later, the children come back with refreshments. Garret is thirstier than he realizes. He takes a small sip of the pomegranate juice and smacks his lips. He then raises his cup and takes a deep gulp, followed by a curious bite of a fig.

Mayreea takes a small nibble of the fig. She silently enjoys the taste. "We need information on a curse."

"A deal is final. Besides, I couldn't lift it if I wanted to. Masika created it, and only Masika can lift it.

"We are seeking information on one particular curse," Mayreea continues.

Jomana's narrow eyes stay focused on her. "Just information?"

"That tree is not healthy. May I take a look?" Garret asks.

"Yes, go ahead." She lowers her eyebrows at him.

Garret walks past the two children and waves them over. "That tree looks sad. Let's see what we can do to help it?"

They both excitedly look back at Jomana for approval. She gives the slightest of nods. They scuttle up to his side.

"Trees need water to thrive, and this one looks like it is not getting enough. Let's say we make it happen."

"But how?" Nubia asks.

Garret pulls out the small glass vial again. He has them hold out their fingers, and he puts a small drop on the tip. "I call upon you Dianeeta to once again allow the water to flow. Give life water back to this tree and those that depend on it. Rense Vann!"

He lets a drip come from the vial. The sparkling blob spins and sinks into the mud.

"Nothing happened," Nubia says.

"What was supposed to happen?" Zahur asks.

Garret has them lower their fingers to barely touch the surface. He whispers, "Let it be so."

Their eyes blink and jaws drop as a tingle surrounds their hands. The mud sinks and the water becomes clear. It slowly spreads out from where they touched. The children stand back in amazement at what they are witnessing.

The gurgling of water comes from the vase as the water flows again. The channels carry the clear fresh water to the small pond and around the sycamore fig tree.

Jomana is awestruck. "This cannot be real." Nubia puts her hands in the cool running water and Zahur stands in it. He wiggles his toes as the water washes off the sand and dirt from his feet.

Garret cups his hands and drinks from it. "Ah. Nice and refreshing."

Jomana comes over and touches it for herself. Her hands glide through the cool water. She hasn't experienced water like this in a long time.

Zahur laughs as he splashes water everywhere. Garret has Nubia go over to the tree. He demonstrates for her how to lightly sprinkle the base and branches with water and teaches her how to tend to trees for the best results.

Jomana calls in the two men to watch over the children and heads back to the table with Mayreea. They look stunned at the flowing water. Zahur splashes one of them. He looks back at Jomana with a teasing grin. She nods approval.

Both men grab handfuls of water and splash Zahur. They laugh and carry on.

Jomana turns her attention to Mayreea. "You are not here to have a curse lifted or cast?"

"No, we seek information on a particular curse."

"Why? Are you recipients of it? Who are you?"

Jomana hears Zahur laugh like he never had before. She glances in the direction and watches the men laugh and splash at the young boy. Nubia is gently pouring water over the tree's branches and trunk.

"I am a witch of spirits. I can see a spirit of happiness rise around you for a brief moment, overtaking the dominant one of distrust and deceit."

Jomana tugs on her earlobe to adjust the earring as her eyes narrow.

"I know Masika was a witch. She was known as the witch of curses. We are not here for anything other than information on one curse."

"And that is?"

"Tangeo."

Jomana squishes her lips together and takes a deep breath. "I'm not familiar with that one. Who are you? What is your connection to this curse?"

"Tangeo is a sad one. The story has been told and variations are out there. So I would like to know more about it."

Jomana sits there expressionless. The laughter and splashing continues. This in turn makes Jomana feel cooperative. "Give me a moment.

I need to go through her library." She walks to the side of the room and slips between a small crevice that was not seen before. The paintings almost hide it depending on the angle you look at it.

Mayreea watches Garret with the children. Moments later, Jomana returns. She has a small brown book with jagged and torn paper. The pages crackle as she turns them one over the other. She eventually spots the curse in question. "Here it is. Tangeo's curse."

Jomana reads over it slowly and, with her head facing down, she rolls her eyes up to meet Mayreea. Her eyes shift towards the flowing water. "Again, why the interest in this curse? And tell me the truth or you will get nothing from me."

Mayreea is hesitant but tells her. "We have a friend that was taken from us by...Well, that doesn't matter. We used a spell to locate her. And we believe she is maybe with...What's her name? Tangeo's love?"

"Ah huh." Jomana nods ever so slightly. "That is most unfortunate, if so."

Mayreea cocks her head, moving the locks out of her face. "What do you mean?"

Lines form on her forehead as she focuses on the script. "This was dated in the year 503. Tangeo embarrassed and robbed the victim in front of his mistress, taunting them about how well of a bladesmith he was. Tangeo's lover clapped and encouraged him on. They boasted about how they are in love."

Mayreea tilts her head, and her fingernails tap the table. "That is not what I heard. But go on."

"The curse is very specific. The victim wanted Tangeo to suffer. He captured Catalina, Tangeo's lover, and brought her to Masika. Part of the curse had Catalina offered to the demoness, Dalzara."

Mayreea rubs her chin. "So that's her name."

"There, she would keep her in a suspended state. Once every year, during the summer equinox and at the rise of the full moon cresting over the ocean, her spirit is set free to visit Tangeo to remind him of what was lost. Then, at their height of happiness, Dalzara would whisk her away, not to be seen for another two years. This will go on forever until he finds her."

"That is a specific curse. Why hasn't he looked for her?"

"It states that the victim wants her to never be found. When Tangeo searches for her, all will be false clues to her whereabouts. If he asks someone to search also, the curse will activate on them as well. If Tangeo and Dalzara meet by accident, he cannot fight her, as a weakness will set in."

"So, will he go on forever? But we know the general location."

"Do you know how curses work?"

"Not really."

"There are two types. One is to protect a place or item from thieves and robbers. Once it is known, fear of its consequence is the most powerful part. Regardless if the power fades over time, the fear remains."

"And the second?"

"Those that bestow a curse on another. Repercussions of a cheating lover, a failed agreement, or even embarrassment. Most are vindictive. Again, the mere thought of a victim believing in the curse allows it to happen."

"With that being said, we know the curse and Tangeo is real. So we cannot find our friend?"

"That's right. But my grandmother always puts in a twist or a way out."

Mayreea sits closer to Jomana to hear over the laughter of everyone splashing now.

"Masika has a side note. She rarely did that. It reads, *This was a difficult curse. My opinion, Tangeo didn't deserve it, but payment is payment. And Anwir Mire paid in gold and blood. To end the curse, one who has no knowledge of this curse must discover the location of Catalina, then defeats Dalzara. Then Tangeo will be free.*"

"Oh, like that can happen." Mayreea shakes her head in disbelief.

"That curse was seventy-five years ago. Sixty years ago, Masika was killed by none other than that man, Anwir Mire."

"What?"

"My mother told me he wanted to make sure no one would ever come here to get the curse lifted. After he killed her, he used her very own book and blood to curse the water of this place so we would abandon our home. We did not leave."

A sad smile forms on Mayreea, and she slumps her head into her hands. A soaking wet Garret comes over. "Why so glum?"

Jomana spreads her hands while standing and grins ear to ear. "Your friend here knew nothing of the curse and set us free. Gave us water back again. Yes, Mayreea, have hope."

Mayreea has a ghostly smile and holds Garret's hand. "We know where she is. We now know the curse. Now the hard part is who can we find that can rescue Abigail without even knowing they are?"

"It's that difficult?" Garret asks.

Mayreea sighs and leans back in the chair. "I guess the others got the simple part today." Mayreea takes a sip of juice. "We best get going to tell the others."

"Do you want the company of my guards to escort you to the oasis?"

"That is alright. I have enjoyed the time Dianeeta has allowed me to be here. I believe she allowed us to succeed in our small journey here, and she will do the same for us to get back to those that need us."

Mayreea feels comfort in what he is saying. "We will be okay. Go join them for some long overdue fun."

Jomana shakes the hands of both of them with palms facing upwards. She walks them to the door. "Stay on the rocks as much as you can. The sandling cannot rise from hard surfaces. You have ended a curse today. Hopefully, that is a good sign for you on your journeys."

They all give faint smiles to each other. Mayreea gives Garret a jealous look.

"What?"

"You are all wet on this dry, hot day. Lucky you." She laughs.

Mayreea's dress sways in the hot dry air of the desert. The water is quickly being absorbed by the dry air from Garret's clothing. Sand sticks to his sandals and lower part of his robe as they walk over and around dunes. They decide not to head back the same way but go northwest and then cut down to the oasis to avoid the sandling by staying on hard rocky areas as much as they can.

Occasionally, they climb a dune to check where they are and where they have to go. They look back at the monoliths that are getting farther away. A few hours of walking again and the heat is getting to them. Garret's robes are dry but the bottom. They come across a small ravine between two dunes to rest in the shade. The sun is setting, and the shadows are long, keeping the ravine cooler than in the sun.

"How did you figure out how to deal with the water back there?" Mayreea asks.

"I just thought of it as a friendly gesture to help lighten the mood."

"But how did you get the water flowing?"

"Ahh. Us followers of faith do not have spells or access to planes of magic, as it was described by Arthygus. It is more of divine intervention through prayer." He grins at her. "And a few tricks I have learned along the way to grant favor. But belief is the strongest part."

Mayreea sits down and leans against a smooth part of the rock wall. She closes her eyes for a quick rest. Garret does the same a few feet away from her in the shade. Minutes turn to hours as they sleep.

Garret is awakened by a clicking sound. His eyes open to see twilight has come. The dust in the air creates a magnificent orange throughout the sky, followed by shades of red. Above that, stars glow in the deep blue of the night. He is mesmerized at the beauty he is witnessing when a shadow moves across the higher dune.

The clicking becomes louder. His heart races as the shadow comes into view much clearer. The shadow of a scorpion the size of a large cargo wagon moves up behind them. He slowly turns to Mayreea. She is awake and frozen in fear, watching another large scorpion come down into the crevice.

Garret quickly scans the area for a way out. Terrified, he leaps across the ravine to grab a large rock. The scorpion crawls quickly at him. He throws the rock at it, hitting it behind the head. It harmlessly bounces off the exoskeleton of the black scorpion.

A darkness covers Garret. He looks up to see the other scorpion straddling the ravine, which is much larger than the one in the crevice with them. Garret turns to run, and a loud snap comes from behind. Garret feels his robe tighten and is lifted into the air by the scorpion's claw.

The smaller scorpion races past Mayreea to grab Garret but misses. Garret is pulled away from the ravine and onto a dune. The night's slightly cooler air allows him to breathe better. He wiggles, trying to set himself free, but his robe is too tight.

Mayreea uses this time to stand and recalls her scepter. She thinks of something to do. She has no spells that deal with sand, nor is there anything else around she can use.

The larger scorpion holds Garret high, arcs its back, and whips its tail. The smaller one jumps up at Garret. The larger one's tail hits the smaller one. Right at Garret's face, he sees the stinger break loose from the hit. He quickly grabs it and rips it off. The larger one twists and leaps in pain, sending Garret and the smaller scorpion tumbling through the air.

Mayreea witnesses this and sees them fly out of sight. She runs through the ravine and works her way up. Using her hands to pull herself up, she flops onto a dune. Sand begins to slide down in front of her. A triangle-shaped dull sapphire about the size of a melon sticks partly out. She catches a whiff of rain and looks to the sky but sees no clouds. She shrugs her shoulders.

Curious, she reaches for it. It feels warm and scaly, unlike a gemstone. *Perhaps a spearhead*, she thinks to herself and gives a harder pull. It does not move. Mayreea is on her knees now and grabs it with both hands, pulling as hard as she can.

Garret impacts the dune side. He slides and rolls down the angled sand until he hits bottom. He lays still for a second, trying not to cough. The scorpions see where he went. He can hear the two snapping at each other, though. He lays motionless, trying to think of what to do.

Mayreea loses her grip, falling backwards into the ravine. She slams against the hard rock side but stops herself from falling the short distance. She spins around and peeks her head out of the ravine.

The scorpions are fighting with each other, making a racket now, but there is no sign of Garret. She hopes they don't see her. Sand falls from the dune in front of her. The sapphire slithers out of the sand.

It is connected to something that has tiny scales of pale blue and violet on the bottom. The diameter gets larger with each two feet of it. More and more comes out. Almost twenty feet in length now and a foot in diameter, the scales are a brilliant hue of blue. Now the tip is a sharp spear point.

Horrified, she realizes what it is. *It's a tail,* she says to herself. Her eyes are the widest they have been in a long time as she watches the dune turn the sand like a wave cresting on a beach. A sparkling, light blue leathery wing unfolds, revealing a deep blue scaled body. A long neck is still buried in the sand. It slowly rolls towards Mayreea.

She ducks into the ravine as the massive body covers her in darkness. She falls against the stone floor. What little twilight is left shines in from the other side of the ravine. Rock and sand fall on her as a huge, scaled arm lazily slides down. The foot-long, bristling, white claws—the size of her arms—rub against her body. She dares not breathe or move.

Garret is finally brave enough to stand. He adjusts his robe, shaking the sand out of him to be a tad more comfortable. While slapping his robe, he looks at the top of the dune. There are the two scorpions looking down at him. He cringes.

The large scorpion shoves the other one to the side and steps in front of it. It crouches down to leap at Garret. His heart races, jaw drops, and eyebrows raise at what he sees. Two large blue scaled claws the size of horses crash down on the scorpions. The small one is crushed under the tremendous weight, and the larger one's tail is pinned into the sand. The tail snaps off as the scorpion struggles to get free.

Two, large, blue, leathery wings spread out to almost seventy feet wide in total. It has a large scaly neck with violet undertones along the chest. Deep blue hues are on the sides and upper part. Its head rises over the scorpions, showing off its dominance over the giant bugs. Its pearly white teeth almost sparkle in the night.

Its massive single horn on its front snout comes to a sharp point.

The fluorescent cyan sclera and the deep dark sapphire pupil of its eyes demand to be watched.

"As I live and breathe. A blue dragon." Garret stands there, mesmerized by the marvel of the mighty dragon.

The blue dragon's massive jaw opens then crunches down on the scorpion, spraying juices and exoskeleton everywhere. The whole time, the eyes do not waver off of Garret.

Garret's hand is grabbed by Mayreea, who escapes from the opening of the ravine. "That's our cue to go."

Garret runs along beside her, looking back at the dragon. He smiles and almost wants to wave at it. The dragon's eyes follow him while it eats the scorpions in the night. Mayreea cringes at the terrible cracking and crunching.

"That can be us. Now keep going."

They scurry out of range, then begin to walk. Hours go by until they make it to the edge of the oasis. Garret stops, gasping for breath with his hands on his knees, wheezing.

"Come on, that dragon can be on us any second if it wants."

Garret raises his finger, wanting to speak, but nothing comes out. Mayreea looks in the night's distance. The desert is surreal as the deep red slowly dissipates, being taken over by the midnight blue of the night. The stars dance in the heat. She looks for any trace of the dragon in the sea of sand.

"Come, we must move to the tree." Fearing there is no time to search, Mayreea goes to the nearest palm tree to get bark and begins crushing it in her mortar.

Garret stands upright and stretches. He, too, was admiring the nighttime of the desert. "In all my years, I never would have thought I would do so much traveling in such a short time... It's like a re-awakening for me... All thanks to the wonderful girl Abigail that happened to fall into our monastery."

A black exoskeleton shell about a foot in diameter lands in the sand behind Garret. He looks down at it, then up at Mayreea with frozen eyes.

The scent of clean ozone after a rain becomes overbearing of the plants at the oasis. Mayreea blinks her eyes at the realization of what that smell is.

The sand parts in small waves like on the beach when a heavy weight, gently sits down upon it. The swooshing of the sand grains falling over each other soothes Garret's ears as he watches. It flattens most of the dune top into an oddly-shaped bowl. A deep, low-pitched, arrogant voice speaks softly over them. "The dark woman is correct. I can be on you when I choose." The words gurgle off to silence.

Shimmering into view is the blue dragon. It sits on its hind legs, using one of its claws to pick out bits of the scorpion from its teeth. Garret stands frozen in fear and curious at the same time.

The dragon picks out another piece of exoskeleton and flings it near Garret. The large head slithers down near him with its mouth ajar. He makes sure Garret sees the shiny sharp teeth sparkle with small whitish purple arcing of what may be static electricity. "Tell me, traveler. Why have you trespassed in my lands?" His voice makes Garret tremble with his low gurgle being so close.

The dragon's cyan eye watches Garret look back at the monoliths in the distance. "Ohhh. How nice." The dragon's head raises high over Garret, making sure he sees its mighty girth of scale and muscle, proudly showing himself off. "You have a purpose."

"Purpose?" Garret asks.

"Do not play me for a fool..." He swings his arm and claws near Garret, giving him a little nudge to show how small Garret is to him. "No one would cross these arid lands to go to Masika's place and back to the oasis on the same day. That's right, little man, I know of Masika's place." The dragon lays down in front of him. "Purpose."

Garret nervously looks around. "Well, I... we..."

The dragon's voice becomes louder and more boastful. "Don't mind the witch getting a spell ready! That's right, I can hear you grinding away. Now tell me the purpose!" His voice lowers to a gurgle again, almost like a purring. "I can tell if words are untrue...false." He gets closer to Garret. "I dislike that. Now tell me some gossip."

Garret takes a deep breath and thinks there is no harm in telling the dragon the truth. "Forgive my manners. I am Abbot Garret. A priest of...Dianeeta. She has granted...no. She has given me the chance to...see how things are compared to what I have known to be the truth."

"I'm curious about this tale... Go on," the dragon softly rumbles.

"My companion over there is Mayreea. And yes, she is getting a tree door spell ready for us to go back home." The dragon lifts its large scaly eyebrows at the revelation he told the truth. "We needed to seek Masika's help, only to discover she passed on years ago."

The dragon rests his head on its front paw and folds its wings along the back. "How sad you didn't get what you wanted."

Garret points his finger at him. "But you are wrong. We got help. From her granddaughter."

The dragon grumbles. "Never tell a dragon they're wrong."

"Oh. Forgive me, great...?" He rolls his hand out, waiting to hear the dragon's name. "I have never had the experience until now to speak to one. Dragons have not been seen for ages."

"That is because people do not seek them out any longer. Or at least for the right reasons."

Garret's voice becomes joyful. "Then let me say, you are very impressive, and I am thankful to Dianeeta for allowing our chance encounter to happen."

"Maybe it's because I let you live?"

"How's that?" Garret rebukes quickly.

"I saved both of you from the scorpions."

Garret claps his hands. "Oh...Yes, you did. I suppose you did. Then a thank you is in order. That was definitely quite a show of power you did back there. Most impressive indeed."

Mayreea has the spell ready but holds off from casting it. She steps to the edge of the oasis. "So, what are you going to do with us now?

"Do? Why would I do anything? I'm waiting for an answer to your purpose."

"Yes, that. We needed information on a curse," Garret explains.

"Gossip! Tell me more...For I grow agitated at your procrastination on purpose!" the dragon roars. His growl echoes over the dunes, and his teeth crackle with blue sparks.

Garret stumbles back, fearing the worst. "Alright, it's a long story."

"You got time." The dragon softly grumbles and smiles.

Garret tells of how he found Abigail. From her showing him different parts of the world and giving a different view of witches to getting taken by a demoness and the curse.

The dragon stays motionless, and its eyes never wavered for a second. He looks over at Mayreea, who is staring back at him.

"That is all I know at the moment. Our time is limited, and we must make haste to get back with the knowledge we gained today. I would be more than willing to tell you more after it happens if we can go now."

The dragon is intrigued. "I have not met a person like you, Abbot Garret. Most want to steal my treasure or take my scales for whatever use. But you...You gave me gossip. Good gossip. How do I know you will come back to give me more?"

"You have my...word."

"No, I will keep your companion. The witch to be sure."

"No. She is an important part in this story also."

"You tell me no?"

"Yes."

"Yes...no?"

"Yes! I tell you no. No, you cannot have her." Garret pulls out the small blue vial. "Here. Hold this in the meantime. It is very important to me. It holds Dianeeta's water power."

He sets it in the dragon's paw. He can hardly hold it because the vial is so small to him. "Fine. I look forward to our next meeting."

Garret and Mayreea look at each with a twisted expression about what to do. "Does that mean we can go now?" Garret asks.

The dragon stares at them. They take it they can and work their way to the tree. Mayreea activates the tree door spell. Garret looks back at the dragon. "What is your name, great dragon, so I can call upon you when I return?"

"Neistablár," he grumbles in the low-pitched voice.

13

Blood and Sand

The darkness of night now intermixes with the shadows of death. Survivors are in a daze, catching their breath. They nervously raise their weapons at the slightest noise or moving shadow. The goblins and gnolls already stank, but now the stench of decay is setting in. Thankfully, it is not full sunlight to make it worse. Klinksly takes one step to go after Olivia. Waldron's hand firmly grabs his tiny shoulder to stop him. His eyes frown, and he hardly shakes his head at the little gnome. Klinksly lowers his head, knowing he is right to let her be. Saddened, he goes over to Glambell and Flingar, who are still holding the wererat. Klinksly stares him down. "You're one lucky rat."

He scoffs at him. "Me, lucky?"

"If it was up to us...you'd be dead," Glambell says. They let go of him. The wererat stands and slowly turns his head at everyone. Trajan and the soldiers are all looking at him. He takes a step back, waiting to be attacked, but no one moves.

"She said to let you go. So we are letting you go," Waldron explains.

"So go," Klinksly says. The wererat walks fast uphill, looking back to make sure no one is after him. He makes it to the top of the hill; the darkness of the night has set in. His face droops in sadness. He sighs in relief and is confused about why they didn't kill him. He shifts into an enormous rat to see better, sniffs the air, and scurries along.

Young Adam approaches Waldron and the gnomes. "Shouldn't we slay all that is evil? Why did we let that creature go?"

The gnomes glance at each other, not knowing how to answer. Waldron cleans his blade, putting it back in his scabbard. He picks up Klatzz's blade from the ground after Olivia dropped it. He puts his hand on Adam's shoulder and taps it. "Sometimes it is just that way. You hope it is for the better outcome."

"Outcome?" Adam asks.

"Yes...That a bit of hope was sent with him to tell the tale of what happened here today." Waldron gazes uphill at where the creature was last at.

"Hope?"

"Hope they learned their lesson and never come back," Waldron says.

Adam wonders what events are now set in motion from all of this. *Was this a moral decision to let it live? What lesson is Dianeeta trying to show me?* he thinks to himself after witnessing Olivia's wrath and kindness all at the same hour.

Prince Trajan gathers his troops. He counts eight surviving archers and nine remaining soldiers. Some of them are injured. His veins are pulsing in his neck as anger grows inside of him that he lost over half of them. His men and women are standing, looking around. Eyes are gazing in the distance, looking at nothing. A few are unaware they are still bleeding. Others stare at the ground and others search over the dead.

Waldron approaches Trajan. "You need to say something."

Trajan shakes his head and tries to speak, but nothing comes out. His eyes are fixed on a dead soldier in front of him.

Waldron grasps Trajan's hand and places the hilt of Klatzz's sword in it. "Here, this is yours now. You earned it." He raises Trajan's hand in the air. "Attention, everyone. You have done well today. You were outnumbered by many. It was unknown about the giants, and the strength of the enemy was greater than you were told." He looks at Trajan to finish.

Trajan lowers the sword, admiring the bluish gleam. He looks up with a grin at his troops. "We are victorious in our first battle. We have lost fallen comrades today. But do not weep yet for them. Check the dead, help tend the wounds of others...You have honored the name of what a Southern Kingdom soldier is all about."

His troops give a Southern Kingdom roar and spread out, gathering weapons and bodies of dead soldiers. Trajan whispers to Waldron. "Why am I so damn angry?"

"That is what you will have to figure out on your own...But that feeling is normal for one that doesn't want war."

Arthygus steps out from a pine tree farther downhill. He has an empty stare at all the dead bodies that lie everywhere, spread out like weeds in a flower garden. Young Adam notices him and makes his way over. Arthygus's face changes into a big grin, and he holds his hands in the air in excitement. "Did you see that? Did you see that?"

"I sure did!"

"Did you see that? I cast a lightning bolt spell!"

"That was an amazing sound. And at the right time."

"No, that was amazing what you did with the light right off the start!"

"It was the only thing I thought of to give us the first advantage."

Silence overcomes them, and Adam softly says, "We survived."

"Yeah, but how?" Adam and Arthygus clap hands together in the air. They look around after hearing a moan. "You hear that? Where is it coming from?" Arthygus asks.

"If we only had a little more light to see."

Arthygus has an idea. "I do a have a common light spell, but if I combine it with a amplify spell, it should be a little brighter." He reaches for a fist-sized rock on the ground. He thinks of the ingredients he needs and holds his hand near his chest. It is too dark for Adam to see that Arthygus's eyes rolled back in his head. He gets wobbly and passes out.

Before Adam can grab him, he hits the ground with a thump. "Arthygus!" Adam reaches down and taps his face. He gasps for breath and moans. "Arty, Arty. Wake up."

Arthygus's eyes open slowly. His vision is blurred, seeing only a silhouette of Adam standing over him. "Wha...What happened? Why am I on the ground?"

"I don't know. Why *are* you on the ground?"

Purgsul comes out from behind the pine trees with an arm full of arrows. He drops them and goes over to Arthygus. "What happened?"

"I don't know? I suddenly feel weak."

The little gnome taps his chin, then grins. "Oh, I remember Farlan talking about when he uses too strong of magic, he needs to rest." He squints, looking into the night sky. "Or something like that."

"Of course," Arthygus says with a disappointed voice. "The stronger the magic spell, the more energy it takes from you."

Adam helps him sit up. "So, what did you do?"

"It has to be the lightning bolt. I've never performed anything powerful like that before."

"And then trying to do a light spell also?" Adam asks.

"Oh, you can't be doing spell after spell. Oh, no, no, no." Purgsul waves his tiny fingers back and forth at Arthygus. "No wonder you passed out. Surprised you lasted this long, you know. After the arrow spell fiasco." He laughs and points back at the pile of arrows.

"At least you are stocked now." Arthygus smiles.

The moan deepens, and their attention is drawn downhill. Purgsul hops over a few dead goblins and raises the hand of a wounded soldier. "We got a live one!" His whiny voice echoes uphill.

Trajan and the others sprint towards them. Olivia hears the gnome's voice right before she goes into Waldron's cabin. With a soft close of the door, she hopes they will be alright. Thoughts of dead soldiers weigh in her mind. The idea of what she did to Klatzz is causing her inner turmoil. *Did he deserve that? Did I have to do that?*

A few soldiers push aside the goblin and gnoll bodies to find their comrade still alive. They begin to clean and bind his wounds. "That is one more alive," a soldier says.

"Still, we shouldn't have lost so many," Trajan sadly states.

"Ehh. Don't be so hard on yourself. They were tough foes, very tough. And we still won," Glambell reasons.

Waldron and Klinksly head downhill and come upon Arthygus sitting on the ground, rubbing his head. "You alright, kid?" Klinksly asks.

"He is. Apparently, he used too many spells, and it wore him out," Adam explains.

Klinksly takes his hat off, wipes his forehead, and teasingly hits Arthygus with it. "Should have been a warlock, kid." He puts his hat back on and taps Arthygus's head. "You did alright though...You did alright." His voice trails off, looking at the giant he killed with the lightning spell, and notices Olivia closing the door.

Klinksly does a slow walk to Waldron's cabin with him not too far behind. He quietly steps onto the front porch and can hear Olivia sobbing inside. Klinksly is about to open the door when Waldron stops him. He puts his finger up against his lips and winks.

"Wow. In all my battles, that was the toughest I have been in," Waldron says, louder than normal.

Klinksly, now getting what he is doing, answers, "How so?"

"Really? You didn't notice?"

"Uhh."

"We were so outnumbered and all we had was what? Almost an hour to get ready? Normally, we would have many soldiers, a few captains, and a veteran leader to guide us into battle... Change the strategy when needed."

Klinksly nods his head and stares in the distance. "That seems..."

"And to top it off, the troops that Prince Trajan brought were never in combat until now. Including himself."

Klinksly snaps his fingers. "And the gnomes! We had them."

"Yes. All, what, eight of them against a horde of seasoned monsters?"

Klinksly again nods in agreement and looks into the distance. "That was a lot of them for sure."

"And Klatzz. Not just some average wererat, but the king himself."

"Yes, there was that too." Klinksly's face turns pale at what he is saying.

Olivia's heart beats rapidly as she listens to them. Tears drip off her cheek and onto the floor. She lifts her hands to see them shaking.

"But in all this mess, you know the saving grace we had on our side?"

"Uhh, you?" Klinksly points at him.

"No...It was Olivia."

Now Klinksly is genuinely enthralled by what Waldron is saying. He takes his hat off and holds it in both hands. "She sure has a way of doing things, doesn't she?"

"If it wasn't for her taking responsibility and coming up with a plan to get help, the gnomes would have perished for certain."

Klinksly remembers Olivia taking charge when Abigail was paralyzed by the ghoul. "Well, when the gems are down and times are tough, I have discovered Olivia comes through. It's like she shines and doesn't even know it. I would follow her into anything, without hesitation...now knowing what she is capable of."

"Even though the Southern Kingdom sent raw recruits to help, it was welcomed help. And for Olivia to bring back...a what? Chimera?" Waldron claps his hands in excitement. "Who would have ever thought of that? And how did she even get that to happen?"

"Olivia did! She is full of surprises, I guess."

"That's right. She had an idea that could help that the rest of us never could have done."

"Yep, that is her. Reacting to a situation just like..." His voice trails off in a sad thought.

Waldron furrows his eyebrows, curious to know what he is thinking. "Like?"

Olivia has worked her way to the door to hear better. She has stopped shaking and wipes tears from her face.

"Just like Abigail...She tries so hard to be like Abigail that she doesn't know her own strengths. She needs to know it is her overcoming these challenges, not someone else."

"You are right. Yet, I suppose attempting to do what Abigail does offers Olivia motivation to do what is needed of her."

A little smile forms on Olivia's face.

Klinksly taps his foot against a cut log. "Why did you help her...You know...with the sword."

"It may not make sense now...or ever for that matter...but she needed to be the one to end it. Not just for us, but for herself, too," Waldron's voice becomes somber.

"What do you mean?"

"I can see she blames herself for causing all this mess." Waldron stops for a second or two, looking into the window and noticing Olivia's shadow has moved near the door. "No one is responsible for another one's actions. So she needed to be the one to finish him and stop this petty madness. For her own wellbeing."

"Wellbeing? That was really hard for her. I didn't think she could do it."

"Deep inside, she knew it had to be done. In time, she will heal. If she had not done it, it may have eaten away at her—not ending Klatzz and the evil he would have spread."

Klinksly remains silent, frowns, then lets out a breath of relief, shaking his head.

"I may be wrong. I don't know her like you do. None of this makes any sense right now... Hopefully it will later. But the main thing is Olivia came through and saved Mushroom Cove."

Klinksly looks up at him. "Yes. She did that."

Olivia has been listening to them talk. She understands now how others see her. *Why is it so easy for Abigail to do things like this? Why do I feel so terrible? I did go get help, didn't I?* She smacks her forehead. *What was I thinking, getting a chimera?*

The fireplace inside the cabin is dimming. Waldron grabs a few logs. "Do you mind getting the door?" Klinksly reaches for the door, but it swings open as Olivia pulls on it. She holds it open for the two to come in. She pivots her head, wipes away the last tears, and sniffles. Klinksly and Waldron purposefully pay no attention and focus on stoking the fire. Olivia closes the door and feels a thump.

"Oww."

Olivia opens the door again, and there is Young Adam, holding Arthygus. She pulls her hands to her chest and taps her feet, worry in her eyes. "Ooo. Sorry. What is wrong with him?" She steps back from them.

"He's okay. The young so-called wizard used too many spells and passed out." Klinksly laughs, trying to lighten the mood.

Arthygus tries to hold himself up in front of her and smiles. "I'm okay, really. Just took some energy out of me." Adam sets him down on a chair.

Olivia frowns. "I could have gotten you killed. It would have been all my fault." She puts her hand on his shoulder; the touch is most welcomed by him. Olivia feels the urge to run and to be alone, like Abigail does. She turns to go out the door. Coming out of the darkness on the left are Prince Trajan and his soldiers. Some are holding torches now so they can see. On the right are the remaining gnomes. She stops with nowhere to go.

Klinksly's little hand grabs hers, and he holds his short sword at them. "It doesn't matter if you blame us for taking Skeel's sword, she gave it to me as a gift...A gift I will treasure for as long as I live. It is special to me. And now it has more meaning to me as she prevented Klatzz's attack on Mushroom Cove. So go ahead...blame us if you must. It's over."

The gnomes take their hats off and use both hands to hold it. Glambell steps forward. "Yeah, we know. We blamed you. But seeing what you did to save our kin at Mushroom Cove... You really do care." All the gnomes bow to her and hold their hats out.

Klinksly whispers to her. "That is a great honor, what they are doing."

Olivia runs up to Glambell and lifts him up. She squeezes his little face against her chest, and his arms fling outwards as he drops his hat. She hugs him tight. "I've always cared...Thank you." She sets him down. Glambell's face is red with a grin. She walks back to Waldron, who is standing in his doorway.

"Will it... Will this feeling go away?"

Waldron stares at her, holding her hands. "For those that care...Never," he whispers. "It only eases with time."

After a few minutes, Prince Trajan steps up. "Do you need us to stay here tonight?"

Glambell looks at the chimera stretching its front paws out behind the cabin. "Nah, I think they got it covered."

"Then, if you can, Olivia, will you do your spell to allow us to take the wounded back home?"

Olivia, still feeling confused and remorseful, nods. Helping the wounded takes her mind off of what just happened. She reaches into her pouch to get the spell ready.

"I will go with you," Klinksly says.

Waldron looks at the weary soldiers. Some are still shocked that they are alive. The prince has a disheartened look about him. He steps out of the front porch and gets their attention. "Listen, there is no glory in battle. Only those that survive will carry the guilt of remembering what has happened here today. But...you should be proud of yourselves. All of you." Waldron turns behind him and points to Adam and Arthygus. "Everyone played a part in the victory tonight." He steps out closer to the soldiers. "I have heard of the bravery and discipline of the Southern Kingdom soldiers." He points at them. "And I saw that from you."

The soldiers' spirits rise, and they smile at each other. Waldron walks up and shakes Prince Trajan's hands. "You survived. Don't look at this as a failure in any way. You...We were outnumbered and overcame these odds of declaring victory. Use this skirmish as a lesson."

"You said you are a knight of old. Where are you from? Your allegiance?" Trajan asks.

Waldron steps back. Everyone is silent, waiting for an answer. He has a lopsided grimace, thinking of what to say. He never spoke of it until recently; Abigail and Olivia only recently found out who he was. Glambell approaches him, but Waldron waves him off.

Olivia steps out. "Does it really matter? He has helped Klinksly and I in the past. Saved us really. And that's why we came back."

"Alright, but I still would like to know," Trajan pushes.

Waldron waves the ones with torches to move closer. He loosens his leather armor and pulls the shirt down that covers his heart. For the first time in decades, Waldron feels a sense of pride in what he is about to say. He clears his throat and pulls down the shirt farther, revealing the white crescent moon with the wavy blade through the center. It has an unnatural reflection; in the torchlight, it almost sparkles white. "I am a Knight of Muun."

"That can't be?" a soldier says.

"I thought they were all gone?" another one says.

"Hey, I thought you hunted witches?" asks another.

The rest question among themselves. Olivia comes to his side. "Despite what you think you know or have heard in tales, the real knights have been deceived by a hidden truth. Waldron is a Knight Protector. So named by the new witch queen, Abigail."

Before anyone can speak, a faint white glow comes from the tattoo on Waldron. The wavy blade becomes straight before their eyes. Everyone is shocked, and in awe, including Waldron. He holds it open for another minute for all to see, then closes his shirt.

Prince Trajan steps up to Waldron, shakes his hand, and raises it. "Without his leadership and determination, we may not have been as successful here today. Waldron is a friend of the Southern Kingdom; I decree it!"

The troops make the southern roar much louder this time.

Olivia puts her hand on Waldron's heart. "I have to believe the tales are true, and this was Muun's way of saying they are. If so, then what lies were spread that we needed to be hunted, and by who? What does the straight blade mean?"

Waldron holds her hand and then lowers it. He curls his lips with no answer.

"Can you open the door spell so I can get my troops home?" Trajan asks.

Olivia nods and looks through the window at Arthygus resting on the chair. "He and Adam can stay behind to rest. I will watch over them," Waldron says with his calm voice.

Olivia stares at the chimera resting behind the cabin. She thinks, *Rest. I'll be back shortly.*

Glambell shakes Trajon's hand and smiles. Prince Trajan was the last to leave through the tree door spell. Adam watched from the porch as the gnomes all wave goodbye and leave to go tell the news that Mushroom

Cove was saved. Arthygus is asleep in the chair. Waldron walks past both of them and closes the door to his little bedroom. Adam sits at the table beside Arthygus and reads through his book to learn more.

He slides a small coffer chest out from under his bed. His hand slowly wipes away decades of dust from the top. With a swipe of his thumb, the latch comes unlocked with a reluctant click. The lid opens with a creaking of the rusted hinges. He stares at the rich red fabric of a well-folded cloak. He pulls back the first fold and there is a fine brooch of the crescent moon and sword. The moon has fine diamonds along its length, and the sword is made from silver.

He removes the cloak and sets it aside. Beneath it is a very light and exceptional chain-mail armor. It was made by the elves from a special alloy. Hardened like steel and light like leather. It still has its shine to this day. The last remaining clothing is gray leather pants.

Waldron lays them out on the bed. *I thought I did wrong. I have done wrong. But what are you trying to tell me must now be done? What is coming? Who is coming?*

*****

Klinksly is the last to exit the oak tree in the darkened courtyard. A few soldiers tell the nighttime guards to get the healers. The injured comrades are laid on the ground. Minutes pass before the healers come rushing out with small bags. Commands are immediately given to help carry the worst injured soldiers inside. Others are encouraging them to hang on, stay awake. The confused soldiers walk around in a daze, trying to process what happened, dragging their weapons behind them. A few others are reenacting what they did to the courtyard guards that look on. A flurry of light post boys sprint out to light the lanterns along with the light crystals.

Olivia and Klinksly remain at the tree. Olivia has her arms crossed, chewing on her fingernail, watching them. Klinksly notices her eyes narrow and become moist.

He reaches for her hand. “It’s not your fault.”

“I know...But why do I feel responsible, Klinksly?”

Klinksly is slow to respond. “Because you care.” He holds her hand to comfort her.

They watch Prince Trajan help with the wounded and those in a daze by getting them to sit. He orders guards to tend to them. A large door opens; four royal palace guards step out followed by King Rashaad. The guards are wearing polished steel chest plate armor and have shields semi hiding the king. Rashaad is dressed in red silk sleeping garments and has thrown a sliver robe over them to ward off the cold of the night.

King Rashaad steps from the guards against their instructions and heads towards Trajan. “Son. You have returned.” His smile turns to a frown as he tilts his head. He has noticed the lack of soldiers. “Really, Trajan? You lost half our soldiers? Or are they left behind?”

What Trajan has experienced in battle, and his father’s tone, finally sets him off. He throws his arms apart in anger. “Really, Father? That’s the first thing that comes to mind?” He gives a hug gesture. “Not oh, hey glad you are back and safe. What happened?”

King Rashaad is taken aback by Trajan's attitude. “Not here, boy.”

“Oh, not here? Now I’m a boy? Then why did you send a boy to do an experienced man’s job? Tell me, Father!”

Rashaad's voice becomes more vocal with anger. “I thought I could trust you to do the job...I see I was wrong.” His voice of disappointment echoes throughout the courtyard.

Trajan turns his back on him. Everyone is watching and is silent. He turns around, points his finger at his father and calmly says, “I still remember the stories that you told me of your first time in battle. How you had generals and officers help guide you. How you had rows and rows of experienced and well-trained soldiers to defeat the orc hordes decades ago.”

Rashaad stands there, crossing his arms. Trajan holds his hands out and pounds his fist into his hand. His voice booms over the courtyard.

“We had none of that! We were outnumbered twenty to one, or maybe even thirty to one.” He throws his hands up in the air. “I’m not really sure how many dead creatures there are!”

“So we got worthless information. I see why it was smart to retreat then." Rashaad reaches out to touch Trajan's shoulder. He smacks his arm away.

"Worthless?! No, Father, you got this all wrong. There was no way of telling what we were up against until it was happening. Those gnomes had no more time to report what was coming. Wererats, hundreds of goblins, orcs, bugbears, two hill giants... and Klatzz the wererat king himself, riding a giant rat the size of a draft horse!"

"Well, you survived by retreating."

"Survived?!" Trajan laughs. "I got my ass kicked. If it wasn't for a young wizard and an acolyte, I would be dead." He holds up Klatzz's sword that gleams a dark blue. "If it wasn't for Levi grabbing Klatzz's sword, I would be dead. The soldiers used it to get the dozen wererats off of me. Did you know normal weapons couldn't harm them?" He smacks his forehead. "I sure didn't! That would have been useful knowledge going into a battle!"

King Rashaad's eyes reflect the blue of the blade. "So...you didn't retreat then? You killed Klattz?" he says with pride.

"Retreat! I'll have you know that, not one!" He points his finger in his father's face. "Not one of our soldiers thought of retreating! Even when getting ripped apart by the giants. We could have, but no! If it wasn't for the gnomes being as brave as they were, Olivia causing an enormous distraction, and that old knight of Muun guiding us..." Trajan walks away from his father and looks at Klinksly and Olivia by the tree.

"No, Father, we did not retreat. We rallied and overcame the odds. And now I know how little you expect of me." He walks towards the open doors. He stops and turns to his father. "Besides...it was Olivia that killed the wererat king... not me." He walks into the darkened hallway.

Klinksly approaches King Rashaad. The royal guards watch him closely. "Your Majesty, if I may?"

"Are you from Mushroom Cove?"

Klinksly removes his flat top hat, holding it with both hands. "No. Olivia and I helped during the battle. Not telling you what to do, but you need to listen instead of assume."

Rashaad's supercilious gaze through half-lidded eyes causes the gnome to rethink what needs to be said. "Come now?" he says in a low tone.

"We were unprepared. Your men were not ready for a battle like this...But you need to hear it from Prince Trajan. For now, you need to console your troops. I expect Farlan Darby will visit soon and show his gratitude for saving Mushroom Cove." Klinksly winks at him. "After all...that was the goal, correct?"

Rashaad stares at the little gnome. He nods. "Perhaps you are right."

Klinksly takes a few steps back, bows, and puts his hat back on. "The prince never once gave up. Even under the dead bugbear he crawled out of and pile of wererats trying to tear him limb from limb."

King Rashaad watches Klinksly walk over to Olivia. He then turns to his troops and shakes each one's hand, congratulating them on a job well done.

Klinksly grabs Olivia's hand. "Time to go."

Olivia wipes her moistened face. Blood from various creatures, people, and who knows what still covers parts of her face and body. It smears across her cheeks, giving her a savage appearance. She wonders if the soldiers will be okay. Her thoughts of Abigail enter her mind again. *If she was here, she could heal them. Oh, Abigail, we are trying to find you.*

Klinksly has Olivia open the tree door. They saunter hand in hand to the Snowcap Keep pine tree that has become all too familiar lately. Olivia scoops fresh fallen snow in the night. The cold feels refreshing as it melts in her hand.

They don't bother knocking. Instead, they open the door and walk inside. Olivia stands looking around, not knowing what to do.

"Great, you're back," Mr. Blaine says, walking around the corner with an opened book in his hands. He looks up and pauses in his steps, squinting at them with perplexed eyes. "And what happened to both of you?"

Olivia speaks with a defeated voice. "I killed the wererat king...Do you have a heated cleaning tub?"

"You what?" Mr. Krew says from the other room.

"Yes, we do, Miss Olivia. Fourth door on your right. Go downstairs," Mr. Blaine instructs. He watches her the whole way with a curious expression. His finger never leaves the page he was reading since the unexpected interruption.

Mr. Krew enters the hallway to see a very bloodied and dirty Olivia walk by with a ghostly expression. She disappears behind the door. Klinksly waves both of them into the library to explain what happened.

When they are about to sit, the front door opens, and they hear Mayreea. "That's it. I got sand everywhere." She storms past the library entrance and stops. She walks in to give Mr. Blaine a kiss.

"I'm okay. I'm going to the cleaning tub." She looks at Klinksly. "And you two had the simple task." She walks out into the hallway, still talking to herself. "Just go and visit the witch of curses, they said." They know better than to ask when she was in one of those moods. They hear Abbot Garret laugh. "I have sand in places I didn't even know I could get sand in."

Abbot Garret stands in the hallway, sand dripping from his clothes. He gives an awkward smile. "Is there a place I could...clean up?"

Mr. Krew, Mr. Blaine, Klinksly, and Abbot Garret exchange what happened with them. Everyone was silent when Klinksly was telling his tale about the battle. Of what Olivia did and what happened with Waldron. And the last part about meeting King Rashaad and the argument with his son.

They were also quiet, listening to every word coming from Abbot Garret and what they dealt with. The sand creature that almost killed them, Jomana, giant scorpions, the dragon, and the curse.

Mayreea strides her fingers through her long hair, shaking the sand out of it. She walks down the stone steps and doesn't realize the dim yellow light crystal is already lit and the tub is bubbling. The large tub room has gray and black stone walls. Wood knobs protrude from the stone to hang clothing on. She slips out of her dress and sand flings onto the floor.

She dips her foot into the tub and slides in. To her surprise, she is startled to see a bloody Olivia sitting there with her knees in her chest and arms covering them. Olivia's eyes stare into a distance that is not there again.

"Olivia? I'm sorry. I didn't mean to interrupt you." Mayreea is about to get up to leave when she sees Olivia's moist, swollen eyes slowly move to meet hers.

"What is it? What's wrong?"

Olivia lifts her head and sighs. Mayreea can see all the scars from the past rat encounters she had and now fresh injuries also. "Olivia...Who...or what has done this to you?"

Olivia doesn't smile. She should have felt comfort in someone asking what is wrong, but she feels nothing. Mayreea notices this.

"How about I tell you what Garret and I just went through and what we found out about the curse?"

Olivia nods, slips into the water up to her chin, and listens to Mayreea's tale.

14

Deceptive Practices

A bright flash brightens Tyrees' darkened room while he relaxes in a chair. Seconds later, a thunderous boom screams through the open window. He expects the wind to pick up soon, followed by the rain. He watches as the dark storm covers the setting sun. *This is a sign that my time has come,* he thinks to himself.

The door creaks open as Brak and Brace sneak in. A splinter of lightning cracks in the distance, and they notice Tyree sitting in the chair. A slight cool breeze blows the curtains aside.

"The time is right, boys."

If Brak and Brace could see each other in the darkness, they would see each other's mischievous grin.

"We're really going to Skylar Castle?" an excited Brace asks.

"What are we getting?" Brak whispers.

Tyree gets out of the chair and grabs a small sack. He slings it over his shoulder. A closer flash of lightning brightens the room and reveals Tyree's sly smile. "You got what you need for this...expedition?" A louder crackle and boom shake the window.

The boys lean inward at each other and do a silent slap of the hands. Tyree leads them downstairs and out into Keskella City. The storm is approaching quickly as they scurry through the cobblestone streets leading to Skylar Castle. They can feel the temperature dropping quickly. The stone and wood buildings are a mix of colors and sizes. Most are two stories tall, while others are as high as five. Homes are intertwined with small businesses and eateries along the way.

Most of the way, shops have closed except for a few taverns, alehouses, and inns. Brak and Brace peer into shop windows as they walk by, noting anything to get into later. This is holding Tyree up. The flash of lightning and rumbles of distant thunder echo through the alleyways of Keskella.

Tyree grabs both of the boys by the collars and whips them into a dark alley with no one seeing them. "Listen, we don't have time for useless thievery. We have a brief window to get what I need. Understand?"

"Yeah, yeah, we know," Brack says.

His tone makes Tyree angry. "I'm giving you the opportunity to show me!" He points his finger at himself. "Me! What you can do." He pokes his finger in Brak's chest. "This is the grownup world now...Can you prove to me I made the right choice in choosing the both of you for this task?"

Tyree pushes them against the wall. "Or should I just kill the both of you now and be rid of your incompetence?" Tyree pulls the red book slightly from his pocket.

The boys' eyes bulge at the site of the book. A flash of the vision they had of themselves burning enters their mind. Brak is the first to talk. "Okay, okay." He holds his hands up in a stopping motion. "We get it. We were just having fun."

"Fun?" Tyree's harsh tone shows them he is not kidding.

"We get it now." Brak straightens himself and a twisted demeanor overcomes him. "So what is it you need us to do? Because without telling us, we won't know how to prepare or...how serious this is." He gives Tyree a friendly elbow tap and a wink. Brace follows Brak's example.

Tyree can see the difference in them; he steps back and pushes the book back into his pocket with one finger. He squints at both of them, looking from head to toe. "Now that is more like it. I guess that is in order."

Another flash of lightning splinters across the night sky. Tyree looks down the alley quickly. Shadows of wooden crates line the sides along with boxes of garbage. A few light drops of rain sprinkle here and there. The thunder echoes eerily through the alleys and streets again.

Tyree grins. “We are going to Skylar to retrieve my family heirlooms that prove I’m the rightful heir.”

The boys glance at each other with a smile of joy. “We are actually going to the castle?”

“Yes. You will need to go to the second floor and retrieve my scepter, a book, and staff.”

“What? How?” Brace asks.

“I will tell you when we get there. For now, we need to move along. Stay quiet and don’t draw attention to yourself.” Tyree’s eyes demand to be followed. “Now...follow but stay about thirty or fifty feet behind me. Got it.”

The boys nod their heads and excitedly rub their hands together. Tyree leaves first and a few seconds later, the boys vacate the alley. The light rain falls more steadily with the cool wind blowing leaves and little trash around.

A figure approaches from the dark seclusion of the alley, where Tyree and the boys previously were. It is a Keskella guard dressed in a brown leather vest and cloth pants with a white and light blue tunic draped over it. He carries a small sword to his side. The brown-bearded man's eyebrows raise, and he grinds his teeth. “Not on my watch,” he whispers to himself, and he quietly draws his blade.

A black-gloved hand reaches out from the darkness behind him, covering his mouth, while a wavy-bladed dagger slices through his throat. The guard’s gurgles are muffled, and he is dragged into the gloom of the alley. Tyree walks on without concern, knowing he has Gullen Mull following them to deal with anyone’s suspicion.

Wind-driven rain has forced most people inside. The streets are empty but for a few city guards here and there. They are taking shelter under porches or inside opened tavern doors. Almost every one of them watches Tyree and the boys scurry by.

“I should have left earlier.” Tyree shrugs and smiles like a fool at each of the guards.

The rain becomes heavier along with the wind. Lightning is now flashing and cracking at the same time. Tyree continues on with the boys in tow. They meander through the alleys and streets. At the edge of town, they come across many elm and beech trees. They are spread out in three neatly organized rows.

A thirty-foot-tall stone wall, adorned with tapestries and vines, stands behind them, encircling the colossal limestone castle. The castle is built on a tall slab of granite that is amazing in itself. At a thousand feet in diameter and three hundred feet almost straight up out of the ground, the castle looms above the landscape, watching everything.

Lightning slices through the sky in front and behind the Skylar Castle. The reflective silver and white of the limestone walls glow in the illuminating flash. Brak and Brace stand there with jaws open at the wonder of how tall the castle is.

"That's right. Take it all in. But let's get a better view." Tyree looks around and chooses a three-story building that has a darkened room on the third floor. They make their way to the building that has two smaller leafless maples in front of it.

Tyree has Brace sneak up and look into the window. He sees two small glow crystals in a far room. There is a man getting the fireplace ready with a stack of wood beside it. Brace comes back. "Just some guy in there busy with starting a fire."

Tyree looks up, and no light appears from the second and third floor. He pulls out a small gold wire that is bent in a loop about the size of his pinky. Attached to it is a three-inch leather string. He grins at the boys. "Keep up with me." He walks over to the side of the building and looks around to make sure no one is watching.

"Levitoida." The gold wire sparkles, then fades. Tyree grabs the side of the building with one hand and pulls himself up. He lifts off the ground and up he goes to the third floor in seconds, hovering beside the wall. He comes to a window and stops.

"Well, that looked easy," Brace says.

"I guess he wants us to go up there?" Brak asks.

They both nod at each other and climb the outside of the building.

It takes two minutes before they get to Tyree. He is standing in the air waiting for them to open the window. Brak feels around the window and pulls out a small file and pick from his side pocket. The window lock clicks, and he slowly opens the window.

Lightning flashes near and rattles the building as Brak slips in. His hand sticks out and waves them in. Brace climbs in, followed by Tyree. He slowly floats down on the floor without a sound on the wooden floor.

Luckily, this is a storage room they snuck into. Brace makes sure the door is locked and that no one is outside the door. "It seems empty, but we must not make a sound." At that moment, Brak bumps into a small wooden crate and knocks it off a table.

Tyree catches it before it hits the floor. He carefully puts it back with his jaw clenched and squinting at Brak. Brak carefully walks to the center of the room, away from everything.

Tyree lets the moment go and has them come to the opened window. He reaches into his pocket and pulls forth a green book. "This was handed down by my father, and his father, and so on." He flips through pages. "Here it is," he whispers.

He pulls a small yellow glow crystal from his pocket to shed the faintest of light onto the page. "On the second floor, there's a room called the Ambassador Room. It is immediately straight across from the stairs that you will go up."

Tyree strokes his fingers across the page, tracing the outline drawing of the room. His mind races back to the memory of what his father said when he handed him the book. *"In this book contains the secret location of our heirlooms that were hidden before our family was wrongly evicted from this kingdom. It may be you or your son or your son's son. Whenever the time is right to reclaim the throne, these objects will give the Mire family the right to once again rule Skylar."*

"It is my time, and no one else's." Tyree's pretentious tone makes Brak and Brace glare at each other.

"Can you describe the room and where to find them?" Brace asks.

"The Ambassador Room is where the representatives of each so-called kingdom of today meet. Every year they gather to discuss meaningless politics." Tyree grinds his teeth. "With me as king, there will be no need for that any longer."

Another lightning flash hits nearby with a thunderous clap. This snaps Tyree out of his vain thinking. "The room should be all gray with a white stripe halfway up the wall and a light blue stripe near the ceiling. There should be a statue of a man holding a book and a teapot in the left corner facing in."

"Statue? Teapot? That's odd," Brak comments.

"Rumors had it that a wizard was turned to stone by accident from his own methods. It is a reminder of something, blah, blah, blah. Who cares? Either way, above him, in the corner, is a secret panel. Slide it to the left, then right, then left again and push."

"Should it open?" Brace asks.

"Yes. Inside, there should be a small silver scepter. That is the most important item I need. There should be a blue book with gold trim. Then there is the staff. It should be made of wood and bone. I'm not sure what it looks like. Bring these items to me."

Brak and Brace lazily smile at each other. "You're not coming?" Brace asks.

"How are we to get in there unnoticed?" Brak adds.

Tyree smiles and puts his hands on their shoulders. "Boys, I do not have the talent you do. I will slow you down."

Their eyes gleam at the recognition.

"I will use an invisibility spell on both of you. That will make the job easier."

Their smiles could not be any bigger. They both rub their hands together in excitement.

"This is very important. Once I cast the spell on you, you will not be able to see each other. You can still hear and make noise. So you will still have to be stealthy."

"What happens if we get separated?" Brace asks.

"Don't."

"How?" Brak chimes in.

"You figure it out. Now there should be enough time to remain invisible to get in, get the items, and leave undetected."

"Will the items turn invisible once we grab them?" Brak asks.

Tyree grins. "Good question. I'm pleased you asked. Yes. Anything you pick up will disappear, and anything you lay down will become visible. And most important. If you hit anyone or take an action against someone, the spell will end and you become visible where you stand...Instantly."

They nod their heads in sync and speak at the same time. "And that would be a bad thing."

"Good. Now that is out of the way, stand there while I cast the spell." Tyree pulls out a thin string of spiderweb, gum arabic, and a drop of clear water. He twirls them together in a ball in his hands. "Katoaa sivustolta."

The ball glows a faint blue light. It then fades into his hands. He touches Brak with one hand and Brace with the other. Their images fade from sight.

"You feel anything?" Brace asks.

"No. I feel normal," Brak answers.

"Same here."

"Alright, time to go. Do your thing." Tyree steps aside from the window. The wood creaks a little as Brak steps out first.

"Hey, what if the statue is not there? It has been a while, right?" Brace asks.

Tyree shakes his head. "If it is there or not, just go to the far left corner."

"Oh, should we meet you back here?"

Tyree lets out an impatient sigh. "Yes, or I will find you near the wall. Now go."

Brace climbs down the wall to the ground. "Brak...you there?" he whispers.

"Yes, over here."

The two work their way through the first two rows of elms and beech trees in the steady, cool rain. Brak walks into the open and emerges from the third row of trees. The rumble of thunder echoes across the open plains, along with another flash of lightning.

"Brak...Psst."

"Brace? Over here."

"Where?"

"By the wall." Brak shakes a vine to get his attention."

"Oh."

Brak notices an outline of Brace crouched over in splashing rain. "Brace...are you sneakin'?"

"Huh. Aren't you?"

"No. I walked down in the open because I'm invisible. Duh."

"Oh yeah, no, I'm not sneakin."

"Sure you are."

"This feels weird not having to sneak," Brace comments.

"Yeah, it does." Brak giggles. "It sure is fun. Let's go over to the gateway to get on the other side."

"Don't we want to climb the walls so we won't be seen?"

"Why take the chance? We are...in...visible."

"Oh, yeah."

They walk along the wall till they come upon the gate. The large wooden doors are closed, save for the guard entrance. The two sneak past the three guards. Two of them are sleeping, and the other is reading a book under an oil lamp. When they get to the other side of the room, they carefully open the door and slip out.

The guard's eyes shift towards the door. "Damn wind." He gets up from the table to shut the door. His eyes peer out into the darkness of the night and see nothing but rain. He closes the door and locks it. Brak and Brace were standing in front of him, standing still.

"Guess the spell works," Brace says.

"Yeah, we could have used this a long time ago," Brak whispers.

"Imagine all that we could have done with it."

"Imagine what we *are* going to do with it," they say at the same time. Brak and Brace are smiling and rubbing their hands together but cannot see each other doing so.

They begin the long walk up the carved stairs into the slab of granite. Along the way, every hundred feet, is a figure carved into the wall. Most are men, but there are also women, dwarfs, gnomes, elves, and one of a dragon. Draperies of past times hang alongside them.

The lightning illuminates the glistening wet statues and makes them look like they move. “I wonder who they were?” Brace ponders.

“Probably important people from long ago.” Brak rubs his fingers across one, admiring the stone carving.

Lightning streaks like a spider’s web across the nighttime sky, and the rain remains steady. They make it to the top of the stairs. Two rows of tall oak trees guide them to the front gate that is a hundred feet away. The trees are small compared to the towering castle that looms over them.

Brak’s voice can barely be heard. “I knew the castle was huge, but not like this.”

They walk down the center, admiring the castle. The ground is lit by another flash of lightning. They briefly notice the stone beneath them. Huge polished stone squares of gold, gray, white, and light blue, are aligned in a crisscross pattern to the gate. Twelve-foot-tall black iron bars hold white light crystals every twenty feet on each side as they walk towards two massive wooden doors.

The doors themselves have magnificent carvings of places of Esalon, from the mountains in the north to the western woodlands. The southern rolling hills and plains to the eastern shores are represented as well in the carvings. In the center is a raised carving of Skylar Castle.

Brak marvels at it. “It’s like an entire map of Esalon.”

Brace rubs his fingers across it, studying the layout, and whispers, “Neat. But how do we get in? I mean, this is a gigantic door. Surely someone will notice it opening up.”

At that moment, a smaller door opens up alongside the stone wall. A young castle guard steps outside. He is wearing a more formal outfit, being inside the castle. The pants are a medium blue along with the silk shirt. The tunic is the same blue except for the white tree and bird wing design. He looks around before a grungy voice inside yells at him.

“Burgman! Shut the door and come back in.”

Brak whispers, "Quick, slip in the door." They both hustle to the door. Brace slips in as the guard's hand misses Brace's backside reaching for the door handle.

They step into a large grand entrance way and stop immediately to marvel at what they see. A room that is a hundred feet wide and the same length. The polished white marble floor has gold and black veins throughout in all directions with no seams. The white walls are adorned with huge, framed paintings of cities, towns, and landscapes throughout Esalon.

The scents of sandalwood and cherry tobacco blend in the warm air. Scent pots hang from the far side of the room near a fireplace. Two night guards sit at a small table playing a card game near the guard door. They are dressed the same but have no weapons.

The light blue painted ceiling is fifty feet high, and a huge, curved staircase is to the right, leading up to the second-floor balcony. At the base of the railings are a gold griffin and a gold dragon. Both have their wings folded. The griffin has deep amber gems for eyes, and the dragon has emerald eyes.

Suspended from the ceiling are ten large white and blue light crystal chandeliers with the center one gleaming a gold color. Brak and Brace never saw a gold light crystal until now. They stare with their mouths open at it.

The walls are adorned with stunning carved stone statues of past kings and queens from the Skylar Kingdom. Between them are fine wooden display cases that are painted in gold leaf. The glass is clear and locked. In them are small trinkets, jewelry, and clothing of royalty from days of old. A few of them have a weapon in them, like a sword, mace, and even a bow. Stamped copper labels tell who they are.

Brace's curiosity has gotten the best of him, and he walks along with his hands behind his back so as not to touch anything. He passes an empty display case. The copper stamp reads 'King Evander Baran's sword...Sliver Brisg.'

The young guard shuts the door. "I was checking to see if any funny business was going on outside, that's all."

"Funny business?" The larger guard laughs.

"Well, to see if anyone was creeping," Burgman says.

The thinner ebony guard was about to take a drink but spit it out, laughing. The larger one lets out a bellowing laugh too.

"Creeping?!" the thinner one says.

"Listen, Burgman. This is, what, your first week here on night duty?" the larger one asks.

"Yes, sir. Albert, sir."

"There is no funny business going on. Hasn't been in decades. You have to be a master thief to get in here, and Keskella has none," Albert explains.

"Really?" Burgman asks.

"That's right. Even then, a master thief would know better than to sneak in here. With all the traps and all," the thinner guard says.

"Now come over and deal another hand." The guard Albert motions for him to sit, which he does.

Brak and Brace make their way to the stairs, each not knowing where the other is. When they get to the top, five more statues stare at them, each one a different dragon. Some have their wings spread and others have their mouths open.

"Psst," Brace whispers.

"What?" Brak whispers back.

"Just making sure you're here."

"Yeah, this place is amazing."

"Hey, there's the room."

"Where?" Brak asks.

"Where I'm pointing."

"Really? I can't see you?"

"Oh, yeah. That's right."

"Come on, let's go," Brak says.

They walk past the dragon statues when a lightning flash hits nearby with a thunderous boom, rattling a few windows. Brak and Brace both jump, reacting to the sound. They make it to the outside of the dark

Ambassador Room. The entrance is blocked by a blue rope at waist level with a small pole at each end.

When they step over the rope, it sways ever so slightly. The gray walled room has the white stripe halfway up the side and the blue one along the top. It is thirty feet long and twenty feet wide, with no windows. In the center is a long, dark brown oak table and chairs with gray and silver pillows. Along the wall are smaller paintings of mountains, pine forests, lakes surrounded by poplar trees, rolling grass-covered hills, and stormy ocean shores.

In the center of the room behind the table is the statue of the man holding a book and teapot.

"Brak, you there?" Brace whispers.

"Yeah," he whispered back.

"The statue is in the center."

"I see that."

"What do we do?" Brace asks.

"He said it was the left corner. I'm going to grab a chair, have you stand on it, and I will stand on your shoulders." He lifts the chair, and the pillow falls to the ground. They are motionless for a few seconds. Brak continues to the corner with the chair.

Brace climbs on the chair, and Brak feels for where he is then easily climbs him. As he balances on Brace's shoulders, he can hardly reach the ceiling trim. He pushes it, slides it, but nothing happens.

"What was it again? Left to right?" Brak asks.

Braces respond in the faintest of voices. "It's push, then left, right, left, and push it again."

Brak pushes hard, but nothing happens. He is still balanced on Brace's shoulders. He then tries pushing slightly and again, nothing happens.

"Maybe it's on the other left corner, you know, the one farther away from the entrance?" Brace suggests.

Brak slaps his forehead in disgust. "Of course. He did say the farthest corner. I'm coming down."

Brace quietly moves the chair to the other corner. Once again, Brace steps on the chair and Brak climbs on him. Brak applies pressure and the panel moves slightly. He pushes harder, and it pops the old paint seal with a cracking sound. They both freeze in caution and delight.

*****

Back at the table, two rounds of cards have gone by. Burgman throws a silver coin on the table, followed by the other two guards. He shuffles the cards, looking around, then pauses.

"What you doing?" Albert says.

"You wouldn't be cheating now, would you?" the thinner guard questions.

Albert smacks the other guard's shoulder. "Now, Hudson, how can he be cheating when we are winning?"

Hudson frowns. "Well then, what you staring at, Burgman?"

"There are wet footsteps on the floor going across the room."

"Well, yeah, you went out in the rain," Hudson says.

"Don't worry about it. The morning cleaners will take care of it. They always do." Albert adds. He takes another sip from his goblet.

"No, you don't understand." Burgman stands up, throwing the cards on the table. "I came straight over here." He forcibly puts his finger on the table. "Besides, there are two sets."

Albert and Hudson look over at the side entrance and they see two sets of wet footprints. "By golly, Burgman is right," Hudson says. The three of them follow them around the room till they lead them to the stairs. But they have now disappeared. The three of them slowly look up at the stairs.

"Ahh, you found em, now go check up there," Albert says.

Hudson and Albert turn to go back to the table. Burgman remains at the bottom of the staircase.

*****

Brak slides the three-foot long, ten-inch wide panel left till it stops. Then he slides it to the right till it stops, then back to the left. He pushes on the panel, and it falls into the ceiling.

"What's in there? Ooo, this is exciting." Brace wiggles, almost causing Brak to lose his balance.

"Keep it steady and quiet down. I'm not sure yet." Brak reaches his hand around and feels a thick stick. He pulls on it. It is long. Once he grasps it, it turns invisible. "This must be the staff." The staff is almost out when it gets caught. Brak feels around, and it seems the staff splits at the top. He can feel two sharp points and a cold gem or stone between them.

He wiggles it and it passes through, but he loses his grip on it. It bounces off Brace's head onto the floor with a loud clack and clattering, rolling to a stop.

Albert and Hudson stop and turn quickly with Burgman looking back at them. "Well, don't just stand there…Go check it out!" Albert yells.

"Ow. That hurt," Brace whines.

"Nevermind that, someone's coming." Brak reaches around inside the hideaway and grabs a cold metal tube and a leather book.

Brace turns to see the staff lying on the floor. In the darkness, he can tell something is reflecting light from the balcony at the split top of the staff. He leans slightly to get a better look when the chair leg snaps. Brak falls past him onto the floor. The metal scepter smacks the floor, cracking it. Brace falls against the table, causing it to screech across the floor.

Brak picks himself up, holding the book and scepter. "Quick, grab the staff and get to the door."

Brace grabs the staff, and it disappears in his hands. He stands there amazed for a second and feels a brush of air beside him. "Come on," Brak murmurs.

Brace takes a step over the broken chair. He takes a few steps with his back towards the entrance, looking for anything else to take. He turns around quickly to step over the rope but bumps into Burgman, who is standing there peering into the darkened room.

They both stand there for a second, not moving. Burgman speaks with a shaky voice. "Who…Who's there?"

Brace is only inches away from him and can feel his breath against his face. He reacts the only way he knows how. Brace turns the staff sideways and pushes the guard backwards. Burgman slaps the marble floor with the back of his hands and pounces up, terrified.

Brace's image shimmers as he becomes visible in front of the guard.

Brak is at the top of the stairs and looks back, stunned that he can see Brace standing there holding the staff. Brace's eyes widen at the sight of the staff. The top two feet are made from bone, with two small spiraling horns about six inches long each. In the center is a dark amber gem with black and olive green swirls in it. The bottom half is made from a twisting wooden vine. Three multicolored feathers are tied around the base of the tip with a copper string.

"Stop the thief!" Burgman shouts, approaching Brace.

Brace's instinct kicks in as he swings the staff from his right to his left. The staff impacts Burgman's side of his head, sending him to the balcony. Brace races over to prevent him from falling over. He grabs onto his tunic only for it to rip. Brace tries to grab his leg but is too slow. Burgman flips over the rail. There is an eerie silence. Not even a scream from the young guard as he flips and tumbles through the air.

Braces closes his eyes in disgust. Brak turns his head. Albert and Hudson are at the base of the stairs, watching him fall. A bone-breaking flop echoes throughout the room, followed by a loud gurgling cry.

"Get him, Hudson!" Albert yells and goes to check on Burgman.

Brak remains still as Hudson runs past him. Brace runs between the dragon statues and tries to open a door. He rattles it, but it won't open.

"Drop the staff now or—" Hudson warns but is cut off.

Brace sprints behind the dragon statues and out the other side, but Hudson beats him. He dives for Brace, but Brace pushes his head down and jumps over him. He makes it to the top of the stairs, only to see four guards coming up. Brace hears Hudson running up behind him and he ducks. This causes Hudson to fly over him and down the stairs, knocking over the four guards.

Brace knows he can't make it past them. He runs back to the door and kicks it with all his might. The door splinters open with the handle and lock remaining attached to the wall. A dark hallway appears. Brace is hesitant until he hears the guards coming up the stairs.

"Get him! Kill the thieving son of a bitch!" Hudson commands.

Brak sashays out the side door they came through. Brace runs down the darkened hallway with the staff in hand. He passes two doors on the left that are locked. The first door on the right opens as he slides by, trying to stop. The silhouettes of guards take up the hallway when he looks back.

Brace slams the door shut, locking it. A flash of lightning illuminates the room. "Great! A window." He slides a table over to barricade the door. Brace rushes to the window. He rubs his hands across it to discover there are no latches or hinges. "Damn!"

The door bangs as they pound against it. He frantically looks around for another escape but finds none.

Brak is midway across the lit entrance from the castle in the rain when he hears the breaking of glass from above. Shards fall from the wall and when they hit, the granite smash into smaller pieces. He stands there watching Brace exit the window a hundred and twenty feet high.

There's no way he can climb that smooth surface, he thinks.

"There's no way I can do this," Brace says, looking down the wet slick limestone side. He notices a small ledge halfway down. He slides the staff between his belt across his back. Brace retrieves thin strips of leather from his pocket that have small metal spikes sewn into them. He wraps them around his palms so the spikes will give him grip.

He's not? Brak thinks. A bell rings from within the castle. *You can do this*. Brak moves once again to the stairs to get away. He steps aside to allow a few guards to go by now and then.

From the edge of town, Tyree looks through a small handheld spyglass from the third-floor window. The extra lights have now gotten his attention. He spots one of the boys climbing out of the window with the staff on his back. "What have you done now? At least you have the staff."

Brace slides out the window, digging the spikes into any crevice he can find. He makes it about thirty feet when he hears the door shatter and men rush in. Hudson leans out the window. "There!" He points down.

"Faster. Must move faster," Brace says to himself. He slides a little as the spikes dig in, creating stone splinters that end up in his face. He stops with a jolt when his hands dig in.

"Get me the crossbow boys...I'm going to stick me a thief," Hudson says with a glorified tone.

"Oh come now, why would you do that?" Brace taunts.

Hudson leans back in and comes out with a loaded crossbow. He aims it at Brace. "Because I can." *Clank!* The stored energy of the crossbow thrusts the bolt forward. It misses Brace's head by a foot.

"Load it again!" Hudson gives the crossbow back.

Brace slides down and is losing grip. Hudson leans out farther this time. *Clank!* The bolt whizzes in front of Brace, hitting the wall and his hand. He pushes off the wall by mistake. His stomach feels like it is going to come out of his mouth. His jaw and eyes are open as wide as they can be.

Tyree watches the boy fall. "Please don't let the staff break. Land belly up." He loses sight of him when he falls behind the trees.

Brace flails his arms and legs in a desperate attempt to grasp onto something. He knows he is going to hit hard and die. He stops flailing his body and right before he closes his eyes, a pale pinkish red light glows from the feathers of the staff. Brace tilts his head and notices the feathers are glowing.

He begins to slow down and softly lands on his back like a feather falling from the sky. He takes a moment to consider what just happened and lets out an enormous sigh of relief. A yelling Hudson draws him back as to what is happening. A bolt shatters against the granite near him.

Brace stands and draws the staff from his back. He looks at it and kisses it. "Thank you, staff." Another bolt hits the stone floor closer to him. He sprints off towards the stairs but sees guards running in all directions. He has an idea. Brace walks out nonchalantly into the opening, pointing and shouting. "Over there! He's over there! Hurry now!"

Most of the guards are fooled, but two are not. Brace scuttles to the edge of the granite. He looks down, and it's over three hundred feet down to the bottom.

"Hey you! Thief, stop!" a guard yells. Those that ran past Brace turn to run back through the trees and crystal light pole. Brace turns around and waits until they are almost near him. He whips the staff around, smiles, and gives a gigantic wave of his hand while falling backwards over the cliff.

Brak is almost to the bottom of the stairs with about a hundred feet to go when Brace flies by him. “Woo hoo!” he screams.

“What the...” Brak said. Now he races down the stairs as he watches Brace float to the ground. By the time Brak gets to the bottom, Brace has already snuck past the guards at the wall and made his way through the three rows of trees.

The rain is still steady, and puddles have built up here and there. Brace remains near a tree as the lightning has become more distant. He swings the staff a little, admiring how light it is.

“I’m glad you didn’t break it,” Tyree says, startling Brace.

“Huh? What? Oh, it’s you.”

Tyree takes the staff from Brace. “And where is the other half?”

Brace rubs the back of his head. “Well uh, I’m not sure.”

“Not sure, huh? I saw you fall out the window. Is he still in there?”

“No. I’m right here.” They both look behind them and can see footsteps splashing in small puddles as Brak walks up to them. “Here you go,” he says cheerfully.

“Brak, we can’t see you,” Brace reminds him.

“Oh, right.” He grabs Tyree’s other hand and lays a book in it and a scepter. As he lets go, they become visible.

Tyrees grins. “They were there... Unbelievable. At last. They are in my possession.” Tyree slips the book and scepter into his pocket. He pulls out that small metal wand he used before. He makes a twirling motion, and a doorway opens up.

“Where you going?” Brace asks.

Tyree smiles. “Why, back to my room, of course.”

“What about us?”

“Night is still young. Find your own way back.” He looks behind him to see castle guards combing the area. He steps in the doorway and disappears. Before Brace can react, Brak pushes him into the portal, and they both slip in before it closes.

15

Necessary Undertakings

It has been two days since Olivia and the others have returned to Snowcap. An early storm has blanketed the area with snow. Mr. Blaine decided it was best not to leave Olivia alone and have someone remain with her. She had trouble sleeping, so Mayreea summoned a sleep spirit to help her rest for now.

Mr. Krew and Mr. Blaine deliberated on what to do about the curse but have no answers at the moment. Klinksly and Abbot Garret have nothing more to provide. After rummaging through piles of books and scrolls, a knock is heard on the front door in the early evening.

Mr. Krew opens it. There is a green cloaked, dirty man covered in snow and a woman in a fancy white and tan fur coat with the hood on and long white boots that are made for royalty. Klinksly is standing in the hallway with one eyebrow raised, tilting his head and staring at the odd couple.

"We bring news, Mr. Krew," the man said.

He waves them inside into the hallway. The woman gently lowers her hood. Her long brunette hair that was neatly tucked rolls out past her chest. Her light caramel brown eyes command respect. Klinksly stands mesmerized by her appearance.

The man's face remains partially hidden by the cloak's hood. The unshaven, pale skin, pointed chin, and pointed nose are all Klinksly can make out.

"What is worthy of this intrusion?" Mr. Krew asks.

The woman peers at the gnome, then back at Mr. Krew. "You know we only show up when important news needs to be said, Mr. Krew."

He nods. "Yes, you are correct. I did not mean any disrespect. I'm a little frustrated at the moment."

"When are you not?" the man quips. The woman smiles and giggles.

Mr. Krew frowns at him, and the man's demeanor changes instantly.

"Two days ago, before the big storm, someone snuck into Skylar Castle and stole a staff," the woman explains.

Mr. Krew nods, and his fingers press against his chin. "Anything particular about that?"

"The way the guards described the staff, it was the Pukahurith staff."

Mr. Krew rubs his chin. "Are you certain?"

"It was described as made with wood and bone and had two small horns at the top. It was said this staff was in possession of Rory Mire, the second generation ruler of the Mire family. The staff disappeared or was hidden. History does not tell."

"And now you say it has been found?"

"Not just found. But specifically stolen. They knew exactly where to get it and nothing else was stolen."

Mr. Krew puts his hands on his sides. "Interesting." He looks at the man. "And what news do you have that is so important that warrants you being here?"

He grins. "Back in Splinteroak, after the zombie incident. Rumors of a Shadow Sect follower was spotted."

"Shadow Sect? Impossible. They were eliminated by the Skylar Knights of old. That magic was banned a long time ago. You cannot tap into that portal any longer."

"Well, I'm not sure what to say, but the way he was tattooed up and the olive green cloak. Looked like one to Frederick."

"Is that so?" Abbot Garret questions them from behind.

"Yes, indeed, Mr. Krew. But that's not all. I was making my monthly rounds to Merchants' Pass. Garnet City soldiers are looking for somebody or a group that killed all the Banda Krada gang near Merchants' Pass."

"Tyree..." Mr. Krew mumbles.

"It has to be him," Klinksly agrees.

Mr. Krew looks back at the gnome. "How do we know these events are related to him?"

Klinksly taps his forehead, thinking. "We know he has the Book of Power in his possession. What it actually does, we don't know. So it would be foolish to push it aside. We know he has a map to Geemend's Seeker and is on his way to it. We know he thinks he is an heir to the throne and must have known about the staff's location from a past family diary or something. He is moving quickly with purpose. We cannot dispute those facts. What his end goal is...Well, that can be debated."

Mr. Krew stands motionless with a fixed gaze on Klinksly. His eyes pierce through any doubt that Klinksly has. "Mr. Blaine?! We need to meet this Waldron fellow now and get them under way...Then we head to Splinteroak."

Klinksly's eyebrows raise. "Uh, Splinteroak?"

Mr. Krew walks past the gnome and into the library. He comes out with two small bottles. "Here you go." He hands the woman and man each a bottle. He also puts a small pouch of gold coins in their hands. "Job well done. Keep eyes and ears out for any word of this Tyree fellow."

The two smile and walk out the door. Klinksly rubs his forehead. "Splinteroak? Why there? For what?"

Mr. Krew walks past him. "I want to look into this 'zombie' issue more closely."

Klinksly stands there, baffled at what is going on. "What about Olivia?"

"She will remain here...with Mayreea. Try to get her to sleep," Mr. Blaine says.

The four of them prepare for tomorrow's brief journey.

*****

Tyree enters his room, holding the newly acquired trophies. He rolls the staff back and forth in his fingers, looking over it. Before the light dissipates from the portal, Tyree is shoved by Brace, stumbling into him. Brak comes through as the portal closes.

"Whew! That was close," Brack says, clapping his hands. "Hey? I can see myself now."

"Of course you can, idiot. You took an aggressive action." Tyree shoves Brace away from him. He glimpses at the two, shaking his head. "I will give you credit for thinking about coming through the portal."

The two stand there soaking wet, dripping on the floor, looking like they are expecting something. Tyree is about to dismiss them harshly when a thought occurs to him. His mother always said to treat the help well because they are the first ones to turn on you.

Tyree lights an oil lamp on the end table. Most of the storm front has passed with little lightning happening now. He reaches into his overcoat pocket. Clinking of glass is heard as he feels around. He produces two small dark green vials about two inches tall.

"Here, take these for your troubles."

"What is it?" Brak asks.

"That potion will enable you to climb walls like a spider for a short time."

Brace's voice squeaks in delight. "Really?"

"Yes, the whole potion needs to be consumed, so use it when you need to. Now leave me be and go get some sleep."

The boys quietly take their prize and slip into the hallway. Tyree sets the staff on the table. He retrieves the scepter and book from his coat pouch that seems to hold more than normal. He undresses to get into something dry before sleeping.

Three hours go by and most of the town is dark and quiet except for the hypnotic raindrops hitting slate rooftops. He still occasionally hears and sees guards running about clueless, but he knows why.

A light knock comes from his door. Gullen Mull walks in.

"Ah, I see you made it. Anything happen tonight?" Tyree asks.

"A guard in the alley overheard you. It has been taken care of."

Tyree tilts his head back, looking at the ceiling. "Ah...good."

"I see the two were successful. I told you they're good."

"Good? Yes, I will admit it... I've been thinking. I have another task for you...If interested."

"What does that entail?"

"Back when we slept the night in that barn by the river?"

"Yes."

"And how the boy read about that other entry? Caden Tavish. Go and find out what that is all about. And if you find anything, take care of it. I want no other claimers...Understood?"

Gullen smirks. "There will be expenses and it may take time—"

Tyree throws a coin purse on the table that jingles when a few gold coins roll out. A coin spins, falling off the table. Gullen's hand catches it before it hits the floor.

"There is a thousand gold. Go when and where you need to. Meet me in Splinteroak in...say three months. Regardless if you have anything to report or not."

Gullen Mull pushes the coins back into the purse and zips it shut with the leather string. Tyree shows him the book so he can write names down. After a few minutes, he leaves. "I will see what I can do." Before he closes it, his eyes scrutinize him. "You really are on to something this time, huh?"

Tyree grimaces while raising his fist. "Ahh, just go." The door shuts quietly.

*****

The morning comes with the clouds parting. A good breakfast fills Klinksly's belly. He still holds a warm buttery biscuit in his hand while the three of them walk to a pine tree through the knee-deep snow. Mr. Krew wears his black dress suit with a thin silver cane. Mr. Blaine enjoys his dark blue dress suit with lighter blue stripes when he goes out on visits. Abbot Garret is once again in his dirty red robes.

The fresh fallen snow crunches beneath each step he takes. He stops in front of the tree and wipes snow from the side of the bark. "Alright, Klinksly. Take us to this Waldron fellow."

Klinksly opens the tree door spell. Little green sparkles flicker and spin differently than how Olivia casts the spell. The gnome guides them around Waldron's cabin. Sitting on the porch is Arthygus. His face lights up at the sight of Klinksly and the others.

"They're here." He tilts his head back and forth, smiling, looking for someone. "Is Olivia with you?"

Klinksly raises his finger and tries to speak. "Ahhh. Well."

"No, she is not, young wizard. She is back at Snowcap, resting. Now I need to see this Waldron fellow," Mr. Krew says.

Arthygus frowns and leans back in the chair, disappointed. "Oh."

Mr. Krew's long face shows no patience in the matter at hand. "Now would be most beneficial."

"Oh, of course." Arthygus stumbles out of the chair and opens the door. "Waldron, you have guests." He holds the door open for everyone to go in.

Inside the cabin is Young Adam explaining to Waldron of how he came across the Amulet of Eloton and mace that was once wielded by Miles Nicolas. They both pause when Mr. Krew and Mr. Blaine walk in.

Mr. Krew firmly asks, "Mr.Waldron, I presume?"

"Yes."

"Good. Have the young wizard or Adam explained to you why they came with Olivia?"

Waldron glances at Adam then asks, "Who are you?"

"You can call me Mr. Krew, and this is Mr. Blaine. You know the gnome already." He doesn't even turn around to look at Klinksly. He taps his cane on the floor in front of him and rests both hands across the handle. His long, aggravated face gazes at Young Adam, expecting an answer.

"Well, we didn't get th—"

Mr. Krew cuts him off with an authoritative tone. "Of course you didn't. So I'm here to do what Olivia failed to ask you."

"Hey! We were but—" Arthygus was cut off by Mr. Krew's hand.

Mr. Krew doesn't even look at Arthygus. "Listen up, you two. We now have new information and time is not on our side... Mr.Waldron...we need you to take Arthygus and Adam to Baladain."

Waldron chuckles. "I must've misunderstood you. It sounded like you said something else."

"You heard correctly; I said Baladain. I do not let people second guess at what I say or make subtle hints. I'm clear and precise in what I said. I will say it again, Mr.Waldron...We need you to take them to Baladain."

Arthygus steps around Mr. Blaine, pointing his finger in the air. "He is correct. That is why Olivia brought us to begin with."

"And why me?"

Arthygus is about to say, but Mr. Blaine beats him to it. "Look at them. You think they'd survive getting there? Much less being in there?"

Waldron leans back in his chair. "This is for not. That place can't be found."

"It has been found. The young wizard boy has shown us through a location spell," Mr. Blaine says.

"What is so important that you need to go... to this place?"

Arthygus speaks up. "There is a scroll we need to get before this Tyree guy gets ahold of it."

"If he does, it will be very bad for us all. You need to go now. Tyree is on the move and is farther along than we thought," Mr.Blaine says.

Mr. Krew's voice is firm and direct. "That's right, Mr. Waldron. I'm sure these two young boys can fill you in on the whys, how comes, and where's on the way. Will you get them there?"

Waldron thinks about going or staying. "The gnomes need my help more than these two. They can take care of themselves from what I have seen." Adam and Arthygus smile at the compliment.

Klinksly slips in between them. "It was Olivia that was going to ask you for your help, explain why it has to be you. But I don't know what she was going to say."

Waldron knows what she most likely would have said now being a Knight Protector. Deep inside, he feels his question was answered. "Alright, I will do it. Let me get ready. How close can you get us there?"

"Unfortunately, the location that was shown to us is on the other side of the Elven Kingdom. We can only get you close to Silver Birch City in the Woodland Kingdom."

"Why not to the edge of the Elven Kingdom? Pass that entirely?" Waldron asks.

"The Elven king, Vindblad, prevents witches from using any magic in his kingdom. We respect that law and don't get near his domain. Unless it is of the utmost importance. Even then, we need to ask permission to walk the paths to Smaragastré, the emerald tree."

"Hum. Alright then, I will need to pack more things." Waldron heads to his little room.

Young Adam asks excitedly, "We are going to the elf kingdom?"

"Presumably, that is the only way to meet the king." Mr. Krew's facial expression tells Adam he should not have asked it like that. "Getting him to grant passage is another thing entirely. Either way, this journey is very important. There is no room for failure." He walks out the door to give them privacy to pack. Mr. Blaine follows him out.

They walk around when the stench of death draws their attention uphill. They come across the hillside where the battle took place. The amount of dead goblins and bugbears is astonishing. The three walk around in silence.

"My story telling could never do what actually took place justice," Klinksly says. He points uphill. "That is where Olivia killed Klatzz."

"I'm at a loss for words," Mr. Blaine says.

Mr. Krew remains quiet as he makes his way to the dead king. Once there, the three of them stare at the decaying corpse.

Mr. Krew speaks with a faint voice. "No witch of a young age should ever have to endure such a traumatic experience as war. Especially our Olivia." He understands now what she went through. He taps Klinksly on the shoulder. "You did well to bring her back...safe. You are a worthy queen's attendant."

Klinksly stands there with his mouth open while the two walk back down the hill. "Was that a compliment? I will take it as one." He grins and follows them. Klinksly does not want to see this place again anytime soon.

"Come now, Klinksly, onto Splinteroak we go," Mr. Blaine calls.

While they are away, Abbot Garret sits down with Young Adam. "I was told all that you went through by the gnome...It seems you were chosen by Dianeeta for a purpose."

"Purpose? Why me? Surely there are others way more qualified than me to handle battle and direction. I sort of fell into place with them."

"Ahh, Young Adam. You still don't see. Look how you contributed to their success. Who knew a little boy that was dropped off to us by his parents would become a holy warrior with an ancient weapon and on a mission with others to stop evil."

Adam grins slightly, not knowing what to say.

"No more sweeping floors when you get back."

"Somehow, I'd rather be doing that now. It seemed peaceful and had immediately satisfying results."

Abbot Garret smiles and lays his hand on Adam's shoulder. "You are growing into a young priest, my friend. But I won't mislead you. Be careful with what you do and say. There are others that don't want the truth to be revealed. Find what you can, do your part, and come back to me safe. I have faith in you."

Adam puts his hand on Abbot Garret's shoulder too. "I will do my best. Thank you, Abbott Garret." They smile at each other, knowing it may be some time before they see each other again.

*****

Olivia wakes to find herself laying on a soft cool moss bed surrounded by a wall of darkness ten feet away from her. The croaking of frogs, along with the trickling of water, cuts the silence near the willow trees that surround her. Her feet sink into a warm pond that smells of algae. She should be alarmed but has no reaction.

Lying on her back, she gazes into the night sky, but she doesn't see any stars. Olivia pulls herself up onto her elbows. The frogs stop croaking and faded whispers begin.

"Hello?" Olivia says.

Whispers become voices to the point she can understand them.

It's all you...

Alone...

Why did you do it?

Olivia panics. "What? Who are you? Show yourself!"

A red glow comes from the darkness. Something thin and long pushes aside the hanging willow branches, and they disappear. Her father's saber comes into view, floating in front of her. The water, frogs, and moss are all gone, and she stands there in nothingness.

Why did you use me like that?

"What do you mean?"

You...Me... We kill so easily!

The bodies of men, women, orcs, and a few gnomes come into view out of the dark. Olivia's skin scrunches around her eyes while she watches an image of her swinging the blade in anger. The scene transforms from the battle to other places and times that have not happened yet.

She watches in horror as she kills a goblin with the saber but continues on cutting into people. Men, women, and even a child. The image of Olivia looks back at her with blood all over her face. *This is why you are alone... You can't be trusted...It is all your fault!* Her left hand holds the blade, and the right brings up Klinksly's decapitated head, while she laughs.

"Stop it! Stop it! Stooop it!" Olivia screams herself awake.

Mayreea rushes into the room after hearing the scream. Olivia is sitting up in the bed, pounding the mattress with her arms. She sits on the bed beside her. "Dear...What can I do to help?"

Olivia breathes heavily for a minute and stares at the wall, afraid of what she has become. She raises her knees to her chest and lowers her head to them.

"You don't want to talk about it?" Mayreea puts her arm around her for comfort. "It has been almost two days. You haven't eaten, you don't speak, and you are not sleeping."

Olivia continues to stare at the wall.

"I will summon a sleep spirit. That will help you sleep without dreams."

Olivia feels nothing. She is not sad, happy, comfortable, or afraid. She is tired and shrugs her shoulders at Mayreea. But she doesn't care if it works or not. Mayreea lays her back in bed and pulls the sheet up to her neck.

"What is going on with you? What happened out there?" She walks out of the room. "I will be right back. I need to get some of my scent oils for the summoning."

Olivia lays there, quiet and motionless. She can't rid her mind of the feeling of killing Klatzz. She can still feel the pulsing of his heart in her hand. His words still echo through her head about how she is a nobody. Now another thought occurs to her as Mayreea enters the room with a lit dark green candle.

Mayreea notices Olivia's eyes are opened wider. "What is it, dear?"

Olivia grabs Mayreea's arm with the candle, causing hot wax to spill on Olivia's arm. She doesn't even twitch. "I manipulated another creature to kill other creatures with my ability...What kind of twisted person does that?"

Mayreea lets out a sigh, calmly sets the candle on the end table, and removes Olivia's hand from her arm. "Olivia...you need to stop thinking like that. You are a kind-hearted person who was just pushed...Get some sleep now."

Mayreea rubs a little mix of mint and lavender oil under her nose. She closes her eyes and chants in a language Olivia does not understand. Moments later, a small green and white mist floats over Olivia. It twirls and twists until it becomes a humanoid shape of a head and torso that is neither male nor female, with no hair and glowing purple eyes.

The spirit's arm wraps around Olivia, and she falls into a mindless sleep. Mayreea gives instructions in a whisper. "Keep this tortured soul asleep for the night. Keep all nightmares and negative thoughts away. Give her peace of mind, sleep spirit." She taps small drops of oil into the candle to scent the room while the spirit does its job.

*****

Tyree has allowed Gullen to leave on his mission, and the group rests for a day, doing whatever they like. It is late in the morning in the town of Keskella the following day. Tyree has invited everyone to his room. Glaive, Ryan, and Kade are there when Brak and Brace arrive late as usual.

"Finally." Tyree huffs. "Let's begin."

Ryan asks, "Wait, where is Gullen?"

"Friends, I'm going to be open with you. I took some gold to pay Gullen to do another task."

Kade tilts her head and snarls. "You what? When?"

"How much?" an angry Ryan asks.

"Our gold?" the boys ask at the same time.

Tyree throws his hands in the air. "Whoa, whoa. It's for the better. And yes, *our* gold. Not your gold...ours." Tyree lays out the map to Geemend's Seeker on the table. "Forgot about the gold. There will be plenty more, or whatever you decide soon."

"So what's this?" Brace asks.

Kade mumbles under her breath, "Great...It's going to take me longer to get home now."

"Come now, sweetie, this map will lead you to what you desire." Tyree smiles and holds his arms out wide.

"A treasure map? A real map?" Brace asks, looking closely at it.

Tyree gently pushes him back. "You see, I have come into possession of my family's relics from when they ruled Skylar." He points to the staff in the corner and lays the scepter on the table over the map.

"Okay. But how does that get us gold, chief?" Glaive asks.

"Oh, Glaive, if it wasn't for your craft of swinging a weapon... This is the map that will lead us to Geemend's Seeker."

"Which direction, north?" Ryan asks.

"Yes. We need to go north for the next two weeks and find a local guide. From there, once we attain the seeker, each one of us will get to use it for whatever you need to find." He points at Kade. "And you too, sweetie. You can find the location of whatever you are looking for."

Brak and Brace clap their hands together in excitement again and speak at the same time. "Well, I'm in."

"You two didn't even think about it," Ryan says.

"Don't have to," Brak starts.

"It's a no brainer. What else are we going to do?" Brace finishes.

Tyree is surprised at how quick they responded. "See, they know a good chance when they see it. So what do you say?"

"I'm in, chief," Glaive says.

"Ahh, you would have been coming along, anyway."

"Alright. Let's go and see what this can show us." Ryan crosses his arms.

"Again, I will follow for now," Kade is hesitant to say. A feeling inside her is saying this is a bad idea. But to get knowledge of where the Black Diamond of Truth is located is worth the risk to her.

"Great." Tyree smacks his hands together. He slips the scepter into his coat pocket; he was ready to use its power of suggestion if they didn't want to go. He will keep that secret with him for a while.

"When do we leave?" Kade asks.

"Glaive, take the boys and get the horses ready. We leave in an hour to ride north."

Kade looks through the gold to see what is left. "Will we get the chance to make more coin along the way?"

Tyree's eyes frown at her. "If we must, but only if deemed necessary. We might have caused too much attention already." He glares at Brak and Brace, who snicker back at him.

Tyree waves everyone to go get packed.

*****

Olivia's mind drifts asleep and is finally blank. After hours of well-deserved sleep passes, Olivia's mind awakens. At first, sprays of color try to come into focus, then are pushed back to darkness by the sleep spirit. A brighter flash of light overcomes the spirit's darkness as it retreats in her mind. Olivia is once again standing along a cool beach in the fall.

Sand reeds and marram grass sway in the salty breeze. The midday sun is behind her, and the dark cloudy horizon of the offshore storm has the roaring waves crash along the shoreline one after another. To her distant left is the seacoast town she dreamed of before.

She is drawn to her right by someone moving. Where the beach ends and the grasses take over, the young blonde-haired boy has turned into a twenty-one-year-old. His worn brown pants and red silk shirt have seen better days, but it is still an improvement over what he had before. A girl of the same age is wearing a fine white cream lace dress with long sleeves that end with ruffles. Olivia thinks this is the little girl from the first dream, grown up.

She watches them hug. She gives him a long kiss, and they hold hands for as long as they can until she steps back. The girl lets go, sobbing, and hastily walks away towards town. The boy stands there motionless with a necklace in his hands. He neither looks sad nor happy.

Olivia watches the girl get into a rowboat and is taken to a ship offshore. She observes the boy watching the ship fade into the distance. Olivia feels a parchment appear in her hands. She unrolls it to see the words...Con Del Mal.

She walks to the boy. Olivia is surprised by how focused his deep blue-gray eyes are. She smiles and hands him the paper.

"What is this?" he asks.

"There is nothing holding you back now," Olivia says.

Olivia jumps out of her sleep, causing the sleep spirit to vanish like steam cooling off. "Holy mother of... I know what needs to be done!"

She lays back on the pillow, unable to sleep again. New thoughts of what needs to be done, memories of the battle, Abigail missing, and her parents' disappearance now circulate through her mind. She tries to focus on the dreams to remember them.

The next morning, she sneaks out of Snowcap before the others awaken. She uses the tree door spell to go back to Waldron's cabin. She finds that Arthygus and the others have left. Rustling of leaves startle her, and she panics. A feeling of happiness overcomes her while she avoids looking uphill where the battle took place.

She glances above the cabin, and there is the chimera looking down at her, hiding behind the cabin. She carefully walks around to it and holds her hand out. The creature carefully creeps around the cabin to her. The head lowers for her hand to touch it.

She feels comfort in rubbing the fur between its ears on the large head. An idea pops into Olivia's head. "I need someone to watch over my home while I'm not there. It's a nice place. You would like it. High in the hillside."

She rubs and pets the beast with both hands. The red dragon head slithers near her with gleaming eyes that look like they want to eat her. "You can see the ocean from my place." Olivia closes her eyes and thinks of the image of her home and location. *Go. Go there. I will see you at my home soon.*

Olivia backs off with one final pet and slips into the tree door again.

16

Grim Decisions

Thanks to Mr.Blaine and his tree door spell, Young Adam, Arthygus, and Waldron enter Vestur Forest, a mile from Silver Birch City. The air is crisp with a scent of fall. Many leaves still cling to trees. Oranges, vibrant yellows, and reds mix in with patches of evergreens.

The leaf-covered soft soil crunches beneath their boots. The breeze whistles through tree limbs with a pleasant tune. They scope around to make sure no one has seen them. It was decided to appear on the west side of the city to avoid any attention to them. The three men travel two days to get to Willowdale, a small village to the west.

They wander along small creeks and walk on short woodsman paths. The trio spend an evening of drink, food, and song with woodcutters in their cabin. Arthygus shares small amusing magic tricks, and Young Adam explains teachings of Dianeeta to the woodcutters. Waldron remains quiet and listens. His thoughts stray to Evalyn and how near she could be.

The tapping of raindrops against the rooftop wakes them. Hickory smoke from the morning breakfast fire arouses their noses. After good farewells, the trio walk through the wet dense forest of poplar, elms, oaks, and clusters of pines. They were warned of strange creatures lurking that haven't been seen for some time. Even the elven scouts have had sightings of them.

The rain intensifies after a few hours' walk, so they pull up their hoods. Waldron leads them to a grove of red maples that still have their leaves to sit under. Arthygus pulls out his glass water bottle from his robe he has over his leather.

"How is it that bottle doesn't bog you down?" Waldron asks.

"Oh this? Nah. It's my magical robe that does it. The pockets are larger than they appear." He sticks his hand in one, reaching around up to his shoulder. He pulls out the gold dagger that Abigail gave him.

"That's a fine dagger. I'd keep that dagger handy, being out here."

His face saddens while glaring at the dagger. "Abigail gave me this... It saved Adam and myself from falling into..." He looks at Adam, who smirks and agrees with a slight nod.

"How are we going to approach the elf lord?" Adam asks.

Arthygus scratched his head. "We could sneak through, couldn't we?"

Waldron shakes his head. "That would not be wise to trespass through his lands."

"But it would be quicker. What if he holds us up or denies passage?" Arthygus asks.

"If he finds out why we need passage, he might not even grant us to leave. They may imprison us," Waldron says.

A hoarse bass voice echoes around them, like talking through a hollow log. "Your only choice is to go around his lands."

The three of them are startled and turn in the direction the voice came. Leaning against a big oak tree is a giant man, who is an amazing eleven feet tall. His bright red beard and hair stand out against his weathered, dark, pale skin. He wears tanned leather sewn together in patches and has two metal armbands around his forearms. A large sword, that would take Waldron's two hands to wield, is stuck into the ground.

"Did he just talk to us?" Adam whispers.

"Yes, he did, and he is a forest giant, a firbolg. I have heard of them," Waldron whispers back.

"Yes, I did. What of it?"

"Remain seated and calm," Waldron says, lowering his hands at them. "Why would we go around when we can ask for permission?"

"Ha." He bellows a strange, deep laugh. "From what I heard you say, you are in a hurry. But the elf lord is not. He will detain you."

"What do you suggest we do?" Adam asks.

"It depends on your time and destination."

"What do you mean?" Adam asks.

"If you're trying to get across the Carnassial Mountains, there are better paths to take in the Southern Kingdom and far north of here. Unless you are seeking to go to the Lifvana Hills. But why go there? No one does."

"Will you take us?" Arthygus asks.

"Bwa, wha...what?" The forest giant crosses his arms. "That is where you are going?"

Waldron stands, gathering his things. "Get up, boys. We need to go." He looks at the giant. "I do not know your name. But thank you for the caution."

"Now hold on...What is that you seek? There is nothing in those hills. Lifvana means lifeless in elvish, you know."

"Lifeless?" Arthygus asks.

Waldron slowly walks through the ferns. "Come, keep up."

"I suppose I could." The giant strokes his beard again.

"Why would you?" a skeptical Waldron asks.

"There are unwelcome guests in these woods coming from the mountains."

"And you deemed us strange?" Waldron asks.

"No, I see you are headed for trouble, and I don't want trouble in these woods."

"Alright then. So guide us. This is Adam and Arthygus. I am Waldron. And who is our guide?" Waldron winks and grins at both Adam and Arthygus.

"I am Gorm. Scout of the clan, Halfgar."

They follow Gorm to the edge of the forest. They are on a ledge that overlooks the elf lord's valley. As far as they can see to the north and south, a lush forest that was once green is now showing its fall coat in all its splendor. What seems like twenty miles away are the Carnassial Mountains rising out of the horizon. The hillside has a slight incline with raspberry and blackberry bushes hugging the top along with thickets of thorn and small trees.

Arthygus explains to Gorm that they need to get to a lone tree in the hills and find the robed stone man. They traveled two hundred miles in twelve days as he guides them to the south and around the elf kingdom. Gorm keeps them from wandering trouble as best as he could. Being close to the Elf lord boundaries, not much was about. A few goblin scouts they easily took care of. They hunt deer and boar to sustain them, and many freshwater streams keep their water supplies full.

They awake in the morning on the western side of the elf lord's lands. The sun is a welcomed warmth on their faces from the night's cool fall air. Adam rises first to stretch. He watches the early light reflect off the mist in the valley below. A slight breeze blows, pushing aside the mist like a horizontal waterfall.

Adam turns to watch the sunrays light up the mountains in the background. They move down the mountain ever so slowly. Soon the rocky wastelands come to light. He is dismayed that there is nothing but rock after rock, sharp and round. No lush trees, streams, ponds, or wildlife that he can see.

His eyes narrow as he focuses on a single dead tree in the distance. "Hey! Get up! I see them. The trees! The dead trees!" He jumps up and down at finding it.

Arthygus stands up quickly. "Where?"

Adam points toward the dead trees. "It has to be where we need to go."

"I do believe so," Arthygus says.

Gorm remains behind, for he does not like the rocky terrain. It is decided to leave the sleeping supplies behind for better movement. Waldron leads over the rocky terrain. At first, the gray and brown rocks are small, like melons. After a mile into the journey, they become a mix of large boulders and huge slabs of black rock outcroppings the size of houses.

They walk around the boulders, climb others, and hop over ones that are flat but have small crevices in them. Arthygus notices the sharp edges and could easily cut him if he slips. Others are rounded from the elements overtime.

“Do you notice the lack of any plant or insect life?” Waldron asks, jumping over a wider crevice. The other two follow him, jumping over the same spot.

“Yes. Why is that?” Arthygus asks.

“I’m just trying not to fall and paying attention to the distance. Not to any plant or bug,” Adam admits.

They take a break as the sun climbs higher. Arthygus sips his water. “Plants and insects can tell you a lot about the terrain you are in, like what's around that can help or harm you.”

“That’s right,” Arthygus agrees.

“What do you notice?” Waldron asks.

Arthygus taps his chin, looking around. “I’m not familiar with this type of land. I would say with the lack of plants, there is no dirt for them to grow in.” He bends over to look closer in the crevice. I do see water at the bottom...Oh wait. I see mosquitos and other bugs crawling in the shadow and edges of the puddle.”

Waldron nods. “Good thing you noticed that. That means the puddle is stagnate and not good drinking water.”

“I was taught how to grow plants, not seek them out. I have a lot to learn.” He looks off in the distance. “I never thought I would be out here or anywhere.” He chuckles. “It’s all Abigail’s fault. If it wasn’t for Dianeeta bringing her to our doorstep, I would still be sweeping floors,” Adam says.

“That's a good way of looking at it. Let’s go, boys.” Waldron turns around, glimpsing a shiny copper flash reflecting the light for a split second, then lowers into a crevice. He pauses. “Be on your guard. I don’t think we are alone.”

The sharpness of the rocks turns into smooth round edges. Along the larger flat tops they walk across, they notice old and new large scrape marks. Waldron leads them down into a crevice, since the gaps are becoming too wide to jump. The gaps are twelve to twenty feet deep and ten to twenty feet wide at spots, while others they barely can squeeze through.

Arthygus's concerned voice questions the decision. "Is this safe?

"It's our only choice at the moment. We will head topside when we can." Waldron is on edge not being able to see far to check for danger. When they leave a larger crevice, a large amber eye with an orange pupil opens along the wall. It watches every move they make until out of sight. The gray and black of the stone slowly turns into dull copper scales as it silently slides into the shadow.

An hour has gone by, and Waldron thinks they are close to the dead trees. "Arthygus, you are the lightest. Climb on my shoulders and tell me how close we are to the trees."

"It's like a maze down here," Adam says, nervously looking around.

"You hear that too?" Waldron asks while Arthygus climbs on him.

The rock ledge is just out of reach, and he jumps to grab it. His hand grasps the rock as hard as he can, and he pulls himself up to his elbows. For a second, he swears he saw what looked like a dull copper rope, half foot thick, slide down a crevice in front of them. "Uh...I can see the trees. They're in front of us. But..."

"Okay, pull yourself up. Adam, climb up next."

"But..." Arthygus says as he gets a push on his feet from Waldron.

Adam swings his mace up; it lands with a clang beside Arthygus. He grabs Adam's arms and helps him up. Both Adam and Arthygus help Waldron to the top of the boulder. They are a few yards from the cluster of dead trees. Arthygus counts eighteen of them that are standing.

His voice raises in excitement and he points. "There! Over there is the fallen tree!"

"It sure is!" Adam says, also excited. "We are close. Do you see the sign?"

"Sign?" Waldron asks.

"Yes, there should be a sign somewhere," Adam informs him.

Arthygus scrambles over to the fallen tree, hopping over crevices. He finds the fallen tree and straddles it like a saddle on a horse.

Waldron tilts his head and his eyebrows curl in. "What is he doing?"

"I'm not sure," Adam says.

Arthygus lays down on the tree and focuses on the length and sights up the tip. At the end of his sight is a rock formation, and one looks like a robed man pointing down. Arthygus grins. "I see it!" He stands up on the dead tree and jumps up and down. "The robed man! I found the entrance!"

Snap! Crack! The dead tree splinters and falls into a crevice with Arthygus screaming like a little girl. His stomach flies into this throat. Waldron and Adam hop and sprint over to him. They stop at the edge, gasping for air. Their eyes roll and they both laugh uncontrollably.

Waldron bends over and sticks his arm out. There is Arthygus laying on his back only three feet down with the dead tree trunk. Arthygus's face reds as he wipes himself off. He points to the rock formation they need to go. Once again, they hop and jump over ravines.

A deep laughter gurgles quietly as a wide copper head of a dragon peers over the rocks, watching them leave with its amber eyes. Its long and muscular head is similar to a horse, only five feet long and three feet wide. Two shiny copper horns arch back on the top of the head and three smaller ones beneath each ear point back as well. It smiles and giggles, sinking back into the crevice.

They reach the bottom where the rock is pointing. Adam removes a few rocks, discovering a slab with markings on it. They stand back, looking at each other.

"Baladain," Adam says.

"It does exist," Waldron murmurs.

Arthygus is in disbelief. "The spell was right."

They take a few minutes to let it sink in. Arthygus readies his spells he had been studying the last few nights. Adam scans through the book of Miles Nikolas for any advice. Waldron hones his blade and puts the sword back in his scabbard.

"What exactly are you getting in here? No one has visited this place since...over five hundred years ago," Waldron says.

"We need to get a scroll before Tyree does."

"Why?"

Adam sighs. "Because he tricked us into getting General Prakdon's Book of Power."

"But he can't read it because it is demon rune," Arthygus adds.

"And the scroll is a demon rune reading spell," Adam finishes.

Waldron shakes his head. He points at Adam. "Lead the way... Arthygus, follow behind me. If there is something down here, it will give you time to do your...you know."

Adam clears a few more rocks out of the way and finds he can lie down and squeeze through. He puts his mace out first, feeling the ground. He slides a few feet into darkness.

"You alright?" Waldron asks.

"Yes." He then speaks in a faint tone. "Tulkoon Valo." A light glows from the tip of his mace, lighting the pathway. "Oh, my."

"What is it?" Waldron can see light coming from the hole. Waldron crawls and wiggles in, followed by Arthygus.

The three kneel and marvel at the black stone staircase carved to perfection. The dull stone hardly reflects the light from Adam's mace. He stands and lowers the mace onto the stairs. The steps are ten feet long and two feet wide. Adam gives an uneasy smirk, taking a step down. His boot slaps the stair with a echo.

He turns and shrugs his shoulders. "Sorry," he whispers.

"Well, if the tales are true, the portal was closed. So there shouldn't be anything down here," Waldron says to lighten the mood and offer Adam comfort.

Arthygus casts a small light spell on his dagger so he can see better around him. Waldron is uneasy being surrounded by light in the darkness. They quietly continue down the stairs, expecting something to move or come at them. Deeper they go until they come to the bottom. There is a solid stone door with exquisite carvings of twisted bodies and skulls of indescribable shapes. The whole door design itself is of a large devilish face, laughing.

"Who would carve such a monstrosity?" Adam asks.

"Something not of this world," Waldron says.

"How do we get in? The door won't budge." Adam pushes against it.

"Hold on. Let me try my knock spell." Arthygus approaches the door and hesitantly touches it. He makes a partial circle with his fingers across it. "Avata." The half circle glows deep yellow and sinks into the black door. Arthygus steps back behind Adam, who glares at him.

The door cracks along the edges. Dust and pebbles fall to the ground as the door slides to the side with a hollow grinding. Stale air rushes past their faces, swirling dust everywhere. They look at each other, and Waldron nods for Adam to go in.

Adam takes a step in, and the others follow. The hallway becomes larger and taller but still the black dull stone. Their light sources brighten the area to show old bodies long decomposed. Along with their rusted armor or deteriorated leather straps, human skeletons still have dried skin attached. A few other bodies have turned to ash, save for a few bones. They spot two bodies with blackened exoskeletons with distorted joints; small, sharp bony spikes, and bony tails. Their lifeless hollowed skulls still instill fear in Adam and Arthygus.

Their eyes dart from side to side cautiously but are not focused on anything. Adam comes across a skeleton that has a bronze chest plate bashed in at several spots. A once white and gold tunic that was worn proudly now is torn and faded. Adam notices the left side of the skull has been cut from the top of the ear down to the shoulder. He has never seen inside the bone before and is shocked. His eyes remain glued to all the little webs of bone.

Waldron nudges him forward. "Move on. Try not to focus on things too much."

"He was wearing the tunic of the Father. It was almost unheard of for a high priest warrior to fall in times gone by. What could have done that?"

"Frightening creatures we dare not speak of," Waldron says.

Adam clears his thoughts and moves ahead. Arthygus gets closer to one body. The shadows from the light make it look like the empty eye sockets are moving. The hallway comes to an end with a large copper door that has been blackened by fire and tarnished with time. When they get closer to the door, faint white bluish letters form in front of them.

Adam stops when Arthygus pulls him back. "Do you see that?"

"Yes."

"What is that?" Waldron asks.

Arthygus's voice pitches slightly higher in excitement. "Lower your light so we can see it better."

"Is that a ward or a warning?" Waldron asks.

Arthygus scratches his head. "I...I can't understand it."

"I can," Adam mumbles in awe. "It's an ancient script that I have been studying." He takes his finger and swipes it through the letters out of curiosity. The letter acts like mist with his energy mixing with the magic.

"What does it say?" Arthygus asks.

"It is more of a description...I think." He steps back to read the symbols and points at them. "Here is where Muun cast aside the undead with a swipe of her hand. She pushed back the spawns of the abyss and closed the portal with her golden spear. With the aid of Matteo Nicholas and Ilmarinen to seal the portal of necromancy."

"Ilmarinen?" Arthygus taps his chin. "I believe that was a wizard that dealt with gates and portals I read about in my studies."

"Matteo Nicholas? I wonder if any relation to Miles?" Adam asks.

"Okay. So how does this help us get past the door?" Waldron asks.

Adam pushes against the door, and a perfect seam reveals two door halves. Adam stops. "Hey...You said Ilmarinen was a wizard?"

"Yes, why?"

"Then why were witches blamed for closing the portals?"

Arthygus stands flabbergasted at that thought. "I...I don't know."

Waldron is getting nervous standing there and not moving. "We must keep moving...but cautiously."

Adam presses the door; it takes a little more force to open it. He points his mace into the darkness, and they stand there, mystified at what they see. The light shines far into a dusty darkness with no end. They can see no ceiling, and the floor is flat black stone. Near them on the left and right are smooth black stone buildings that have no seams, doors, or windows. Each one has only a small gap between them of two feet. Inside is a darkness that the light cannot penetrate.

The walkway between the buildings is at least fifty feet from left to right. The floor is void of any object or body. Arthygus and Adam's eyes do not blink in fear of what may lurk in the shadows. The trio walk slowly in a semicircle. Waldron has an extremely sharp-tipped arrow ready in his bow. Adam grips his mace, and Arthygus pulls a spell ingredient from his leather. The dagger in his hand wobbles.

The air is still and smells like stagnant decay. While walking by, they peer into openings, ready for anything. Their hearts pound from the unknown fear that is invoked in them. Step by slow step, they get closer to a wall of gray stone. Adam holds his mace higher to brighten the area. A gray, stone, gazebo-like structure with two opposing openings with stairs sits in the middle of the walkway. The pillars on the side are of human husks twisted and bent, holding the roof.

Adam dims the mace when he notices something odd. The faintest pale olive green light radiates from within. They make it closer to the entrance. Waldron climbs the first stair to peek inside.

"What is it you say we are looking for?" he asks.

"A scroll," Arthygus says.

Adam looks around the structure. The light shines upon a great stone statue lurking over the gazebo, paralyzing Adam. He has seen the goat-like torso with hoofed feet, a large human-like bloated belly, and fat meaty arms with hands the size of a small gnome before. The claws are like small knives. But the head is half human, half unknown demon. The large bulbous eyes have a vertical raised rib carved into the center. It has veins carved on the outside of its face and two large spiraling horns swept back. Huge wings with two spikes in the center spread out. The arms are reaching out over the gazebo at ten feet high.

"Arthygus...Arthygus...It's the statue."

Waldron and Arthygus scurry over to him and are stunned at what they see. "Not that again."

"What do you mean again?" Waldron asks.

"Uh...We saw that at the sunken tower...Before Tyree." Arthygus shrugs his shoulders at not wanting to repeat what happened.

"Alright...I think the scroll is in there." Waldron taps Arthygus.

They turn to walk up the steps, and Adam stops them before they enter. Inside is a pair of huge thin arms protruding out of the floor. They are carved from black stone, while everything else is gray. The tree finger hands hold a brown and green parchment that is the source of the pale light.

"Let's get it." Arthygus leans forward, but Adam jerks him back.

"Hold on. Something is telling me..."

Waldron smiles. "Go on, trust yourself."

"More like Dianeeta's saying something's not right here." Adam looks around and notices more script carved into the wall's edge near the ceiling. "Clever hiding."

"What is it?"

Adam reads it and drops his mace. "No...Let me read that again."

Arthygus darts his gaze at Adam, then at the writings. "What?"

Adam's mouth drops open, and his eyebrows pull to the center in disbelief. "This can't be."

"Tell us," an anxious Arthygus pushes.

"It basically reads, *Those who sin can pass without restriction, and the portal will remain closed.*"

Arthygus nods his head. "Okay. Okay. That's not bad."

"But...*Those that are good at heart will break the portal seal.*"

Waldron and Arthygus both say at the same time. "What?"

Adam looks around, reading it one last time. "If we leave the scroll, Tyree will walk up and get it, and the portal remains closed. If we get the scroll, we break the seal to the portal."

Arthygus scratches his head. "What do we...do?"

Everyone's unfocused gaze is expecting an answer. An eerie silence takes over the room while they think about the dilemma they are in.

*****

Olivia remained sleepless for nights. The others are concerned as she hardly leaves the guest sleeping room at Snowcap. Klinksly has taken Abbot Garret back to the monastery. Mayreea, Mr. Krew and Mr. Blaine are sitting in the library when Olivia hastily walks by. Klinksly chases after her as she walks to the front door.

"Olivia, wait. Where are you going?" Klinksly asks.

She turns to him with her head looking down while avoiding eye contact. She takes a deep breath and slowly lets it out, as if all these questions are annoying. "I'm going to go to my house to get a change of clothes. I will be back."

"That's a good idea. Let me get my coat."

"No!" she screams.

Mr. Krew and Mr. Blaine peer into the hallway.

"Why not? You shouldn't be—"

"Shouldn't be what, Klinksly!" Olivia stomps her feet, crosses her arms, and her voice becomes very frank. "I'm tired of waiting. I'm tired of not knowing what to do about Abigail. Tired of looking through old books and papers. Tired of these images of the battle in my head...I'm just...tired." She opens the door and heads outside. "Now I am doing something about it."

Olivia leaves Klinksly standing in the cold doorway, looking confused. Mayreea comes from behind him. "Leave her be. Nothing we can do for her until she is ready to talk to us."

Olivia angrily starts the tree door spell, but in her state of mind, it misfires. She screams with a high pitch and kicks the tree. "No! No! No!" She punches it harder and harder. Olivia feels a helpless anger grow inside of her she has never felt before. Soon, blood drips from her hands from pounding the pine bark.

"Olivia!" Klinksly screams, running over to her. He grabs her hands, still beating the tree. With a slight struggle to get them to stop, Klinksly takes the mortar and pestle from her.

Tears run down her face as she looks at her bloody knuckles. "I need to go," she firmly whispers between her teeth.

Klinksly doesn't say a word. He grinds the bark, activates her tree door spell, and hands her mortar and pestle back. Her trembling hands take it from him. She looks back to see Mayreea watching on, then looks at Klinksly.

He is drawn to her eyes. The dark circles around her eyes seem to go from remorseful to determined as she squints at him. Olivia doesn't smile or say anything. She steps into the tree door, and Klinksly watches the yellow sparkles fade to the floor.

Klinksly turns towards Mayreea. “I think I will visit home for a bit…It’s been too long since I was there.”

Mayreea smiles and nods. Klinksly disappears into the tree.

*****

Olivia makes it home to change into a long green mint dress. She grabs her dark green cloak and brown boots. The saber gets put back where she found it, and she heads back outside to the ash tree. Olivia stares at the tree again, thinking of when she was mad at Abigail and how she was trying to teach her the tree door spell. Her head shakes to clear the thought.

She glances over the hill and the scenery seems different, like it doesn’t bring joy anymore. She calmly opens the tree door. “I can do this…but I don’t know if I should.”

Olivia steps out of a grove of black walnut trees. The branches reach out in all directions. The salty breeze catches her attention. A few hundred yards through sand reeds and marram grass lies the sandy beach on a cloudy day. A storm is offshore, causing waves to crash one after another with loud plops when they crest upon themselves. There is a fishy smell from the sand crabs being turned and pummeled by the waves.

Olivia slowly walks to the beach, letting her hands caress the grasses. Occasionally, she plucks a sand reed. She holds it, then tosses it aside to grab another. Her ghostly stare watches the waves roll.

I shouldn’t be here. What if this is the wrong thing to do? She lets her hair down to let the breeze do what it wants. She slumps over as if she has given up when a shadow approaches from her side. Her eyes barely move to see the shadow of a man with flowing long hair.

“In my dreams…this was a more pleasant encounter,” a regal, silvery voice says.

Olivia shrugs her shoulders.

He steps beside her and sets down a brown backpack, looking at the waves. “I have had many dreams. Some I still remember when I was younger. And some recently. I thought they were just dreams. But one thing was constant in them." He stands silent for a few seconds. "You. The lady in green with the brunette hair. You have been in a lot of my dreams, and I don't know why."

She turns to him, and her eyes are swelling. Olivia does not trust herself in what to say. She does not want the curse to do its thing.

He points out to the horizon. "See that ship out there? You told me—"

"There is no reason to stay any longer," she says sadly. She hands him a small rolled up parchment. "Go...Go find your adventure."

"I don't know who you are or what these dreams mean. Here is reality staring me in the face. What am I to do? Trust a dream? Trust someone I have never seen but in dreams?"

Her black hair sways in front of her face from the ocean breeze. His hand gently brushes her bangs aside. Olivia's eyes beg for an unspoken help. His dark blue-gray eyes show a ray of hope. "Vock. My name is Vock, in case you were wondering."

He unrolls the parchment. "Hum. It's a starting point."

"Olivia." Is all she says to him as she heads back to the black walnut trees.

He watches her walk through the grasses and fade into the trees. Vock studies the town one last time before walking south along the beach.

Appendix 2

Appendix 2

For the magic words in this story, I decided not to make words up that can't be pronounced and confuse the reader. So I used the Finnish language for them. It is a very fluid language for magic words. For elvish names and places, I used the Icelandic language (IS). I felt it worked. And a few Gaelic (GC) words also. Below is how to pronounce them and their meaning. Enjoy.

Book one Abigail
Se'allt = (IS) Name of wild elf. See's all (sea alt)

Varita = guard (Vart tia)
Vedä = pull (vid da)
Jaatya= Freeze (yat ya)

Book two Tyree
Muuttaa = change (moo ta) Diamond to cane
Meikila = make (may key la) cane into sword
Liekki = flame (lee ay key)
Shokki = electric shock (shocky)
Vedä = pull (vid da)
Unohda tänään = Forget today (oo no tan ann)
Lopeta hengitys = Stop breathing (low pet a hang git is)
Kutistua = Shrink or reduce size (koo tiss two wa)
Suurentaa = Enlarge (sir rin taa)
Paikantaa esine = locate object (pie can taa es in a)
Sagoil = Release (sa goil)
Nahda lapi = See through (na da la pee)
Hidas = Slow (he daas)
Lífvana (IS)= lifeless (lee van a)
Djöfla gardur = Devils garden (jeer fla gar door)

Pimeys kuluttaa = Darkness consume (pee mose kul lou taa)
Maaginen Ehdotus = Magic suggestion (ma gin in eh do toose)
Tulkoon Valo = Let there be light (too kun val o)
Tyontaa= Push (toon taa)
Palauttaa voimat = Restore strength (pal lou taa vot mutt)
Salama = lightning (sal la ma)
Hengen Valtikka = Scepter of spirit (hen jen val teeka)
Lage Vann = Create water (la ga von) Norwegian
Rense Vann = Purify water (rance von) Norwegian
Levitoida = Levitate (Lev e toy da)
Katoaa sivustolta = Disappear from site (Ka tow wa see vos tolt a)
Avata = Unlock (Ava ta)

Witches Agenda evolved from the author's passion for fantasy writing. Since the mid 1980s, Greg has been writing exciting fantasy adventures for role-playing games and has now created a fantasy series. Greg invented Tomes Of Auhere as the home for his imaginative tales to be brought to life. Here, you will read tales of dastardly deeds, found courage, triumphs, and blossoming romances.

Greg is no stranger to writing. He also released a short psycho thriller story in Ebook form, The girl In The Lemon Yellow Dress in 2022. Greg also contributed two historical fiction stories for the Gettysburg Writers Brigades anthology in 2021 and 2022. He owned a motorcycle business (CWR) from 1996 to 2017 and wrote several articles for a local off-road magazine. As a motorcycle enthusiast, he loves riding in the countryside for views and ideas for stories. Greg is also an aviation buff that enjoys flying planes. His main passion is painting small fantasy figurines and has been doing so since the 80s. He has also illustrated some of his own Witches Agenda characters on his website, tomesofauhere.com. He has lived just outside of the Gettysburg area since 1997.

Look for the rest of the Witches Agenda series.

Book one, Abigail...July 2023
Book two, Tyree......November 2023
Book three, Vock .....January 2023
Book four, Cecilia...March 2024
Book five, Olivia.....June 2024
Book six, Marcella...September 2024
Book seven William...December 2024
Book eight, Jareed...January 2025

www.ingramcontent.com/pod-product-compliance
Lightning Source LLC
Chambersburg PA
CBHW021619030826
48979CB00033B/318

* 9 7 8 1 9 6 1 9 1 8 0 4 7 *